Praise for Donita K. Paul's
# DragonKeeper Chronicles and Chiril Chronicles

"The writing is crisp and the setting imaginative. This series will speak to all ages of Christian readers."
—*Publisher's Weekly*

"Donita K. Paul never fails to satisfy the imagination and delight the soul.... This is fantasy that truly illuminates reality."
—JIM DENNEY, author of the Timebenders Series

"Donita K. Paul's vivid imagery and startling plot twists will delight fans."
—KACY BARNETT-GRAMCKOW, author of the Genesis Trilogy

"I wouldn't expect anything less from Donita K. Paul, as she always gives us a delightful read: intriguing, challenging, and full of blessing."
—KATHRYN MACKEL, author of *Vanished*

"Donita K. Paul possesses a unique talent for instilling deep wisdom and spiritual truth in a story that is engrossing and satisfying.... She is one of my favorite authors."
—HANNAH ALEXANDER, author of *Silent Pledge*

"Donita K. Paul's inventiveness never ceases to amaze. Fresh ideas for new races of people and unusual creatures keep flowing from her gifted pen."
—JILL ELIZABETH NELSON, author of the To Catch a Thief Series

"Shut your eyes, hold your breath, and plunge into the unshackled imagination of Donita K. Paul."
—LINDA WICHMAN, author of *Legend of the Emerald Rose*

# Dragons of the Watch

# Donita K. Paul

A NOVEL

# Dragons of the Watch

WATERBROOK
PRESS

DRAGONS OF THE WATCH
PUBLISHED BY WATERBROOK PRESS
12265 Oracle Boulevard, Suite 200
Colorado Springs, Colorado 80921

ISBN 978-1-4000-7341-2
ISBN 978-0-307-72960-6 (electronic)

Cover design by Mark D. Ford

Published in association with the literary agency of Alive Communications Inc., 7680 Goddard Street, Suite 200, Colorado Springs, CO 80920, www.alivecommunications.com.

Published in the United States by WaterBrook Multnomah, an imprint of the Crown Publishing Group, a division of Random House Inc., New York.

WATERBROOK and its deer colophon are registered trademarks of Random House Inc.

Library of Congress Cataloging-in-Publication Data
Paul, Donita K.
    Dragons of the watch : a novel / Donita K. Paul. — 1st ed.
       p. cm.
    ISBN 978-1-4000-7341-2 — ISBN 978-0-307-72960-6 (electronic)
  1. Dragons—Fiction.  I. Title.
    PS3616.A94D7295 2011
    813'.6—dc22

                                                2011020648

Printed in the United States of America
2011—First Edition

10 9 8 7 6 5 4 3 2

*To those readers who take the time to write encouraging words.*
*You brighten my days and make my work worthwhile.*

# Contents

Acknowledgments  ∽  xi

Map  ∽  xii

1: Invitation  ∽  1

2: Departure  ∽  8

3: Within a Cloud  ∽  16

4: A Beacon  ∽  22

5: No One at Home  ∽  28

6: Within the City  ∽  36

7: Rumbard City  ∽  43

8: Pickles and Mustard  ∽  51

9: In the Library  ∽  57

10: A Walk in the Night  ∽  66

11: A Good Night's Rest  ∽  74

12: Meet the Dragons  ∽  82

13: Sing, Sing a Song  ∽  89

14: Daggarts and Danger  ∽  97

15: Home, Sweet Hovel  ∽  106

16: In Search of Flour and Eggs  ∽  114

17: A Picture Tells a Tale  ∽  124

18: Pickles and Calamity  ∽  131

19: Clean Up  ∽  140

20: A New Start  ∽  149

21: A Diary's Account  ∽  155

22: The Bells Did It  ∽  164

23: Old One and Orli  ∽  173

24: Escape ⌒ 183

25: Discovery ⌒ 190

26: First Duty ⌒ 198

27: Sticks and Stones ⌒ 207

28: Good? Good! ⌒ 216

29: Snips and Snails ⌒ 223

30: A Goal, No Two ⌒ 231

31: Realization ⌒ 236

32: Morning Revelations ⌒ 245

33: Tuck ⌒ 253

34: Birth Day ⌒ 258

35: Where Is Porky? ⌒ 266

36: Rescuing Porky ⌒ 271

37: Gray Phantom ⌒ 277

38: Sighting a Wizard ⌒ 282

39: The Gang ⌒ 290

40: Run! ⌒ 297

41: Sanctuary ⌒ 304

42: Fairy Tale ⌒ 311

43: The Clan ⌒ 320

44: Keys, Keys, Keys ⌒ 327

45: Doors, Doors, Doors ⌒ 334

46: The Bottle Wizard's Bottles ⌒ 340

47: A Wizard's Way ⌒ 347

48: Journey to the Other Side ⌒ 355

49: Rendezvous ⌒ 362

50: The Ball ⌒ 368

Epilogue: In and Out of the Bottle ⌒ 377

Appendix (People, Glossary) ⌒ 383

# Acknowledgments

Mary Agius

Kacy Barnett-Gramckow

Evangeline Denmark

Beth Devore

Jani Dick

Jim Hart

Kathy Hurst

Hannah Johnson

Heidi Likens

Shannon, Troy, and Ian McNear

Carol Reinsma

Rachel Selk

Faye Spieker

John Case Tompkins

Beth Vogt

Rebecca Wilber

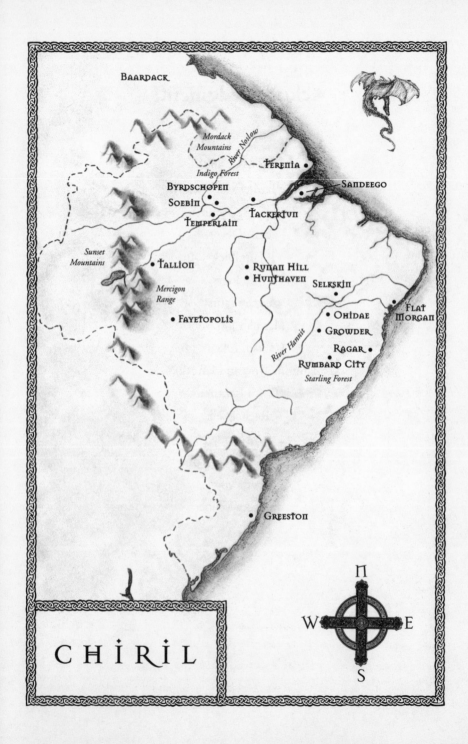

# Invitation

Ellie sat on her favorite boulder and looked Tak right in the eyes, telling him what was on her mind. "Gramps shouldn't have taught me to read."

Tak responded as he usually did when he received Ellie's confidences. He lowered his head, placing it on her knee for a rub.

Ellie obliged her pet, stroking the white hair between his nubby horns with one hand while digging in the pocket of her homespun pinafore with the other. The mountain breeze toyed with the paper she withdrew. With difficulty, she smoothed the small poster out on her other knee. Dirty and wrinkled, it still made her heart beat a little faster.

*Royal Wedding and Coronation*
*Princess Tipper*
*and*
*Prince Jayrus, Dragonkeeper and Paladin*

*All invited to the celebration*

"All invited. But Ellicinderpart Clarenbessipawl and her goat Tak can't come. No chaperone, no travel. Ma and Da aren't interested. And Gramps just laughs. 'You'll see. You'll see,' is all he says. He should take me himself."

Her younger brother's shrill yell came from the knoll rising out of the river to the east. "Ellie! Ellie!"

He stood on the hill, grinning like a bear with a paw in the honey hive and his face red from running. His stubby tumanhofer body bounced with excitement. He held his fists above his head and whirled them around in circles. Something had set him off.

She stood and hollered back. "You best be calling me by my proper name out in the open 'n' at the top of your lungs, Gustustharinback. Ma will tan yer hide if she's finding out you disgrace the family with such shabby care of our dignity."

When he saw her, he cupped his hands around his mouth and shouted, "Yer wanted at home. Itta be good news."

That information didn't impress her. Probably a delivery of the bolt of muslin ordered, which meant she'd be cutting and dyeing lengths for making new clothes. Not exciting news at all.

"Can it wait?" She gestured behind her to the scattered goat herd. "I'll have to gather Tak's clan if I'm to come home now."

"I'll come help you." Gustus charged down the hill toward the footbridge across the river.

Ellie stared at him for a moment with her mouth hanging open. The good news had nothing to do with cloth. Her brother would never voluntarily help bring in the goats for something as mundane as new clothes. He scurried down the path, slipping some on the loose rocks. But the precarious descent did not slow him a bit. Even in the narrower patches, where exposed roots of arranndon bushes tripped careless hikers, her sturdy brother skidded downward.

Folding the royal celebration notice into a small square, Ellie stuffed it back in her pocket. She turned away from watching her brother's progress and nudged the goat. "Come on, Tak. You find the nannies, and I'll find the billies."

Ellie went one direction and Tak another. In a few minutes, she located the fifteen goats that formed the herd. Mostly young males, these animals preferred the rockier terrain. She suspected it had to do with their perpetual game of I'm-up-highest.

She clicked her tongue and tapped her staff on a rock. Their heads rose as if all attached to the same string, though they didn't come right away. Each one chewed what was in his mouth and casually left his place one by one. Taking a serene amble down the hillside, they passed her, heading toward the bridge and home.

When the last one clomped by, Ellie rested her staff on her shoulder and followed. Tak already had the nannies plodding along the bank toward the footbridge. Gustustharinback trailed the nannies and carried the smallest of the baby goats in his arms.

He shouted when he caught sight of his sister. "Hurry! Aunt and Uncle Blamenyellomont are at the house. I can't tell you the surprise, and I'm gonna burst with keeping my tongue from waggin' and you from knowin'."

She tapped her staff on the rock beneath her feet. The billies scampered before her, picking up her impatience and gratefully heading for home. Even after eating all day, they appreciated the handfuls of button grain they got from the farmer's younger children.

With the goat hoofs pounding on the wooden bridge, Ellie couldn't hear or be heard. So she waited until she'd caught up with her brother on the other side.

"What's with all the falderal, Gustus?"

She watched as he forced a glare onto his face, erasing the impudent grin he'd been wearing. "You are to call me by my proper name if I have to call you by yours."

"There's a difference between shouting 'Ellie' and speaking 'Gustus' quietly." She grabbed his arm. "Now tell me, or I'll toss you into the river."

He pressed his lips together and gave her his most obstinate glower. The corners of his lips twitched, and she knew he wanted to laugh. She let go. She couldn't really dunk him while he carried the small kid.

"Why are our aunt and uncle here?"

"Can't tell you that either. But they's only stopping, not staying. We'd better hurry."

Ellie lost Gustustharinback's help as soon as they came in sight of the pens. He scuttled down the last hill and opened the gate but then ran through the goat barn, across the yard, and into the house.

The herd followed the leader through the opening and took up different places to observe their world. Ellie and Gustus had put many odd things within the goat pen for the animals to climb on. Old wooden benches, barrels, a huge thick branch they had pulled with the donkey's help, and crates littered the ground. The goats enjoyed scrambling up, over, and around the obstacles.

Tak stayed at Ellie's side as she put water in the trough and fastened the barn door securely open so the animals could come in if they wanted. He followed her out the door on the other side of the barn and waited patiently while she latched it shut.

Entering the back door so she could wash before meeting their visitors, Ellie noticed that the kitchen showed signs of serving tea. Her mother must have prepared refreshments to carry into the common room. Through the pantry door, she could see empty spots on the shelves, which meant the good china pot and the blue glass dishes were being used.

Warm water sat in a tub in the sink, and she used that to wash her face and hands. She pulled the scarf off her head, gathered her long, curly black locks into a ponytail and used the scarf to tie it in place. Wisps of hair immediately escaped and framed her tanned face. She washed her face again as if she could rid herself of the look of a farm girl. Hopefully Aunt Tiffenbeth wouldn't make that tired old comment: "Your blue eyes would be more attractive if you scrubbed away some of that mud you use for face cream."

Voices from the family's conversation drifted through the partially open door. Aunt Tiffenbeth quarreled with Ellie's father.

"Brother, you are wrong in this. Ellicinderpart is your eldest child and way past the age to be in the village looking for a husband."

"If there's a man good enough for her, he can just come courting here." Her father's voice rumbled in the wood-paneled room, and Ellie did not even have to strain to hear him. She stepped closer to the door in order not to miss a single word her aunt spoke.

"You are the most vexing man. That is *not* going to happen. It isn't the way of things, and you know it. You're selfish and your mind is rootbound."

Only his older sister could get away with talking like that to Ellie's father. She probably ought to go in before the discussion escalated to verbal warfare. She finished wiping her hands and draped the towel over one of the kitchen chairs around the square table.

"The girl is needed here."

"The young woman is your unpaid servant."

"She has obligations to her family. None of the other children are old enough to take over her chores."

"And it's not her fault five years passed before you begat another child. She should not be punished for Boscamon's whim. Besides,

Letterimdebomm is quite old enough to take over the goats and the dressmaking."

Her father said nothing. Ellie held her breath. Would she get to go live in the village, get a job, earn her keep, and possibly attract the attention of some young man?

She heard the rustling of a skirt. "Would you like another cake, Tiffenbeth? Letterimdebomm made them just yesterday afternoon." Her mother, trying to divert the tension between brother and sister.

Ellie knew it was pointless. Uncle Stemikenjon cleared his throat. Her father never cleared his throat before he spoke what was on his mind. He just blurted it out.

"I'll have another piece," said Uncle Stemikenjon.

"And—," said Aunt Tiffenbeth.

Ellie flinched. Her aunt was going to ruin it. Her father's silence might mean he was contemplating what she had said. But if her aunt pushed too hard, he'd turn stubborn.

"—all your children can read," continued Aunt Tiffenbeth.

"That's not my doing."

Ellie could imagine her father tossing a glare in her gramps's direction. The old man would smile that toothless grin and keep stroking the cat, whichever cat happened to be on his lap. He couldn't sit down without attracting at least one.

"Reading will be a great asset in the village," said Aunt Tiffenbeth. "It's only up here in these hills where it's not customary to teach all the children to read."

"There's no sense in taking the time to teach them all. One or two could be the readers and that could be their contribution to the family. Ridiculous waste of time to teach them all."

From behind, Ellie heard the unmistakable sound of Tak's footsteps on the wooden floor. Before she could turn, she felt the hard butt of his head on her backside.

She whirled and shook a finger at him. She spoke as forcefully as she could in a whisper. "Tak! You know you aren't allowed in here. Go back outside."

Ellie followed Tak as he made his docile retreat, but she watched scornfully the arrogant sway of his hips and the self-satisfied bounce of his head. His white coat gleamed as he entered the sunlight. Once he'd tromped down the stairs, she shut the door and latched it. That goat was too cunning.

Ellie straightened her shoulders and passed through the kitchen once more. With fingers on the doorknob, she drew the door toward her and stopped.

"I suppose she can go."

"Da!" She rushed into the room and flung her arms around him. "I'm going to the village?"

"Nay, not that. Yer going with your aunt to Ragar, to see the coronation and celebrate the wedding."

Ellie tried to breathe, but her lungs had expelled all the air from within and seemed paralyzed. She pushed out of her father's arms and looked around at the faces that stared at her. Gramps grinned. Her mother's face wrinkled in concern. Aunt Tiffenbeth arched eyebrows above twinkling eyes. Uncle winked. Her seven smaller siblings sat around the room with hands folded primly in their laps but eyes dancing with excitement.

Ellie made a strangled attempt to speak.

Her father thumped her back. "Breathe, you silly girl. You can't go anywhere if you expire on the spot."

# 2

# Departure

Three days later, Ellicinderpart knew for sure that the world was a beautiful place and her aunt and uncle were the most generous of tumanhofers. She sat in the second seat of their carriage with Aunt Tiffenbeth and gazed out the window. She wore a new dress her aunt had purchased in town, part of her new wardrobe. The coachman had strapped two carpetbags full of new things to the roof of their vehicle. Her uncle sat across from them with his face hidden in a book.

A warm glow spread through Ellie as she thought of the two gowns she'd carefully packed in the larger carpetbag the night before. She'd tried them on one more time and admired the dresses in her aunt's tall mirror. She had never thought to own one gown so lovely, let alone two. One for the coronation ball and one for the wedding reception.

In the mirror, a sophisticated young lady had laughed at the sight of herself, a farm girl dressed in such finery. In the pale yellow dress, Ellie felt like a delicate flower. In the soft azure gown, she could have floated up into the sky and drifted among the clouds.

Aunt Tiffenbeth patted Ellie's knee and pointed out the opposite window. "There's the road we take to go to your home. I bet you don't travel that road often."

"Not at all. We take the path to Glenbrooken Village on the other side of the mountain."

"This road is closer for us and is wide enough for the carriage." Her aunt frowned and pointed. "Isn't that your goat?"

On one of the cliffs, a white goat stood straight and tall against the blue sky.

"Tak!"

Ellicinderpart's shout brought her uncle out of his book.

"What's wrong?"

His wife answered before Ellicinderpart had a chance. "Her goat is up on that ridge. What is he doing there?"

Uncle Stemikenjon leaned forward to look out the window. "It's not so far from their house."

Aunt Tiffenbeth whipped around to face Ellie. "Do you come this way when you take the goats to pasture?"

"Never. The path to this side of the mountain crosses Crooked Gorge. You have to walk all the way down and then climb all the way up the other side. Very few plants grow in the gorge, so the herd doesn't feed well."

Uncle Stemikenjon glowered out the window. "Who took over your job as goatherd?"

"Gustustharinback."

"Would he be foolish enough to cross Crooked Gorge?"

"I think he's foolish enough," answered Ellicinderpart, "but too lazy."

Aunt Tiffenbeth took a turn leaning forward to improve her view of the rough hillside. "Stemikenjon, you must have the driver stop. Ellicinderpart must do something about Tak."

"Nonsense!" her husband blustered. "The goat got here on his own, and he can very well find his way back."

"But this goat is special, like my Niffy. You know how distressed I would be if dear Niffy were in danger."

"Indeed I do. You treat that cat as if she were worth something, and I tell you, she's not."

Ellie smiled as her aunt and uncle bickered over her aunt's spoiled feline. Ellie had met the cat when the family journeyed all the way to the relatives' house for a feast day. Niffy, looking fluffy and elegant, had never shown any friendliness to her family, and the family had no opinion of the cat. But Aunt Tiffenbeth made a great deal over the pleasure and companionship the cat bestowed upon her. Ellie didn't feel a "great love and admiration" for her goat as Aunt Tiffenbeth felt for her cat, but she didn't want anything to happen to Tak either.

"Silly goat," she muttered. The last thing she wanted was to interrupt her trip before it had barely begun to take care of a goat that should be at home, or at least in the pasture near home, with Gustustharinback.

Uncle Stemikenjon used his cane to bang on the front of the carriage above Ellie's head. The driver hollered, "Slow!" in a loud and long, stretched-out way. The coach lost speed and came to a stop.

"Oh no!" Ellie looked frantically from her aunt to her uncle. "What are we going to do?"

"You," said her uncle as he opened the door, "are going to see to the goat. Take Tak home."

Ellie felt all the joy drain from her, leaving a sad, hollow shell that wanted to wail. She was much too old, of course, to disgrace herself with sobs and rivers of tears.

"No, no," said Aunt Tiffenbeth. "Home is too far from here. You would never catch up. Take Tak to the Hopperbattyhold family, and pay one of those boys to return your goat to the farm."

Ellicinderpart relaxed a little. Taking the goat to the Hopperbattyhold home would only take a little time. She could get there and back in under an hour if she scampered.

"I don't have any money," she said.

Aunt Tiffenbeth dug deep into the folds of her elaborate skirt, where a pocket held her cloth coin purse. She opened it and reached through the narrow neck with two fingers, pinched a coin, and brought it out. "There." She placed the copper piece in Ellie's hand and took a moment to carefully return her money to its hiding place.

Uncle Stemikenjon had already descended from the coach and stood on the road, waiting to hand Ellie down. Ellicinderpart placed her small hand on his broad fingers to steady herself and jumped.

"Will you wait for me here?" she asked. "I shouldn't be too long."

"No need to wait." His gruff voice raked across her resolve not to cry. "After you leave the goat at the Hopperbattyholds', continue around Nose Point and down the hill. You should reach this road again just about the time we've traveled the long way around. We'll pick you up at the crossroads near Pence."

"Look at the clouds, Stemikenjon," said Aunt Tiffenbeth. "She should take a cloak in case it rains."

"Right." Uncle Stemikenjon shouted to the coachman. "Toss down the blue carpetbag."

The servant loosened the ropes, slipped out the needed luggage, and hoisted it in the air.

"This one, Master Blamenyellomont?"

"Aye."

Half of Ellicinderpart's new clothes came over the edge of the rooftop in a small valise made of heavy cloth. Uncle Stemikenjon caught it and handed it to Ellie.

"Get your cloak out, dear," said her aunt. "Oh, and you'd better take a change of clothing in case you get rained on."

Ellicinderpart opened the bag and pulled out her cloak. The clouds in the distance did look ominous, black and brewing. She gladly put the beautiful brown and black patterned wool around her.

A chill wind swirled up from their feet, and road dust pelted her face. She put a protective arm over her eyes. When the little tempest had passed, she looked up the stony hillside at Tak. He shifted his feet and kept an eye on her. She got the impression that the goat waited impatiently.

"Oh my," said Aunt Tiffenbeth as she struggled to close the window, pulling on the thick, opaque waxed paper that provided shelter. "Perhaps you won't make it to the other side of the mountain before the storm hits."

Uncle Stemikenjon leaned over, snapped the carpetbag closed, and handed it to Ellie. "Take the whole thing. If you can't make it to the crossroads, spend the night with either the Hopperbattyholds or the Dabryhinckses. Tiffenbeth, give her a few more coins to give the neighbors for their trouble."

Her aunt obediently dug through the abundant material of her skirt to find the cloth pouch.

"Ellicinderpart," said her uncle, "if you were a young flibbertigibbet, I'd be worried. But you have a sensible head on your shoulders. If you get lost, follow us to the capital as best you can. Once on the main highway, you will be able to stay in reputable taverns, and you can probably find a ride."

Aunt Tiffenbeth stretched her hand out to deposit a few more coins in Ellie's palm. "Keep those safe, dear. The clothes in that bag are for everyday. The better gowns will stay with us." She sighed, carefully depositing the purse back in the deep pocket. "We would wait while you take care of this little chore, but we are to meet up with my sister and her family in Bellsawyer day after tomorrow. Maybe we can wait for you there." She turned to her husband. "Stemikenjon, why don't we wait for Ellicinderpart in Bellsawyer?"

"We can wait an extra day there, but if we tarry too long, we'll lose our accommodations in Ragar. Better give the child more money for meals and lodging. And a tad more for emergencies."

Ellie's mind skittered over the words—emergencies, reputable taverns, Bellsawyer. The possibility of actually getting to Ragar to see the coronation and join in the festivities for the royal wedding flew into the bank of threatening clouds that approached from the west.

"Give her a handkerchief to tie up the coins, Stemikenjon. And young lady, you put the little bundle where no one will suspect you have it. Take the money out when no one is looking, and put just the amount you will need in your pocket."

"Yes ma'am." Ellie watched as her aunt once more went through the time-consuming process of finding the pouch, pulling it out of the complicated skirt, pursuing a few coins that rattled at the bottom, and bestowing them upon her with great solemnity. The procedure took too long and tested Ellicinderpart's patience. But how could she utter, "Please hurry," between clenched teeth to her generous aunt and uncle?

A second paper window shield snapped into place as Aunt Tiffenbeth returned to shutting out the elements.

Uncle Stemikenjon patted Ellie on the shoulder before returning to the cozy interior of the carriage.

"Hurry along," he said as he climbed in. "Take care of that goat and join us, either at the crossroads or in Bellsawyer if you're a day behind us. If you fall farther behind, you can find us at the Strolling Minstrel in Ragar."

Ellie answered, "Yes sir," just as the door slammed shut.

The coachman leaned over the edge of the roof with a concerned look on his face. He tipped his hat to her and clambered over the luggage to regain his perch above the horses. He hollered, "Go on," and flicked the reins. Ellie jumped back as the huge wheels turned beside her.

She watched the coach for only a moment, then turned her gaze to Tak. The silly goat pranced as if delighted she'd been left behind.

Ellie lifted her skirts to avoid the brambly bushes and trudged upward on a hill with more rocks than grass. She didn't want to get her new dress dirty or torn, and she had on soft leather boots that shaped attractively around her ankle. Not only that, she had real stockings on. The fine knit of the hosiery itched, but her legs looked very pretty.

Her cloak caught on a branch. "Oh! I'm going to ruin my beautiful clothes." She cast an angry scowl at the goat, but Tak looked away. The cold had deepened, and her stiff fingers fumbled with the fabric clinging to a row of thorns. The material came away, and she examined her fine cloak for any damage.

"Yer a very, very lucky goat, Tak. If'n I'd found a tear, you would notta been shown to a nice warm barn."

Ellie heard the country accent in her words and repeated them as she clambered over a rocky patch. "You're a very lucky goat. If I'd found a tear, you might not have been escorted to a nice warm barn." She smiled. She could talk right when she needed to. That was due to her ma.

Tak scampered toward her when she reached the ridge, then abruptly changed directions and trotted away.

"Oh, no you don't, Tak. I'm not in the mood for playing catch-me."

Cold, damp wind whipped her cloak aside. She shivered and put down the carpetbag to button against the chill. The valise fit under the ample width of her new cape.

Holding the precious valise of clothing, Ellie looked for Tak. He'd disappeared.

"Tak!"

She heard his bleat and hurried toward an outcropping of rock. Tak stood in a patch of green grass, plucking the blades and chewing. Huffing and puffing, she crossed the level ground and sat on a boulder close to the goat.

First she made sure her cloak protected her new dress, then she looked out across the landscape, getting her bearings. The road her aunt and uncle were traveling wound between hills. In some places, she could see the brown ribbon, and in others, woods or hills blocked her view.

After she caught her breath, she'd take Tak down this mound and into the valley she could see just to the south. The distance to the Hopperbattyholds' didn't amount to much. And they'd be going downhill.

The clouds darkened the land to the west, but something caught the light in the hills across the vale. The sun still shining in the east sent shafts of light through clouds not yet amassed for the storm. For her to see it from this distance, the object must be the size of a house. The glint of reflection winked on and off as the sky collected billows of thick vapor.

A clap of thunder punctuated the last glimmer. Tak raised his raucous voice in protest. Her goat hated rain, hated rain with a will. Tak bolted down the mountainside. Ellie grabbed her carpetbag and scrambled after him.

3

# Within a Cloud

Ellie muttered as she followed the goat. She'd been left on her own with a mixed-up set of directions. "If this happens, do this. If that happens, do such and such." She knew her aunt and uncle held her in affection and wanted to do something nice for her, but Ellicinderpart realized that it was up to her not to be a bother. She must not cause an inconvenience. Well, she hadn't. Tak had.

The air thickened with a fine, cold mist. Tak hated to get wet. "Serves him right. What is he doing so far from home?" She called to the goat rushing down the mountainside. "I bet Gustus is scrambling over the hills trying to find you, Tak. Da will be mad as a pig in a crate when he finds out Gustustharinback let you wander off."

Tak bleated a grumpy retort and continued dashing down the rocky terrain.

He wanted to get to shelter as soon as could be. Ellie shifted the carpetbag from one hand to the other. The load got heavier with every step, and the bulk of the valise made it hard to keep her balance. "I'm going to fall down this mountain and never see the coronation."

Just as she reached a level spot near the base of the mountain, the rain changed from a light sprinkle to a torrent. Tak bolted for a cluster of huge rocks, and Ellie followed. Tak leaped over the smaller boulders. To follow, Ellie had to climb and squeeze and struggle with her carpetbag. The hood of her cloak fell back, and rain poured on her head like she'd stuck it under the water pump at the kitchen sink. She fell off the last rock, which was barricading a cave, hit dry dirt, and rolled away from the entrance.

She peered into the dark recesses of the cave. Creepies crawled over her skin, making the fine hair stand up.

"Where are you?" she whispered.

"Maa."

One of the shadows shifted. Ellie tensed, ready to run. Tak took a step forward.

"Oh, you scared me, Tak." She unbuttoned her cloak. "We'll have to stay here. Not exactly what I'd like, but you don't care for rain." Pausing, she waited, thinking she might have heard a squeaky noise from farther back in the cave. "And I don't like closed-in places." She listened again, then whispered, "Probably a bat, and bats won't hurt us."

She turned and faced the entrance, snapping the water off her cloak. She then laid it over a rock to dry. Sitting on the ground, she took off her new boots and sopping stockings. Tak took a few steps closer and looked over her shoulder as she worked to wring some of the rain out of the hem of her skirt.

"It's no use. I'm going to have to change." She reached for her bag and pulled it closer.

Tak nibbled at the ribbon holding a wet hank of her hair.

"Stop!" She batted at him without hitting him. He responded to the signal to leave her alone by plopping his backside down. He looked like a very big, ugly dog. He chewed his cud, and his eyelids drifted half-shut over his horizontal pupils.

Ellie paused in rummaging through her valise to ponder his contentment. "You're wet and stinky." The observation did not disturb his unfocused gaze.

Ellie stared at the sheets of rain soaking the boulders across the front of their shelter. The rivulets all flowed away from the cave entrance. They wouldn't be flooded.

With a big sigh, Ellie pushed her new clothes back into the carpetbag. Changing her wet and mud-splashed dress for another would only get two outfits grubby instead of just one. She laughed a little at herself. At home she had two dresses. She'd have to be more than just a little dirty and uncomfortable to warrant putting the second dress on. She scooted back to the stone wall, arranged the carpetbag for a pillow, and snuggled down for a rest.

Two nights before, she had been so excited about going with her aunt and uncle that she couldn't sleep. The next day in town had left her worn to a nub. She'd discovered that shopping was hard work. Keeping up with Aunt Tiffenbeth had been exhausting.

And that night, when she'd finally fallen onto the soft feather mattress in a room she had to herself, she couldn't sleep. No sisters snored. No little bodies on either side of her squirmed and wiggled and dug at her with sharp elbows and toes.

She couldn't hear the breeze in the stand of quaken trees outside the farm window. The windows stayed shut in town. Aunt Tiffenbeth said burglars might be tempted to come through open windows.

Homesick. And she wasn't even five miles from home yet.

She concentrated on the beautiful clothes Aunt Tiffenbeth had insisted on buying. She envisioned herself in each outfit. She planned what she would wear in the carriage, what she would wear to the street festival, what she would wear to the coronation parade, and what she would wear to the reception that would take place in the streets around the palace. Finally, she drifted off to sleep.

Ellie awoke with a start. Her elbow hurt from being pressed into the hard ground. The muscles in her neck complained of the inadequacy of a carpetbag for a pillow. A rumble came from her stomach, and her nose discovered that the wet goat was still a very wet goat.

She sat up. Thick, moist air clung to her skin. The rain had stopped, but now it seemed the cloud had settled on the mountain. She must have slept a long time. Getting to her feet, she shook out her skirt and found that one side was almost dry. She tiptoed to the front and took in the gray and soggy world.

Tak rose to his feet and pranced to her side. "Maa."

"We're going to the Hopperbattyholds', and you aren't to bellyache about having to go out in this squelchy weather. I've already missed my chance to meet them at the crossroads." She snatched up her hosiery and boots. "I can't wear wet stockings. I'd get blisters." She opened the carpetbag and pulled out thick socks. She dropped the stockings, and Tak picked them up.

"Oh, no you don't." Ellie carefully worked them out from between Tak's teeth. "You aren't going to ruin them."

She hurried to get her shoes on and her bag repacked and herself looking as decent as possible considering she wore damp boots, a damp dress, and a damper cloak. She clambered back over the rocks and stood for a moment trying to figure out where she was.

Tak reluctantly came out. He spied a tasty bush and wasted no time indulging in an afternoon snack.

"I'd almost eat that bush with you, Tak." Ellie placed a hand on her hollow stomach and rubbed as if the pressure would ease away hunger.

She looked over her left shoulder but could hardly see the mountain, let alone the line of their descent. Fog blanketed everything. "We came down from there, and we were heading that way." She turned back toward the direction they'd come from and turned again toward the path she thought they should take.

"The Hopperbattyholds' should be easy to find. We'll keep the mountain close and keep bearing to the west. I don't want to spend the night up here, cold and wet and hungry. Let's go, Tak."

She headed the direction she'd chosen. Tak nipped off a last mouthful of leaves and chewed as he followed.

The thick fog hid every bush, rock, and landmark behind swirling gray mist. Noises echoed. The fragrances of soil, flowers, and grasses drifted past Ellie's nose.

"Do you smell mint?" she asked Tak. He came up beside her and gave her a friendly head butt on the side. "It's you! You found a patch of mint growing. Oh, I hope it wasn't too far behind us. Where is it, Tak?"

He stood looking at her, and she groaned in frustration. "It wouldn't have filled my belly, but chewing on it would have made me feel better."

Seeming to agree with her, Tak worked the vegetation in his mouth, then swallowed.

"Come on." Ellie sighed and continued their trek.

The ground leveled out so that they did very little up-and-down climbing. Ellie felt they had walked for hours. She hiked a lot doing her chores. But now her muscles ached as if she'd trimmed hoofs all morning and bailed hay all afternoon.

The cloud thickened, settling on the land. Ellie and Tak trudged up a rise, and Ellie laughed when her head popped out above the mist. A few more steps, and they stood on top of a knoll. As far as she could see, a haze like a gentle sea eddied over the land. Tops of hills poked out like islands.

Ellie turned a full circle, looking at the murky world.

"Tak," she said.

The goat came close and leaned against her leg.

"I have no idea where we are."

# 4

# A Beacon

Tak made a guttural noise, tossed his head, and moved out as if he knew exactly where he was going. With no better options at hand, Ellie followed.

The land undulated in knolls and elongated hills. Ellie and Tak dipped into the mist and climbed out again at the next rise many times before Ellie saw something she recognized. A thin shaft of sun cut through a high cloud and pinpointed the same glint she had seen early in the day. With a sigh of relief, she figured the Hopperbattyholds' house was just to the south of that landmark.

Tak disappeared within the hovering cloud, and Ellie hurried to keep up. At the next hillock, she realized the shining object would be directly in their path if Tak didn't veer off to one side or the other. The goat trotted on with determination, and she had no objection to letting him be her guide, as long as he headed for the glint on the hillside.

Her only complaint bumped against her legs as she walked. She pictured the goat cart in the corner of the barn and wished Tak pulled her carpetbag. The abundance of new clothes didn't seem quite such a boon, the valise seeming heavier as they crossed the foothills.

A little breeze kicked up, and the mist swirled and eddied, clearing in some patches and stretching thin through others. Across the distance, the object that had attracted her attention took on a shape. Wide at the base with straight up-and-down sides, and narrowing to form a neck, the gleaming object looked like a large bottle. It would have to be an impossibly large bottle to be seen from such a distance.

Tak jogged through the hollows now that the breeze had cleared the way. At the top of each knoll, Ellie spotted the glint she was using as a landmark. The large object grew larger. Ellie squinted. Of course, things appeared bigger as one drew nearer, but this bottle, in comparison to the boulders next to it, actually expanded in height and width.

Tak barreled down another slope into one of the remaining pockets of mist. Ellie lost her footing and slid on wet grass. She held tight to the handle of her carpetbag with one hand while she hugged it to her chest with the other arm. Nothing hindered her slow roll down the hill, but the thought of grass stain smudges on her new dress made her moan. Tumbling to a stop against a rock, she took a minute to determine whether the fall had physically hurt her, checking the places that felt battered. Finding nothing serious amiss, she sat up and felt her carpetbag, making sure the latch had held.

Tak came to her side and butted her arm.

"Okay, I'm coming." She set the valise aside and got to her feet, vexed at the clinging leaves and long pieces of brown grass on her skirt. The wet debris stuck, and she impatiently tried to brush it off. Tak head-butted her on the backside as she leaned over.

"Stop it! You nearly knocked me off my feet, and then I'd have to start cleaning up again." She lifted her arms and let them drop. "What's the point? There's no one out here to see what a mess I am."

"Maa," said Tak.

"You don't count." She grabbed her carpetbag, skimming her shoulder along the tall rock that had stopped her tumble.

A current in the mist cleared the air around her head. The sharp features of a dragon appeared at her side—shiny, pointed teeth, blazing eyes, hot breath, and scaly skin.

Ellie jumped back and looked again. Stone. The frightening visage was not real, but a lifeless statue. A standing stone. She'd heard of them but thought these ancient relics existed in faraway places, not in the hills near her home.

Breathing deeply, she tried to steady her heart and force the lump of fear in her throat to dissolve. The dragon teeth were gray like the rest of the head perched at the top of the rock. Not sharp, but somewhat rounded, as if over hundreds of years the weather had filed away some of their fierceness. On second examination, the blazing eyes appeared glazed over, cold and unfeeling. And the hot breath turned chill as the mist swished past her face.

Imagination. She had a wonderful gift of imagination, fed by the books Gramps had given her to read. Ellie turned away from the object that had scared her witless and resolutely marched after Tak.

She found a second standing stone as she came out of a hollow. What had appeared from the last rise to be a tree and two tall stumps turned out to be a tree, a tall stump, and another vertical rock, deliberately placed by some intelligent beings. The head carved out of the top fifth of the stone depicted another malevolent dragon.

Ellie had heard few tales of dragons. Chiril didn't regard the beasts as intelligent, and their numbers had been hunted down by ugly beasts from the north long before Ellie's gramps had been born. No one she knew had ever seen a dragon except for pictures in books.

She averted her eyes as she passed the standing stone. When she looked directly at it, it was obviously a skillful sculpture. As her eyes slid closer or moved away, the features seemed animated. Just her imagination, of course, but very unsettling. She preferred not to look at the beast at all. Better to be on her way and escape the creature's gaze.

The next part of their journey would bring a ridge to their right. This would block the view of the glinting bottle-shaped thing. The outcropping jutted straight up and looked like a long, spiked tail planted among the green hills. They'd follow along the base, and the bottle should be to the east as they came to the end. Now would be the appropriate time to angle off to the south to reach the Hopperbattyholds' farm.

Surely the farmer and his family would know about the odd sights so close to their property. Two standing stones stood three or four miles from her own home, and that gave her shivers. She wished she'd read more about them and the theories surrounding their formation. She'd ask Mr. Hopperbattyhold.

Calling Tak, she moved away from the ridge and headed toward the small farm, the nearest safe place to leave her wayward goat. The silly goat had taken her out of an exciting ride in a real coach with four horses pulling it. What did she get in exchange? A most uncomfortable hike. Unpleasant weather. Scary standing stones. A dirty dress. Arms that ached from carrying her carpetbag. And only a slim chance of catching up to her aunt and uncle in Bellsawyer.

Ellie wanted to go to Ragar, to a wedding reception and a coronation. She didn't want to explore the highland hills or discover ancient standing stones. She had a plan. Take Tak to the Hopperbattyholds', spend the night with a warm dinner and friendly chatting this evening, leave early in the morning, and hurry to catch up to her aunt.

The goat stood his ground and made no attempt to come with her.

"Tak, this way."

"Maa." Tak shook his head and turned away, then trotted toward the end of the ridge.

"I should just leave you," she shouted.

The goat trotted on, disappearing around the giant stone tail of the sculpture-like beast. Ellie fumed but stomped back the way she'd come with a mind to capture that pesky Tak. She'd known the goat longer than she'd known some of her youngest brothers. As much trouble as Tak could be, she counted him as not just a pet but a friend. And so she doggedly trudged after him.

The gentle breeze that had blown away the last of the grounded cloud stiffened. Ellie squinted to protect her eyes and hurried to catch Tak. She planned to tell him what she thought of him when she had a firm hand on his collar. She skidded to a stop when she rounded the last ridge that would be the tippy-tip of the rock tail.

In front of her, beyond what appeared to be a glass wall, the sun shone on a bright road winding through a meadow of tall grass and wildflowers. Tak sat beside the thick wall and licked it.

Ellie approached cautiously. Pushing the handle of the carpetbag up her arm, she put her hand out to feel the solidity of such a thing. No one, ever, had said one word about a towering wall made out of glass. Everything on the other side looked huge, like things did when you looked through the bottom of a bottle. Ellie tilted her head back and gazed upward. Huge. Monstrous. Colossal.

She pressed her nose against the glass, cupped her hands around her eyes to see better, and peered at the land on the other side. On this side of the wall, gray clouds and the late afternoon drained all light from her surroundings. But on the other side, the sun shone as bright as noonday. Her side was rocky hills with sparse vegetation. The other side teemed with flowering green bushes and long grass waving before a gentle breeze. The wind whipped at her cloak, and Ellie leaned closer, feeling the cold solid glass press against her cheeks.

"Maa."

Tak shoved her from behind, and she fell. She fell *through* the glass wall, feeling its cold hardness touch her arms and legs just as she had felt it on her nose, forehead, and cheeks. It didn't break, but it didn't stop her fall. She sprawled on the lush, cushy grass and gasped for air.

"Maa." Tak folded his legs and settled beside her.

She rolled over, sat up, and stared at where she had just stood. She saw no glass wall. The pleasant countryside stretched on to a band of trees, and the road passed through the woods and went on to the horizon. Not a prickly bush or a scrawny shrub of her world. Only the lovely, serene landscape that had appeared on the other side of the wall—the glass wall that was no longer there. Ellie felt her nose tingle, her eyes water, and a horrid sob waiting to escape her chest.

Now she *really* did not know where they were.

# 5

# No One at Home

Ellie fought rising panic as she examined the unfamiliar terrain. Rocks from tiny pebbles to huge boulders spotted the fields around her home. But grass covered this place. Trees with full heads of soft green leaves lined one horizon. Even the shrubs dotting the landscape appeared to be less rugged than the rough and thorny bushes of home.

Tak jumped to his feet and trotted off, following the impressive road going toward a line of trees.

"Wait!" Ellie scrambled to gather her carpetbag and stood. "Tak!"

She hoped they would pass through the glass wall, even if she couldn't see it, and be back at the end of the ridge. Within a few steps, she knew that crossing over to the other side was not going to happen.

She ran to catch up. Tak jogged along at a brisk pace. Ellie, huffing and puffing, finally got close enough to grab his collar.

"Stop!" She jerked on the goat and fell to her knees beside him. Tak looked at her, the pupils of his yellow eyes mere slits. He thumped his hindquarters down. His disgusted look lingered on Ellie for a long moment before he turned to stare toward the trees.

The wide road could accommodate three wagons side by side. Ellie had never seen anything but dirt tracks, or paths covered in shale. Compared to those country lanes, this highway represented something she might see in the grandest of cities. She sighed, thinking she should be on an old dirt road headed to Ragar, probably the grandest city in Chiril.

She brushed her fingertips across the pavement. The satiny smooth surface surprised her. The odd creamy yellow looked like butter. She and her goat were the only dirty spots on the road.

Still holding on to Tak's collar, Ellie put her arm around his neck and leaned heavily against his side. "I'm so hungry."

Tak tilted his head back and rubbed his chin against her arm. Absent-mindedly, she scratched the spots around his head that gave him pleasure, behind his ears, around his ruff, and under his chin. The mist from the other side of the wall still clung to his coat. The odor wrinkled her nose, but she cuddled him anyway.

Her clothes were damp, flecked with mud, and smeared with grass stains. Cold, wet shoes trapped her feet and made her feel like she'd crammed them into a laundry bucket. She used one foot to push a shoe off her heel, then wiggled that foot out and used it to remove the other shoe. Blue dye from the leather stained her socks. She stretched her legs out in the sun, hoping to dry a little.

So much for elegant clothing.

Her stomach grumbled.

So much for eating fancy meals with her aunt and uncle in roadside taverns.

She could have gone to sleep in the warm sun, leaning against the goat. His coat was drier than her skirt. After a time, she forced herself to straighten.

"Well, collapsed in the road is not going to get us any closer to food." She tied the laces of her shoes through the handle of the carpetbag and walked in the ruined socks on the smoothly paved yellow road.

With a firm grip on Tak, she let him pull her toward the horizon lined with trees. They walked for a long time before they entered the shade of the forest. The warm breeze dried Ellie's clothes and hair and the outside of the carpetbag.

She had to change to Tak's other side occasionally and shift the heavy valise to the other hand. He walked along sedately, and she finally decided to let go of his collar and sighed her relief when he didn't bolt.

Tired and hungry, she trudged down the middle of the road.

"The reason this road is so nice is that no one travels on it. How could it be worn with no use? I thought we might flag a carriage for a ride, or at least pass a traveler who could tell us where we are."

"Maa," Tak answered.

Between the towering trees, they passed in and out of shadows that fell across the wide highway. Tak gave a loud bleat, darted off to the side, and tore into a bush, ripping off tender green branches and chewing contentedly.

"I wonder if I could eat those." Ellie followed the goat and dropped her carpetbag with a delighted exclamation. Berries grew on several bushes. One bush hid blackberries under broad leaves. Another bent under the weight of berries that looked much like the black ones, but the fruit was smaller and yellow. Ellie sat in front of the bushes and picked the berries as fast as she could put them in her mouth and swallow.

With her mouth full and juice running down her chin, she told Tak, "I would have walked right past these. Thank you, Tak."

Remembering the time Gustustharinback had eaten a bushelful of fruit from their parnot trees, Ellie made herself stop as soon as she felt full. Gustus had had a stomachache for two days. She looked at her purple fingers with alarm. A glance down at her dress confirmed her fear. "I'm as messy as a pig."

"Maa."

"I am! Look at me. I *belong* in the country, not at a coronation or a royal wedding."

She looked around her at the lovely road, the towering trees, and her goat. "This is probably my punishment for leaving where I belong and chasing after a glittery life. Just because something sparkles, Tak, doesn't mean it's good for you."

The goat looked askance at her and then turned away, gazing down the road.

"Maa!" He took off, leaving Ellie to jump to her feet, grab her bag, and follow at a run.

Just before Ellie caught up to him, the carpetbag fell out of her hand. She didn't stop but ran faster without its weight. Finally she latched on to Tak's collar and pulled him to a stop.

"Whatever is the matter with you?" She dragged him back to get her valise, then once more started the uncomfortable business of hauling the carpetbag and keeping a firm grip on Tak's collar.

In the distance, Ellie spotted the tops of many buildings.

"A city!" She hurried for a bit but soon realized that miles separated her from the metropolis. She slowed to a plod and dragged the carpetbag beside her.

She finally reached the first house on the outskirts of the giant city. The berries were just a pleasant memory, and the long afternoon walk an unpleasant reality. The enormity of the home matched the enormity of her dismay. Tak head-butted her off the road and toward the path leading up to the house.

The bottom step to the porch came up to Ellie's waist. From corner to corner, the house was longer than any block in Glenbrooken Village. And as for its height, Ellie could not even begin to estimate.

Perhaps as tall as the tallest tree she had ever seen. And in the city beyond, buildings stood shoulder to shoulder, stretched to the sky.

Ellie listened. The wind rustled the leaves in a nearby tree. The tree had grown no bigger than it should have, and for this, Ellie was grateful. The tragabong tree looked just like the tragabong trees at home, and the sight of it comforted her.

Of the birds and insects she'd seen, none were oversize like the giant buildings. Now when she looked at the very wide road, she realized it matched the proportions of the other man-made structures.

The sun slowly sank to the west, and crickets tuned up for a nightly serenade. All good and normal, except for the monstrous house in front of her.

Ellie left her carpetbag in the grass where Tak nibbled a presupper snack and hauled herself up on the first step. Unfortunately three more steps confronted her. By the time she scaled the last one, her breaths came in deep pants. She collapsed on the wooden porch until breathing came normally again.

Who would be in the house? All of the natural landscape seemed normal-sized. Surely the people would be too. However, why would normal-sized people build such enormous houses? She strained her ears to pick up some noise from behind the front door. Nothing.

"Nobody's home," she whispered.

The idea that no people lurked within gave her courage. She sat, listened, heard nothing but the sounds of nature, and got up. Rapping on the door with a closed fist, she hoped no one would answer the knock. If someone did, what would she say?

She looked down at her feet and saw a bundle-up bug crawling in front of her toes. "Small, like a bundle-up should be. The people will be normal as well. Or maybe not. Even so, I will not scream, no matter how big they are."

No one answered. She knocked louder, and still no one came. Stretching and standing on tiptoes, she jiggled the doorknob. Locked.

With a sigh that expressed both relief and frustration, Ellie left the door and stood under a window. If she stood on tiptoes, she could grasp the windowsill. She jumped to look inside. The sun shone in the west windows, illuminating the room. In the brief moment she could look in, she saw big furniture. The next time she jumped, she noticed a huge coat hanging on a hook on the wall. Next she saw a teacup on an end table, but it looked more like a soup bowl. And the last time she jumped, she saw Tak standing in the center of the room.

She jerked around to look where she'd last seen him. Of course, he was not in two places at the same time. Only her carpetbag remained at the bottom of the giant steps.

Ellie scrambled down the stairs with much less care than she had used coming up. Her landing on the grass didn't contain one iota of dignity. Aunt Tiffenbeth would have been displeased.

She stood and raced around the house. The distance to the corner was just as she had surmised, about a half a village block. The side of the house seemed to stretch forever, but this was not true. Her sore legs protested as she rounded the next corner, and the sight of the back entrance allowed her a brief moment of relief.

Instead of steps, a ramp tilted from the ground to a huge open door. She slowed going up the incline, not because she feared what hid in the house, but because her body protested the long day of walking and the dash to get to the back door.

Tak welcomed her with his usual comment. "Maa."

He whirled away from her, and she followed at a walk, craning her neck to see all the fascinating features of the room. She walked under the rough-wood kitchen table. A spoon the size of a ladle lay on the floor. Everything looked just like the things at home, only on a larger scale. She passed through the door into a dining room. The eating table here was grand, with carvings on the legs. She guessed they had been polished at one time, but now dust coated everything.

Tak trotted down the hall, and his hoofs clumped on the thin carpet runner. Ellie came to the front room and stood in one place, staring. Cozy chairs and sofas surrounded a much shorter table, with playing cards sprawled across its surface. A basket of knitting sat at a corner, within easy reach of one of the stuffed chairs. Empty shelves stood beside a comfortable chair, and she wondered briefly what they had once contained. A pillow rested on the floor next to the smaller sofa.

Ellie resisted the urge to lie down. Instead, she made the long journey back around the house to fetch her carpetbag. After bringing it inside, she searched for anything from which to make a meal. Dishes and empty canisters cluttered the shelves but offered no sustenance. She found no food or water, so she would go to bed hungry and dirty. But she had four walls and a roof, enormous walls and a massive roof. She took off her filthy dress and slipped a nightgown over her long underwear. She brushed her teeth as best she could, then unbraided and rebraided her hair.

"It might get chilly tonight," she said.

Tak swung his head to look at her, but didn't offer a comment.

Rummaging around in her carpetbag produced a voluminous skirt to use as a blanket. The pillow on the floor wasn't quite as big as her bed at home but was twice as soft. The light faded, and Ellie made one more search for something to eat. Under the counter in the kitchen, she found an enormous cupboard door that she had overlooked. Several jars and boxes tumbled out. In all the disorder, she found nothing edible.

She made her bed on the pillow and climbed in as twilight gave way to night. For some time she lay very still, listening to every noise. But soon her thoughts overcame her awareness of the old house, and she pondered her unusual circumstances.

She tried to shut down a flow of questions, but found it impossible. *Where am I? How do Tak and I get back? Does anyone even know I'm lost?*

This pesky quizzing cycled through the main queries and occasionally added or subtracted one or two questions. Since she interrogated herself and she had no answers, the exercise became boring.

Tak settled beside her, and his outline in the light of the moon helped her forget the strange happenings of the day.

When she awoke in the morning, his chin rested on the pillow-bed beside her. He opened his eyes and greeted her.

"Maa."

"Tak, I think I feel brave enough to go into the city. Last night I wasn't sure. But I was tired. Maybe we'll find someone to tell us where we are and how to get home. That would be nice."

She glanced around at the room they'd slept in.

"It would also be nice if this helpful person is no taller than I am."

# Within the City

Dew still clung to the grass and bushes as Ellie and Tak walked deeper into the city. The space between houses became shorter, and the structures loomed larger. A string of homes changed to shops, with only an occasional residence. Still no signs of life. Each building appeared to be deserted. A shiver ran up Ellie's spine from time to time as she walked. Sometimes the frisson was caused by her awareness of being alone except for Tak. Sometimes, an eerie feeling of being watched caused her to glance around at the empty windows.

Birds and butterflies flew among the gardens and, on the commercial streets, among the flower boxes and planters. The streets at one time had been well cared for, but now an air of neglect marred their beauty. Dry leaves filled the street gutters. The wind occasionally picked up dirt and swirled it around in dust devils. No one had trimmed the bushes or cut off wilted flower heads. Ellie put aside a fearful thought of a perished city with dead people decaying in these many buildings.

The road ended at a paved circle. Streets branched out from this center like six spokes on a wheel. In the middle, water splashed in a fountain. Seven statues of women in flowing gowns poured water from elegant pitchers into the base they stood in.

Tak leaped up on the side of the pool and drank from one of the streams of falling water from a stone lady's urn. Ellie climbed the carved rim and eagerly quenched her thirst too. Wiping dribbles of water from her chin, she sat with her legs dangling over the outside of the fountain's containment wall.

Somehow this area of the city impressed her as different. She studied her surroundings, trying to discern just what made her feel more at ease in the wide-open circle. A slight wind picked up an abandoned scarf, and like a marionette responding to the puppet master's strings, the thin cloth performed an aerial dance. Tiny brown dowdy birds fluttered about like scraps of paper just as they had along the route to the center of town. But the flower boxes looked beaten, as if someone had whipped the puny plants with a stick.

Tak bumped her as he hopped down, and she almost fell.

Her complaint against him died in her throat as she saw the plate of food up ahead of them. She jumped and tried to reach it before him. She lost, but the pile of oversize muffins would satisfy them both. Dark muffins, white muffins with nuts, yellow muffins with fruit, and a blue muffin that didn't look like anything she had ever seen before.

After eating a half dozen, the odd blue muffin attracted her attention. This one didn't smell as rich as the others, and it was half the size. Cautiously, she nibbled at the edge. Flavor burst in her mouth, something tart like lemon but balanced with just enough honey. She slowed down to enjoy the chewy texture and the wonderful tang.

Tak went back for another drink. Ellie returned to her carpetbag and opened it, trying to find a clean handkerchief to wrap up the leftover muffins. A child's loud shout brought her head up with a snap. Into the circle, a huge child, taller than Ellie, barreled from one side, snatched the muffin plate, and tore down another street.

As he passed between the corner buildings, he shouted, "There's another one. She's got a dog. Catch her!"

A chorus arose from all around. "Catch her! Catch her! Catch her!"

Tak took off the way they'd come.

Ellie had pulled her things out as she'd searched for the handker-chief. Now she stuffed clothing in as fast as she could, but the mess stubbornly refused to be crammed inside. She tried to close and fasten the latch. A primal scream from somewhere behind Ellie sent her after Tak, leaving her belongings behind.

More childlike voices echoed the first yell. Even the cry of a mountain cat couldn't compare to the war shrieks of the child savages.

Tak slipped between two buildings, and Ellie hurried to keep him in sight. The thought of being alone in this strange land, in this huge city, with monstrous children scared her. Tak was just a goat, but he was her only ally.

They came upon an alley, and the goat cut to the left. Ellie followed. Tak pushed his body behind a pile of rough pine boxes, and Ellie shoved on his backside to make room for herself. They waited, panting. The wild calls scattered and came from all different directions.

Tak's tail flicked and slapped Ellie in the face. She ignored the goat and leaned toward the opening of their box cave. Were the shouts congregating in one direction? They were. A few minutes passed, then the fanatical screeches resumed.

"I think they're coming this way, Tak."

She scrunched in as far as she could and pulled a pine flap out of one box, shielding the hole to their cave. A splinter impaled her thumb, and she stuck the wound in her mouth.

The horde charged past them. Some still chanted, "Catch her!" but most put their energy into bloodcurdling yells. Their pursuers' feet pounded on the pavement, and the boxes rattled as they went past. Hearing a *whop, whop, whop, thud* against the top of the pile from one end to the other, Ellie imagined one child wielding a club.

Finally, the noise diminished. The mob had moved on.

The goat's stubby tail whipped across her face, and he began backing up. When she wouldn't budge, he kicked her. Not too hard, but enough to make her move out of his way. Once in the alley, the goat stared steadily in one direction and then the other.

"Maa!" He ran back the way they had come and away from the pack of giant children. To Ellie's confusion and dismay, the city became a maze of alleys and streets that reminded her of the labyrinth she'd read about. Several times she and Tak caught sight of child gangs some distance down the way. Tak found places to hide when they couldn't outrun the children.

The chase lasted all morning. Ellie tried to direct Tak to a path that would take them out of the city altogether, but the stubborn goat turned back toward the center over and over. Again, they heard the clamoring of the pack, and Ellie chose the turn they'd take to escape. The alley looked promising, but she soon saw she had led them into a dead end. A huge door into the building stood open, so she ducked inside with Tak at her heels.

The door slammed shut, and Ellie whirled with a start. Before her stood a gentleman tumanhofer. Definitely a city dweller by his fine, though a bit torn and dirty, clothing.

He clicked his heels together. "Allow me to introduce myself. Graddapotmorphit Bealomondore of Greeston at your service." He bowed. "You and I are presently the only tumanhofers in Rumbard City."

Ellie returned a bobbing curtsy, realized it was a very country form of the pleasantry, and switched in the middle to a deeper dip. She lost her balance and steadied herself by grabbing a barrel, which tipped over with a bang.

All three stood still for a moment, listening to see if she'd revealed their whereabouts.

After a moment, Ellie curtsied again. "Ellicinderpart Clarenbessi-pawl from, well, not anywhere in particular. Outside of the village, Glenbrooken Village." She'd done that badly. Embarrassment warmed her cheeks.

"Maa."

She glanced at her goat. "And this is Tak."

A noise from the alley caught their attention. The knob on the door turned. Graddapotmorphit Bealomondore grabbed Ellicinderpart Clarenbessipawl's hand. "Run!"

He guided them between giant hanging clothes, and Ellie realized they were in a store. She panted as she tried to keep up. "Where do all these ready-made clothes come from?"

"Cottage industry, and it would seem the urohm ladies believe in stiff competition. I'll show you the fancy labels inside the clothing some other time. Right now, I hear the stomping of enemy forces."

The children swarmed through the shop. Bealomondore led Ellie and the goat to a counter and ducked under the edge. They followed him into the empty space behind the counter front.

Dust tickled her nose. Ellie rubbed it. "It's stuffy in here," she whispered.

"Don't sneeze," Bealomondore ordered. He climbed a stack of boxes arranged like a staircase. Darkness covered him from the waist up. "Come on up. We're going to hide in this locked drawer."

Tak quickly scaled the makeshift steps. Ellie followed more care-fully. At the top she could see the narrow opening along the side of the drawer. The distance from the highest step to the underside of the counter provided a bit of a challenge in wiggling into the safe haven. The tumanhofer gentleman helped Ellie climb into the deep drawer and then lifted Tak in.

Scarcely any light filtered into their hiding place, but she recognized huge coins and paper money. Ellie heard scraping noises below, then Bealomondore's hands gripped the side of the drawer, and he soon maneuvered himself in beside her and the goat.

"This drawer is locked," he explained. "The only way to get in or out is the way we just used. And that way can only be used by people our size."

"What is this place?"

"A money depository, like a safe." He put a finger to his lips.

"They won't find us?" Ellie whispered back.

He shook his head. "They'll give up soon. It's almost time for noon-meal, and they know better than to be late."

"What happens if they're late?"

"The food will be gone, eaten by those who got there first."

With his face turned toward the light filtering in through the crack running between the lip of the drawer and the underside of the countertop, Ellie could see the tumanhofer's frown.

"They go hungry?" she asked.

"If they are horribly late, the leftovers, if there are any, dry up and blow away."

"So there *are* adults someplace who care for these wild things?"

"There's only one adult left, and he lives in the library. They call him Old One. He has the doors locked and won't let them in."

"But..."

"I know. It boggles the mind."

"Who are they?"

"As far as I have been able to ascertain, they are the last of the urohms living in Chiril."

Ellie let out a loud sigh of relief and then froze. A child's steps neared their hideout. The drawer rattled but didn't open.

"Whatcha doing, Phee?"

"I heard a noise."

"How d'ya think they'd get in a locked drawer?"

"I forgot it was locked."

"It's locked every time we come in here."

"I know. I just forgot. I want to see that dog. Tolly says the wee one has a dog. I've never seen a dog."

"Neither have I. Come on, Phee. I'm hungry. Let's go to the circle."

"It was fun though. I had fun. We almost got 'em, didn't we? I hope we snatch 'em next time."

"Yeah, me too."

"What are we going to do when we catch her and the dog?"

"Same thing we'll do when we catch that wee man."

"Eat 'em?"

"Yeah, eat 'em."

# 7

# Rumbard City

"Let's go." Bealomondore started to climb out of the drawer.

Ellie grabbed his coat sleeve. "Is it safe?"

"Yes, they've gone for noonmeal." He went over the edge and disappeared. She heard a thud and then his voice. "Hand me the goat."

Ellie hoisted Tak over the side and into Bealomondore's waiting arms, then climbed out with a little assistance from the tumanhofer.

"I left my belongings in the fountain circle. Can we go get them?"

Bealomondore gave a humorless laugh and shook his head. "We may be able to gather your things as time goes by, but the hordes claim everything they find. And they're all in the circle now eating."

Tak stamped his hoofs on the wooden floor.

"He wants to go out," said Ellie.

Bealomondore led the way. "You mindspeak with the goat?"

His back didn't tell whether the tumanhofer joked or asked a legitimate question. She liked it better when she could see his face while he spoke. On the other hand, his sincere expression had her believing everything he said. Perhaps it was better not to see his kind eyes while she debated whether he was trustworthy.

His comment was odd. No one she knew had ever claimed to mindspeak. Maybe he meant something else.

"Talk without words, in your mind?" she asked.

He nodded without looking back.

Mindspeaking! Ellie had learned over the past day and a half that the rules of Chiril didn't seem to apply to Rumbard City. Of course, she'd heard of mindspeaking, but only in stories. Those tales arose out of wizards and dragons, rarely sighted even in Chiril. This tumanhofer had answers. He had experience in this strange place. She wouldn't scoff at the things she found absurd. She was going to remain respectful to get as much information from him as she could.

Cautiously, she phrased her question and chose a neutral tone of voice. "Mindspeak with an animal?"

He paused at a place in the wall where a crack let in sunbeams. Nudging a loose board to the side, he peeked out.

"All clear." He removed two boards, stepped through, then handed Ellie out. "Don't trip on that baseboard."

Tak hopped through the hole. Ellie waited, glancing up and down the alley, while Bealomondore returned the boards.

When he finished and brushed his hands on his pant legs, she asked again. "Do you mindspeak with animals?"

"Only dragons."

Ellie pulled in a breath, but it did nothing to tamp down the sudden anger that surged through her. All her good intentions scattered before the familiar feeling of being teased by rascally brothers. "That's enough!"

Bealomondore's eyes widened as he spun around to face her. "What?"

"I know it's obvious that I'm a country girl, but I'm educated. I don't know what pleasure you derive from throwing ridiculous statements at me, but I don't appreciate it. I'm lost and scared and late." She struggled to keep her tears at bay. "I was supposed to meet my aunt and uncle in Bellsawyer. We were going to the coronation and the royal wedding reception."

"Now that's a coincidence. So was I."

For a moment, Ellie's ire cooled. "You were? You haven't always lived here?"

"It seems like forever, but I've only been here two months."

"Why were you going to Ragar two months before the festivities?"

He hesitated. "I know Paladin and Princess Tipper. I was asked to do the wedding portrait."

Ellie stared at the tumanhofer. He painted? Did he really know royalty? He looked earnest, but no one knew royalty. No one! Well, she guessed somebody had to.

Bealomondore tilted his head toward the end of the alley. "If you want to see the horde at feeding time, we have to get moving. We don't have a lot of time to get there."

He turned and hurried away.

Tak gave her a look that said, "Come on," and fell in line behind the tumanhofer.

Ellie couldn't think of exactly the right word to describe the fickle goat. She'd raised him from a bottle-fed kid and had never had any trouble with Tak until recently. Her beloved pet now seemed intent on leading, or pushing, her into trouble.

Ellie did want to retrieve her carpetbag and clothing, so she hustled after Bealomondore and her goat.

They came to the circle from another direction and entered one of the surrounding buildings. Bealomondore's confidence eased her fear of being so close to the young giants. He led them directly to the front of the building and positioned them behind a broken door where they could observe the circle and not be seen by the children. Ellie didn't need to be on the same side of the center to see her things.

Various children had donned most of the garments she owned. Of course, nothing fit. Her beautiful green skirt hung around a dirty boy's neck like a cape. Several children used her stockings as sashes.

A lovely dress with a wide, swaying skirt draped over the back of a girl like a hat. She'd crammed her head, down instead of up, through the neck hole. At present she had two pieces of fruit in her hands and took savage bites out of each, chewing and wiping the juice from her mouth with the sleeve of her shirt.

Ellie's aunt had said the blue gown was walking apparel and they would promenade along Palismon Boulevard with other fashionable ladies while in the city. Ellie now doubted she'd ever reach Ragar, let alone spend a morning promenading. She blinked back tears as she further examined the fate of her beautiful clothes.

Not all the children had chosen to wear something from her carpetbag. Some items must have been tossed into the air. Her shoes dangled from one of the watering ladies. Her lace slip had landed ringed around a broken bench. Someone had stuffed one of her caps onto the head of another stone woman. The carpetbag floated in the fountain pool like a colorful sea ship.

Ellie sank to the floor and put her face in her hands.

Tak pushed his nose into her neck and huffed. His warm breath comforted her a little, and she put an arm around his neck.

"We'll be able to get some of the things back," said Bealomondore. "They'll play all afternoon and discard the items as they go. We just need to snatch them up before another child lays claim."

Ellie turned enough in her sitting position to peek out again. All of the children ate like swine, smashing the fruit into their mouths and taking huge, slurpy bites.

Bealomondore sighed. "You don't want to get close enough to smell them."

"If Old One in the library provides the food, why doesn't he guide them at all, teach them?"

The tumanhofer shook his head. "Old One never comes out. I don't think he's the one providing the food. I can't figure out any logical means by which the meals can be assembled and delivered. Added to that, I haven't even seen Old One yet, though I've explored the library. I only know of him by eavesdropping on the little jackanapes."

Ellie watched a child run in from a side street and check the baskets placed around the rim of the fountain. The enraged boy threw down each empty container and roared. The others ignored him. He didn't bother with the last few but approached a busy eater, grabbed his portion, and shoved him into the fountain.

"Oh my!" exclaimed Ellie. "They need some discipline."

"I doubt it would do any good. This lot is incorrigible."

Ellie raised an eyebrow and asked, "Have you tried?"

"No, and I don't intend to. I've been trying to discover a way out of this place."

"Really?" She pondered his response. While it would be honorable to try to reach these lost children, it certainly made wonderful sense to escape the city. "You think we can get out?"

He grimaced. "Wait until you see the library, then you'll understand the enormity of the problem."

He didn't sound very hopeful. Ellie returned to her study of the children. "How many are there?"

Bealomondore sat down beside her, his back to the door. "On some days when I count, I get fifty-eight. On other days, I get sixty-three. They move around too fast to get an accurate tally."

"I don't understand." Ellie stretched up a little to get a better view. "They all look like they're around the same age. There are no babies, no older children?"

Bealomondore shook his head, agreeing to the negative.

"How old are they?" asked Ellie. "Do you know?"

"They are all six, every last one of them."

"Six?"

"Six."

"So someone has been feeding them for six years."

"No."

"No?"

"I have found documents in the library, written by hand, probably by Old One. Rumbard City is under some kind of wizardry. Those rapscallions have been six for several centuries. But they don't remember that they were six last year and will be six again on the next birthday. Therefore they never mature, never learn from their experiences, never grow up physically. They are little hooligans suspended in a perpetual state of selfish rebellion."

Most of the children had finished their noonmeal. They wiped sticky hands on their clothing and ran off, some in groups and some alone.

Ellie sank to a sitting position again and turned to share the door as a backrest with Bealomondore.

"If Old One does not provide their food, then who does?"

Bealomondore shrugged. "I have no idea, but whoever it is supplies me as well." He sat up straighter. "All that running and hiding this morning made me hungry. Would you like to share whatever has been provided?"

"Yes, please, and I'm thirsty too."

He stood and extended his hand. She grasped it and easily came to her feet.

He nodded his approval. "You're strong and agile. That will come in handy. And I have nothing against country girls." He smiled. "Princess Tipper lived most of her life away from any city."

The comment pricked that doubt Ellie had laid aside. She followed the tumanhofer but didn't ask him any more questions. She didn't know if she could trust his answers.

The vent they had used to enter the building still stood open. Bealomondore stopped before exiting and listened. He held up a finger, indicating "wait a minute," then pressed it to his lips. With his hand on her shoulder, he gently pushed her to the side of the huge crack.

"One of the hunters is coming."

Ellie's eyes widened as she heard shuffling feet coming down the alley. The lone hunter did not stop but continued on until they could no longer hear him.

Ellie whispered, "Why did you call him a hunter?"

"Because they spend a great deal of time hunting me. And now, it would seem, they are intent on hunting you as well."

"They're just children. I have brothers and sisters around their age. It's a game."

"Didn't you hear them express the desire to eat us? Recall, if you will, the savage way they tore into parnots, berries, melons, and apples."

"Just play-talk and rudeness." Ellie looked into Bealomondore's eyes. "They need a mother. They need an adult. They are children without anyone to care for them."

"Miss Ellicinderpart Clarenbessipawl, they are children, but they've gone feral. Wild beyond taming. Dangerous to anyone smaller and weaker. We are the wee ones. There is nothing we can do except stay out of their way."

# 8

# Pickles and Mustard

Bealomondore chose the shortest route to take his visitor to a fountain a few blocks from the town's circle. On one hand, it was good to have company, but on the other, he would have to protect her from the hooligans and make sure she had a safe place to stay.

And then there were the proprieties to consider. She was lovely and single. He was single and a good prospect for matrimony.

Even with purple berry stains on her chin and fingers, she had a certain unsophisticated charm. Better if she would have come to him as an old crone near death's door. But they were both young and eligible, and they had no chaperone. The squirmy heathen kids did not count. The goat didn't count. The mysterious Old One in the library didn't count. And they might be here for months. He hadn't found any useful information in the library on how to leave Rumbard City, and the answer might not even be among the bookshelves.

The goat kept close to his mistress but made forages to the side, poking his nose in places that must look interesting to one of his species. He gazed down alleys and seemed to listen. What a goat would listen for, Bealomondore did not know. He had no experience with barnyard animals and found that the pet acted like a dog in many ways. The urchins thought it was a dog, but he wasn't surprised since they were sorely uneducated.

Ellicinderpart kept up with him, even though he set a quick pace.

And she climbed well. Rumbard City, built exclusively for urohms, presented plenty of opportunities for tumanhofers to climb up, over, and down what the giants would consider ordinary steps. Bealomondore thanked Wulder that He had not sent him a prissy society girl who would cringe at such athletic pursuits.

A couple of urohm blocks made a long hike for tumanhofers. Ellicinderpart uttered no complaints as they traveled. And she quickly hid without a fuss when noises from the gangs reached them.

She definitely was not an ordinary individual. She had many superb qualities, but he feared some of them would be inconvenient. She clearly suspected him of outrageous lies. She would remain skeptical of anything he said, wanting full explanations. He couldn't blame her. When he'd first met Tipper and her father, he had been full of doubt.

He wondered for a moment if his preoccupation with Ellie stemmed naturally from two months of his own company. He couldn't remember any time in which he had been so isolated. His life had been full of cultural events with the upper crust of Chirilian society. Then he had accompanied Paladin and others on adventuresome quests. He'd met many unusual people in his journeys around Chiril, but he'd never met a traveler who had a goat for a companion.

After a long walk, they reached the fountain they sought. The deserted square held a patch of grass with the artful monument in the center. Once tidy flower beds now held a riot of colored blooms in a helter-skelter array.

"This is where the provider leaves my meals."

"It's beautiful." Ellicinderpart walked slowly around the metal art. Flowers, small animals, and birds clung to a central cone, three feet wide at the base and culminating in bubbling water at the top. The fountain cascaded over, through, and around the metal wildlife. The pool at the bottom was smaller than the huge, elaborate fountain in the middle of the city.

The girl's goat ignored the water and trotted over to the doorway of a butcher's shop. On the stoop, in a dark corner, stood a box carved and painted with chickens, pigs, and cows. Tak butted the box.

"Tak!" Ellie ran to grab his collar. "What are you doing now?"

Bealomondore laughed as he joined her. "I wish I'd had Tak with me two months ago. This is where our noonmeal is hidden. I almost starved before I found it."

He reached to open the lid and laughed again when Ellicinderpart peered over his shoulder while the goat tried to push between him and the box. He used his knee to shove Tak out of his way.

"How did you find it?" asked the girl.

He didn't hesitate in answering. She would soon learn that he spoke the truth. "The dragons of the watch took pity on me." He pulled out two bottles and a package wrapped in brown paper. "Aha! Whoever leaves the meals knows that there are two of us now."

"Dragons of the watch?"

"Yes, they patrol the entire city. It's a large city, and you can go days without seeing one."

He gestured for her to have a seat on the bench between the butcher's and shoemaker's shops. She climbed the wrought-iron side and sat on the wooden slats. He handed up the package and then the bottles. She waited until he climbed up and settled beside her before handing back the parcel of food.

Bealomondore stifled a sigh. He knew from her arched eyebrows that this would not be a comfortable noonmeal with inconsequential chatter. He untied the string on the package.

"Tak and I," she said, "walked from the very outskirts of this city to the center, and we never saw a dragon. How can huge flying beasts not be visible? And even before we got to the city, surely we would have seen them above the buildings as we approached."

"Look, sandwiches." He picked up one to examine, knowing he would not divert her attention. "This one has pickles and mustard." He offered it to her. "Do you like pickles and mustard?"

She took the sandwich without comment, but Bealomondore saw the suspicion in her eyes. He tried to win her with a little cordial conversation.

"What? If you don't like pickles and mustard, there's another sandwich." He picked it up to check the contents. "Oh dear, more pickles and mustard."

Her attention shifted to the sandwich in her hand. She lifted the top piece of bread a bit. "There's greens, tomato, and some kind of meat as well. You needn't go on and on about the pickles and mustard."

"Then you do like pickles and mustard?"

She turned to look at him, her eyebrows scrunched down and her mouth pressed in a firm line. "It doesn't really matter whether I like pickles and mustard. It really doesn't! I wish you'd stop talking about pickles and mustard and sandwiches."

Bealomondore did his best to sound sympathetic. "Aren't you hungry?"

"I'm starving!"

"That explains it then."

"Explains what?"

"Why you're a bit peevish." He smiled even though she showed signs of inflicting violence on him. Her empty hand had balled into a fist. "Let's eat, and then we'll both feel better. Do you mind if I thank Wulder for our food?"

"Wulder? Who's Wulder? I thought you didn't know who left the sandwiches."

"I'll give you a complete explanation of Wulder after we eat, and all good things come from Wulder, either directly or indirectly. I've often thought He might be the provider. But that's a discussion for after we eat." Bealomondore pointedly bowed his head to cut off any further comments. "Oh, Wulder, I thank You for this meal and for bringing Ellicinderpart Clarenbessipawl to Rumbard City. Help us to work together to find a way out. Thank You for meeting our needs even before we ask. And bless this food."

He lifted his eyes to find her staring at him wide-eyed and slack-jawed. He took a bite of his sandwich and winked at her.

"Delicious. Try it."

Raising the sandwich to her open mouth appeared to be an automatic movement. But once she chomped down on that first bite, an expression of delight came over her. She chewed, swallowed, and took another bite. Leaning her head back, she closed her eyes and breathed deeply.

A feeling of satisfaction filled Bealomondore. She was enchanting in that unguarded moment. And his tension over their circumstances fled with the pleasure of a good meal. Perhaps he would be able to gain her trust. They could work together to solve the mystery of Rumbard, although by that time the coronation and wedding would have passed. He took another bite of his sandwich and hoped for a myriad of solutions to his varied problems.

The first to tackle would be the most immediate. What was he going to do with Ellicinderpart for the whole afternoon? He didn't regard being her bodyguard as a productive way to spend his time. But he couldn't let her roam around on her own.

"I usually go to the library in the afternoon. The horde runs wild, and they get tired and cranky. I prefer to be out of their way, and since Old One won't let them in, it's a good time to do research on the city."

She took out a handkerchief and wiped breadcrumbs from her lips. "I'd like to see the library, but I don't know if I want to see the librarian."

He took the two bottles and paper wrapping and jumped lightly to the sidewalk. "I don't know that Old One is legitimately a librarian. But he does live there."

"Did you search for him?"

She swung her legs back and forth while he deposited the trash in the butcher's box. Stained blue and riddled with holes, her socks ought to be discarded.

"What did you do with your shoes?" he asked.

"Oh, my feet were sore from all the walking and the shoes were wet, so I took them off."

"It doesn't hurt your feet to run like we've been doing all morning?"

She blushed.

Bealomondore cringed inwardly at his social blunder. How could he, the suave portrait painter for the rich, be so insensitive? It must be the result of being a warrior in Chiril's defense against Baardack. "I didn't mean to offend you."

"No, it's all right." She lifted her chin. "I take the goats out to the mountain pastures every day, and when the weather is fair, I go without my shoes."

He nodded and moved to stand in front of her. He held his arms up and smiled. "Jump, and I'll catch you."

She slid off the bench, and he caught her waist easily, then lowered her to the ground.

He pulled his hands back, and turned to survey the fountain and the small park around it. "Well, where's Tak? We have a bit of a walk."

# 9

# In the Library

Ellie's eyes fell on the words blazoned in gold across the front of the huge white building: Rumbard City Library.

Bealomondore led her around to the back of the building to a vent, and she watched as he unscrewed one of the two bolts that held the cover. The two other holes for screws were empty. Once he removed one, he slid the slatted metal sheet down. The grate made a steep and slippery stairway to climb. After Bealomondore helped her navigate the slats, he went back down to help Tak enter.

Ellie assisted the tumanhofer in lifting the cover into place and then holding it while he reinserted the screw. The tumanhofer wedged the loose bolt in between the wall and the cover in such a way as to keep it from swinging down and revealing the secret entrance.

Darkness shrouded the immediate area, but Ellie could see light in the distance. Tak trotted between stacks of wooden boxes. Ellie hurried to catch up.

Sunshine poured through a circular skylight in a round room surrounded by bookcases. Around the edges of the rotunda, plants in huge pots overflowed with thick, tangled vegetation that climbed the walls on its way to the ceiling. Some of the foliage qualified as trees in Ellie's opinion.

In the center of a white marble floor, sofas and comfortable chairs sat on a lush patterned rug. Several small tables nestled up to the seats.

Books were piled high on one table, with more books stacked by the chair next to it.

Drawn to the place where someone obviously spent a lot of time reading, Ellie tiptoed as if she might disturb the unseen patrons of the library with her footsteps. She started at Bealomondore's voice directly behind her.

"Old One has chosen a varied selection of reading material."

She put her hand to her chest and spun to face him. "Don't do that again," she whispered.

"Sorry, I didn't mean to startle you." Bealomondore pulled a contrite face.

Ellie didn't trust him when he looked so abashed and preferred his cavalier demeanor much more. She could label him vain and arrogant and not have to fight the urge to depend upon him. She feared that he would gain her confidence only to trick her somehow.

In Glenbrooken, strangers, sophisticated strangers, were watched until proven proper, moral, and reliable. The villagers, her family, all the neighbors, everyone had manners, but no one was as polished as this well-to-do tumanhofer. She knew family and friends would readily lend a hand, but could Bealomondore be trusted? In Rumbard City, she was without the counsel of older, wiser voices. She would have to discern on her own from the evidence before her.

Bealomondore scaled a stack of books and climbed into the chair. "It's here. Come on up."

Curious, she followed his route to the top and peered over the arm of the chair to where Bealomondore struggled with a huge book. He dragged it to the back of the chair and propped it up against the cushion.

As he opened it, he glanced up at Ellie. "I think this is Old One's journal."

"His private journal?"

Bealomondore had the grace to look a bit embarrassed. "Well, yes. But he has to know someone is reading it because I never put it back in the position I found it. Some days it isn't here. And sometimes I think he is writing *to* me because he mentions things that happened years ago like he wants me to know the history."

"Then why doesn't he just sit down here and wait for you, then tell you to your face?"

Bealomondore shrugged. "Perhaps if we ever find him, we can ask." He looked at the open pages and back to Ellie. "Come down and read with me. See what you think."

She slid down the upholstered arm and landed on the soft seat cushion. Her raggedy socks looked extra shabby next to the rich fabric of the chair. She sat cross-legged with her feet tucked under her skirt.

"Are we going to start from the beginning?" she asked.

"No, I'm looking for the last entry I read." Bealomondore turned pages with effort. The small task involved walking from one side of the book, grasping the paper's edge, and dragging it back. "Ah! Here we are."

He stood back a few steps and looked up, then read the tidy script. *"The silence weighs heavily on my soul. When I can stand it no longer, I go to a window on the second floor and open it. Sometimes I can hear the birds. It is best at night, when insects serenade the cool breezes. It is worst when the remnant is close enough for me to hear their coarse screams, horrid laughter, taunts, and threats. Of course, they don't bother me. None of their jeers are directed toward me. But they heap scorn upon each other. I've not seen an act of kindness in a century or more. But then, I don't watch them as I used to. Observing their conduct saddens me beyond what I can* bear. *To think that the mighty urohms are represented by selfish, grubby little fiends.*

*"I wonder when I die how long they will go on in their perpetual childhood."*

Ellie let out a long, slow breath. "He doesn't sound very happy, does he?"

Bealomondore sat down with his back against the arm of the chair. "No, he doesn't."

He clasped his hands and rested them on his knees. He appeared to be lost in thought, and Ellie did not disturb him. As he puzzled over whatever was on his mind, she read the second page in the book. *"I think perhaps Wulder has sent someone to take my place as guardian of the library. A tumanhofer—"*

"Bealomondore, look." She pointed to the lettering. "He does know you're here. He's mentioned you."

The tumanhofer started and followed her pointing finger. He jumped up and read aloud. *"A tumanhofer visits the library. For almost two months now. At first I thought he was my overactive imagination, a vision of a dream of mine come true, or perhaps a thief who stumbled upon our bottled city. I can't bring myself to talk to him. It's been so long since I've had a conversation with anyone but myself. But since he came, I find I don't talk to myself as much. I fear he will overhear me and jump out of some shadow to confront me. That would be most uncomfortable, and I am old. Surely he wouldn't frighten an old man."*

The entry in the journal ended.

Ellie giggled. "I don't think he wants you jumping out at him and scaring him to death. He obviously wanted you to be forewarned. Scare him, and he won't answer any questions."

Bealomondore took hold of the page and hauled it to the other side. He glanced up and smiled. "Good guess. Listen to this. *'I fear I would be scared to death. I am no longer striving to live longer, but my idea of a pleasant passing would be to sleep and not wake up.'*"

"That's sad," said Ellie.

"He often writes about years of being alone. I've only been here two months, and I have had too much of my own company."

"So you are glad Tak and I showed up?"

He studied her for a moment before smiling. "You aren't too bad."

"You sound like one of my brothers."

He winked at her. Her brothers never winked at her. Something passed through his expression that did not look like a brother at all. She looked away and wondered if the warmth in her cheeks meant she was blushing. Did the amount of heat determine the height of the red coloring? She looked back at him, but he didn't seem to be aware of her discomfort. Perhaps he was as obtuse as her brothers.

He studied a fingernail on his hand. Her brothers would have had half a yard of dirt under their toenails and the other half under their fingernails.

Bealomondore put his clean hands on his thighs. "I have sisters and one brother. I enjoyed giving my sisters a hard time. My older brother did not take well to teasing."

She laughed, then sobered. "I have lots of younger brothers and sisters, and I miss them. Bealomondore, we must find a way to get out of Rumbard City."

He nodded, then turned, stretching out a hand to help her rise as well. "There are older journals on the floor. Shall we go down and see what we can find?"

Tak had been busy while they were occupied high on the chair. He munched on long, spindly leaves from one of the ornate plants. Holes in the greenery indicated he had snacked from almost all the pots. He stamped his feet when he saw Ellie.

"There's a park behind the library," said Bealomondore. "I'll take him out there."

"I want to go too." She went to Tak and rubbed his ears. "It's not dangerous, is it?"

"The park isn't, and the mob rarely comes close to the library." Bealomondore walked between two bookshelves. "This way."

As Ellie followed with Tak, she craned her neck to survey the towering bookcases. Elaborate leather bindings covered most of the books. The rich colors with embossed lettering outnumbered the plainer jackets. The size varied from books she could almost handle to ones that might kill her if they fell from the shelves and landed on her. Suddenly she laughed.

Bealomondore stopped and turned around, tilting his head in a quizzical gesture.

Ellie smiled at him. "I just remembered what you said earlier— that once inside the library, I would realize the enormity of the problem." She glanced around at the books. "Now I understand."

Bealomondore laughed and gestured for her to follow. At that moment, she thought the tumanhofer made a good escort. Tak tugged, and she skipped a step as they maneuvered between the library stacks.

A black wrought-iron gate gave them entrance to the block-sized yard. Statues lurked among overgrown shrubbery. Ellie heard but couldn't see a fountain among the bushes gone wild.

She let Tak go inside the fence and explored on her own. Bealomondore stayed close, and she appreciated his presence. Her little brothers would have chosen a place such as this to jump out and scare the wits out of her. She understood Old One's aversion to being surprised.

When she came upon several sculptures, she shook her head in wonder. "There are so many statues."

"From what I've seen," said Bealomondore, "Rumbard City was a cultural center. There's a museum, an opera house, and a university. All empty. The architecture of the city, and the numerous parks with fountains and statuary, indicates an interest in higher forms of civilization. The restaurants represent different ethnicities and speak of refinement and sophistication. And even the quality and variety of the books in the library signify a concern for philosophy and opportunities for broad education. This was by no means a backward society when it met its end."

"What could have caused it?" Ellie climbed on a bench to sit down and studied her tumanhofer companion. "There's no sign of death or destruction. It's as if a portion of the populace just left, taking nothing with them and leaving behind one man and a crew of untamed children."

"No," said Bealomondore. "I've read enough to know that the city was separated from the outside world. The adults grew older and died. The children matured to the age of six and then remained that age."

"That still leaves the questions why and how."

"Correct. And I believe when we find those answers, the key to our escape will be close at hand."

"I certainly hope so."

They spent the afternoon spreading the books out on the carpet in the library and opening them one by one. Many contained lists and summaries of books Old One had read. Some of the books had Old One's concise opinions of their literary worth. Both Bealomondore and Ellie were confused by entries such as, *Imanderron is a worthy friend, one who begs my attention and calls me back for more musing over the worth of life and the injustice of time.*

*Imanderron* turned out to be one of the books by the chair and clued them in to Old One's habit of sometimes referring to favorite volumes as friends.

Ellie and Bealomondore each took a journal to peruse, hoping to cover more territory and find something that would help. Occasionally one would call to the other to share an interesting entry, but most of Old One's accounts detailed tedious days with nothing relevant to their predicament. They discovered that the older journals had much more lively reports.

"He probably hadn't yet succumbed to the melancholy of being alone," said Ellie.

Bealomondore stood and stretched. "It's time to collect our dinner."

Ellie looked up to the domed skylight. "Oh my! It's gotten dark." She frowned and looked around. "Where is our light coming from?" The tops of the pillars glowed.

"Lightrocks. The library is almost too well lit at night. I have to find a dark corner to sleep in."

"You sleep here?"

"Yes, it is the only place I know the grimy masses will not invade. If I oversleep in the morning, I won't be awakened by grubby paws mauling my person."

She looked again at the dark sky. "But we have to go out to fetch our meal?"

"Not to worry," said Bealomondore in good humor. "The brats must be afraid of the dark. I've never seen one after the sun goes down."

He came and offered her his arm. "Would you care to go for a stroll, Miss Ellicinderpart Clarenbessipawl?"

She smiled and nodded as she took his arm. She was hungry, and the prospect of dinner with Bealomondore delighted her. Bealomondore would also protect her from naughty children should this be the one time they ignored curfew. Tonight she could relax and enjoy the moment. Tomorrow she would put more thought into how to escape.

# 10

# A Walk in the Night

When they left the library, they found the pavement wet and raindrops clinging to leaves and flowers.

"The evening shower," said Bealomondore. "Most nights—not all—a gentle rain washes the dust from the air and waters the plants."

Tak attacked a bush, munching the vegetation, clean and sparkling with raindrops. Ellie looked up, watching wisps of clouds trail across the sky. The moon backlit the ethereal tresses, causing them to glow. She tilted her head and studied the moon.

"It's bent," she said.

Bealomondore stood beside her and followed her gaze.

"Yes, I've noticed that from time to time. As the evening progresses and the moon's position changes, it will lose that odd shape."

"What causes it?"

"The bottle effect."

Ellie shifted her eyes to examine the tumanhofer's face.

"I found it in a book in the library beside Old One's chair. I think he has researched the phenomenon, and it is fortunate for me that he left the books out. Can you imagine climbing the bookshelves, locating a book, then trying to get it down?"

"The bottle effect?"

"Remember I said that Rumbard City is under some kind of wizardry?"

"Yes."

"It would seem that whoever cast the spell put the city in a bottle. We're looking at the moon through the glass, and when the moon is positioned so that it is beyond a corner, it looks bent."

Ellie admitted to herself that at one time she had thought the glinting object she'd seen in the distance looked like a bottle, but the whole thing in reality was absurd.

She didn't try to keep the sarcasm from her voice. "The rain comes through the neck of the bottle and spreads out to make a shower?" She arched her eyebrows. "Are the clouds inside or outside the bottle?"

He chose to answer her question without rancor. "The climate within the bottle is delivered in the same manner as the food—the right kind, in the right amount, at the right time."

"But we don't know who delivers the food and weather?"

He shook his head slowly. "No, we don't. But we shall continue to explore the possibilities."

The two tumanhofers and one goat strolled toward their destination. Ellie strained her ears, but heard nothing more than night sounds, mostly insects, with the occasional hoot of a nightflyer.

During the day, even in the safety of the library, she'd felt uneasy, as if at any moment the children might break in and ransack the solemn stillness and order of the building. Her other fear stemmed from the possibility of Old One suddenly stepping out from between the stacks. While he'd hinted that they might scare him to death, she was more concerned that he would frighten a year or two off her own life.

Nighttime in the city had a different feel, serene and pleasant. She thought of all the six-year-olds, tucked in bed and sleeping soundly.

"Where are they?" she asked.

"Who?"

"The children."

"In bed."

"But where?"

Bealomondore looked around as if the buildings would give him a clue. "I don't know."

"You've never looked for them?"

He shrugged, furrowed his brow, and shook his head. "Why should I?"

"So they are probably sleeping in boxes, or on the floor, or some-place totally unsuitable."

"As long as they are asleep, what does it matter?"

"It does matter. Children should have their hands and faces washed, if not a whole bath. They should have a good-night story and be tucked into a cozy bed. They should have a kiss on the cheek or forehead and someone to smile at them. The last thing they see at night should be the happy face of someone who loves them."

"These children would bite the hand that tucked them in."

"Maybe not." She paused as they walked past several shops. "Per-haps they might bite the first night or two, but I bet they'd like being loved."

Tak trotted ahead and reached the fountain first. He drank and then, with water dripping from his beard, went to investigate the box on the butcher's stoop.

For dinner they had hot bowls of stew, a loaf of buttered bread, and two peaches. They sat by the fountain to eat, then cleaned up by returning things to the box.

"Shall we go home by a different route?" asked Bealomondore. "I thought we could go by the town circle and collect your carpetbag if it is still sailing the turbulent sea around the stone ladies."

"And you're sure the children won't be lying in wait?"

"Positive."

Ellie called Tak to leave the bush he was chewing on and come with them. They traveled a street she didn't think she had seen during her frantic route that day. She and Tak had crisscrossed much of the inner city during their attempts to elude the children that morning. Bealomondore's guidance brought them back to the central fountain after only a ten-minute walk.

The moon was no longer bent, and lightrocks glowed from the tops of lampposts. Along the way, they picked up a few of her discarded garments. She hoped to find enough garments to change her clothes when they reached the library.

They came to the empty circle. Ellie sighed her relief. She trusted her tumanhofer companion more and more as she grew to know him, but the lengthy chase that had begun her day had her wary of running into the hunters.

Her valise floated low, having taken on water. Bealomondore took off his shoes and socks, rolled up his trousers, and waded in to rescue the listing ship. He then climbed several of the statues to retrieve her shoes, a bonnet, and her lacy slip.

As he returned her slip, she blushed in the moonlight and dropped her chin to avoid his eyes. He laughed and made a sweeping bow. "I consider this to be the sail to the ship, milady, nothing more."

She wrapped her clothes in one skirt to make an easily carried bundle. None of her new clothes would ever be the same, but at least she'd have a change of clothes again. She carried the clothing while Bealomondore held the carpetbag away from his side to prevent the drips from staining his trousers.

Feeling much better about Rumbard City, Bealomondore, and

their chances of finding an escape, Ellie walked happily beside her escort as they made their way back to the library.

Tak wandered ahead of them, poking his nose into whatever interested him and nibbling whatever grew from the flower boxes. Bealomondore stopped at a corner.

He motioned toward Tak, who had gone on in a straight line.

"We turn here."

"Tak," Ellie called. "Come back. We're going this way."

The goat turned his head and started back, then stopped. He looked at them and then down an alley.

"This way," Ellie insisted.

Tak shook his head so that the hair on his whole body shimmied in the moonlight, then took off down the side alley.

Ellie turned to look at Bealomondore with a shrug. "I'm sorry. But I can't leave him out here. When the children come out tomorrow, they would love to catch the 'dog.' "

"I understand." He put her bag down and took her bundle to place next to it. "We'll leave these here. It'll be easier to give chase without any encumbrances."

The goat let out a plaintive "Maa!"

"He sounds upset," said Ellie.

They hurried to the point where Tak had disappeared around a corner. Tak stood just a few feet into the alley. At his feet, a pile of clothing lay in the shadow of the building. The moonlight touched the white hair of the goat and part of the cloth.

Ellie didn't recognize any of the visible material as part of her missing garments. She walked forward with Bealomondore right behind.

"Maa!"

She stopped beside the goat and leaned over. Tak shifted, and the moonlight he had been blocking fell on the clothing. Ellie saw a dirty hand and stood up abruptly. She turned to Bealomondore but could not utter a sound. He hurried to her, put his arm around her shoulders, and turned her away.

Her voice trembled. "Is it…?"

"Yes, I think so." He let go of her.

Ellie thought she would faint. She'd never fainted, but as Bealomondore's arm left her, she thought she would crumple. She stiffened her legs and felt the tumanhofer crouch beside her.

"Is she…?"

"He, I think. And yes, I'm afraid so. There's a lot of blood." He stood and looked up. "He must have fallen from that catwalk up there."

Ellie took a deep breath in. She glanced up at the ladderlike structure that crossed the alley from one building to another. Three stories up, the narrow planking with rungs passed from one window to another.

She felt the world tilt and dropped her chin to her chest. Bealomondore had stood, so she took hold of his arm, willing the dizziness to subside.

She swallowed hard and hoped she wouldn't throw up. "What should we do?"

"I don't think there is anything we can do."

"Tell the other children?"

"No."

"Do you think they know? Do you think they saw him fall?"

"I have no idea."

Bealomondore's answers angered her, but she realized his tone held sorrow and sympathy. He wasn't being heartless, just answering her truthfully. She fought the horror of a child dying from such a fall and the bitter words that sprang to her tongue.

"Bury him? We can't just leave him here."

He put his arms around her and guided her face to his shoulder. "It's all right, Ellicinderpart. All the urohms in this city have died, yet there are no bodies, no skeletons, nothing. Whoever brings the food and rain takes away the dead."

Tears coursed down her cheeks, and she embraced Bealomondore, holding him tight. She cried for the big child and for all the little ones cowering in the dark, perhaps sleeping, perhaps too upset to close their eyes.

She sobbed as her companion urged her to leave the alley and continue to the library. When they reached the corner, he whispered, "I'll come back for your things."

They entered the library by the rear vent, and Bealomondore had her sit on a cushion near the storage room.

"I'll return as soon as I can."

He left, and Ellie wiped her tears on her sleeve. She needed a handkerchief. Getting up, she followed a light and found a room with lots of tables of books in various states of repair. She climbed a stool and took a rag from the tabletop. It smelled of turpentine, but she shook out the dust and used a relatively clean corner to blow her nose.

She sat on the edge of the stool and waited. Her tears dried and left her with sadness squeezing her heart. She wanted to talk the situation over with her mother. She wanted to hold her little brothers and sisters.

Bealomondore came back and easily found her. With both arms filled with her belongings, he looked up to where she sat perched and waiting. "Are you going to be all right?"

She nodded. "Did you know they have…accidents?"

"I figured it out. Old One's mentioned that there used to be over a hundred children. They don't die of old age. He's said he never had any illness. I thought that if he didn't have colds or stomachaches, then probably the children would be protected as well. But they are wild and do what they want, and they don't show much common sense."

"With no one to warn them or scold them, they are bound to do dangerous things."

"Yes." His simple answer held a mountain of regret.

He'd thought about all this during the two months he'd been captive in this city. She could hear his despair. It echoed in her heart.

"No, Bealomondore." She flipped over and started her climb down the stool. Wrapping her body around one of the legs, she slid to the last rung before the floor, then hopped down.

"What do you mean by 'no'?" he asked.

"I mean that we are not going to let any more children die."

His face took on a wary expression. "What are you planning? They're dangerous, wild, ruthless—"

"Children. They're children. I agree they are a bit wild." She tapped his chest with her finger. "But we're going to tame them."

# 11

# A Good Night's Rest

Bealomondore knew his guest's crusade to save the children could be laid at the door of the tragedy. He'd given up trying to reason with her and just nodded his head once in a while. The fact that she still had the berry juice stain on her face didn't help him take her more seriously. He realized she'd be humiliated if she saw the purplish red goatee painted on her chin.

Tak lay beside Ellicinderpart, sound asleep. He made little noises, as if a dream occupied his nighttime thoughts.

Bealomondore envied the goat. He wished he could stretch out and go to sleep. He stifled a yawn. It had been a long, eventful day. Much more challenging than many of the days he'd spent in Rumbard City. He began to think Ellicinderpart would never wind down when suddenly she yawned. He jumped at his chance to move them toward retiring for the night.

"Let me show you where you can wash, and I'll drag a pillow into a little nook where you can have some privacy as you sleep." He stood and gestured for her to follow.

She blinked and stared at him for a moment before she stood. "You said you sleep here?"

"Yes, in the children's section. There are cushions on the floor."

"Blankets?"

"Yes." He smiled at her. "I appropriated them from a doll cradle.

It doesn't get very cold at night. I doubted the baby doll needed the covering more than I did."

She gazed at him. The humor had not registered.

"You must be very tired," he said.

She still did not move.

He tried to sound patient. "Are you coming?"

She nodded, and he led the way to the children's room, where bright colors dominated the décor and chairs and tables were more in line with the size they needed. In a corner behind a librarian's counter, a door remained open to the pint-size rest room.

"I never close the door all the way," he explained. "I don't know if I could open the door once it was shut. I'll leave you here, and I'll see about locating an appropriate spot for you to call your own."

She went into the room and pushed the door, but not shut. He scratched his head. One minute she chattered with plans to win the children's trust, and the next she changed into a docile, quiet—pleasantly quiet—guest. The ordeals of the day must have caught up with her.

He glanced around the room. His bed was between the science and mathematics shelves. He moved to the opposite side of the room, latching on to a pillow as he passed the middle, where he assumed children had sat to listen to stories. He dragged what would be Ellicinderpart's mattress to the area where a cradle held the wooden baby. Behind the books that displayed colors, shapes, alphabet letters, and numbers, a shadow provided a dark enough spot to facilitate slumber. He crammed the pillow in the tight corner and turned his attention to acquiring a blanket.

The baby's bed had a small pillow and a sheet. He stole them from the cradle and then went looking for something to serve as a heavier cover. Under the librarian's counter, he found a stack of folded cloth. He chose a soft, thick flannel, wondering how the librarian had used it.

Ellicinderpart came out of the rest room, her chin scrubbed clean. He made no comment, not wishing to embarrass her.

"I've found a cozy spot. First let me show you where I sleep so you'll know where to find me if you need me during the night. I can't imagine why you would, but just in case."

He led her to his corner, then swiftly moved on to where he'd put the cushion for her bed. "I hope this will be comfortable." He handed her the flannel.

She took it and looked at the sheet he'd spread over the cushion. "I'm sure I'll be fine."

"All right then. Good night. I'll see you in the morning."

He took several steps away, but she called his name.

"Bealomondore?"

"Yes?"

"Thank you." She sighed, and he thought for a moment that she would dissolve into tears again.

But she lifted her chin and batted her eyes to ward off the onslaught. He recognized the same type of bravery his sisters had exhibited when told they would have to dine with their father.

"Thank you for everything. It would have been horrid to encounter all of this alone. Or rather, with just Tak. I don't think I could have handled it well at all."

Not quite sure how to react, Bealomondore bowed in his most elegant manner to honor her statement. "I have to admit, searching for clues will be more fun with a partner."

She smiled, and Bealomondore forced himself to turn away and head for his quarters. Was it the extended solitude that made him susceptible to her charms? Or was Ellicinderpart Clarenbessipawl the most appealing country miss he'd ever encountered?

Ellie thought she would not be able to sleep, but soon after she snuggled into the cushion and covered herself with the flannel, she fell into a deep slumber. When her eyes opened in the morning, she couldn't remember any dreams plaguing her, but her first thought was of the unfortunate child. She should have dreamed of him. How could such a thing not cause a deep unrest?

Before her callousness raised a specter of guilt, she realized that some of her clothes had been returned. Someone had scattered bits and pieces of her belongings over her bed. These were not the things she and Bealomondore had recovered, but things that had still been missing when she went to sleep.

The children?

No, Bealomondore said they never ventured out at night.

She sat up and rummaged through the assortment, glad to see the green skirt and mismatched stockings.

Bealomondore?

Could he have gone out again?

No, he was tired when they parted, and she felt confident that he'd gone to bed.

Old One then?

She shook her head at her theory. Nothing she knew about the old urohm indicated he would go out of the library at all, let alone at night, to retrieve her things.

She got up, folded her clothes, matching up what outfits she could conjure out of the bits and pieces at her disposal, and finally chose what she would wear that day. After changing in the rest room, she went in search of Bealomondore. She found him, still in the children's section of the library, sitting at one of the tables designed for small giants.

"Good morning," she said.

He looked up from a book, stood, and smiled as he bowed. "Good morning. I brought our breakfast back from the butcher's shop. Will you join me?"

"Oh, so you have been out." She sat in the chair he pulled out for her. "Thank you for bringing me more of my things. We just might get it all back."

He gave her a quizzical look as he reclaimed the chair he'd been sitting in. "I didn't find anything but toast and jam this morning."

Ellie picked up a slice of bread and bit into it without the jam. Rich with whole grains and butter, it tasted wonderful. But it didn't capture her whole attention. As soon as she swallowed, she pursued an answer to her questions.

"Who gathered my things and deposited them on my bed then?"

"I imagine it was the dragons of the watch." Bealomondore relaxed in his chair. "They come to the library quite often. It is a central building, and I think they're curious as to what I'm doing in their city."

Ellie chewed on her toast and eyed her companion. Most of what he'd told her had proven to be true, but this claim that dragons roamed the city didn't sound feasible. And dragons had entered the library? And she didn't wake? Perhaps kimens or o'rants or emerlindians, but *dragons*? Not likely.

Bealomondore fiddled with a cloth napkin on the table. "And then there is the fact that two of the dragons came with me into the city two months ago."

She didn't say anything but stopped chewing.

He looked sheepish, and he should. He was about to unload some fanciful tales and actually expected her to believe him.

"Det and Laddin," he said. He bravely made eye contact, but she squinted in what she hoped was a discouraging manner. It didn't work. He plunged on.

"Their names are Det and Laddin. Paladin gave them into my care, or maybe me into their care, during the war. I was on the front lines, and Det is gifted in geography. He can recall maps he has only glanced at. He saved me and my men more than once by knowing where a ravine ended or what lay downstream." He glanced up at her, then back down at the napkin. "And Laddin is a green dragon...healing. Green dragons are healing dragons."

Ellie resumed chewing and swallowed.

"There's tea," said Bealomondore.

"Thank you. I'd like tea."

He stood and walked behind the librarian's counter, where he fetched a teakettle and two teacups.

After he poured, he offered sugar and cream. She shook her head and took a sip of the warm, dark brew. It wasn't a tea she recognized, but her mother had only brought home one of the two varieties available in the village.

"Delicious," she said.

"It doesn't come with our meals. It's always here. I suppose the librarians fixed tea during their workdays. Or perhaps they had little tea parties for the children."

Ellie set the cup down on the table. "Possibly."

She looked at the teakettle. "That is such an unusual contraption. Does it sit on a stove?" She turned toward the counter behind the librarians' desk.

"No." Bealomondore pronounced the word slowly. "As with many things in Rumbard City, I am at a loss to explain how this works. If you fill the kettle with water and put it on a circle that looks to be part of the counter, the circle turns red and the water boils. So you could cook there if you wanted to." He laughed. "I'm a better cook over a campfire."

That made her cast him another inquiring look, but he chose to change the subject.

"Det and Laddin don't particularly care for sifting through all these books, so they joined the watch. It suits them to nose around the city, flying a routine inspection tour every night. And it helps the overworked members of the watch."

She refused to ask a question since it would only encourage him to invent more falderal. He didn't need any encouragement.

"There are five dragons in the watch. With Det and Laddin, they have seven. They keep an eye on things. That's how I knew you'd entered the city. They told me, and I went looking for you."

She nodded and finished her tea. She wiped her mouth with a napkin and stood. She wanted to say something extremely clever to put this prankster in his place, but she couldn't think of anything other than, "I don't believe a word you say," which seemed unsatisfactory as a stinging rebuff.

She stood straight, trying to look as dignified as Mistress Clamber did when she walked down the sidewalk of the village. She turned to stride off in a stately manner but stopped short. Along the top of one of the short bookcases, seven dragons, no bigger than kittens, sat staring at her. They were many different colors, quite beautiful. Their wings either folded against their bodies or extended out from their torsos as if at a casual stance. They looked intelligent.

Ellie finally managed to think of something to say. She curtsied. "Good morning."

# 12

# Meet the Dragons

The dragons flew into the air, did flips and dazzling acrobatics. The flash and dance of the display mesmerized Ellie. One of them sang, and although Ellie didn't recognize any of the words, the tune reached into her heart and created a bubbling wellspring of joy.

Bealomondore came and stood beside her.

"Can you hear them speaking to you?"

She started. "No, they aren't saying anything. That purple one is singing—you can see her lips move. But the others are silent."

"Well, you wouldn't see their lips move when they communicate with you. They mindspeak."

"Oh."

The dragons enlarged their performance by spreading out across the children's area. They flew around Bealomondore and Ellie and did their fancy moves above, between, and around them. At first Ellie ducked and dodged the speedy dragons but soon learned they would not bump into her. She relaxed again and allowed their exuberance to stir a thrill that urged her to join in the dance.

Bealomondore stepped in front of her, bowed, and swooped her into a rollicking country dance. The two tumanhofers whirled around the open space and then up and down the aisles of books. When the dragon song and dance came to an end, she and Bealomondore collapsed, sitting on one of the child-size tables, panting and laughing.

The dragons settled around them, two on Bealomondore's shoulders and the others on nearby furniture.

When he'd caught his breath, Bealomondore lifted one dragon off his shoulder and held him out for her to greet.

"This is Laddin. He's a healing dragon. He's been with me for two years."

Ellie dipped her head. "Pleased to meet you."

"Did you hear him?"

Ellie twisted her mouth and gave Bealomondore an impatient look. "Of course not."

"Well, he says, 'Pleased to meet you as well,' and for me to be patient with you. One of the dragons will stay with you today and awaken your ability to mindspeak."

She looked from the dragon to the tumanhofer and back to the dragon and again to Bealomondore's sincere expression.

"How do you know I have any ability to talk to the dragons?"

Bealomondore shrugged. "Why do you assume you do not?"

"Perhaps tumanhofers from my family, or from my part of the country, are stifled in this area. You say you have an artistic talent—"

"When did I say that?"

"You said you were asked to do a wedding portrait for Paladin and Princess Tipper."

"Oh yes, I remember mentioning that."

She quirked an eyebrow at him. "Was that not true?"

He looked her in the eye and spoke calmly. "I'm not a liar, Ellicinderpart."

She ducked her head, unable to meet his earnest gaze. "I'm sorry."

He took her hand and squeezed it. "I have to admit that when I first met Princess Tipper, her family, and friends, I often thought they were crazy. And Lady Peg gave me a word to describe liars who mean no harm."

"Liars that mean no harm?"

"When you meet Lady Peg, you'll understand. She has a very unique perception of the world." He smiled and Ellie thought he must be fond of the woman. "She's Tipper's mother and the wife of Verrin Schope, scholar, artist, and wizard."

"I don't think I've heard of either one."

For a brief moment, his face registered amazement mixed with dismay. His expression returned to polite interest so quickly that she wondered if she'd imagined his reaction.

"Lady Peg is the daughter of King Yellat and Queen Venmarie. She married Verrin Schope. He is a stunning intellect versed in everything from mechanics to anatomy. And his artistic abilities—he astonishes the world with paintings, sketches, sculpture, carvings. There's no end to his genius. He fell through a portal fifteen or so years ago and ended up in Amara. There he developed skills as a wizard under the tutelage of a very old wizard named Fenworth and his librarian, Librettowit, a fine tumanhofer. And he was introduced to Wulder, the one and only true and living God."

Ellie felt her eyebrows stretched above her eyes and deliberately brought them down, trying to compose a look of acceptance to these wild declarations.

"So Boscamon is a myth?"

"Yes!" He seemed pleased with her question. "Boscamon is fiction, made up to fill the need we have to believe that there is an ultimate authority in the universe. His tale is a placeholder waiting to be replaced with truth. Wulder has been unknown to us, and Paladin has been charged with establishing His followers in His truth in the land of Chiril."

His enthusiasm stirred a desire to know more, but one statement Bealomondore made did not hold true. She had to point it out. "Old One knows of Wulder."

Bealomondore frowned at her for a moment, then a memory brought wonder to his face. "The journal! He mentioned Wulder in the journal."

She nodded. "Why does he know who Wulder is? And it sounded as if Old One regards Wulder as someone in authority. What does he know that the rest of Chiril doesn't?"

Bealomondore rested his palm across his chin and stroked his jaw with the three lower fingers. He puzzled for a moment before speaking again. "This is most intriguing. And let's add to the list of questions. Why were the urohms concentrated in this city? Why was the populace exclusively urohms? That's not true of any other city in Chiril. The kimens keep to themselves for the most part, but they're not isolated. They do interact with the other races."

"Why is the urohm city so grand?"

Bealomondore turned his attention to the dragon on his shoulder. "Det says there is no poor section of Rumbard City. There is no evidence of poverty."

Ellie cleared her throat. "You said Lady Peg gave you a word for lying with no harm intended."

"Ah yes. It is *fibberlating*. The person had fibbed but intends to tell the truth later, when it is more convenient. Mind you, she doesn't approve of fibberlation. And if you ask her why, you will get a long and complicated explanation, at the end of which you will still have no idea of the reasons for her conviction, but you will be thoroughly convinced of her basic goodness."

"Really?"

He nodded his head vigorously. "Most assuredly."

"Are you fibberlating to me at this very moment?"

He stood straighter and laid his hand upon his breast. "I am of the same opinion as Lady Peg. To fibberlate is to stoop below the dignity Wulder has bestowed upon us." He relaxed his stance and leaned forward to whisper in a conspiratorial manner. "But truly I think that last bit is Lady Peg echoing a sentiment she has heard Verrin Schope espouse." He rolled his eyes. "Please don't ever use the word *espouse* around Lady Peg. That is one of those words that is sure to set her off."

With a grin on her face, Ellie slowly shook her head back and forth, totally bewildered. "I will probably never meet Lady Peg, and I don't think I could truly understand what you mean unless I did meet her face to face."

Bealomondore dropped his bantering air and looked quite sincere. "You will meet Lady Peg, Ellicinderpart. I will introduce you to her myself."

Before she could think of a reply, the dragons burst into noisy chittering.

"What are they saying?" asked Ellie.

"They have to go out on their rounds, and they want to be introduced before they go."

The dragons lined up on the bookcase as they had when they first came that morning.

"You've met Det and Laddin. Kriss, the light green one—"

The little dragon did a flip on the bookcase.

"She's a procurer of food, which isn't needed much in Rumbard City, and it makes her sad that she cannot enjoy her favorite pastimes of gardening and cooking."

Ellie curtsied to each dragon as Bealomondore introduced them.

"Maree predicts the weather."

The blue dragon dipped his head.

"His skills are underused as well. And Amee"—the dragon hopped at the mention of her name, and her scales shone with markings black as ebony and creamy white that looked like ivory—"is a wonder at communicating with animals, securing their cooperation, and negotiating disputes among them."

Ellie's eyes widened as she curtsied. A dragon diplomat to the animal kingdom! Her eyes shifted to the next in line, an orange and yellow fellow. The dragon wiggled in a funny dance, and Ellie giggled.

"Soosahn is a laughter dragon, able to see humor in most situations and dedicated to lifting the spirits of those around him."

"And," said Ellie, "the purple dragon sings."

"Yes, Airon is musical."

"I am very pleased to meet you all. I'm sorry that I don't hear you when you mindspeak. I hope I can learn how."

All the dragons turned to look at Airon.

Bealomondore smiled. "Airon has been chosen to be your tutor. They feel that she is most likely to be able to reach your mind and begin the communication lessons."

The dragons leaped into the air and flew in a circle.

"They're saying good-bye."

"Will I see them again?"

"Yes. They like you."

She grinned. The dragons flew in a line toward the stairs to the upper levels, all except Airon. The purple dragon circled around Bealomondore and Ellie. With each turn her circle became smaller.

"She's going to land on your shoulder. Try not to cringe."

"Do her claws hurt?"

Bealomondore laughed. "She says her claws do not hurt. Do your toes hurt?"

Ellie gasped. "She understands me."

"Yes, you're the one with the problem, not her."

She made a face at him but didn't really feel any annoyance. The prospect of getting to know real dragons, learning to mindspeak, and perhaps convincing the dragons to help her gain the respect of the children outweighed any petty grievance against her tumanhofer friend.

Even with the warning, she flinched a little as Airon landed on her shoulder. She didn't feel the pinprick of tiny claws, only the slight pressure of Airon's small body. Very cautiously, the purple dragon stretched out her neck and laid her cheek against Ellie's. The young tumanhofer girl's heart capitulated.

She had to turn her head at an awkward angle and pull back in order to look at the dragon on her shoulder. Airon seemed to recognize the problem and moved out to the top of her arm. Now Ellie could look straight into the beautiful dragon's eyes.

"How are we going to do this?" she asked.

Bealomondore rocked back and forth on his feet, a pleased expression taking over his features. "I suggest you sing."

# 13

# Sing, Sing a Song

Ellie doubted that singing would help her understand when the dragons tried to mindspeak with her. But Bealomondore had suggested it, and she didn't have any other ideas. He went to pore over the books in the rotunda. She and Airon settled at one of the child-size tables. Airon stood in the middle of the table, while Ellie sat comfortably in one of the four matching chairs. Tak claimed a cushion beside a fish tank containing no fish or water, just colored gravel in the bottom with a small castle and some shells.

Watching the little purple dragon, Ellie wondered what she thought of this experiment. Airon looked interested in her but hardly took on the role of teacher. Well, if Ellie wanted to know what the purple dragon was thinking, she had better learn how to mindspeak. She started by singing a simple lullaby that she had sung to younger siblings as she rocked them to sleep.

In the sky, in the sky
Stars and moon say good night
Sleep, my baby.

Day has gone, day has gone
And sleep says ah, come on,
Little baby.

Close your eyes, close your eyes
And I whisper good night
Sleep, my baby.

Morning comes, morning comes
And you'll greet the new day,
Little baby.

She repeated it several times. Airon joined on the second verse and sang along without words, at least not words Ellie recognized. The purple dragon's intonations matched perfectly with her own, but the syllables sounded like nothing more than *dah*s, *lah*s, *mee*s, and an occasional *ray*. Tak nodded his head, not quite to the simple beat. He would go to sleep if she sang for any length of time. He always did at home when she sat in the porch rocker and crooned to a baby.

Ellie started again at the beginning of the song, and when she reached the end of the fourth verse, she continued with more lyrics she didn't recall ever having heard before.

Rest all night, rest all night
Knowing I'll hold you tight.
Sleep, my baby.

Dreams so sweet, dreams so sweet
Fill your heart and your life,
Little baby.

Learn and grow, learn and grow
Safe with us in our home,
Sleep, my baby.

Soon enough, soon enough
You will follow your road,
Little baby.

She frowned as she looked at her singing partner. "Did you know those verses? Because I certainly didn't."

Airon ducked her chin and then raised it to point to the ceiling. She sprang up and did a flip in the air and landed with her feet doing a *rat-a-tat-tat* on the wooden tabletop. Tak tilted his head and watched her with his yellow eyes.

Like a whisper in her mind, Ellie heard, *"Yes!"*

She jumped to her feet and did her own version of Airon's celebration dance. The purple dragon flew in circles above her head. Together they twirled out of the children's section and through the many aisles of bookcases to the rotunda. Tak followed but refused to join in their exuberance.

When the three entered the round hall, Bealomondore stood with a book in his hand. "I heard you coming. I gather you've had some success."

"I heard her. She told me more words to the song I was singing." She came to a complete halt and lifted an eyebrow. "How did she do that? Not the mindspeaking, but knowing more words to a song I taught her minutes before."

Airon flew to Bealomondore's shoulder.

"All minor dragons collect information from the people around them," he explained. "Singing dragons collect songs, as well as musical history. You might have heard the other verses, and the lyrics were buried in your brain. In that case, she dug the words out. Or she recognized something she had learned somewhere else and mined the information she had stored."

Ellie smiled at her purple tutor. "It's an interesting talent."

"That's only the surface," Bealomondore said. "She can use her music to soothe anyone. She can mesmerize an assailant. Musical dragons have been known to unify dissenting crowds, bringing them to a common ground. Music, in their capable care, is medicine."

"Oh!" Ellie clapped her hands together. "She can help reach the children."

Bealomondore looked at the dragon and then at Ellie. "You didn't hear what she just said?"

"No." Her spirits fell. "She spoke, and I didn't hear it? Have I lost the ability already?"

"Don't be dismayed. It'll take practice to get good at mindspeaking."

Ellie went to Old One's stack of books and sat on the floor beside them. The disappointment threatened to sweep her joy clean away. But that possibility could be thwarted. She chose to refuse the frustration and concentrate on improving her skill. She gave herself a lecture. This setback was no more taxing than getting to the goat barn and finding that she had to go back to the hills to find a stray member of the herd.

Tak came to her side and placed his head in her lap. She absentmindedly rubbed behind his ears.

After a moment, she lifted her chin and asked, "What did she say?"

"She said, 'We will practice, practice, practice until your mind's ear is sharp. And *then* we'll sing to the untamed masses.'"

Ellie smiled at the prospect of having a partner in reaching the children. She knew all too well that Bealomondore did not relish the task. She wanted to know more about Airon. Had she once lived outside this captive city?

"Has Airon ever seen an emerlindian with their pointed outside ears?"

She'd directed the question to the tumanhofer, but the dragon answered with a series of clicks and chittering.

Bealomondore nodded to Airon and turned to translate. "She says she has seen emerlindians, but it is the heart that opens the mind, not the shape of the ear."

Ellie smiled at her two friends. "You know, I was determined to go to the royal wedding reception and the coronation. But if I had to be stuck someplace"—she tilted her head toward Bealomondore—"I'm glad it is here with you." She smiled more broadly at Airon, who made noises she suspected were happy words. "And you."

"So you had your heart set on Ragar," said Bealomondore, "and quite frankly, I had no idea of where I would be going after Ragar. I had the invitation to the Amber Palace to paint the portrait. My parents, who used to be ashamed of me, wanted me to come to Greeston and enter their circle of friends. That would have netted a bounty of commissions for more portraits." He sat on a stack of books. "What's left of the troops I fought beside in the war want to spiffy up their uniforms and gear to march in the coronation parade. I should join them. I didn't finish my study of the kimen village—another place I'd like to go. And the Valley of the Dragons always holds an appeal. The stunning landscapes make it easy to get lost in capturing the beauty on canvas. Too many choices and none of them having that final, persuasive allure."

He looked sad, and Ellie scooted to sit on a cushion close by. She leaned toward him and peered up at his downcast expression. "Couldn't you do all of them, one at a time?"

"I could." He averted his gaze, staring up at the skylight until she thought he had forgotten her. A big sigh escaped him as he refocused on her. "I could, but I am ready to pick one thing, one place to get to know extremely well. Perhaps even one lady with whom to share the experience of settling down."

"Surely among all the people you know there is someone who interests you."

He tried to muster a grin. "There was one who caught my eye, but she was my good friend, and she never saw me as someone who could be more than that."

"Maybe that's where you should go. To renew the friendship? Encourage a romance?"

Now his full smile broke out, and the room felt lighter, easier to breathe in. Ellie leaned back and watched him.

His eyes twinkled, and he chuckled a bit. "No, I've moved on, and she's moved on. She found someone who gives her that urge to build a nest and raise little ones."

He straightened his shoulders and grinned. "Do you know what I would like to do?"

She shook her head.

"I should like to sketch you and Airon as you sing, as you practice." He bent over to pick up a large pad of paper and a box that rattled. "I have the things I need. You two set up wherever you like. Try to stay in the light."

Airon did an airborne somersault and flew to a chair across the room that soaked up the morning sun from the skylight.

Ellie followed and climbed into the oversize seat. She sat sideways with her back against one arm, while Airon sat on the other arm. Shy at first, she sang a slow song about cherries and chickens and cabbage. The artist took off his jacket and stood as he sketched. One arm held the pad of paper, and he made bold strokes with the pencil in the other hand. He'd then sit and, with great concentration, make smaller marks. He drew several pictures from different angles.

Ellie longed to see them, but singing with Airon captured her attention. The songs varied from ballads to nursery rhymes to frolicking party melodies. They came to a short children's song.

> The sun comes up each morning.
> The sun goes down each night.
> And if the sun doesn't shine today,
> His job, I'll give away.

They repeated it several times, and Bealomondore joined in. Then they sang it as a two-part round until they achieved the desired effect. Next, Airon suggested they try it in a three-part round, and Ellie heard the mindspoken words. When they tried the harder version, Bealomondore and Ellie got their words all tangled up. Airon, of course, only sang in her style of syllables and didn't have a problem. They ended up laughing, all three of them. They tried to start the song again but couldn't make it past the third line before all three voices were on a different tune.

Ellie fell over onto the seat cushion. She wiped tears of laughter from her eyes. Bealomondore was in a similar state, leaning against a table and holding his side.

"Hear now! What's all this commotion?" A loud voice boomed from one of the balconies above that ran around the rotunda's open space.

Ellie sucked in her breath and stopped laughing immediately. She squinted as she looked up, realizing by the angle of the sunbeams pouring in that it was noon.

"Who's there?" asked Bealomondore. "We're sorry to disturb you, sir."

There was no answer. Ellie detected a slight movement. She jumped from the chair and scurried to stand next to Bealomondore.

"Did you see him?" she whispered.

"No, did you?"

"I saw something move. There. Beside that painting of horses."

"Ah." Bealomondore made a bow in the direction of the shadowed figure. "May I issue an introduction? This is Ellicinderpart Clarenbessipawl. I am Graddapotmorphit Bealomondore."

He bowed. She curtsied.

No response.

"Do we have the pleasure of addressing Old One?"

"Go about your business," came the loud, gravelly answer, "and I'll go about mine."

The shadow moved away.

"Wait," called Ellie. "Please don't go. We'd like to know you. Can't you come down and talk to us? We could have tea."

"Tea's no good without daggarts, and there haven't been daggarts for years."

He shuffled off.

"Should we go after him?" asked Ellie.

"Have you seen the grand staircase?" Bealomondore shook his head. "He'll have to come to us."

# 14

# Daggarts and Danger

As Ellie and Bealomondore walked to the butcher's shop, Airon flew above them, circling back whenever she got too far ahead. Tak moseyed along, munching on plants from the flower boxes and poking his nose in piles of trash. They occasionally had to stop and wait for him to catch up.

"How long do you suppose Rumbard City has been under the wizard's spell?" asked Ellie.

"Four hundred years."

"Exactly?"

"No, approximately. Rumbard City's been around for four hundred years. Old One's journal recordings did not give a year until later on, so I estimated by how many earlier journals I found."

"You really have learned a lot in the two months you've been here."

"Necessity. Desperation. Boredom. Three instigators of industry."

Ellie mulled that over in her mind. She could see how that was true. But the poor children and lonely Old One crowded out other thoughts of Bealomondore.

"Do you know what I want to do?" she asked.

"Eat noonmeal?"

"Yes, that. I'm starving. But after noonmeal I'd like to look into making daggarts. These children don't ever have daggarts, do they?"

"Not that I've seen." He smacked his lips. "Daggarts. Our cook used to bake daggarts in the early afternoon, and we'd have them with milk. Now *that* was a treat." He shook his head. "An excellent idea, but where are we going to get the ingredients and a working oven?"

"We could look in the bakery."

Bealomondore smiled at her, the twinkle in his eye gleaming. "That sounds like a reasonable place to start."

They emptied the box on the butcher's stoop and hurried through their meal. After disposing of the leftovers, they went to the other side of the fountain to the bakery. Ellie had full confidence that Bealomondore would be able to gain entry to the closed shop. However, his skills were not needed. The back door lay on the ground, and the state of the interior testified to ransacking done by the roving horde of six-year-olds.

Tak meandered around the room, sniffing and sneezing at care-lessly tossed flour. Ellie crossed her arms over her stomach, looking down at the white piles of flour on the floor and childish footprints marking trails in every direction. "Well, the supplies used to be here."

"Maybe we can find something on a top shelf." Bealomondore began to climb up to a counter. "What kind of daggarts did you want to make?"

"I know recipes for oatmeal, chocobit, and butter daggarts."

Bealomondore took hold of a book with two hands and lowered it over the side of the counter. "A recipe book. Watch out. I'm going to let it fall."

The book landed flat and poofed the old flour into the air. Ellie waved a hand in front of her face and backed away. When the air cleared, she returned to the book and opened the cover. "There's a sec-tion on desserts."

"Good," came Bealomondore's answer from high above.

Airon chittered wildly, and Ellie interpreted her distress. She looked up and gasped. Bealomondore climbed a long, thick string of garlic that looked brittle and ready to break.

"Be careful!" she shouted.

He reached a cabinet, wedged his fingers under the door, and opened it. Once inside, he gave a hoot he must've picked up from living with the kimens. "We hit the mother lode! I see baking powder in a tin, an unopened bag of salt, a box that has spices in it, and some colored sprinkles you put on top of birthday cakes. You know, the kind that goes on the icing."

She put her hand over her eyes, shielding her sight from the glare coming in the big front window. "Any sugar? Flour? Lard?"

"Nary a speck. Are eggs in your recipe?"

"In the oatmeal and chocobit."

Bealomondore came to stand on the edge and leaned out to speak to her. "We'll have to go to the outskirts and see if there are any wild chickens. We might find a house with an oven and supplies."

"It took a long, long time to walk into the city."

Bealomondore sat on the edge of the cabinet. "I'll ask Det to scout out a house so we can go straight to it instead of searching."

Tak stood at the door, looking out of the building and into the alley. He stamped his feet and glanced over his shoulder at Airon. The dragon let out a shrill whistle. Bealomondore grabbed the rope of garlic and hurried down.

"They're coming!" said Ellie. "They're coming down the alley. We'll have to go out the front."

Bealomondore hopped down and ran to the big window. He ducked and peeked through the displays. "I don't see anyone out here."

He crouched as he approached the door. Ellie also stooped as she joined him. Tak and Airon stayed at the back and kept their eyes on the alley. Bealomondore manipulated the large deadbolt.

As the door swung open, Ellie whispered loudly, "Come on!"

They raced past the fountain and down the street that would lead to the library. Airon flew in front. Tak brought up the rear. Ellie kept pace with Bealomondore.

The chase reminded Ellie of the first morning she had spent in Rumbard City. Every time she thought they had lost the boys and girls, another group popped up and sent their little party of visitors fleeing again. Someone ought to take these children in hand and teach them how to be civilized.

While she and Bealomondore panted from the exertion of escaping, the hunters giggled, shouted, laughed, and called out the despicable things they planned to do when they caught the two wee ones, the bird, and the dog. Ellie didn't believe a word of their cannibalistic plans. They didn't know how to cook, for one thing. For another, she suspected they had never actually caught anything and had no idea what to do if they should, by chance, take prisoners. The children seemed woefully ignorant.

One of the reasons the countryfolk didn't encourage reading was the expanded imagination that resulted from books. She dreamed of going to a big city and seeing the royal wedding celebration and dancing in the streets at the coronation. Books describing such things had awakened a longing in her heart. Many of the older folk saw this as a danger, not a blessing.

But Gramps said, "Education means you can think bigger. Thinking bigger is a good thing, more fun than having thoughts that are pinched and scrawny."

Ellie read to her younger siblings, and they developed wild schemes, much wilder and more detailed than those proposed by these children. Her brothers made up grand stories and acted them out. Her sisters staged operas, even though they had never seen one. And they imagined wearing ball gowns, even though they'd only seen black and white sketches. This bunch of six-year-olds didn't go much further with their devious plots than "catch 'em," "tie 'em up," and "eat 'em."

Bealomondore found a break in a building wall, and they climbed over a pile of bricks and into a cool, dark room with no windows. After Tak climbed in and Airon swooped through the hole, Bealomondore pulled some of the loose bricks closer to make a barrier. They sat back in the darkness and listened as the hunters stormed right past their hiding hole.

"Can we stay here for a while?" asked Ellie. "My shins hurt. And Tak looks all in."

The goat had collapsed near a sidewall. Ellie could just make out his shaggy white coat. Airon perched on a box and chittered. She heard the dragon's agreement in her mind.

"Yes," said Bealomondore. "If they don't spot us for a while, they will probably lose interest."

For a long time, no one spoke. Various groups of children passed from time to time. They no longer ran but trudged past. Disparaging remarks about the wee ones, the bird, and the dog became softer, less vehement. The last pack made muttering sounds and dragged their feet. When no more came by, Ellie wondered if they had found comfy spots to nap. She could have used some water, a more comfortable room, and a good sleep.

"How far are we from the library?" she asked.

"Not far, but these little brutes can be intuitive. They probably have guards along any route we would take. If we can get past a certain point, we'll be safe. They don't like to get too close to Old One's territory."

After some time, Bealomondore suggested they make a dash to the library. Ellie agreed. Airon went out to scout and came back to report the main street clear. Ellie beamed.

"What?" asked Bealomondore.

"I hear almost everything she mindspeaks now."

He returned her smile, and she basked in his approval. Not everything about being stuck in a bottle city was bad.

They entered the alley and made their way to the corner and the main street. Tak lagged behind, and Ellie wondered if he was hurt. She asked Airon, who related that Tak wanted food, water, and no more running. That sounded like a good plan to Ellie. Airon added that Tak was being particularly grumpy.

She put her arm around the goat's neck. "As soon as we get to the library, we are going to rest a great deal."

After they moved two blocks closer to their sanctuary, Airon again scouted ahead and brought back a report that several children sat in an alley they would have to pass, but they looked very sleepy.

"Shall we try it?" asked Bealomondore.

Ellie nodded. "I'm game."

They tiptoed down the street, keeping an eye on the alley Airon pointed out as the trouble spot. They passed on the opposite side of the street and could see the slumping forms in the shadows. When they were clearly out of danger, Bealomondore quickened the pace.

The library loomed at the end of the street. Ellie couldn't take her eyes off of it. She strode beside Bealomondore, forgetting how tired her legs had been only moments before. Far ahead of them, Airon flew into a third-story window. She smiled when Tak offered a "Maa!" He was happy to see home too. But the second "Maa!" had a different tone.

She whirled around and saw two urohm boys standing between Tak and her. Tak stood his ground, lowering his head a trifle and staring. He looked too angry to be captured, but she didn't trust the boys to have good judgment. She tiptoed back and felt Bealomondore close behind. Two boys lunged out of the side street.

"Tak, run!" she called.

Tak bounced back and forth, pivoting on his back legs, unsure which way to go. The two boys in front of the goat let out a screech and tackled him. The other two piled on top.

"Let him go!" She ran forward.

Bealomondore snatched at her arm, but she shook him off. "Let him go!"

Three more children rushed her from one side and grabbed hold of her arm. She tried to wrench herself free.

Another child came out of nowhere and locked on to her other arm.

"We got the dog!" screamed a child from the arms and legs twisted together on top of Tak.

"We got a wee one!" yelled her captors.

"Where's the other wee one?" cried a child with curly hair and pouty lips.

Ellie struggled to look behind her, but still another child appeared, fell at her feet, and locked its arms and legs around her.

"He ran in the castle," said one of the boys holding her arm.

"Old One'll get 'im."

Ellie closed her eyes and breathed a sigh of resignation. She'd been caught. Tak was captured. For some reason Bealomondore had deserted them. She'd welcome Old One appearing on the scene and roaring at the naughty boys and girls.

"You look funny," said one of the children in a nasty voice.

"*I* am a tumanhofer. *You* are a urohm."

"You don't have a stink," said the child wrapped around her legs.

Ellie frowned down at the top of its head. She wasn't sure, but she suspected the child was female. "I would assume no stink is a good thing."

"Nah," said the tallest child as he got off the top of the Tak pile. "We'll stink you up some before we take you into our secret fort."

"You don't need to do that on my account," said Ellie. "I'm perfectly content to be at odds with your traditions."

Several children said, "What?"

To Ellie's ears it sounded like a perfectly natural response from small children.

Small children? These children were taller than she was.

She made her face stern and used the voice that made her younger siblings cringe. "You will let me go. You will let Tak go."

"Why?" The tall one sneered.

"Because *you* are a child. *I* am an adult. Your behavior is unacceptable. You will treat me with respect."

Ellie didn't like the tone of the laugh that spread through the captors.

"Maybe we'll respect you," said the tall one. "After we eat you."

That pronouncement raised a round of snickering and wicked giggles.

"We gonna eat the dog?" asked the child at her feet.

"No, dummy. You're supposed to play with a dog."

"Tak is not a dog," said Ellie. "He is a goat."

Tall One looked at her with squinty eyes. "He better be a dog, or we'll eat 'im. And if you give us trouble, we'll eat you twice."

"We could eat the bird," said the vocal child now sitting on her toes.

"Stupid, we didn't catch the bird."

Ellie refused to inform them that the bird was a dragon.

The child below sniffed. "I wanted to hold the bird."

Tall One threw a disgusted look at the whiny child, but answered with unexpected compassion. "You can hold the dog."

Ellie felt the clamp of arms and legs loosen, and the child darted off to join the pile on Tak.

Ellie wondered if Tak would come through this encounter with wild children without harm.

"You be nice to Tak," she admonished the children in general.

One of the boys pinched her.

"Ouch!"

"You shut up." He glared at her from just an inch away. "We're going to wrap you up in ropes and drag you to our fort. Then we're going to hang you. Then we're going to eat you."

"Can we do all of that before bedtime?" asked a familiar voice from the Tak pile.

"Sure we can," said the boy, twisting the bit of Ellie's flesh he held between two fingers. "We're the bad guys."

Ellie put on her most intimidating big sister face and growled at the six-year-old. "You need someone with a stiff brush to scrub the dirt off of you. And that same someone might put a bar of soap in your mouth if you aren't careful. I don't like your tone of voice. I might just be the one to teach you some manners."

"Are you going to do that before or after we eat you?" he asked with a sneer.

Ellie pasted a sweet smile on her lips. "Before."

# 15

# Home, Sweet Hovel

The children tied Ellie's hands together with one of her own stockings. After several attempts, they had another stocking, hers, tied around her head as a blindfold. She could look down and see through a gap in their handiwork, but she didn't feel any obligation to tell them.

The boys pushed and shoved her through the street. She recognized some of the planters where Tak had nibbled a snack, which clarified which street they marched her down. She could hear higher voices, and she assumed they were girls, talking baby talk to the goat. She could just imagine the disgusted looks Tak was bestowing on the silly children.

She became aware of Airon's presence and received the reassurance that the dragon followed and would return to tell Bealomondore her exact location.

*Where is he?* she asked.

The image of Bealomondore swashbuckling with an impressive sword came to her mind.

*He went to get a sword? That's insane. These are children. He can't spring on them and dispatch six-year-olds at the point of his sword like soldiers from an enemy army.*

She listened. The thought formed in her mind.

*You tell him he is not to scare these little children with a sword.*

"There's the bird," yelled one of the children. "We'll catch you, bird! You're doomed to be bird stew."

Ellie wondered why the children always threatened to eat whatever they caught. "Are you children hungry?"

"Nah." Ellie recognized the voice of Tall One. "We get food, but we never eat anything fun."

The statement made Ellie smile. Maybe daggarts would work in softening the attitude of her captors. Of course, a few obstacles stood in her way. She'd have to escape. She and Bealomondore would have to find the ingredients and an oven.

She got pinched again. "Don't you smile!" She recognized this voice too. The pincher shoved her forward. She stumbled, but so many hands held on to her that she didn't fall.

"You don't smile when you're a prisoner."

"I'm sorry." Ellie tilted her head toward the one she'd offended. "I forgot the rules."

He grunted. Her little brothers would have said, "That's all right. Just don't do it again." These children didn't know the customs that made playtime fun. If she and Bealomondore were stuck here forever, she would make sure these overgrown six-year-olds learned some manners and rules.

The small procession of captors and two captives came to a building, and Ellie spotted the raised threshold she would have to step over. None of the children warned her, and none noticed that she did not trip. Inside, the cool air smelled musty.

Her handlers took her through several rooms and then made her sit on a box. They untied her hands, then retied each hand to two posts beside the seat.

"Take off the blindfold," ordered Tall One.

The stocking was yanked off the top of her head, pulling her hair. She blinked and studied the dirty faces surrounding her. It seemed to her that they were trying to outdo each other in a fierce glowering contest. Several got bored and wandered off. Others followed. It didn't surprise her that Tall One and the pincher tied for last-to-give-up at looking mean. Ellie stopped watching the contest and surveyed her surroundings.

A dozen children still surrounded Tak. They petted him and cooed and talked nonstop. No one listened to anyone else, and poor Tak closed his eyes.

"The dog wants to go to sleep," said the girl with curly hair and a permanent pout. She started jostling the others, making them surrender their positions next to Tak. The others gave way, proving to Ellie that this girl had earned her place of boss by being tough.

"We should give him a name," said the child who previously clung to Ellie's legs.

They turned in unison to their captive.

"What's his name?" demanded Pouter.

Ellie used her calmest, kindest, most nonthreatening voice. She would not give them the satisfaction of losing control. She would speak like an adult, even if doing so tied a twist in her tongue. "His name is Tak."

"That's no good." Pouter turned back to contemplate the goat. "If he's going to go to sleep, he has to lie down. Make him lie down."

Six children rushed forward to obey the command. They grabbed Tak's legs and pulled them out from under the frightened animal.

"Stop!" Ellie fumed. "You're going to hurt him."

Tak hit the floor on his side with a thud and a grunt.

"You don't know much," said Tall One. "He's not hurt."

The announcement from their male leader ended the contest. Pincher plodded across the floor, making as loud a noise as he could.

His footfalls sounded like he weighed three hundred pounds. He threw himself down on a pile of dirty blankets.

Tak lay still. Ellie figured pretending to be docile was a good strategy. With a little difficulty, she scooted back on the wooden box so she could relax against the wall.

Tall One and Pouter left the room together, whispering and looking very much like they were conspiring to do evil. Ellie reminded herself that children didn't plot with much efficiency. Even the knots that bound her to the pillars failed to totally restrain her movements. She could probably loosen them and escape if no one was watching. Only a dozen children remained in the room. But each and every one of them kept sneaking peeks at her while they pretended to be absorbed in their games.

She studied them as much as they watched her. For the most part, they behaved much like her younger siblings and their friends. But the urohms' simple games erupted into slapping and shoving fights for no apparent reason. The matches consisted of moving objects like stones and sticks in a pattern she could not discern.

Leg Clinger came to sit close to her but twisted a cloth in her hands and did not speak. The rag represented something. The child wadded the material into several shapes and finally clasped it tight in her arms and cuddled it, rocking slightly.

Ellie spoke very softly. "My name is Ellicinderpart."

Leg Clinger stopped all movement.

"What's your name?" Ellie asked.

The child's head dropped closer to the rag she embraced.

Ellie tried again. "I have little brothers and sisters."

Leg Clinger's head tilted slightly, and Ellie got a brief glimpse of one eye.

"How long have you lived here?"

The child shrugged, and Ellie felt she'd made one step closer to reaching her. "I come from a place outside the bottle."

"There isn't a bottle." The girl shifted so she faced Ellie. "That's a fairy tale."

"I see." Ellie searched for a topic that wouldn't shut off the flow of conversation. "Who gives you your food?"

A shrug and the head dropped, leaving Ellie to stare at matted hair. Mud caked the child's shoes, and stains covered her skirt, blouse, and apron. But in contrast, none of her belongings looked old.

Ellie decided to try one more topic. "You have nice shoes."

Leg Clinger straightened out her legs and looked at her feet. She nodded.

"Where did you get them?"

Another shrug.

"Do you have a name?"

The look she got from the urchin said Ellie was incredibly dumb. "Yeah."

"Mine is Ellicinderpart. What's yours?"

"Gardie. Yours is too long."

"You can call me Ellie." She waited, but Gardie didn't comment. "Who takes care of you?"

Another disgusted look. "Me."

"When I was six, I had a mother and father to take care of me. What happened to all the mothers and fathers?"

A shrug. A sigh. "Old One took care of us, but he got mean."

Another child lifted her head from a pile of stones he played with. "That's another fairy tale, Gardie. You know it is. He never was anything but mean." He glared at Ellie. "We aren't supposed to talk about it."

Gardie ducked her head.

The stone-piling child motioned to Gardie. "You come over here and leave the prisoner alone. You probably aren't supposed to talk to her."

Gardie stood and shuffled over to stone-piling child.

Ellie looked at the one with the stones. "Do you have a name?"

"I won't talk to you."

"What is the game you play with your stones?"

A pause. "Trickery."

"I don't know how to play Trickery. Will you show me?"

"Long as I don't have to talk to you. I bet we aren't supposed to talk to you."

"Who will tell you if you aren't allowed to talk to me?"

"Yawn," said Gardie.

The boy was moving his stone pile closer to Ellie. "Yawn's top bad guy."

"Are you all bad guys?"

Both children nodded.

"Why? Why not be good guys?"

Both children shrugged. Ellie despaired of ever getting information out of these two. She watched as they played with the stones and could not make any sense of the game. If she asked questions, they shrugged. The game went on and on until the boy who would not speak to her scooped up all the stones and crammed them in his pockets. Gardie didn't seem to care.

With no cue that Ellie could detect, the children sprang to their feet and bolted from the room. Tak raised his head, looked around, and stood.

"Maa."

"I don't know where they went. Oh! I bet it's dinnertime."

Gardie ran back into the room and halted just inside the door. "I can't bring you anything to eat."

"That's all right."

"I gotta go, or it'll all be gone."

"That's all right. Go ahead."

"We'll come back. We have to be inside before the sun goes down."

"Why?"

"If we don't go to bed, there's no food in the morning. Everyone has to wait until noonmeal, and if they figure out who wasn't in bed…" Her eyes grew wider. "I gotta go."

She dashed away.

"Maa."

Ellie twisted her wrists against the stockings binding her to the posts. "Just a minute, Tak, and I'll go with you."

"Would you like some help?" Bealomondore stood in the doorway, looking very dapper, a sword strapped to his waist.

"Yes, I would. I don't want to be here when they come back. And I certainly don't want you brandishing that sword at them."

He came across the room and quickly undid one knotted stocking. "I wouldn't hurt a child."

He untied the other stocking, and Ellie took it. She stuffed the unmatched pair into her pocket.

Her voice broke in the middle of her next declaration. "I know you wouldn't hurt them." She stood rubbing her wrists.

"What's the matter?"

"There's one named Yawn that *I* could very well hurt if given the chance. He's a bully."

Bealomondore put his arm around her shoulder and guided her

toward the door. "You don't think munching on daggarts will bend Yawn to your will?"

She giggled. "I think it would take plum pudding, birthday cake, daggarts, and iced parnot slush to even get his attention."

"Sounds like a hard case. We'll start with daggarts."

"Thank you for rescuing me. What took so long?"

"You told Airon I couldn't use my sword. I had to wait until the children cleared the building."

"Thank you for that too."

He smiled, stopped, and bowed to her. "Miss Ellicinderpart Clarenbessipawl, would you do me the honor of going to dinner with me?"

She smiled back and felt tears well up. She batted them away. "Yes, I will. Your kindness overwhelms me."

He gave her a quizzical look and merely exclaimed, "Ha!"

# 16

# In Search of Flour and Eggs

Bealomondore and Ellicinderpart pored over the journals the next morning. They waited for Det to come back with news of a house that might supply their daggart-making needs.

Bealomondore cast glances up to the balcony where they had seen the shadow of Old One. He didn't appear to be watching them today, or he was being careful to keep out of sight. Airon had gone out with the watch, and Tak had stubbornly refused to come in after they walked to get breakfast. The goat roamed the fenced-in park behind the library. His nibbling of overgrown shrubbery could only do the landscape some good, and the children never came that close to the library.

Ellicinderpart had on an unusual combination of blouse, skirt, and vest. Obviously parts of the original outfits were still held hostage by the horde. She didn't complain, and that made her very special in his eyes.

His mother would have hid in a closet. Even his more sensible sisters would not have gone out of the house. But the young tumanhofer lady took it in stride and wore what she had available without a fuss. In fact, he was impressed with her relaxed attitude about almost everything that came their way. He had been more irritable when he first bumbled into Rumbard City.

If she'd get over this crazy scheme to tame the wild ones, he'd be happier. Mixing with that immature gang could lead to disastrous misadventures.

Right now, her intent gaze fixed to the pages of a book, she showed him a profile of innocence and determination. He reached for a pencil and stopped, remembering his duty to find information about anything. That goal superseded all other considerations. They knew practically nothing, so anything ranked as valuable information. He would have years to sketch her likeness.

Bealomondore looked back at his book, a history, *The Migration of Urohms.* He flipped through the pages until he came to a chapter titled "Transformation." He read the first sentence and then read more rapidly, his attention caught. When he finished, he called Ellicinderpart to take note.

"This is remarkable. Listen. The urohm race is exclusive to the land of Amara. Those who came to Chiril came as diplomats. But their origin is in Amara, where they unselfishly stepped up to help defend a group of kimens who were under threat of annihilation.

"The account is stunning. They went to bed determined to fight the overwhelming odds and knowing it was probably a lost cause. In the morning, they awoke to find that Wulder had enlarged their bodies to match the bigness of their hearts. Their clothing and horses and weapons were also large, but they kept their houses and furniture on the small side to keep themselves humble."

He and Ellicinderpart both raised their heads and looked around. The huge furniture and grandiose size of the rotunda—all the architecture in the city—sure didn't measure up as small.

"Well," said Ellicinderpart, "the urohms in Amara may have normal-sized homes, but these urohm diplomats must not have believed as strongly in humility."

Bealomondore scanned the upper balcony again, wondering if Old One eavesdropped. He raised his voice just in case. "I sure wish Old

One had the itch for company. Imagine the details he could clear up for us."

He turned as the sound of flapping leathery wings came from the storage room of the library. Det swooped into their sanctuary and landed on the back of a chair. Ellicinderpart closed her book and leaned forward. This morning she had revealed that she had trouble understanding all the dragons except Airon. Apparently she was determined to tune in to Det's report.

Bealomondore saw the look on her face change from concentration to joy. She heard.

Det had two houses designated as possibilities, both in a neighborhood close to the edge of town and therefore out of the range of the roaming hunters. To go to either house would require spending the night away from the library, perhaps two nights.

Bealomondore watched Ellicinderpart to gauge her reaction to this news. He was sure she hadn't realized that being alone in his company without a proper chaperone sealed her fate. She would be his wife or be relegated to a single life, probably on her parents' farm.

She stood and put her book down on the top of a pile next to Old One's chair. "I'll pack a few things."

He nodded and watched her scurry off. He certainly wouldn't take advantage of her lack of sophistication, but he did wonder how she would react once the situation became clear to her. He closed his eyes and sighed. Of course, they might be stuck in the bottle city until they were both old. That would solve the problem of what society thought. What did he think? How did he feel? He opened his eyes at the revelation in his heart. He felt grateful.

In the past two years, he'd given his heart to someone who loved someone else. He had to admit that they, his former ladylove and her intended, were a perfect couple. But loneliness and a lack of destiny had descended on him at the end of the war. Painter? Soldier? Society dandy? Diplomat? What was he? Falling through the bottle wall had not devastated him as much as it might have. After all, he had no particular path to take. But with the coming of Ellicinderpart Clarenbessipawl, all that changed.

He looked to the skylight and whispered, "Wulder, bless my soul, You've provided, and although it's going to take some getting used to, I'm pleased You've brought me a young lady I can admire."

He needed to pack a few things as well. And he wanted to strap on his Sword of Valor. So far the only dangerous beasts he had come across in Rumbard City were six-year-olds. But venturing farther from the center of town might uncover something more sinister. This information was another thing they might acquire from Old One if the ancient urohm would just speak to them. Bealomondore headed for his private corner of the library.

Ellie waited with Det at the back entry to the library. As Bealomondore approached, he saw her eyes widen. Her glare fastened on the sword belt and scabbard.

"Why are you wearing that?" she asked.

"Just to be prepared."

Her frown turned fearsome, and he bit off a laugh he knew would offend her.

She spoke through tight lips. "You will remember these urohms are children, won't you?"

"Yes, Ellicinderpart. On my honor as a gentleman, I promise not to pierce the heart of one of the scalawags."

She looked doubtful for a moment, and he hoped she would not belabor the point. Of course, he wasn't looking for the chance to cross swords with a child. And besides, from what he'd seen, most of their weapons were made of wood.

They went past the butcher shop to pick up their noonmeal and were surprised to find twice as much food.

"Enough for dinner," said Ellicinderpart, shaking her head in wonder. "Who is it? How does he or she know what we are planning?"

Det chittered. She gave him a sharp look, then turned to Bealomondore. "Wulder? He says Wulder provides?"

"That has been my conclusion. The Tomes record His principles and some of His history. Those accounts speak of His sending His people into barren lands but providing a sweet bread served in small bites and scattered on the ground each morning. And at dusk, He caused birds to gather in the camp for the people to capture and prepare for the evening meal."

"Why did He send them to a barren land?"

"Punishment for disregarding His power and His will."

Ellicinderpart tilted her head and wore a thoughtful expression. "So He interacts with His 'people' more than Boscamon?"

"Since Boscamon does not exist, then of course He does."

Tak came and nudged Ellicinderpart's arm. Absent-mindedly, she pinched off a piece of bread and fed the morsel to her goat.

Det reminded them of the long journey. They put their trash back in the box and stowed the extra food in Bealomondore's satchel. Det led them quickly out of the center of the city, where they would be most likely to run into a band of children. Once they felt safe enough to slow their pace, Bealomondore engaged Ellicinderpart in conversation, learning about her family, her siblings, her many aunts and uncles, and the farm that had been in her father's family for many generations.

"I find it odd," he said, "that there is no legend of a city of giants in the land. Your family has been in the area for almost as long as the city has been in the bottle, yet no one tells tales of its existence."

Ellicinderpart's face brightened at the topic. "Did you see dragon posts before you came to the glass wall?"

"I did."

"No one has ever mentioned those monuments to me. No one talks about the city, the urohms, or the stone dragons."

Bealomondore offered his hand to help her over a rough bit of pavement. The cobbles shifted underfoot, and he didn't speak until they passed the obstacle.

"I've read of other standing stones. They're typically said to be centuries old, which would fit our theories about Rumbard City. And they typically have their origins shrouded in mystery. Something so obvious in the countryside should garner interest and be honored with at least an oral tradition of history."

Ellie broke in. "No! No one has said a word about dragon stones. My family often goes to the festivals within walking distance. Among all the singing of ballads and stories of lore, I have never heard anything about the city or the standing stones."

"It is my opinion," said Bealomondore, with a finger in the air for emphasis, "that something prohibits the populace from recalling anything from the past. Such was the case in the accounts I read. And more interesting is that even when the local people acknowledged a standing stone in their vicinity, they failed to recognize the significance of these monuments. More often than not, they forgot these oddities are among them."

"I think I've missed something. What *is* the significance of the standing stones?"

"My point exactly! We don't know!"

Ellicinderpart shivered, even as they walked in the warm sun. "That doesn't seem natural, does it?"

"No, and neither does a city in a bottle. I would say that either Wulder Himself or one of His wizards cast the spell that is Rumbard City."

"Wizards are connected to Wulder?"

She looked at him with curiosity. Bealomondore hesitated. How much could he tell her without sounding like a fool? So many times when he tried to explain what he had learned about Wulder, people thought it foolishness. But those who knew Wulder marveled at the miraculous and didn't discount the wonders Wulder had performed. Bealomondore would spend many years with Ellicinderpart, one way or another, so he made the choice to feed bits of knowledge to her in little portions.

"Yes, they derive their skills from an intimate knowledge of the way Wulder designed the world."

"We don't have wizards in Chiril, just stories about such men."

"We do have wizards now. And some wizards are women. At least Librettowit, Fenworth's librarian, says there are female wizards in Amara. In Chiril, Verrin Schope is a wizard. Paladin is somewhat like a wizard, but apparently more. And Fenworth, if he hasn't traveled back to Amara, is a wizard."

"The stories have good and bad wizards, so is Wulder good and bad?"

"No, men are good and bad. Sometimes, when people are given a lot of responsibility, they use the power to make themselves even more powerful. A principle in the Tomes says, 'He who forces his gift to fill the world will suffer the loss of the gift and the world.' "

Airon flew in from one of the side streets and announced that she was going to accompany them on the rest of their journey. With her along, the conversation soon turned to singing. The sun set, and they had a meal on the front porch of a small house. The only one who seemed disgruntled with the plan to move on was Tak. He wanted to be done with walking for the day, and he made that complaint clear through the two dragons.

After an hour's rest, the moon came up and provided plenty of light, so they continued, following Det to the first house he had discovered.

Inside, they found an oven, stores of food, and huge baking sheets to make daggarts.

"Do you think the things in this kitchen are still good after four hundred years?" asked Ellicinderpart.

"I don't believe it can be that old. Remember, the urohms died off naturally of old age. And I would suppose that Wulder provided fresh staples until the only food needed was enough to sustain the children and Old One."

"And us."

"And the dragons of the watch," Bealomondore added.

"What happened to the people in the barren land? Are they still roaming around without a home?"

"No. According to the Tomes, they could not go into the good land until the generation of scoffers died off. Then the next generation would be allowed to enter."

The goat came and stood beside Ellicinderpart and leaned into her leg, almost knocking her over. She smiled and rubbed the top of his head. "I'm so tired I can hardly stand up," she said. "And so is Tak."

They left the kitchen and found a room with a thick area rug, a couch, tables, chairs, and throw pillows. Bealomondore climbed an end table and hopped onto the sofa. He shoved a pillow to the edge.

"Look out below!" he shouted and heaved the plush cushion over the side.

He pushed another pillow off, then jumped, landing on what would be his bed.

Ellie giggled. She put a hand over her mouth and sobered. "Oh my. I'm getting silly, I'm so tired."

"Well, then," Bealomondore said. "Let's turn in and discuss Wulder, wizards, and the world more tomorrow. And in addition to contemplating large issues, we can be practical as well. We'll be able to see better in the morning light and take inventory of the cabinets."

"If we find the ingredients we need, you know I'm going to insist on baking the daggarts."

Airon and Det flew in, circled the room, then settled on an overstuffed sofa.

Bealomondore dragged a pillow through a doorway. "I'll sleep in here. And yes, I figured we'd have to bake."

"If we find eggs."

"If we find flour, sugar, salt, and all those other ingredients."

"If we find a working oven."

He laughed. "Maybe we won't have to bake after all."

"Don't count on it. I know a recipe for iffie pie."

"Never heard of it." He raised his voice to reach the other room. He removed his coat and sat to take off his shoes.

"It is my grandmother's recipe. *If* you have an ingredient, you put it in. *If* you don't have it, you don't put it in."

"*If* you don't mind, I'd prefer to stick to daggarts."

"How is that an adventure in living?" She sounded as if she had lain down, her voice muffled.

"Believe me, I've had enough adventure. I'll be happy if tomorrow is nothing more than a day of baking."

"Good night, Bealomondore."

"Good night, Ellicinderpart Clarenbessipawl."

"My family calls me Ellie."

"Good night, Ellie."

"What does your family call you?"

"Graddapotmorphit."

She responded after a short pause. "Good night, Bealomondore."

# 17

# A Picture Tells a Tale

Ellie turned over again and greeted the lightening sky with relief. The cushion did not make a satisfactory mattress. Her bed in the library was much more comfortable. She'd tossed and turned most of the night. Tak raised his head and then put it back down quickly, as if to say, "Oh no! I'm not getting up. It's too early."

Ellie couldn't stand the lumpy bed any longer and gave up any notion of sleeping a few more minutes. She changed out of her night-gown, folded the garment her aunt had purchased, and put it away in the little bag she'd brought with her. She figured the library must have given out the bags since Rumbard City Library was emblazoned across the front. The light cloth sack was easier to carry than her carpetbag.

She washed her face and crept to the back door. The closed door momentarily stymied her desire to go outside. She didn't have a clue as to how to open it. Following the wall, she came to the opening they'd crawled through the night before. She pushed halfway through and stopped to gape at the garden. Gorgeous, lush bushes crowded the yard, and each had bright flowers of different sizes and colors. She hadn't seen any of this splendor when they arrived by the light of the moon. Everything had been shades of gray. She twisted to lie on her back for a better view.

For several minutes, she reclined half in and half out of the small portal. A flock of heliotrope birds fussed at each other in a tragabong tree. Butterflies with shimmering wings flitted between the flowering bushes. A breeze rattled a chiming tree, and the little bell-like leaves quaked. The musical jangle rose and fell, sounding a pleasant natural percussion in the early morn. Later in the day, the leaves would soften in the heat of the sun and no longer sing softly to the world.

Ellie felt Tak pushing her from behind. She wiggled out and sat on the grass as the goat followed. "So you decided to get up after all."

A rooster crowed.

Ellie sat up straighter. "Did you hear that? Where there's a rooster, there are chickens. Where there are chickens, there are eggs." She jumped to her feet. "Come on, Tak."

Det and Airon joined the two early birds.

"Are you coming with us?" Ellie asked.

Airon assured her that they would be back soon. At the same time, Det mindspoke their intention to check for news from the watch. Ellie found she received the simultaneous messages with a little less confusion than before. Perhaps she would become skilled at communicating with the little messengers. The dragons flew off toward the center of town.

Ellie and Tak followed the sounds of clucking down the alley and came to a huge lawn behind a mansion. A barn stood on one corner. Two giant horses grazed in a pasture beyond. Dozens of normal-sized cats scooted around the paddock and outbuildings.

"It must be perilous to be a mouse around here," she said to Tak. "I don't see any goats or cows or pigs. I guess this was not a working farm but more of a hobby." She looked again at the mansion on the hill. "No farmer I've ever known lived in a house like that."

The rooster ran in front of them on an urgent mission. He challenged a smaller bird that had the audacity to strut in front of his hens.

"I'm glad they're not giants like the horses. I think I'd run." She glanced around the barnyard and stopped to consider the small wooden hutch. "I don't think they've been laying in that chicken coop. Let's look in the bushes."

She examined the shrubbery nearest the alley with Tak right behind her, who was plucking green leaves for his breakfast. There she found dozens of eggs. Many eggs were clustered, and the grass and foliage around them showed obvious signs of a hen's devotion. Having run off from the house without a basket of some sort, she tucked up the hem of her skirt, making a pouch to put the eggs in.

She and Tak meandered back to the house where they'd slept, enjoying the early morning feel in the air and fascinated by the trappings of the urohm neighborhood. When they finally made it back, Ellie sat beside the hole in the wall and, one by one, put the eggs inside. With her skirt pouch emptied, she stretched out on her stomach, reached through the skinny portal, and carefully moved the eggs aside. Finally, she crawled in, and Tak followed.

An empty flowerpot stood against the wall, and she loaded her find into the makeshift bowl. In the kitchen, she placed the pot on the seat of a chair and brushed twigs and bits of dirt from her clothes.

"Is that you, Ellie?" Bealomondore called from somewhere in the house.

"Yes."

"Come here. I want to show you something."

She followed the sound of his voice and ended up in the room where her lumpy pillow-mattress lay. Her venture outside had been filled with color, light, and beauty. Now the darkness of the empty house made her skin prickle with bumps. "Where are you?"

"Through here."

Tak darted in front of her, and she gladly followed.

A light beckoned her from the end of a hall. Bealomondore had opened the shades in a room filled with paintings.

"Aha," she said as she came through the door. "What a fine collection. Are the paintings good or merely pretty?"

"Mostly good. A few excellent." He pointed to a picture of a ship on the sea and then to a depiction of a woman reading to children around her.

He pointed out a six-foot-tall painting of two men standing side by side, a tumanhofer and a urohm. "But this is the one that astonishes me."

"Oh!" Ellie moved to the picture as if drawn by a rope. "Is it right? I mean, the proportions? The shorter man comes up to the other's waist. Surely one is too tall or the other too short."

He took her hand and pulled her along with him as he sped down the hall and into another room. Dropping his grip, he crossed the room and pulled on a shade, which zipped up and twirled several times at the top, making a *whopping* sound with each turn. Sun poured in through the window, and dust motes floated in the air.

"This is a nursery."

She'd already surmised that from the furniture and childish pictures, toy trains, and stacking blocks.

"I'm four feet five inches tall," Bealomondore said.

She had no idea why that was relevant but decided to not reveal her obtuse state.

Bealomondore strolled across the room to a wall that had one decoration, an embroidered height chart. Several places were marked with ribbons. Bealomondore fingered one of the lower trimmings. "Haddy, age two." He straightened out another to read. "Gelay, age five." Another strip said, "Haddy, age four."

Ellie shrugged. "My family records our heights on the wall in the mud room. Don't most families keep some kind of record?"

Without a word, Bealomondore turned and backed up to the measuring chart. "How tall am I?"

Ellie came closer to look. Her eyes widened, and she shifted her gaze to his solemn face. He already knew what it said.

"Three feet five inches."

He quirked an eyebrow at her.

She corrected for more precise accuracy. "Five and *a half* inches."

He moved out of the way and nudged her in position to be measured. "How tall are you?"

"Four feet one inch."

He glanced at the number at the top of her head. "Three feet two inches, and I'm giving you a bit on the inches."

"So the urohms don't have the same standard of measure as we do?"

Bealomondore pursed his lips and let out a breathy whistle. "On the contrary, my guess is that their twelve-inch foot would match our twelve-inch foot."

He took her hand and led her back to the art room and to the portrait. "In that picture, the tumanhofer comes up to just above the urohm's knee. Look at the background. What do you see?"

"Shelves of books, a table, a lamp, a globe, a desk, and papers."

"I believe this is a painting done in Amara and brought here."

"Why?"

"The size of the furniture is small in comparison to the urohm figure. The globe shows the Eastern hemisphere, where Amara is located. And the style of clothing is foreign."

Once he pointed out the details, Ellie could see what he meant.

"So tumanhofers and urohms got along well in that land? Well enough for two men to want a portrait together?"

"I hadn't thought of that, but yes. My point is the size of the tumanhofer." He moved to stand beside a chair in the room. He reached up to put his hand on the seat of the chair. "This chair is designed for a urohm." He patted the edge of the seat. "The urohm's knee would bend right here. I'm a foot below that point. We're smaller, Ellie. When we came through the glass wall, we shrank."

Ellie let out a nervous giggle. "That's not possible."

"Nothing about this place is possible. Why would you doubt a simple case of 'Shrink the Visitors'?"

"Bealomondore, why? Why would someone bother to make us smaller?"

"I doubt it was aimed at us in particular but affects anyone who passes through the wall."

Ellie took in a deep breath and let it out. "Wulder? Could it be like the legend of the urohms? We were made the size of our hearts? We're smaller, because our basic personalities are selfish? We don't care about others?"

Bealomondore shook his head sadly. "I hadn't thought of that." He pinched his upper lip. "No, that can't be it. At least not for you. You have a heart for these beastly children. It could certainly be true of me, however."

"No, you've taken care of me. You care about Old One."

Bealomondore gave a dismissive snort. "I am interested in Old One because he might be able to help us get out of here. And of course I've watched over you. You are a pleasure to have around. You rescued me from wretched loneliness. So my care also has a self-serving motive."

He frowned and looked away from her, his gaze moving to the window and beyond. She walked over to his side and took his hand. "What you need is a good breakfast and something to occupy your mind other than these depressing speculations."

He looked down at her, squeezed her hand, then brought it to his lips to kiss. "What shall we do for breakfast?"

"I found chickens, and therefore I found eggs."

"That sounds good."

"And afterward, you and I shall bake daggarts for naughty children and a grumpy old man."

He laughed. "See? I told you your heart is not small."

She smiled but kept the words flowing through her mind to herself.

He made her heart swell. She felt the expansion in her chest every time she looked into his eyes, heard him speak, or felt his presence. She liked this tumanhofer very, very much.

# 18

# Pickles and Calamity

Tak found a shady corner in the yard and settled in for a day of resting and eating. When Ellie invited him to come in with them to explore, he pointedly turned his head away and chewed. She and Bealomondore passed through the small opening and plowed into the task they had set before them, the locating of ingredients and appropriate bowls and cooking pans.

Ellie bubbled with enthusiasm. Her partner in raiding the kitchen was the most amusing companion she'd ever known. And tackling the difficult task of baking with oversize equipment would be full of surprises. Ellie giggled with anticipation, then glanced at Bealomondore to see if he'd heard. The door he was opening required all his attention. Each big urohm cupboard provided a challenge to little tumanhofers.

She and Bealomondore both explored the pantry, shoving boxes into unsteady stairs so they could reach the upper shelves. They found dried fruit and stores of nuts, as well as sugar, flour, and salt. They both climbed on the counter and investigated the cabinets. A small bag of baking powder, some spices, chocobits, and bowls added to their found treasure.

And they laughed over many of their discoveries.

"Look." Bealomondore held up a glass jar of pickles. "This urohm housewife kept jars of pickles in every nook and cranny."

Ellie laughed and held up a jar she'd just found. "This makes my sixth hidden pickle stash. How many are you up to?"

"I'm ahead of you by three."

"Someone in this house must have had a passion for pickles."

"You mean the mother hides the jars out of necessity?" Bealomondore examined the pickles more closely.

"I suppose she'd have to if the woman wanted her pickles to last through the winter. My mother hides her razterberry jam."

"Perhaps we should sample these. They must be uncommonly good."

"Mother's razterberry jam is." Ellie smiled at the memory of her brothers fighting over a jar. For a brief moment, her home tugged at her heart.

She swallowed, put on a smile, and said, "We'll have to find mustard if we want pickles and mustard on our sandwiches."

Bealomondore reached in the cabinet in front of him and held out a yellow bottle. "Mustard!"

Ellie laughed.

In many of the drawers, bunches of soft hemmed hand towels covered the contents. Delicately embroidered cloth rested on top of forks, spoons, and table knives. Measuring cups and spoons nestled under a thin sheet of patterned material.

"Whatever is the purpose of this, Ellie?" Bealomondore asked. "Do all housewives feel the need to conceal the contents of their kitchen drawers?"

She shrugged. She had no idea what possessed the mistress of this house. "I don't know, but I can tell you that all this handiwork is of the best quality."

"The habits and traditions of the urohms may forever be a mystery to us."

"When we get out of Rumbard City"—she chose the word "when" instead of "if" on purpose—"we can ask your friends, Wizard Fenworth and Librettowit, if they have stayed after the wedding. Or Verrin Schope, if they've gone home."

Bealomondore's face brightened. "Exactly, and Librettowit left a library at the underground cathedral in the Valley of the Dragons."

Ellie plied Bealomondore with questions and learned a great deal about his last two adventures with his friends. This time she hung on every word and then realized that she'd turned a corner in her regard for Bealomondore. She no longer suspected him of teasing her, telling her outlandish stories to prove her gullibility.

They went outside to collect wood for the stove and then laughed at their clumsy attempts to light the fire in the belly of the oversize oven. Covered with soot but successful, they lined up their ingredients to begin baking daggarts.

By the time the sun reached the zenith of its daily journey, they had located all the items they would need to make several batches of the crunchy treats.

"Time to begin this intrepid endeavor?" Bealomondore nodded to the warming oven.

"It would be better to wait for coals. The wood is burning too hot."

"Then perhaps we should eat our noonmeal first."

Ellie grinned. "We could have pickles."

Tak came in from the backyard, stamped his feet, and nodded his head in the direction of their exit.

"What's the matter, Tak?" asked Ellie.

Bealomondore headed for the back entrance. "I'll check it out."

Tak trotted over to Ellie and leaned against her. Ellie rubbed the goat's neck and the crown of his head between the two stubby horns.

Bealomondore's voice beckoned from outside. "Come on. Noonmeal has arrived, and I assume Tak was announcing our supper."

Ellie and Tak squirmed through the hole. Bealomondore stood next to a wrought-iron table with a glass top. A picnic basket sat in the center.

Ellie pointed to the table. "This wasn't here before, was it?"

"The noonmeal wasn't here, but the table was."

"I don't remember it."

"Just the same, it was here." He pointed to a row of potted plants. "The table and two benches were covered with these flowers and things."

She vaguely remembered the jumble of plants. "You moved all that?"

"No." Bealomondore pushed a crate closer to one of the benches. "Whoever brought the noonmeal cleared the table."

"Don't you find that a bit odd?" she asked.

"Ellie, I find it odd that our meals are provided. Why should clearing the table be odder?"

"You're right." She responded to his gesture and clambered up onto the crate and, from there, onto the bench.

She opened the lid of the basket and pulled out two jars of cold lemonade. She unscrewed the lid on one and handed it to Bealomondore.

He took a long swig. "Ah, that is excellent." He smacked his lips and looked at the basket. "What else is in there?"

"Sandwiches, something in a bowl, and two pieces of pie." Ellie handed him a paper-wrapped sandwich.

"Let's see what's in the bowl."

Ellie pulled it out and took off the cover. She laughed and tilted it just a bit to show Bealomondore.

"What is it?" he asked.

"Button grain for Tak. It's his favorite, and he hasn't had any since we left home."

With a flip of the tail, Tak made the leap from the ground to the bench, bypassing the crate. "Maa!"

"I don't understand," said Ellie. She held the bowl steady while Tak devoured the grain. "This is so unnecessary. Just like the pie, it's nice but an extra, not essential."

Bealomondore sat cross-legged on the bench and opened his sandwich. "My premise is that the food is provided by Wulder."

"I know that."

"And in the Tomes, it is written, 'Like a good father, Wulder delights in the pure pleasure of His children's hearts.' "

Ellie waited. So far, she didn't see his point.

Bealomondore spoke around a bite of sandwich. "Did your parents ever blow bubbles for you on laundry day?"

She smiled. "Yes, and I blow them for my little brothers and sisters."

"And these bubbles serve no purpose?"

"Well, they're fun to chase. And they have a sheen of rainbow colors on the surface. That's pretty."

Bealomondore held up a finger. "Number one: I contend that fun and beauty are required for a full life. Joy has purpose." He held up a second finger. "Number two: The parent, or in your case, the big sister, and in my case, the laundry maid, go to a little extra trouble to give something that produces only pleasure, nothing else. Wulder gives us pie. He gives Tak button grain. Why? Because He delights in our enjoyment of simple pleasure."

Tak cleaned out the bowl, huffed into it as if to uncover any stray bits, then jumped off the bench. Ellie put the bowl on the table and perched on the edge of the bench with her legs dangling over the side. She folded back the paper wrapping her sandwich. Salty ham and cheese blended with thick tomato slices and crunchy lettuce for a satisfying noonmeal.

Ellie concentrated on what Bealomondore had said about Wulder giving good gifts. She took that thought and related it to their experience. "We make daggarts to show that we would like to care for Old One and the children."

"Ah, and our conversation comes full circle." Bealomondore plunked his trash in the picnic basket. "You are the altruistic one. I am merely along for the ride."

Ellie rolled her eyes at him, and Bealomondore chuckled. He passed a piece of pie to Ellie and forked a large bite of his own. When they'd finished, he returned the bowl, forks, and plates to the basket and snapped the lid shut.

Ellie hopped down from the bench. "Come on, curmudgeon, oh surly fellow who does not lift a finger for another's pleasure. Let's make those daggarts."

The grin on Bealomondore's face couldn't have been any wider. Ellie remembered her brothers. She was the oldest, but Nabordontippen, who was born next in line, was the orneriest. He made mischief and delighted in leading the twins and Gustus into more. And that self-satisfied smile graced the lips of all four of her impish brothers when they'd executed some roguish misdeed.

But Bealomondore gave her little trouble as they stoked the fire, mixed the dough, and shaped enormous daggarts on the baking sheets. He proved to be a helper when working, not an instigator of mischief.

The heavy pans required the strength of both tumanhofers to maneuver the daggarts into the oven. Pulling them out challenged them even more. But clever Bealomondore rigged up a stool in front of the oven, and they managed to slide the daggart sheet onto the wood platform.

Ellie shoveled up the large daggarts with a metal spatula and put them on a plate while Bealomondore held the tray steady. Then he put the new daggarts on a cooled sheet, and they both lifted them into the oven. The door closed from one side to the other instead of up and down. If it had been one you had to pull down, Ellie doubted they could have made daggarts at all. By the end of the afternoon, they had several piles cooled and ready to be wrapped.

She collapsed on the kitchen floor and leaned against a cabinet. "I am so glad we're not going to try to get back to the library tonight. I don't think I could walk to the chicken yard, let alone clear across the city."

Bealomondore sat beside her. "If we find it is impossible to get out of this bottle, I propose we make our home out here rather than in the heart of Rumbard City."

Ellie didn't answer immediately. She weighed his words in her heart. Oddly, the prospect of being in Rumbard City without a way to get out didn't paralyze her like it once had. "I believe we will get out. Someday. I don't worry about it like I used to."

Bealomondore put his arm around her shoulders and gave her a gentle squeeze. "You are one spunky lass, Ellicinderpart Clarenbessipawl."

"Thank you. I think."

"Yes, that was a compliment." He withdrew his arm and waved a hand at the messy kitchen. "Shall we attempt a cleanup?"

She sighed and nodded. "My mother's upbringing would haunt me if I left this borrowed kitchen in such disarray."

"Your diction is that of a city gal, yet you say you have always lived on the farm."

Ellie stood. "Oh, we can talk country when we're among ourselves. But my mom and Gramps set store on book learning. Not so much my father. But he let us have our way, only teasing us about being highfalutin two or three times a week."

She looked around, assessing all that needed to be done. "Do you want to wash dishes or counters and floor?"

"Counters and floor."

"Fine!" She climbed the cabinets to the sink. Bealomondore took time to help her get the water hot and all the dishes within reach. Even though they had used the smallest bowls available to mix the dough, the heavy ceramic made it difficult to maneuver them in and out of the soapy water and then into the rinsing basin. She lined up the clean dishes upside down on a towel to dry.

When she finished, she sat on the edge of the counter and watched Bealomondore mop.

He glanced up, stopped, and pointed to the stack of bowls. "That one looks like it's going to topple."

She turned and saw which one he meant. Getting up on her knees, she pushed a plate farther away from the edge, making room for the bowl to rest more securely against another larger bowl.

Bealomondore shouted, "Watch out!"

The creak of one glass object rubbing against another warned her that the dishes had shifted. Something heavy hit her shoulder. She grabbed the dish she had just moved, but it tilted toward her and thrust her over the edge of the counter. She hit the floor before she even had time to scream.

Glass shattered around her. Pinpricks of pain assailed her exposed skin. Another dish somersaulted through the air, coming right at her. She ducked to the side, covering her head with her arms. It hit her shoulder and then the floor, exploding into flying shards. Broken pieces crunched as she shifted just a little bit.

"Don't move," said Bealomondore from beside her head. "Let me get some of this away from you so you won't get cut."

"Too late," she groaned and exposed the arm beneath her. She gritted her teeth. A long red line ran from the inside of her elbow to her wrist. Blood bubbled out the end of the gash.

Bealomondore clamped his hand over the wound. "This is deep. You must have nicked an artery."

"That's not good," she whispered. She knew his other hand moved quickly. He searched for something, but she couldn't summon the words to ask what he was doing. That seemed odd to her but not strange enough to break through this sudden malaise. The malaise seemed odd as well. Perhaps the combination of heat and the physical effort to make the daggarts had drained her.

"Not good, but we can fix it. I have some battleground experience."

"Oh, aren't I lucky?"

She heard him laugh, but the last words he spoke were mumbled. Or maybe she just couldn't hear through the darkness closing in on her.

# 19

# Clean Up

Bealomondore kept his hand over the wound while Ellie's blood poured through his fingers. Why wasn't the flow stopping? He shifted his grip and breathed a sigh of relief as the worst of the gushing changed to a slow trickle. With his other hand he searched his pockets for a handkerchief.

His jacket! He'd tucked the square of cloth he wanted to use in the breast pocket of his jacket, which hung on the back of a chair clear across the kitchen.

Tak looked at him and then at the brown coat. Without hesitation, he trotted across the wooden floor, took the back of the jacket in his teeth, and tossed his head. After two tries, he yanked it off and brought it to Bealomondore. The goat dropped it beside his mistress and immediately sank to position himself along her other side. Bealomondore winced, but apparently the shattered crockery did not penetrate Tak's thick white hair.

Bealomondore pulled out the white linen, put one end in his teeth, and twisted the fabric with his free hand. He then let loose of the wound and quickly wrapped the handkerchief around Ellie's wrist. He jumped up and ran to the lower drawers and pulled out several of the cloth covers that had puzzled them earlier. He folded them into a pile of squares a little larger than Ellie's wound.

He untied the first bandage, placed a square on the seeping blood and applied pressure. When that cloth soaked through, he added another on top and held it firmly, hoping to stop the flow.

He shifted his position, wondering how to sit amid the debris. What should he be doing to ensure Ellie's recovery? No medic roamed the streets of Rumbard City. King Yellat had provided many medics in the last war. He'd done that one thing right. The old ruler had not been a competent leader in time of war. But one shouldn't speak ill of the dead.

Bealomondore closed his eyes tightly. "Oh, Wulder, I could use some help right about now. Laddin would be the best dragon to send, but of course, You know that."

Tak sprang to his feet and ran for the back entrance.

"Did that goat just leave to get the dragons?" he asked. "Impossible."

Ellie groaned. A bloody stain spread beneath his hand. He added another piece of pretty linen and reapplied pressure.

Tak had not been gone a minute before Bealomondore heard him coming back in. The goat crunched through the broken glass. Behind and above him flew Airon.

Bealomondore breathed deeply. "Airon, do you know where Laddin is? Can you get him here quickly?"

The tumanhofer heard no reassurance in his mind, but Airon took off on the mission. Help would come. It was just a matter of time.

Tak sat down on the shards of broken glass again.

"You're going to get cut." Bealomondore also sat down, carefully. He put Ellie's injured wrist on his leg. "We have to keep this elevated. Wound higher than the heart." He glanced at the goat and caught the animal's intense gaze. "You're listening to me, aren't you? I wonder how much you understand."

"Maa!"

"That much, huh?" Bealomondore used the back of his free hand to itch his nose. "I think it's the smell of blood. My nose gave me lots of trouble on the battlefield. Of course, I only noticed it in the brief moments of respite."

He looked down at Ellie's face. "She looks too pale. With that dark tan it's hard to tell, but she looks pasty."

"Maa."

"You think so too? Well, don't worry. As soon as Laddin gets here, she'll start healing so fast, you won't believe it."

She stirred. He stroked wisps of fine black hair away from her face. "Ellie, can you hear me? You're going to be all right."

Her eyes didn't open, but her lips curved just a tad. "You're talking to Tak."

Bealomondore jerked a little but not enough to let go of the hand he held while applying pressure to the wound. He added another square.

Ellie breathed a little deeper. "Don't feel silly. I talk to him all the time."

"He's kept up the conversation better than you. You've offered no opinions for almost half an hour. You're going to be all right. Airon has been here, and she's gone to get the healing dragon, Laddin."

She licked her lips. Her eyes remained closed, and she grimaced.

"Are you in a lot of pain?" he asked.

"There's a piece of glass sticking into my shoulder, right side."

Bealomondore tried to see from his position but immediately knew he would have to move. "I'm going to put a tourniquet on this wound so I can clear some of the glass and see what other wounds we should be tending. I don't think there are any other big cuts. I looked you over as soon as I got to you."

She barely nodded her head.

He used a longer towel, tore a strip off of it, and bound yet another clean square to the top of the stack protecting her wound. He rolled up his jacket and propped her arm up. Standing cautiously so he wouldn't shower the broken shards clinging to his clothes on his patient, Bealomondore kept an eye on Ellie. Her color still bothered him.

"Wulder, send help. Quickly."

He got out the broom and dustpan he'd spotted in the pantry earlier. Ellie remained still. Heat from the oven radiated through the room. He dripped perspiration as he swept away the shattered dishes, then got on his knees and used a towel to gather up the bits and pieces closest to Ellie. He found scratches on her ankles and two on her neck. The piece that she'd felt against her shoulder hadn't penetrated her skin or even her blouse. He carefully removed it and several other shards under her. Then he washed the places where she'd bled a little from the scratches.

"That feels good," she said. "It's so hot."

He washed her face and hands again, just to make her more comfortable. He looked at the windows and door and knew he could not open them. A breeze would be refreshing. Perhaps he should move her to a cooler spot. He needed some ideas.

Sitting next to her, the tumanhofer again asked Wulder to speed Laddin to their assistance. He'd seen the healing dragon in action many times. Ellie looked so pale.

"Ellie, can you hear me?"

She whispered, "Yes."

"Can I get you something? A cool drink?"

"I'm too hot. Yes, please. A drink."

Climbing the cabinet took him but a moment. He'd developed

some skill at scaling the urohm fixtures. He searched for the smallest glass he could find. Getting down with a glass of water took a little more effort.

He put it down beside her. "I'm going to help you sit up."

She managed to pull herself to a sitting position with his support. He held the glass to her lips, and she gladly drank.

"Thank you, Bealomondore." She leaned back against him.

"I think we should get you out of this furnace."

She looked around, puzzled.

"Just a figure of speech. But I really think you'd be more comfortable outside in the shade."

"Oh, that sounds wonderful, but—"

"I'll help."

She managed to stand with Bealomondore supporting most of her weight. He held her close as he waited for her to get steady on her feet.

"My head hurts." She rested her forehead against his shoulder. "Oh no. I'm going to throw up."

Bealomondore grabbed the bucket of water he'd used when he mopped the floor. She nearly fell for that brief second as he leaned away from her to snatch the pail. He got it under her chin in time.

"Done?" he asked.

"I think so."

"I'm going to sit you on the footstool while I get your water and the washcloth."

"All right."

He pushed the stool with his foot until it touched the leg of the kitchen table. When she sat, she latched on to that leg, her arm wrapped securely around it.

He bent to look in her face. "Can I let go? Are you going to be all right?"

"Leave the bucket."

He did. He scrambled up the cabinet again to rinse out the washcloth with cool water. Ellie was still clinging to the table leg when he returned. He washed her face and gave her a sip of water.

"Are you ready to move outside?"

"Yes," she whispered between only slightly parted lips.

Tak stayed too close as they made their way.

"Move, goat," ordered Bealomondore.

The goat scooted ahead and disappeared around a corner.

Twice on the way to the back entrance, Ellie had to stop to gather the strength to go on. Bealomondore carried the bucket, and she lost what was left in her stomach. They rested.

"What's wrong with me?" she asked. "It's only a little cut."

Bealomondore didn't argue the point that it was significantly more than a little cut. "You're overheated," he explained. "And I think you may have a concussion."

"I didn't land on my head. My shoulder."

"I heard something harder than your shoulder whack against the floor. I'm not saying you're hardheaded, but…"

She smiled, but it turned into a grimace. "I can't laugh, Bealomondore."

He noticed that she stumbled over his name. "All right." He gave a theatrical sigh. "I'll tell you what my brother called me in private." They reached their exit. He guided her to a box where she could sit for a moment. "My first name is Graddapotmorphit. My brother called me Phit. If you wish to call me by something shorter than Bealomondore, I will not be offended."

He heard a faint giggle and thanked Wulder.

"You're going to be all right, Ellie." He helped her up again and eased her through the gap to the backyard. Tak waited outside and resumed his position at Ellie's side.

Bealomondore kept up his encouragement. "Laddin will be here soon, and he's a remarkable healing dragon." Now he was chattering just to keep her alert. "I don't know many dragons, so I wouldn't know if one healing dragon is better at healing than another. I have heard other singing dragons sing, and some are better than others." They walked across the lawn to the shade of a large tree. "So it stands to reason that some might be more gifted than others of the same talent."

He eased her down on the grass. Tak settled beside her on the less injured side.

Bealomondore explained what he wanted done. "We need to keep your arm elevated and still. Lie down, and I'll sit next to you with your hand propped on my leg."

Once she was situated to his satisfaction and before he took up his position, he asked if he should go back and get the glass of water.

"I'm fine. Keep talking. Tell me how you got into the bottle city."

"All right." He thought for a moment as he loosened the tourniquet and applied a new pad of cloth. He then lifted her arm to rest along his thigh. "I told you I was on the way to Ragar to do the painting, right?"

"Yes."

"I was traveling by cart, with a splendid old nag named Stemmore pulling it. I stopped to give her a rest. Across the glen, the landscape turned rough. Green grass ended among a scattering of boulders, and just beyond, an interesting ridge of stone rose out of the ground. I thought the contrast would make a fascinating painting.

"I left Stemmore grazing and walked around the glen, looking at the prospect from different angles. I went back to the cart, pulled out my painting supplies and my case of clothes. If I was going to paint, I would protect what I had on with a smock."

"But you needed to get to Ragar."

"Yes, well…I often get distracted when I see something that must go on canvas or paper."

"So you decided to camp and draw?"

"I don't think I decided anything. I just followed an instinct." He rubbed his chin. The notion to paint the ridge that thickened into a dominant hill and then just as quickly diminished to another string of protrusions from the earth had been too much to resist. He'd thought a number of times that the lure to that area had been more than a whim. Something pulled him.

"Bealomondore?"

"Oh, where was I? Returning to the glen with my things."

"Yes."

"When I got to the place I had previously chosen as the best angle, I saw something I hadn't seen before. The bottle. Of course, I didn't recognize what it was at the time, only an anomaly that I simply had to investigate. I approached the glass obelisk and realized it was much bigger than I originally thought. I could see a countryside, green and lush, inside. I had my hands full, so I leaned forward. Some invisible force pulled me straight through the glass."

Ellie nodded and closed her eyes. "The force that pushed me in was Tak."

"Maa."

She grinned. "He won't deny it."

Bealomondore concentrated on a sound coming from a distance. A chorus of chirps and chitters sounded like an assembly of squirrels voicing their opinions. The entire watch of dragons flew into sight.

Laddin reached them first. He landed on Ellie's stomach and stretched out so the front side of his entire little body pressed against her. Ellie turned startled eyes to Bealomondore.

"He's checking the function of your vital organs."

Her eyebrows went up. Bealomondore almost laughed at her reaction to the minor dragon's methods. But he noticed the color returning to her cheeks, and that was more satisfying than humorous.

Laddin hopped up, ran to her head, and draped himself over her forehead. Ellie giggled. The minor dragon frowned. A few seconds passed, and he skimmed down her side to the injured arm. There he stayed.

"Now you can just relax, Ellie," said Bealomondore. "Laddin has assessed your injuries and has gone to work on the one he deems most urgent."

"I feel something," she said.

"You feel better, I hope."

She looked at him with a puzzled frown. "You know…I think I do."

# 20

# A New Start

Ellie sat up on the edge of the pillow she used for a bed. The sun streamed in and serious dust motes performed ballet in its beams. Laddin had already left. He'd slept with her for two nights, completing the healing of her broken head and slashed wrist.

Pulling back the sleeve of her nightgown, Ellie examined the inside of her arm. No scar marred her skin from the elbow down to just above her wrist. There, the skin puckered slightly in a white line. She closed her eyes and moved her head cautiously from side to side. No dizziness.

She opened her eyes, took in a big breath, grinned, and stood up. Today she and Bealomondore could go back to the library. Maybe this evening they could have tea with Old One. Maybe tomorrow she could feed the children daggarts.

After dressing, she went to the kitchen to see about breakfast.

"Bealomondore?"

He didn't answer, so she checked outdoors. He sat on the bench next to the glass-topped table.

She watched him for a second before speaking. "There you are!"

Tak bleated and ran to greet her. Bealomondore started, then smiled. "You're well enough to be sneaking around, scaring people."

"I wasn't trying to be quiet." She rubbed Tak's head as she moved closer, trying to see what Bealomondore had in his hands. "What is that?"

"It's a tiny diary."

"Tiny? It's pretty big."

"No, no." He shook his head and turned the pages to the beginning. He read. *"I start this tiny diary to record our trip crossing the sea and settling on the distant continent. Mother says I have to because we are making history. That is why I picked the smallest diary in the bookshop. I do not want to write lots and lots. I want to run along the deck of the ship and explore the hold. That's in the belly of the ship, and I am strictly forbidden to go there."*

Ellie started her climb up to the bench. "So for a urohm, it *is* tiny." She sat beside her friend. "Is it interesting?"

"Very." He flipped a few pages. "Listen to this: *I hid today among the lime barrels. I couldn't find my brush, and my hair is in tangles. I put a bonnet on, but Mother is sure to ask why. Memorizing the principles is boring. Papa says we must know the words by heart so we can answer anyone who asks questions. Why can't the grownups do that part? I want to play with new friends there. Porta Mellow says they will be so impressed with us that they will hang on our every word. Strangers from Amara don't go to Chiril often. No wonder! This is a boring trip. But when we get there, I want to brag about crossing two oceans. It's going to take a long time. I don't have to memorize principles now. I'd forget them by the time we land. Good! I'm running out of room to write."*

Ellie picked up a muffin from the table and peeled back the paper. She nibbled on the puffy top. "Mmm…pumpkin."

"There's warm amaloot too."

Two butterflies danced around each other on the way to a flowering bush.

Ellie smiled as she watched them. "Where'd you find it?"

"In the basket."

Her head snapped around to look at her companion. "The urohm diary was in the basket?"

"No, the amaloot was. The diary was in the room next to the nursery."

Ellie reached in and found her drink still warm in a glass jar with a lid. "This is good."

"I agree. It cleared the blur out of my eyes and the fuzz from my brain."

"Not the drink, the diary. The diary is good. We'll learn a lot."

"Much more interesting than Old One's journal."

Ellie mumbled agreement, sipped the amaloot, and nibbled the muffin.

"And there are a dozen of the diaries."

Intrigued by the prospect of following the little girl's life, Ellie said, "We should take them with us to read. We're going back to the library today, aren't we?

Bealomondore looked her over. "Do you feel well enough?"

She straightened her spine and gave a decisive nod. "I feel wonderful." She frowned at her wrist. "That itches a bit, but my mother would say that means it's getting well."

"My nanny said the same thing."

"How are we going to get the daggarts and diaries all the way to the library? And our bags? That's a long walk without lugging anything extra."

Bealomondore pointed to a red wagon by the garden shed. "I pulled that out this morning. Fortunately it's a toy. We'd never be able to pull the big wagon or push the urohm's wheelbarrow."

"Do you think we could take some eggs as well?"

Bealomondore turned to face her, his eyes wide. "We need eggs? We sometimes get eggs with our breakfast."

"I was thinking how much my gramps likes a soft-boiled egg on toast at teatime. Not every day, but once in a while as a treat."

"So Old One might like the same?"

"Possibly."

"You're probably right. But he asked specifically for daggarts. And we don't know what Wulder has provided for him these many years."

"Apparently not daggarts." She frowned in concentration.

Bealomondore responded cheerfully. "Just so."

"Why?"

"Why what?"

"Remember we talked about Wulder giving us things just so we have something to enjoy?"

"Button grain for Tak. Pie for us."

"Yes, that discussion. Why doesn't Wulder give Old One daggarts?"

"That one is easy."

"Easy, huh?" She gave him her best skeptical look. "Then explain it."

"A long, long time ago, when Wulder planned this urohm expedition, He knew that there would one day be an almost empty Rumbard City, wild and dangerous little heathens, and a grumpy old man holed up in the library. Wulder also knew that Ellicinderpart would fall into this bottled city and bake daggarts. If He had been feeding the small riffraff and the curmudgeon daggarts all along, then the daggarts the lovely young tumanhofer baked would not be so special and wouldn't dent the armor of Old One or soften the hearts of the ragamuffins, convincing Old One to come out of hiding and the young ones to be nice and not bite."

Ellie laughed. "I'm not convinced."

"You will be. Once you accept Wulder as your creator and provider, you will change your tune."

"You did say you were going to tell me more about Him."

"I will. Maybe as we walk back to the library today."

Ellie came in from the kitchen and sat down to fold the linens Bealomondore had washed. "This is my last chore," she called. "I wish we could iron them."

Bealomondore pulled a cushion back into the room and placed it where he'd found it the first night they stayed at the house. "I think I'm done, Ellie."

"Good. We can leave soon."

He sat down beside her to help. "Have you figured out why we are doing this?" He waved his hand with an unfolded towel in it, indicating the whole room and the house beyond.

"Respect for someone else's property?"

He tilted his head to look at her. "This house is actually no one's property. They're all dead."

She scrunched her face and continued folding.

"Well, almost all," said Bealomondore.

"That's right." She thought for a moment. "So I guess I'm doing it because I was raised to leave things tidier than when I arrived."

"Really?"

"Yes." She put the last folded cloth on the stack. "Why are you doing it? You haven't exactly been a mule, too stubborn to cooperate. In fact, you've done more than I have."

He stood and helped her up. "I like your reason. Leave things better."

She shook her head. "Can't have it. That's my reason, not yours."

He shrugged. "Well…in the last few years, I've grown to appreciate order. The quest to put the three statues together so Verrin Schope would quit falling apart. Simultaneously, the world unraveling. The war with Baardack. The awful, muddy, bloody battlefields. Wulder opening my eyes again to the beauty around me."

He pinched his lower lip. "All right. I'll make a stab at it." He placed his hands on her shoulders and looked straight into her eyes. "Wulder created this world and everything in it. He expects us to take care of it. When events occur that put things in disarray, He appreciates our trying to right wrongs and do the best we can to restore order, His order." He gestured with his head, looking at the room around them. "Someone built this home. They created it. It's fitting to restore their home as closely as we can to the original state."

Ellie smiled. "Minus several dishes, ingredients for daggarts, a stack of diaries, and one small wagon."

"We only took what we needed, like a hunter takes the life of an animal only if he needs the meat for his family."

"Or if the animal is a marauder who does harm and can't be reasoned with."

He paused for a moment. "Oh dear, I think you've hit on the only reason for war." He kissed her forehead. "Let's go. This conversation has gone too deep."

He picked up the stack of linens and walked away. Ellie put her hand lightly to her brow as if she might tarnish the warm spot left by Bealomondore's kiss. A smile broke out on her face, and she brought her hand down to cover her mouth. She gave herself a shake and willed composure. She would enjoy the long walk to the library. She had an excellent companion.

# 21

# A Diary's Account

Ellie stood beside the loaded wagon. She still would have liked to bring some eggs but recognized that they would not survive the journey. That irritated her, and the fact that Bealomondore had on that sword as if they might run into crazed vagabonds instead of six-year-old children also pinched her patience. Laddin landed on her shoulder, and she felt a rush of contentment.

Ah! So that was it. The healing dragon informed her that although she looked physically fit, her core still suffered from fatigue, both from the injury and from the body's work getting well. She eyed her tuman-hofer friend again and didn't feel quite as snappy anymore. He worked hard to keep her comfortable and out of harm's way. He'd be pulling this wagon all the way back to the library.

"Maa," said Tak.

Ellie raised her eyebrows. "Is there a harness in that shed?"

Bealomondore looked from the wagon to the goat to the shed. "Not a harness that would fit Tak. Does he pull a cart at home?"

"Most definitely. My father does not believe in having animals for pets. So I had to train Tak to pull the goat cart or give him up. It would be convenient to have Tak help."

Bealomondore rubbed his chin. "I could go look in the barn where the chickens are. That place seemed to have just about everything."

"I'm coming with you."

Leaving the daggarts and diaries in the wagon, Ellie, Bealomondore, and Tak made the short trek to the mansion. The chickens
squawked their disapproval at strangers poking around their outbuildings. Ellie found harnesses for a pony trap. Bealomondore found much
larger leather straps that must have been for a very big carriage. Tak
stood beside one of the empty stalls, watching their every move. Occasionally he bleated, sounding impatient with their efforts.

"I guess we will have to pull the wagon ourselves," said Ellie when
they'd looked through each small shack and the barn.

Bealomondore slapped his hands against each other, knocking off
some of the dirt and straw that clung to them. "Rigging a harness to the
wagon might have been difficult anyway."

"Let's go," Ellie gestured to Tak for him to follow.

The goat lowered his head and stayed where he was.

"Oh no," said Ellie. "Don't go all goaty on me. Just come on."

Tak turned his head away in his typical I'm-ignoring-you pose. Ellie
started toward him, but he leaped in the air and darted into the empty
stall.

"There is nothing for you here. No button grain. No nannies to impress." She followed him into the boxed enclosure. "Bealomondore?"

"Coming."

He stood behind her and laughed. In a dark corner of the stall, a
red harness with bell trimming hung on a hook.

"That's what I think it is, isn't it?" He put his hand on her shoulder.

"Yes." Her face warmed. The goat had shown her up many times
before, so it wasn't his antics that caused her to blush. The desire to lean
back just enough for her back to rest against Bealomondore's chest did
a lot to make her uncomfortable. Uncomfortable in a very pleasant way.

She cleared her throat. "Well, let's see if we can figure out a way to hitch it to the wagon."

Bealomondore took a basket down from where it hung on the wall and stuffed it with old hay.

Ellie grinned. "Eggs?"

He winked at her. "It can't hurt to try to take some back to the library."

It took them only a few minutes to gather a dozen eggs. Ellie already knew the hens' good hiding spots. They returned to the house they'd been staying in. Bealomondore managed to rig up a decent apparatus to attach the wagon to the harness, even with Tak sticking his nose as close as possible to the work being done. When the straps were in place, Tak sidled up to the cart's front end and waited patiently to be connected.

Bealomondore obliged. "He sure seems to like this idea."

Ellie shook her head in bewilderment. "He has always been a friendly goat, but since I found him by the road after we had begun our trip to Ragar, he's developed an uncanny ability to be useful."

"Pushing you into the bottle?"

She laughed. "Well, not that, but other things."

"Considering we are living in an enchanted city, imprisoned in a bottle under some mysterious spell and dealing with children who stay children and an Old One who doesn't want anything to do with us, I can accept a goat's sudden propensity to observe, reason, and deduce."

"I don't think I'm ready for that. If he starts mindspeaking to me, you are going to have to lock me up somewhere where I can't hurt myself or anybody else."

Bealomondore raised his eyebrows. "Planning to go berserk?"

"*Fearing* the probability, not planning."

Bealomondore patted Tak on the rump. The goat understood the signal and started forward. "Let's go before he asks us to read to him as we go along."

The load jostled a bit, and Ellie reached up to balance the basket of eggs more securely in a nest of daggart packages. The diaries lined the wagonload, extending the sides of the wagon bed up a few inches. One was in her hand.

She and Bealomondore took turns reading aloud, not to Tak but to each other. Ellie took the first few pages of the diary, holding the book open with one hand and resting her free hand on top of the piles of daggarts wrapped in packets of a dozen each.

"Do you think you can keep them from falling?" asked Bealomondore tilting his head toward the wagon's load.

Ellie looked up and laughed. "I think I'm keeping *me* from falling. I can feel when the road is rough beneath the wheels."

"Very clever. You shall be useful to have around."

She smiled at him, not quite sure how to respond to that statement. In lieu of saying something clever, she went back to reading.

They learned the girl's name in the next entry.

*"Mother says, 'Tilly, do something useful.' But when I ask what I can do, Father says, 'Stay out of the way, Tilly Genejolly.'"*

"A couple more syllables and Tilly Genejolly would make a good tumanhofer name," Bealomondore said.

Ellie read the part about two women dying on board the ship, one in childbirth, and one just wasting away, too seasick to eat. Ellie cried, and Bealomondore took the book and read a couple more entries. The third entry after the unfortunate deaths revealed that the baby had survived.

"Now why didn't she say that right away?" asked Ellie.

"She's young," Bealomondore said. "In all likelihood, it was her first experience with death but not with someone in her circle of friends having a new baby in the family. She wrote about what touched her the most."

Ellie stretched out her palm and wiggled her fingers. Bealomondore placed the book in her hand. She turned back a few pages and read again the page that had upset her.

"*Mistress Cannust hasn't left her bed for over a week now. I don't really know how many days. My mother says ten days, and Porta's mother says fifteen. My mother is probably right. Porta's father says if she doesn't get up soon, she'll die, just like when an animal on the farm goes down. He says Mistress Cannust will be the first death we've had on the ship. 'Halfway to Chiril and only now losing one of our own.' That's what he said. Those words.*

"*My father grumbled at him. Two sailors have died. Though they aren't one of us, my father says it is uncaring not to count them.*"

Ellie turned the page.

"*Mr. Mellow is right. It's horrible. Kimbin Erllee screamed a lot. Her baby was coming. I went up on deck so I wouldn't have to listen. I could still hear her some, so I moved to the stern of the ship. I curled up into a tight ball and put my hands over my ears. The wind wasn't blowing, the sails weren't flapping and snapping, and the waves weren't splashing much against the hull. Sailors called it a doldrum, nothing much happening. But in the belly of the ship, that wasn't true. I wish it had been.*"

Ellie took a deep, steadying breath and turned another page. "*Last night, Mistress Erllee was still screaming when my mother made me go to bed. Porta came to sleep with me because we were both crying. Her mother went to help Mistress Erllee, though she said there wasn't anything she could do. Not really. My mother went to sit with Mistress Cannust. She said there wasn't anything she could do either. So it happened. Mistress Cannust died.*

*As soon as my mother got back to our cabin, word came that Mistress Erllee had a puny runt baby. That's not the words they said, but that's what I saw in my head and remembered.*

*"So one was dead and one was born.*

*"I figured the baby would die next. But I was wrong. Mistress Erllee died. She'd quit screaming, even before the baby came. Now Mr. Erllee stood in the hallway. I could see through the open door. He cried. My father hugged him and patted his shoulder. My father looked like he might cry too. I did cry. Porta didn't. She'd gone to sleep. I don't think you should sleep when someone is hurting in his heart so very, very bad."*

Ellie closed the book and stopped walking. Bealomondore stopped as well, but Tak stepped forward without a care. Ellie turned to Bealomondore to see him studying her.

She pushed a bit of curly hair away from her face. "That last entry was more than her usual one page. She didn't even write big to fill up the lines faster." She sniffed, but no more tears fell. "I hope her mother found her crying and scooped her up in her arms and rocked her. That's what she needed. She needed to be held."

Bealomondore and Ellie walked in silence.

The bells on Tak's harness jingled softly. He looked striking with red straps, tarnished gold bells, and his pure white coat. He did love to pull the proper goat cart at home, but he seemed to be much more conceited about pulling the toy wagon. He held his chin high, and he pranced. After several hours, he still strutted in a high-step that should have worn him out.

Ellie watched him. What was going on with her dear pet? He didn't act like himself, and she greatly needed him to be good old Tak. She needed someone to hold. She needed to bury her face in his long white hair and whisper all her troubles. She knew it was ridiculous to unburden herself on a "dumb farm animal." But she'd done it many times. And Tak had never made fun of her disappointments. He didn't discourage her from dreaming big dreams. He never revealed her secrets to another. He just listened.

She hadn't noticed Bealomondore crossing over to her side, where she walked by the wagon. But his arm came around her, and he guided her off the road into a little overgrown park. Tak followed, jingling those ludicrous bells.

"We all need a break," said Bealomondore. "We'll rest in the shade while it's hot and finish our trip in the late afternoon. We can probably time it to get to the library after the horde has turned in for the night."

He gently pushed Ellie down on a bench and sat beside her. With his arm around her, she naturally leaned her head against his shoulder.

"Ellie, it's time I told you more about Wulder. You don't need to whisper to Tak when times are hard or when you're excited about something. Wulder won't make fun of you, or discourage you, or tell your secrets to others. He truly listens, but He also has the power to change things. Maybe the circumstances, or maybe you, so you can handle the circumstances."

Ellie leaned back. She felt her eyes go wide. "You listened to my thinking. How? Why? I don't like that. I don't. How could you do that? Why would you do that? I didn't know you could mindspeak to me. I didn't know you could hear me thinking." She pulled farther away from him.

His expression surprised her. He looked shocked. He shook his head in a small, steady, and intense motion. "I never have before. I didn't even know I was doing it. I mean, I heard, but it seemed just like you were talking to me. Only I knew you weren't. That you were thinking. But it seemed so natural."

He paused. He looked so confused and genuinely perplexed that Ellie almost took pity on him. But her outrage at his intrusion sat like a block between them.

"I'm sorry," he said, then shook his head. "No, not really. Somehow it was right."

"It was wrong," said Ellie. Her voice amazed her. She didn't sound angry. She was angry, wasn't she?

He nodded vigorously. "You're right. It was wrong. But it wasn't." His speaking came to a halt. After a few seconds he started again. This time with more of the confidence she enjoyed hearing in his every bit of conversation.

"It is wrong because it is an invasion of privacy. But it is not wrong, in this case, because we're supposed to learn something from this. We are supposed to step up to a new level in our relationship."

"Relationship?"

"No longer strangers who met in a bottle city. No longer co-workers, surviving and gathering information to allow us to escape. No longer just friends who enjoy each other's company."

Ellie merely gazed at him, not sure what to expect.

"I didn't intentionally listen in on your thoughts. I don't want you to be angry with me for something that came so naturally. I didn't even notice the oddity until it was over. Let's be patient, Ellie. I think we are going to have an unusual relationship, something powerful and astonishing. Something Wulder has ordained."

He picked up her two hands in his. "Can you forgive the trespass?"

Speechless, she nodded.

He dropped her hands and pulled her into a hug. "And the first thing we are going to do together as something stronger than a team is gain Old One's confidence with tea and daggarts. Then we will tame the wild ones." He paused. "That may take more than daggarts."

She started laughing.

"It's going to be all right, Ellie."

She nodded and giggled and leaned into his embrace.

# 22

# The Bells Did It

They resumed their journey, but the wound and the healing took its toll on Ellicinderpart's stamina. After two hours of steady walking, she staggered and almost fell. Her hand on the side of the cart kept her upright. "I've got to stop and rest, Bealomondore. I'm accustomed to hiking, but not while talking nonstop."

"There's a shady spot ahead."

Beneath a huge spinet tree, they paused for a break, and Bealomondore tucked Tilly's diary into the cart.

Ellie sat in the cool grass. Bealomondore checked the harness on Tak to make sure the unusual device wasn't wearing on his hide. He then went to sit beside his lady tumanhofer.

She picked a small purple wildflower and sniffed it, then offered it to Bealomondore. "I've never talked like that to anyone."

He took it and threaded the stem through the buttonhole on his lapel. "Do you mean for that length of time?"

"No. I guess I mean the content. I've never had a friend to share ideas with. Big ideas. Most conversations seem to be about crops, recipes, and what's come in at the mercantile."

"Ah, in the circle I came from there were two distinct groups. In one, it was considered notable to be able to debate the issues of the time. In the other, esteem was lauded on those who were fluent in speaking of art, fashion, and the current tastes of society."

"You listen to me."

"Of course I listen to you."

"There's no 'of course' about it."

He poked her in the side. "How do you know I am really listening?"

"Because you answer with practical ideas about the matters I've brought up."

"So tell me, dear lady. Do you agree with me to keep the peace?"

"No, we agree on most things. I am rather intent on gathering bits of a more sophisticated viewpoint. If I make it to the coronation ball, I do not want to act like a country bumpkin."

"I think your books have taken care of that."

"Then I'm grateful to Gramps for insisting that we learn to read. Gramps listens to me at home."

"So you do have someone to talk to."

She pointed to the goat nibbling on a bush. "Tak and Gramps. Tak stays awake longer."

The breeze shook the leaves of the tree. Both tumanhofers leaned back and enjoyed the beautiful day. They talked about the different cultures within Chiril. She regretted the intellectual loss to children when country tumanhofers did not educate their children except in animal lore, farming, wild plants and their uses, and homespun skills. Bealomondore agreed and championed expanding the arts among all strata of Chiril.

Bealomondore rose. "We'd best move on. Are you rested enough?"

She took his extended hand. "Yes." She went to Tak's head and stroked his favorite spot between his ears. "How about you, friend? Ready to go?"

"Maa."

Their conversation restarted as they walked. Bealomondore had many ideas for the development of Chiril under Paladin and Queen Tipper. He would propose more communication between different slices of their culture. The countryfolk could teach the city dwellers a lot about homemade instruments and lively dance music. Society from the upper ranks could introduce complicated instruments and printed music. Ellie thought his ideas to be grand and practical.

"It's like us, Bealomondore." She shoved an errant lock of hair behind her ear. "You have so much knowledge of the world that I want to learn. And I could show you tiny bits of beauty in the countryside that most people walk right past. Some of the things the animals do are beyond fascinating. Watching a butterfly emerge from a chrysalis is too wonderful to explain."

Bealomondore put his hand on Tak's harness and tugged to bring the goat to a stop. He stood looking up at the buildings.

"What's wrong?" asked Ellie.

"We must have been walking faster than we needed to. We've reached the center of town too early."

"Too…" A chill went up Ellie's spine. "Oh."

"The callous masses have not tucked themselves into their beds for the night."

"Perhaps we should seek a nice place to hole up while we wait for dark."

Bealomondore's mind was obviously elsewhere. He turned a complete circle, studying the street and structures on it. "I'm not familiar with this part of Rumbard. We'll have to look for an entrance to one of these buildings."

He scanned the windows up and down both sides of the street. "This would be a convenient time for the dragons of the watch to come by. We could ask them to scout."

Ellie searched the shadows. Did some of the children lurk nearby, ready to pounce?

Bealomondore went to the goat's head and spoke quietly. "This way, Tak."

Ellie followed them into an alley. Since they'd quit talking, even the breeze seemed to have stilled. In this late afternoon, the birds were scarce in the center of Rumbard. Ellie wanted to know why. She missed the flap of a bird's wing or a trilling chirp. A bird's tweet while fluttering in a dust bath would have eased the tension.

She heard the bells on Tak's harness and nothing else.

"Bealomondore," she whispered.

He turned his head her way. She made a ringing motion with her hand and mouthed the word, "Bells."

"Hold up, Tak," he said and began to search his pockets. He pulled out a slender blue object, unfolded a blade from the side, and cut through the leather cords holding the bells. Ellie held each bell taut so the knife would sever the ties easily. She also kept her hand wrapped snugly against the metal to lessen the jingles.

"Where should I put them?" she whispered.

"On the pavement. Put them down gently, and make sure they aren't going to roll."

She followed his directions with one hand while she held the next bell with the other. When she straightened, she thought she saw motion out of the corner of her eye. She jerked her head, trying to catch a glimpse of whatever it was. Nothing in sight. She put another bell down and surreptitiously glanced toward the place where movement had been.

When she stood up, she whispered, "I can't shake the feeling that we are being watched."

Bealomondore continued working. Only three bells left on that side. "Could be nerves. At night, after a battle, I always felt as if someone skulked just outside the perimeter of the camp."

She put another bell on the street. Now she had a line of them following a crack.

Bealomondore worked on the next cord. "Your nerves are in a heightened state. Fear does that, and in most cases it's a wonderful thing. As an extra alert soldier, you might save your life and the lives of your friends."

"Did you save many lives in the war?"

"Oh yes." He moved to the last bell on that side. "And my life was saved many times by the soldiers around me." He paused and looked into her face. "Ellie, the war is something I don't like to talk about. I'd rather certain memories did not surface, and the only way I can keep that from happening is to look the other direction. Instead of back, I try to look forward, to keep my mind settled on the future. It's been hard."

He switched sides, giving Tak's forehead a rub as he passed in front of the goat. Ellie held the next bell, and he sawed at the thong.

"The reason it's been so hard," he continued, "is that I couldn't latch on to what I wanted that future to be."

"And now you have?"

"I think the choice is being sorted out. I only need to be a little more patient."

"What are your choices?"

"I could continue on in the service of my queen and Paladin. I could return to Greeston and go into the family business. My father would be amazed at that. And the ironic thing is that now that he is willing to let me be who I am and do the things I think are important, I'm actually considering the Bealomondore Mines as a reasonable choice."

"You said you have a brother who enjoys business."

"Yes, but he is a little cold-hearted, like my father. Neither of them considers the hardships of the workers. And he took an extended holiday during the war. Last I heard, he had not returned."

"What about your portrait painting?"

"Now that is an attractive notion. Portraits are my least favorite type of art to create. But it pays well. It would be nice to be independently situated so I could delve into all the expression of my craft without worrying about what to eat. And to have the money to buy supplies. That's been a problem from time to time in the past." He stood and looked in her eyes. "So you see I am a man without a destination, and that is not a good thing to be."

He tilted his head and smiled in such a way that she lost her train of thought. She'd never met anyone who had so many openings before him. Most were farmers or merchants and would remain farmers and merchants.

"So what is your destination, Ellie?"

She blinked hard. Did he mean the library? They were trying to get to the library, weren't they? No, he didn't mean right now. He meant outside of today, the bottle city, and their present predicament.

"Ragar." She knew her answer was a little short of his meaning, but that was where she had her heart set on going, and afterward, she would probably end up in the village, looking for a husband. Somehow that sounded pathetic, and she didn't want to see a look of pity in his eye.

Did she deliberately avoid his question? Probably not. Ellie did not know how to dissemble. Before turning his attention to the last row of bells, Bealomondore made a quick survey of their surroundings. Often the hushed streets of Rumbard City emphasized the isolation of their dilemma. Whoever heard of a city of this size—meaning the ability to accommodate many residents, not the size of the structures—being so eerily quiet?

He sliced through the leather cords quickly. He too felt as if eyes behind the dark windows tracked their every motion.

"Shall we go?" he asked his companion.

"Maa!"

"I wasn't speaking to you, Tak, but yes, you must come as well. I think we're close to the center of town. In a few blocks, we may be able to hear the water splashing in the fountain."

Just as he patted Tak on the rump, a war whoop pierced the air, followed by the tromping of dozens of little feet on the road.

"Run!" he commanded Ellie and drew his sword.

Tak spontaneously jumped into action, tearing down the street, away from the screaming pack of wild animals Ellie called children. The basket of eggs tipped onto its side. Eggs rolled out, bumping down the hill of daggarts. Some bounced out of the cart, and some became wedged in tight spots.

Bealomondore turned away from the sight. It seemed the hellions poured from every building. "Run, Ellie! Get to the library."

"Don't you hurt them with that sword, Bealomondore." Her voice sounded too near. Hadn't he said to run?

"Go, Ellie. I'm not going to hurt them, just scare them. I can't keep that promise if you're in the way."

He felt rather than heard her retreat. Their bond was proving useful. He had just enough time to glance at the Sword of Valor in his hand. One of the sword's peculiarities was that it changed its shape according to the needs of the battle. A shorter, thicker blade now reflected the setting sun. He would have liked to read the inscription on the hilt. Perhaps he could get a clue about this battle, some advice from Wizard Fenworth.

A big bully ran right up to Bealomondore and reached forward as if to tackle him. The tumanhofer ducked, spun, and landed a sharp blow with the flat side of his sword against the child's rear end. It sounded like the impact of a paddle stick. The ageless, intrepid warrior howled, much as Bealomondore and his brother had when receiving correction from their father.

"We can take 'im!" A lad led a charge of four more boys. Bealomondore whacked arms, legs, backsides, and stomachs, all with the flat of his blade. He doubted the showy sword would even cut in its present state. The thought gave him comfort. He really did not want to injure any of these children, especially now. A band of girls set upon him. He battled the nasty mob until they ran on.

He sighed his relief and then realized that these hoodlums were chasing Tak and Ellie. He pursued them. The children ran after the cart and stopped to pick up packages of daggarts. One would snatch a fallen treasure, and several would surround the lucky one. Perhaps lucky did not describe accurately what happened. A weaker child had everything jerked from her hands. Stronger ones had to share in order not to be tackled by all those who surrounded her.

Bealomondore jogged past numerous children who had given up the chase to have their first taste of daggarts. He stopped to pick up the diaries that littered the street. Every now and then he passed a smashed raw egg. Evidently Tak pulled the cart at great speed. At every turn, the objects in the cart's bed had bounced out. Ellie would be disappointed.

He recognized the streets around him now. Only a block or two to the library. He sheathed his sword. The children did not like being this close to Old One. Old One! *Oh, Wulder,* Bealomondore prayed, *let there be enough daggarts left to have tea with the old man.*

As he turned a corner, he looked up, and there on the third floor of the library, the window framed a white-bearded urohm. Bealomondore could not see the man clearly, but from his stance, he guessed Old One was angry.

# 23

# Old One and Orlí

Bealomondore met Ellie at the back of the library. She had unloaded the remaining diaries and a few packets of daggarts. Now she concentrated on loosening the harness from Tak's back and shoulders.

"Are you all right?" he asked.

She nodded. "You?"

"I'm fine." He showed her the diaries he'd rescued and put them down on the walkway. Then he helped lift the leather straps and hung them over a fence that ran next to the building. "I'm sorry about the eggs and the daggarts."

"Did you hurt any of those children?"

"I dusted the britches of several. And protected myself from each one that attacked. None are maimed."

She turned away to rub her fingers through Tak's hair, flattened by the harness. "I've been thinking. The plan isn't ruined. We need to adjust a bit. That's all."

She went to the gate of the library park and let Tak in.

"So what's the revised plan?"

"This might even work better than the original plan."

The vent squeaked when Bealomondore opened their hidden entry. He stood aside for her to go through first. "Well? Tell me. I'm curious." He gathered up the diaries and passed them in to her.

She took them and made a neat stack as she talked. "Now that the children know what daggarts taste like, they should be eager to please us and be rewarded with more of the same treat."

Next Bealomondore handed over the daggarts, one package at a time. Out of ten dozen-count bundles, only four packets remained. He dreaded the trip to make more. Couldn't they just abandon the effort to win the children and give these to Old One?

He crawled through the opening. No, he had to be truthful and admit that the daggarts had potential. "The ruffians were absorbed in gobbling them up as I passed. None of them put the daggarts down to chase me. Obviously your baking is a big hit."

She sighed and looked woefully at the remaining packages. Without a word, Bealomondore helped her carry them to the rotunda. He nearly dropped his load when a loud voice thundered from above.

"I'll have a word with you."

Ellie regained her composure before he did. She whirled around and dropped a perfect curtsy toward the balcony.

"We'd be honored if you'd join us for tea, sir. We do have daggarts now."

"Humph! I knew that. You sat there planning to go off and bake. You leave and come back with packages. Any fool could figure out you have daggarts. But that's not why I command your audience."

Bealomondore searched the shadows of the upper story and finally spotted a shadow that moved.

Ellie bobbed a simpler curtsy. "I'll put the kettle on."

After putting her armload of diaries down on one of the tables, she ran off toward the children's section.

Bealomondore set his burden on the same table and bowed to the old man in the balcony.

"Will you be coming down, sir?"

"Yes, yes," he grumbled. "Might as well get started. It takes a while."

Something glimmered for a moment, and Bealomondore glimpsed long, straggly white hair draped over a black coat. The urohm had already turned away. A glow came from a lumpish figure on Old One's shoulder. The urohm stepped farther into the shadows, and Bealomondore could no longer see him.

A light dragon. Bealomondore puzzled over the possibility. Old One had a light dragon? None of the dragons of the watch had mentioned another dragon in Rumbard. Not even Det and Laddin had revealed this one's existence. Bealomondore concluded that either he was mistaken and the glow had not been a light dragon riding the old man's shoulder, or the light dragon was as reclusive as his companion.

He knew minor dragons to be a very social group. On top of all the questions that had been stirring his thoughts for the months he'd been here, a whole new set strung out along this line of reasoning. He hoped Old One had suddenly become communicative.

"Bealomondore," Ellie called.

He followed the sound of her voice. The kettle boiled. She'd put cups and saucers and the fancy china teapot on a tray and arranged six daggarts on a pretty plate. She held spoons in one hand and a sugar bowl in the other. Her face showed signs of a tearful eruption about to surface.

She pointed with the spoons to the tray. "It's too heavy for me to carry it all."

Bealomondore wondered if he should reassure her that everything would be all right. Somehow those words had never made him feel better. "I'm sorry. I should have offered to carry it."

She clenched the spoons until her knuckles turned white. Leaning closer to Bealomondore, she whispered, "What do you think he's upset about?"

"I have no idea." He thought about the old man for a moment. "It might be he's made up something to justify his accepting the opportunity to have tea and daggarts."

She put the sugar bowl and spoons on the tray. "He did say he knew we had the daggarts. Do you suppose he was watching for us to return?"

"Perhaps. He was looking out the window when I came toward the library. However, he looked outraged and not the least bit glad."

"Oh, I hope this wins his friendship. Everything would be so much more pleasant then."

"We'll give tea and daggarts a try."

He lifted the tray, and Ellie, carrying the plate of daggarts, followed him to the rotunda. The gentleman had not yet appeared. Bealomondore returned for the kettle and a small chair.

Ellie scurried behind him, carrying the second seat. "I'll feel more dignified sitting in a chair my own size."

Bealomondore agreed, although on his own he probably wouldn't have thought of his dignity being compromised by huge furniture.

This time, when they rounded the last corner, Old One sat in the chair they had always assumed was his favorite. Ellie caught a gasp before it flung itself out of her mouth and embarrassed her.

She had expected him to be huge, but she doubted her head was much higher than his knee. If he struck a blow to one of them, there would be no waking up. But he looked peaceful enough, even with his sour face.

He wore old-fashioned clothing that reminded her of the mayor of their little village. That should have made her less timid, but she'd never liked the mayor. Old One's shoes were polished, and his hair gleamed in the light of the afternoon sun.

Blinking, Ellie focused on Old One's shoulder. A truly ugly minor dragon perched there, looking Ellie over as much as Ellie stared at him. While brilliant clear colors sparkled in the scales of the dragons of the watch, this poor thing had only gray highlighting his wings. The dragon looked like a dirty old rag. It turned its head away.

A horrible thought went through her head. *Oh, dear. I hope I haven't hurt its feelings.*

His head jerked back.

*"His feelings,"* she heard in her mind. *"I am male. My name is Orli, which means 'light unto you.'"* The dragon winked. *"You shall see beauty when and if I ever shine in your presence. It will be worth the wait."*

Ellie swallowed what felt like her heart in her throat and tried to look brave and unconcerned as she followed Bealomondore to the table. He placed the kettle on the center table next to the tray and bowed to Old One. He made a second bow to Orli.

Ellie clasped her hands and curtsied first to the urohm and then to his dragon.

The performance of a common curtsy made her feel less timid. She decided to test to see just how unobliging this old man was.

"Would you pour from the kettle to the teapot?" she asked. "It's too heavy for us when it's so full."

Old One narrowed his eyes and stared at her for a moment. He then grasped the kettle, lifted the lid on the teapot, and poured in the steaming water. He put the lid back and set the kettle down.

"There," he said. "I've done your duty as hostess."

Ellie lowered her chin to avoid giving away her annoyance. She bit her lip and willed Bealomondore to take over the conversation. He jumped in immediately, and she wondered if he'd heard her thoughts as he had earlier. Or was his intervention coincidence?

Bealomondore talked easily, never allowing a long silence to become uncomfortable. He spoke of Chiril and the recent war, the wizard from Amara, and Paladin, who strove to introduce ignorant Chirilians to their Creator. Several times, Ellie felt tension in Orli, though she heard no words. And when she glanced at Old One, his face appeared to have frozen in a disapproving glare.

The tea steeped. When the aroma tickled her nose and told her the flavor should be just right, Ellie poured from the teapot to the cups. She worried that Old One would be hard to please and remembered all the things her mother had said about a proper tea. She offered Old One sugar. He took two spoonfuls. She passed the daggarts, and he took three.

That left a daggart apiece for her and Bealomondore. And one more. She offered the plate to Orli first. He looked up at her in surprise. She broke the daggart into pieces and put them on a napkin on the table. Orli flew down to enjoy the treat.

Ellie handed the plate with two daggarts to Bealomondore.

"Would you like tea as well, Orli? I'm sorry I did not think to ask before."

She got his answer. *"Yes, in a saucer, please, with a little sugar."*

"What is this?" demanded Old One. "How do you know his name?"

"He told it to me, sir."

Orli concentrated on the piece of daggart in his hand, or rather, claw. Ellie thought his concentration was a little overplayed.

Old One glared at her, then at Orli, who didn't appear to notice. Finally he expelled a growly sigh. "I shall not let this subvert my enjoyment of this tea. But I have not forgotten nor put aside this irregularity."

Ellie bobbed her head, fixed a saucer of tea for Orli, and hurried to sit in the chair next to Bealomondore.

She held her teacup with two hands and enjoyed the warm brew. Her daggart tasted just as fresh as the ones she and Bealomondore had eaten from the oven. All the trouble they'd gone to paid off with each crunchy bite.

They didn't converse while they ate. She brewed more tea, and they each had another cup. Orli had another saucerful.

When Old One finished his last daggart, he put down his saucer and cup, folded his napkin, and reestablished his crotchety expression.

Clearing his throat, he produced a voice to rival any judge of doom in a courtroom. "We must talk of what is allowed and what is not allowed. You have upset the citizens of Rumbard City."

"Do you mean the children?" asked Bealomondore.

"Of course I mean the children."

"I thought perhaps you referred to yourself and Orli. And maybe the dragons of the watch."

"Bah! A worthless crew, that watch. They quit reporting to me a century or more past."

A picture of Old One throwing shoes at the tiny dragons entered Ellie's mind, and she gave a start of a chuckle that she tried to hide. Orli barely glowed, but with a pink pearlescence. Bealomondore snorted a wayward laugh as well. Ellie looked at him, caught him looking at her, and they both burst into laughter.

Old One's voice rose. "I've been watching you two. You have deplorable manners. Rummaging through my things. Cavorting and giggling and retaining no dignity, which is supposed to be displayed at all times in the great hall of books."

His eyes went to a pillar, and a fiercer frown darkened his face. He stood and marched to the column, grabbed hold of an overgrown fern, and wrenched the branches downward. While holding the fanning leaves aside, he pointed to a sign.

With authority deepening his already impressive tone, he read. "A quiet voice and attitude are welcome in the library."

Bealomondore managed to compose himself. Ellie chose to stare at her hands.

"So," said Bealomondore respectfully, "you wish to speak to us about our treatment of the children and our lack of decorum in the library."

Old One let go of the branches. They snapped back, whacking the pillar. An unusual sound followed as the sign tilted, then slid down to the floor, where it clunked.

"Yes!" Old One shouted. "The citizens of Rumbard City were left under my care, and you shall not distress them."

Fire raced through Ellie, and she stood, her head tilted back so she could look directly in the urohm's face. If she'd had time to clamber to a higher post, she would have. But anger fueled her tongue, and outrage spurred her on.

"*You* are in charge of those poor children? You're responsible for their welfare? Sir! It is disgraceful. They are neglected. They've had no guidance. They live as animals in a pack, like wolves and muskoxen."

"Muskoxen?" Old One looked at Bealomondore, who shrugged.

Ellie shook a fist toward the old urohm. "Those little children have no concept of right or wrong. They're forced to fight for a portion of food. No one washes behind their ears. No one tucks them in at night. No one cleans a skinned knee and applies a bandage. *You* are in charge? You should be ashamed."

Tears rolled down Ellie's cheeks. She backhanded a swipe to get rid of them, but they flowed too heavily.

Still riding on a flow of fury, she asked, "Who put you in charge?"

"I don't rightly remember. I think maybe it came to me by default. I'm the only adult left, you see. They're an unruly bunch, you see. I gave up."

Bealomondore stood and put his arm around Ellie. She tried to control the quivering of ire, and his warmth calmed her.

"We are aware of your status, sir," said Bealomondore. "Perhaps we could be of assistance to each other."

A glimmer of hope crossed the old man's face. "Could be. Could be." He paused, giving them an appraising stare. "Help to one another? Could very well be the best thing that has happened to me, your being trapped. But I don't expect you to think of that as a good thing."

Bealomondore looked at Ellie and smiled. "I've discovered that good things are found in the most unusual places." He turned to the old urohm. "How may we be of service to you?"

"My first act of cooperation should be welcome in your eyes and a service to me. You see, I know of a place to bake daggarts, not nearly as far away as where you went. You should have asked. No harm in asking. Lot of difficulties when you run off, thinking you know it all."

Ellie started to react, but Bealomondore squeezed her a tad, and Orli's thoughts interrupted hers. The minor dragon reminded her that old age was a trial that Old One had borne all alone for far too many years. *"Mercy. Compassion. Patience."*

She turned to Bealomondore and knew he'd heard exactly the same counsel. They might grow old together stuck in a bottle city, but at least they would have each other. They could give to this old man what didn't cost them but a little kindness.

# 24

# Escape

Today seemed like any other day in the library. Except for Old One sitting in the rotunda instead of lurking in the balcony shadows. Orli lay across the back of the old man's chair. Ellie tried to concentrate on the reading before her, but she just couldn't. She shifted in the overlarge chair, pulled a pillow on her lap, and rested the book against it. Her hands became sore after holding even the smaller books for several hours. She wouldn't let that happen today.

She glanced back down at the handwritten pages. Why would she want to read a diary about things in the past when Old One sat right there in his chair? Why wouldn't he answer questions? Bealomondore had gone to get breakfast, and she was left to pry some information out of the reticent old gent. Only the old gent wouldn't cooperate. He wouldn't answer even the simplest of questions.

She looked up and caught him looking at her out of the corner of his eye.

"Are you ready to tell me your name?" she asked.

He humphed. "I told you yesterday."

"You did not."

He humphed again and turned a page in his book. "Why should I tell you my name when you haven't had the courtesy to tell me yours?"

Ellie closed the diary and plopped it down on the cushion in her lap. "We told you our names when you first spoke to us from the balcony. And we told you again yesterday after tea."

"I've never spoken to you from the balcony. Never spoke to you at all until you invited me to tea."

She sighed. Old One was much more stubborn than she was. This conversation had gone a couple of rounds already, and they hadn't had anything but tea yet this morning.

"My name is Ellicinderpart Clarenbessipawl. My friend's name is Graddapotmorphit Bealomondore. And your name is?"

"What use is a name when no one is around to use it?"

"Bealomondore and I are here to use it."

"You probably won't stay. I wouldn't stay if a way out presented itself." He lifted his head. "Someone is coming."

He looked disoriented, perhaps a bit scared. Orli stood and watched, apparently ready to spring into action. Ellie's irritation dropped away. "It's Bealomondore. He went to get our breakfast."

"Breakfast is served upstairs. Always is."

"So you've already eaten?"

He narrowed his eyes at her as if she had asked a trick question. Bealomondore came into the room with a large basket, the curved handle over his arm. "Lots of food this morning. I assume we are sharing with our host."

"Me?" Old One closed his book. "I'm not your host."

"Why not?" asked Bealomondore as he put his load down by the table and opened the lid.

"Because in order to be a host, one must have invited guests." He looked pointedly at them. "I don't recall inviting anyone."

Bealomondore had his back to Old One and took advantage of his face being out of sight. He pulled an exaggerated grumpy expression that caused Ellie to stifle a laugh. To hide her merriment, she put the pillow and diary aside, scooted to the edge of the seat, and dropped to the floor.

"What do we have this morning?" she asked.

"Muffins and oatmeal," Bealomondore said as he handed the first muffin to Ellie. "Fruit and hard-boiled eggs."

"Old One says his breakfast is served upstairs. So he's already eaten."

"I didn't say that." He sounded gruff.

She turned to look at him. He always seemed so angry. She thought about their earlier exchange.

"You're right. You didn't say you already ate breakfast."

The old urohm looked relieved, but like many of his expressions, the attitude passed so quickly that she wasn't sure she'd seen it. His scowl decorated his face almost constantly. Of that she was sure.

"I know I didn't eat because my stomach says it isn't so." He reached past them and began lifting things to the tabletop.

Her eyes caught Bealomondore's, and again the feeling that he had thought the same thing she did fluttered in her mind. Since that first time when he had heard her thinking about talking to Tak, the feeling had repeated itself. Now he puzzled over why Old One phrased that last statement as he did. And she puzzled right along with Bealomondore. Didn't the urohm know whether or not he had eaten? Did he need proof of an empty stomach to decide the answer?

Bealomondore shrugged and offered to give her a boost up. With his help, she climbed the wooden chair. He came after her, and they each sat on a book to lift themselves high enough to reach their breakfast comfortably.

Bealomondore commented on the walk he and Tak had taken that morning. He'd seen a few birds closer to the center fountain but not actually in the circle.

"I've rarely seen the birds land there," he said, speaking directly to Old One. "Why is that?"

Orli turned his head, ears alert and seemingly interested in the conversation.

Old One bit into a parnot. "At least I still have all my teeth. Things don't wear out. Shoes, clothes, beds, books, furniture, drapes, and rugs never get old or too shabby to keep. There's always food, three times a day, unless those urchins don't go to bed when it's dark. Then there's nothing the next day. Sometimes all day. Only thing that makes them follow a rule."

Ellie and Bealomondore exchanged mystified glances. Was Old One deliberately avoiding the question, or was the gentleman confused?

Bealomondore's gaze went back to the urohm. "Did you make that rule, sir? About going to bed?"

"No, I don't make the rules around here. I don't even try to follow them. Can't remember half of them."

He snapped his mouth shut on the last word.

Orli came to perch on Old One's shoulder, snuggling close to his chin as if to comfort the old man.

Ellie smiled at Bealomondore. "I'd like to take a walk this morning."

"Right."

He was in tune with her. He knew she needed a talk more than a walk. This bond came in handy.

Bealomondore nodded. "Perhaps Old One could tell us about that place to bake daggarts. We could check it out for ingredients and equipment."

"No need to go on a walk for that," said Old One. "It's upstairs, in the living quarters for the custodian."

Ellie raised her eyebrows. "Are you the library's custodian?"

"Guardian," he said. "Not the custodian."

"So you live in the guardian's quarters."

"Said I did, didn't I?"

Ellie looked at Bealomondore, and the same thought blended in her mind with his. *No, I don't believe you did.*

Bealomondore walked beside Ellie as they followed Tak along the pathways through the library park. The foliage still grew wild, but the goat had done a lot of nibbling and seemed to choose plants that needed cutting back. In a few more weeks, he'd have the area looking decent.

Bealomondore tucked Ellie's hand into the crook of his arm. "I don't think Old One is being obstinate. I think he's curt and not forthcoming because he doesn't know the answers."

"Senile?" Her tone sounded worried, filled with compassion for the man who growled in all his communications.

"I don't think so. I think it's part of the spell of the bottle city."

"I'm getting mighty tired of this spell."

"I sympathize."

"What did you try in attempts to get out?"

"Everything I could think of. What did you do?"

"Not much, really. I confess I was so disconcerted and frightened that I didn't have orderly thoughts. I came through the glass wall, but when I turned around, there was no glass wall. From the other side, I could see the pastures and road, but from this side, I couldn't see the trail I had just been on. The ridge, the fog, the scrubby bushes were gone. I took a few steps in the direction I had come from, expecting to walk through the wall again. I didn't, so I followed the road farther in. When I saw the city, I knew I might find help here."

"And you did, but I don't know if this help can get you out of here. I've failed in every attempt."

"What did you do?"

"The first thing I did was the same as you. I tried to retrace my steps and walk out of the bottle in the same spot I'd walked in."

"And that didn't work."

"Obviously. So I came to the city. I explored and discovered that the natives are not friendly. And no one offered me suggestions for getting out. So I headed out of town in the other direction. I walked for several days. In case you are wondering, food is not provided for those who are trying to escape."

"I ate berries." She blushed at the memory.

"Ah yes, the adorable purple beard that decorated your chin."

"Adorable?" She tried to pull away from him, but he held firm to the hand at his elbow. She relaxed and asked a question more to the point. "So you traveled in one direction a great distance. What did you find?"

"Rumbard City."

"Really? You got turned around."

"Yes, really. And no, I didn't get turned around." He frowned. "I experimented two more times. You can walk as far as you like away from the city, but eventually you find yourself approaching the city, but from the other side."

"Frustrating."

"Yes, frustrating."

"Adorable?"

"Right now you have a teasing twinkle in your bright blue eyes and a dimple quivering at the corner of your smile. I say, 'Yes, adorable.' Everything about you has struck me with adjectives I don't usually use."

She lifted her chin a bit and looked at him askance.

"It is true, dear lady. You might as well know it. If we were in the outside world and I made your acquaintance, I believe I would soon be asking your father for permission to court you."

Now she really did turn red, and Bealomondore felt a pang of conscience. Outside of the bottle, the likelihood of their meeting was next to nothing. And outside the bottle, his self-absorbed interest in all things Bealomondore, his lack of direction, and his thwarted love would have made it impossible to acquaint himself with Ellie's charms.

On the other hand, if he had met her, and if he had been forced by some odd circumstances to remain in her company for an extended period of time, he probably would have noticed how comely she was.

She was quiet, and suddenly the quiet seemed too pronounced. Had that bond that had developed between them just given away all his thoughts?

He stopped and gently pulled her around to face him. She looked down. He tilted her chin up with one hand. Her eyes held tears. The sight tore through his heart like a knife through canvas. He didn't deserve such a sweet woman. He wrapped his arms around her and lowered his face. He kissed her on one cheek and then the other. He leaned back, fully intending not to carry his desire into action. A tiny tear rested at the corner of one of her closed eyes.

"Oh, Ellie, I never intended to make you cry."

He leaned in again and placed one tender kiss on her lips. She trembled. His arms tightened. Her lips moved under his. He was lost.

# 25

# Discovery

"Ellie, are you awake?" Bealomondore called from several aisles away. Ever since he'd kissed her in the library park, he'd been trying to keep a certain distance. He'd had to explain that society didn't approve of a bachelor getting too familiar with a young lady when there was no chaperone. He didn't go into the necessity for them to wed. One step at a time.

"I'm awake."

"You've slept late. Breakfast is here, courtesy of Old One."

He heard her sit up, or was that the bond? Could he possibly know that she sat up and ran her fingers through her tangled locks?

"Old One brought us breakfast?"

"Yes. Come to the rotunda when you're ready. I'll try to keep him from eating it all."

A few minutes later she arrived in one of her outlandish outfits. He really needed to go look for more of her belongings. She smiled shyly at him, and he guarded his thoughts. He didn't need her to misconstrue his opinion. Ellie wore odd combinations, but she managed to look comfortable, not self-conscious. He admired that trait immensely as he recalled the display of despair exhibited by society ladies when something minor jeopardized their elegant getup.

Old One sat in his chair, a plate in his lap and a tankard in one hand. He raised the tankard, toasting the new arrival. "Here's to the lady who bakes. We eat whatever she makes. Her daggarts are scrumptious, without any lumps such…as would chase her lovers away."

Ellie's eyes grew big, and a smile quivered at the edge of her mouth, as if she didn't quite know how to react to this type of poetry.

She contained her lips in a prim line and answered. "I'm hoping to lure some children into our care. And I've never had lovers who objected to my cooking."

"Ah," said the old man with mischief lighting his face. "So your many lovers didn't object to your cooking. Very wise of them."

Ellie clasped her hands together and twisted. "I meant that I hadn't any lovers. Not ones who objected. Not ones who didn't object. No lovers. My family liked my cooking well enough."

"Well, quit dawdling," commanded Old One. "Climb up to your breakfast so we can get on with the day." Pushing against the chair arms to aid his struggle, he stood. "I'll just go upstairs and get things ready."

"Thank you, sir," said Bealomondore. "Ellie, stay there. I'll bring things down to you."

A pot of tea and cups already sat on one of the stacks of thick books. Bealomondore balanced a plate as he descended from the wooden chair.

"Bacon!" Ellie took the plate and sat on a shorter stack of books. "I haven't had bacon for a long time."

"The toast and jam is good too."

She took a bite. "Mmm. Razterberry."

Bealomondore poured tea and then sat opposite her with the book table between them.

"What did he mean, Bealomondore? About getting things ready?"

"He seems to be in a jolly mood this morning. He plans for you to bake daggarts in his kitchen."

"I don't mind baking, but how do we get up there? I'm not eager to climb two flights of stairs."

"He's worked it out. There's a dumbwaiter."

She quirked an eyebrow at him. "I don't know what a dumb-waiter is."

"It's a box that carries things between different floors. In this case, it was meant to carry books. Someone pulls on a rope. There's a pulley at the top, so it greatly reduces the amount of strength needed to haul something upward or lower it."

"So Old One is going to do the hauling?"

"He's very keen on having more daggarts."

"Do you think he's strong enough to pull us up to the top floor? He looks weak to me. And he moves even slower than my gramps."

Bealomondore pondered the danger involved. He certainly couldn't put Ellie in the dumbwaiter if there was any possibility of it being dropped. "I'll go up first, and then maybe there would be some way for me to help him if his strength gives out."

"It would be handy to have one of those wizards you talked about here."

"Ellie, I believe it is because of some wizard that we are in this predicament. I don't know what would happen if a different wizard came along and stuck his finger in the pot."

"Guess you're right—too many cooks spoil the broth," she agreed.

They tidied up a bit after they finished breakfast. Then Bealomon-dore led Ellie to the workroom she'd seen before. In the corner, a box sat in a cubby in the wall.

Bealomondore patted the floor of the enclosure. "This is the car. It's guided by two rails so it won't tip during the trip up or down."

He pushed an empty wooden crate to the cleared space under the dumbwaiter. After stepping up, he reached for and tugged a rope. A bell clanged from high above them.

"It rings on the third floor," he explained.

Ellie nodded, but her expression conveyed little confidence that this was a good idea. She surveyed the contraption as if looking for cracked wood or frayed ropes.

"Remember," said Bealomondore, "Old One said things do not wear out in Rumbard City."

"I think *he* is wearing out."

"Point taken."

Old One's voice boomed through the shaft. "Are you in there yet?"

Bealomondore hopped into the box. "Ready!" He winked at Ellie. "Your turn next. There's nothing to it really. Not nearly as daunting as riding on a dragon's back."

The dumbwaiter jerked, then started upward. Bealomondore sensed the question in Ellie's mind.

"Not on the back of a minor dragon. A riding dragon is bigger than a horse." The dumbwaiter lifted him behind the wall, and he could no longer see her. "I'll tell you about it later."

Ellie watched the dumbwaiter slide upward in the shaft. When Bealomondore passed out of view, she saw the two rails that the lift followed and two ropes that moved, one going up and one sliding down. The apparatus whined as if protesting against the weight in the car. Through their bond, she knew that he sat in the car with no qualms. Perhaps his calm demeanor would transfer to her when it was her turn.

She climbed onto the crate and leaned in to see the bottom of the car rising above her. A screech made her jerk back. It sounded as if the box rubbed against the side of the shaft. In a moment, the grating sound diminished, and she could again hear the constant whine. A loud thud cut off the high-pitched complaint.

She sighed her relief as she realized Bealomondore had climbed out and stood next to the urohm.

The dumbwaiter began its downward journey, groaning and protesting with a much-diminished cry. It thumped against the floor of the shaft when it reached bottom.

Bealomondore's voice carried down to her. "Climb in, Ellie."

She hopped aboard and called, "I'm in."

When an initial shudder signaled that her trip had begun, her muscles tensed as if she were about to fall. But the adventure of doing something entirely new grabbed her, zinging through her body. A happy glow replaced the trepidation from a moment before. The whine reverberated in the car, and she covered her ears. But even that added to the thrill. She wanted to tell Gustus about the dumbwaiter. She knew if he were here, she wouldn't be able to keep him out of this contraption.

The image of her brother's ecstatic face sent a wave of homesickness through her, squelching her enthusiasm. She wanted to tell her mother and sisters about Graddapotmorphit Bealomondore. She wasn't as sure about introducing her suitor to her father. What would Da think of an artist?

She'd best start with Bealomondore's service in the war. Then approach the subject of his talent. Perhaps the subject of his unusual friends would not come up at all. Her father was not likely to ask, "Has this young man spent any time living with kimens? Does this suitor associate with wizards? Can't have any odd associates if he wants to court my daughter." She sighed. Mother would understand, and so would Aunt Tiffenbeth.

The car continued to move up past the second floor, where the opening revealed a room of bookshelves in orderly rows. The sides of the dumbwaiter scraped against the walls of the shaft. Ellie clenched her teeth against the grinding noise. Once past the tight spot, Ellie noticed the dim light giving way to stronger illumination.

When she saw a square hole in the wall like the one on the first floor, she could almost imagine having returned to the same spot. But Bealomondore and Old One stood in this room. The tumanhofer greeted her with a grin and held her hand as she climbed out.

He gave her a quick hug and a peck on the cheek. Ellie's eyes darted over to Old One, but the urohm concentrated on applying a clamp to the rope, which she assumed would keep the dumbwaiter in place. Orli sat on the back of a sofa. This morning, his mottled white and gray scales looking more like moldy clotted cream than oatmeal.

Old One put a hand to his back. "That wore me out. I'm going to lie down." He pointed to the opposite side of the room. "Kitchen's in there." He limped to another door and entered the room. Orli slipped in just before the urohm closed the door behind him.

As the latched clicked, Bealomondore pulled Ellie into his arms. "Old One is a completely inadequate chaperone."

Ellie thoroughly enjoyed his kiss. His arms around her made her feel safe.

She could get used to this.

She pulled back. "Did I think that, or did you think that?"

He planted a quick kiss on her forehead and stepped away. "I think *we* thought that."

Taking her hand, he pulled her toward the kitchen. "Let's get busy."

The kitchen surprised Ellie. Smaller furniture made the room seem bigger. Old One had already put ingredients on the one table in the center. He'd stoked the stove and put manageable-sized bowls out for them to use.

Bealomondore walked around the room, reading small pieces of paper scattered on counters, pinned to the walls, and stuck to cabinets.

"What do they say?" she asked.

"Most of them label what is in the cupboards." He touched one hanging by the doorframe. "This one is interesting. *Two tumanhofers downstairs.*"

"Why would he write that?"

Bealomondore shrugged. He read the next slip. *"Name— Bealomondore."*

Ellie looked at a note next to the window. *"Goat—park—girl."* She shook her head. "Tak is not a girl."

"No, but he belongs to a girl." On a cabinet, he found another cryptic note. *"Daggarts—girl—dumbwaiter."*

Ellie glanced at the many flags of paper around the place. "What do you think all these are for?"

"I think they are reminders. I don't think he remembers things."

She looked out the window and saw Tak strolling among a bank of flowers in the library park. "So when he figures something out, he writes it down?"

"And the next day he doesn't have to figure it out again."

She took a moment to digest that possibility. What would it be like to have to rely on written messages for memories of the day before? How would one decide what was important to record? "I wonder if he knows how to get out—"

"—of Rumbard but forgot."

She moved over to the table and climbed up to examine the ingredients. "The spell is such that the children never get past six and don't remember enough to learn from mistakes and mature."

Bealomondore continued to read the notes as he toured the kitchen. "And Old One doesn't remember details, so he can't plan to escape."

"That's probably why he doesn't leave the library."

Bealomondore put his finger on one of the notes and then turned to look out the window. From this spot he could see the labyrinth of city streets beyond the jumble of a garden. "He's afraid he wouldn't remember how to get back."

"Yes, and no notes to help him." She thumped a bag of flour and saw a fine puff of white powder escape the weave of burlap. "He has all the ingredients. Shall we begin?"

Bealomondore nodded and climbed the wooden chair. "I have the feeling that if we could put the things we know together like we combine these ingredients, we might have a solution to our problem."

"That sounds optimistic."

"I'm hoping I am not being too optimistic." He paused. "Wulder provides."

That puzzled her. What did that have to do with daggarts or escaping? "I don't—"

"From the Tomes, 'All things are provided but not all work is done.'"

"So we have to provide the labor?"

He maneuvered onto the seat and stood beside her. "Exactly, so we can share the satisfaction."

"Do you think we'll ever get the right clues put together in the right way?"

He winked. "As sure as we're going to make the best daggarts this city has ever seen."

# 26

# First Duty

Old One came out of his room just as Ellie and Bealomondore prepared the first baking sheet to go into the oven. He did a double take and stood for a moment with a belligerent look on his face, but then his eyes fell on the daggarts, shaped and ready to be baked.

"I'll put that in for you," he said. "My things are smaller than the furnishings in most of the houses. But still, the oven door would be hard to handle. Most everything in this room came from Amara, on the ship that brought us to Chiril."

Ellie raised her eyebrows and grinned at Bealomondore. Maybe they were finally going to get some history out of the urohm. Orli flew to the windowsill and looked out.

Old One slipped the daggart sheet into the oven and closed the door. He then moved around the room looking at his notes while trying not to look like he was looking at his notes. Bealomondore and Ellie busied themselves with preparing the next batch in order to look like they did not notice that he was looking at his notes.

The old gentleman eventually sat down at the table, dug a spoon into the bowl of dough and commenced nibbling the gooey concoction. Between bites he asked Ellie, "Is your goat a nanny or billy?"

"Billy."

"Shame. Goat milk is good. Goat cheese is better."

"We make goat cheese on the farm."

Old One nodded. "Bealomondore, there's a kettle in that cupboard. Put some water on to boil for tea, if you would."

Ellie sat opposite the urohm. "Would you tell us about coming to Chiril?"

"Yes." He paused, then gave Bealomondore's back a quick glance, where he stood at the pump, filling the kettle. The old man winked at Ellie. "My memory's clear if you go back far enough. I suppose you've figured it out, the two of you. You're young and clever."

Ellie smiled with understanding. Her gramps had the same troubles at times. "You don't remember things from today or yesterday or a couple days ago. And as the day goes on, you get too tired to think, and you forget more. At least, that's what my gramps says is the case."

"He's got the right of it," Old One said around a dollop of dough in his mouth.

"Would you tell us how Rumbard City came to be in the bottle?"

He looked so sad and weary that Ellie regretted having prodded him. She wanted to tell him it didn't matter. But of course, it did. She contemplated telling him to keep the tale for another time. But he heaved a great sigh and began.

"We were sent here by the paladin of Amara. We were chosen because our race, the urohms, had demonstrated once before that we could stand honorably. Alas, this time we failed the test."

"How?" asked Ellie.

Bealomondore sat down at the table while waiting for the water to boil. "Why did Paladin send you to Chiril?"

"Paladin knew of Chiril and that the people here had lost the knowledge of Wulder." He looked at them sharply. "Do you know who Wulder is?"

Bealomondore nodded. "Our country has been visited by a wizard and a librarian from Amara. And our own Verrin Schope visited Amara and came back with the truth of Wulder. Now Chiril has its own paladin. Our people are beginning to learn of Wulder and the teachings in His Tomes."

Old One's shoulders drooped, and he looked down at his hands. He'd polished off the spoonful of dough, so he slowly turned the spoon around and around. "That was our job, our first duty. We were to tell the people of Chiril the truth. A very simple task, but we managed to bungle it."

The kettle called, loud and shrill. Bealomondore jumped to take it off the heat. The shriek lost momentum and became silent. The tumanhofer hastily poured the tea, and while it steeped, the three companions in the kitchen removed trays of crisp, hot daggarts from the oven and replaced them with trays containing lumps of dough. With Old One to handle the oven and the heavy baking sheet, Ellie and Bealomondore could manage the other chores easily.

Soon they each had a cup of tea and a daggart.

"I'm glad you came," said Old One.

Ellie reached to pat his arm. "I'm glad we got to meet you. But the truth is, we would like to leave. Perhaps we can all get out."

Bealomondore looked intently at their host. "If you can tell us more about why we are in the bottle, we hope we can discover how to get out."

Orli came to roost on Old One's shoulder. The urohm broke off a piece of the daggart and handed it to his dragon companion. "I suppose I could, but I don't see how it will help. We had a wizard traveling with us, Wizard Pater and his dragon, Salm. The wizard rode the dragon while we sailed in a great ship. I suppose that was the beginning of our demise. The wizard would visit the ship and give us lectures about how we were to conduct ourselves to further the cause set before us. Then he flew off, not suffering the daily rigors of a life at sea."

"Lectures?" asked Bealomondore. "That doesn't sound very encouraging."

"Exactly." Old One broke off another piece of daggart for Orli. "We began to resent his intrusion. But it was his desertion that rankled most. It placed a barrier between him and us. He rode comfortably on his dragon while we suffered seasickness, cold, wet gales of the northern ocean, and then as we came south, times when heat almost smothered us and no winds billowed our sails."

"But where was the wizard?" asked Ellie. "He and the dragon would have had to rest. They couldn't fly continuously, could they?"

"Wizard Pater used his knowledge of the way Wulder had made the world to slip through holes in the sky to land. He visited various places and would tell us about them when he called upon us. We didn't really appreciate the descriptions of his stopovers."

As they once again tended the baking daggarts, Old One continued the tale. "During his long absences and our uncomfortable voyage, we began to devise our own plans for relating the wonderment of Wulder. We knew that these Chirilians had never seen a urohm. We forgot our first duty as it had been revealed to us."

The old urohm grimaced, his wrinkles creased in an unhappy mask of tragedy. "We saw a better way. The ignorant people of Chiril would undoubtedly be impressed with our size. We would go another step and impress them with our sophistication.

"We planned to build a huge city with cultural attractions like a theater, a museum, a library, and industry. Once they were dazzled by our superiority, we would invite them to join us in our worship of Wulder, the Maker of all things, the Giver of all that is good. They would be able to see with their own eyes just how much our people had bene-fited by serving Wulder."

"You obviously built the city," said Bealomondore. "What went wrong?"

"Before we landed on Chirilian shores, one more horrendous storm beset our voyage. Wizard Pater had just left us. And we were particu-larly glad to see him go because he had outlined a plan that empha-sized being humble and having a servant's attitude. We were full of rage and bitterness. The storm seemed to match the fury of our umbrage against the wizard and his plans.

"I now believe that if we had relied more on Wulder, focused our devotion on Him instead of stewing over the injustice of being made to withstand all the elements of nature, all would have been well. Dur-ing the storm, we feared for our lives yet survived.

"And when we saw that we had not perished, we assumed it was be-cause our party of urohms was great. We'd defeated the sea's attempt to slay us one more time. We deserved all the good things that would be-fall us. And I am sorry to say, we assumed that Wizard Pater had per-ished. He'd never returned."

"So," said Bealomondore, leaning across the table and completely caught up in the story, "you landed and built your city."

Ellie thought about how no one, not one person she knew, told the story of Rumbard City and the urohms. She had never heard a minstrel sing of them. There were no plays given by traveling performers re-counting the things Old One talked about. The bottle city, the stand-ing stone dragons, nothing whatsoever tickled the ears of even the closest neighbors.

"We did," said Old One, and again his tone was of defeat. "We proudly invited the citizens of Chiril to visit our grand metropolis and experience the goodness of Wulder."

"Did they come?" asked Ellie.

"Oh yes. They came."

She wanted to know everything, and he stalled, not completing the tale just as it was becoming more interesting. Patience deserted her. "Were they impressed?"

"Yes, though we hadn't gotten around to explaining much about Wulder. Our first duty had slipped somewhere down an imaginary list to an obscure slot somewhere near the bottom. We attributed everything to Wulder but didn't speak of His principles. We would have plenty of time to do that, or so we thought."

Ellie felt like one of the children when a storyteller visited and deliberately paused to build their anticipation. But Old One had no thought of artificial dramatics. He truly seemed distressed. She leaned forward, and just as she touched his arm, Bealomondore lightly grasped the old man's other arm.

Bealomondore asked, "What happened?"

"Wizard Pater found us."

"His anger roiled the clouds in the sky. The citizens of Chiril ran, and as they escaped from the city, the wizard took all their memories of us, the buildings, and the civilization we presented as better than their own. He pulled the memories from them and placed them in a bottle."

Ellie blinked and looked at Bealomondore. Neither one of them spoke. Ellie wanted to know if the city was in the same bottle as the memories, but that didn't quite make sense.

"Our leader, Gordman Rumbard, faced down Wizard Pater and claimed that he no longer had the right to dictate what we do." Old

One's voice dropped to a whisper. "That's when the wizard, the spokesman for Wulder, assigned our punishment. We would be in Chiril but not allowed to be a part of Chiril.

"None of the adults would be entrusted with the treasure of the knowledge we had of Wulder. We would not be able to distribute the gems of life to these people. Only when this generation, my generation, had perished. Even if it were to take four hundred years, none in the city would be released from the bottle. The children would not mature until that time. We would be taken care of, but even being taken care of would be a curse."

Ellie's heart ached for the urohms. Their folly had brought them down. "How is it that the provisions would be a curse?"

"Boredom. No fruit of our labors. No task to do that gave a sense of satisfaction. Nothing we could give of our own to a neighbor to express friendship."

He sat for a moment, dejected. "This has worn me down. I cannot continue." He moved to get up. "I shall go to my room."

"No," said Bealomondore. "One thing has changed. You are not useless. We need your help to make the daggarts."

Old One looked at Bealomondore as if he could not quite understand the words he had just heard.

"I will die soon," he said. "Then perhaps the bottle will dissolve."

Orli chittered, a scolding sound.

Ellie could almost make out the dragon's words. "He doesn't approve."

Old One laughed without humor. "He believes there is one urohm left with honor in his heart. He believes I can change what is meant to be. He thinks too highly of me and too little of justice."

Ellie didn't want to part with his company until they had lifted his spirits. To go off to his room in this state of mind could not be good for his health. "Stay and help us."

"Time to take out the next batch of daggarts," said Bealomondore. He handed two hot pads to the urohm and opened the oven door. Old One allowed himself to be brought back into the job of baking. Later he helped them package the treats. Then he and Bealomondore worked the dumbwaiter, with Ellie at ground level emptying the car of its load.

Late that night, Ellie and Bealomondore walked to the butcher's shop to see if a meal had been left. They assumed the box would be empty since food had been deposited in the library. The box was gone, the butcher's stoop empty.

Ellie stood with her hands on her hips and scowled at the sight. "I don't know if I like the idea of not having to come to get the food."

"I know," agreed Bealomondore. "When Old One told us of the futility of living with nothing to do, I thought of my dilemma. I have more than one thing that would satisfy my need to be of use. Instead of seeing that as a blessing, I regarded it as an annoyance."

Ellie pushed her arm under his and grasped his hand. They stood for a while, linked and comfortable with the closeness of body and soul.

"What do you think our first duty is, Bealomondore?"

"I think we may have already done the first thing on the list."

"Making contact with Old One, bringing him out of his isolation."

"Yes, I don't think Wulder approves of turning our backs on others."

"Do you suppose the children are next?"

He leaned closer and kissed the top of her head. "I know you think so."

"I don't want to get caught up doing my list and not paying attention to what should be first duty for us."

Bealomondore turned to face her. "I thought we did first duty—Old One."

"Yes, but once you've done first duty, it's taken off the list, and the next thing down becomes first duty."

"Well, until we get the list and can read it, why don't we work on getting the daggarts to the ragamuffins?"

"That seems like a logical course."

Bealomondore embraced her and hugged tight. "No, my adorable tumanhofer. A logical course would be to avoid the monsters altogether. That way no one would get hurt."

"No one would get better either."

He mumbled, "Good point," right before he kissed her, but Ellie, at that moment, didn't much care whether he thought her logic held up.

# 27

# Sticks and Stones

Old One refused to leave the library to participate in the Great Lure of the Children. Bealomondore didn't blame him and wished he, too, could forgo the experience, calling the enterprise the Great Trap of the Horrible Horde.

Bealomondore met Ellie at the back entrance. He carried bait and so did she—an appealing treasure of daggarts in two baskets, a cloth covering the contents.

"I'm excited," said Ellie.

"I'd rather you limit your expectations to a reasonable outlook. These children are not civilized. A daggart will not make them docile, sweet-tempered, and obedient."

"I'm not expecting all that. I just want them to associate good things with us."

Bealomondore studied her face for a moment, wondering if there was any argument that would knock that innocent hope out of her head. Then he decided he didn't want to erase the glow in her eyes. He held the grate open for her and helped lower the baskets to the ground outside.

"Maa!" Tak stood at the gate to the library park.

Ellie stopped to scratch between his horns. "You can't come this time."

The goat stamped his front feet and butted the gate.

"No, I'm not taking you. Don't you remember the children being unkind to you? We have to teach them manners before I will let them get near you again."

Bealomondore looked sternly at the goat. "I back your mistress, Tak. This is a dangerous mission, and you need to stay here. We'll be back in an hour or so."

Ellie scoffed at his words. "Dangerous? They're only children."

He took her arm and headed her toward the circle fountain. "You're to humor me and be ready to run for your life if I yell, 'Go!' "

They did no running. For more than an hour, they walked the streets where the children usually played. At one corner, Bealomondore climbed a drainpipe to retrieve a blouse belonging to Ellie. She looked it over carefully once he handed it to her.

"They haven't been rough with it." She turned it over in her hands. "It's a bit dirty but nothing I can't wash out."

She folded it and put it on top of the cloth in her basket. They strolled down the street of shops until she paused to look in the window of a clothing store. "You know, I really admire all the things the urohms have in their shops. In the village, the mercantile had one rack of ready-made clothes. Old One mentioned industry. Is it industry that makes the difference? Everyone at home spent time making for themselves, with little time left over for making things to sell."

"In my explorations before you came, I found that many of the urohm homes on the west side of Rumbard have a cottage at the rear of the property where different things were made—cloth, candles, furniture, clothing, hats, boots, anything one might need. Those homes are more modest than the ones we've visited."

"So as a town, they were pretty much self-sufficient. My gramps says that when the first farms were built, they were so far apart that each family took care of their own needs."

"I suppose that's so." Bealomondore gently nudged her into once again walking down the sidewalk in front of the stores. "And I suppose those in Rumbard City were intent on displaying their accomplishments in all areas."

Ellie pursed her lips and shook her head. "That hardly seems the way to make friends."

"I doubt it ever crossed their minds to make friends with the people of Chiril."

"No?"

"Paladin gave them the task of explaining the ways of Wulder to the people of Chiril. It would have been a better method to ask the urohms to come and help in any way they could, to serve the people."

"Is that how Wizard Fenworth, Librettowit, and Verrin Schope told you about Wulder?"

He laughed. "They didn't tell me much at all. We were busy saving the country. They talked among themselves about Him. But basically, they never laid out rules and facts at all. I became intrigued by the way they acted and how they helped one another...and me."

"So how did you learn about this Wulder?"

"Once my curiosity was aroused, I began to listen more carefully, then I asked questions, then one of them gave me a copy of Wulder's Tomes. Actually, a set. There are three of them."

"Do you have them here? May I see them?"

"I left them outside the bottle. Of course, I would have brought them with me had I known I was going to be trapped in Rumbard City. But I had just walked over to find a spot to paint. My moonbeam cape, my books, my luggage, and all my personal effects are in the cart beside the road I traveled."

He walked for a moment in silence. "That was over two months ago. I'm sure someone has taken the horse and cart to the nearest town."

Ellie ignored his lament over the horse and his things. "What is a moonbeam cape?"

The memory made him smile. "The cape was presented to me by Winkel, one of the matriarchs of a kimen village. It's woven from the fibers of a moonbeam plant and has the impressive property of camouflage. If you remain still, you blend into your surroundings, except in bright sunlight. And inside they sewed hollows, deep pockets where anything can be stored."

He looked at her puzzled expression and knew he had to do more explaining. "Anything that fits in the opening of the hollow disappears. When you wear the cape, you can't feel the weight of all that the hollows hold. No bulges or lumps or sagging material give away the fact that you carry weapons and food and clothing. Librettowit once produced a raft out of his hollow. In pieces. We had to put it together."

Ellie remained silent.

Bealomondore let out an exasperated swoosh of air. "You haven't gone back to not believing me, have you?"

"I...I believe you, but I would like to see these marvelous things. My mind would more easily picture such a thing. Seeing would make it *easier* to believe, but I do believe you, Bealomondore. Don't you understand that I could imagine these marvelous things if I had at one time seen something like them?"

"Not necessarily." Bealomondore noticed a movement at the corner of the next building. He slowed down. "I wore the cape and would forget its ability to hide me. I would put things in the hollows, which just looked like pockets, and then marvel over the lack of evidence that the items still existed. Many times I plunged my hand back in to draw the object out just to prove to myself that it hadn't disappeared."

He edged closer to his companion and spoke quietly. "Ellie, I think we have finally found the children. At least one. Ahead of us, at the corner of the music hall."

Ellie looked ahead. "I see her. I think I've seen her another time. Yes, I noticed her before when I was the guest of the children."

Bealomondore made no comment about her use of the word "guest." She'd been abducted. Right now he focused on not allowing that to happen again.

Ellie's voice came in a breathless whisper. "She's smaller than the others, and I thought perhaps she was younger."

"She must be small for her age. She's still taller than either of us."

"True."

The girl came out in full view and sat on the edge of the wide step into the large hall. The front of the building had huge glass-covered posters of programs. The child watched them approach. Bealomondore inspected the surrounding buildings. "Careful," he whispered to Ellie. "She may be the enticement for an ambush."

Ellie drew near with caution. "Hello, my name is Ellicinderpart Clarenbessipawl. I remember you."

The girl looked up but didn't return the smile Ellie had given.

"What's your name?" asked Ellie.

"Soo-tie."

"I've just recently met a dragon named Soosahn. He's a laughing dragon and is funny."

The child stared at Ellie.

Ellie tried again. "I'd like you to meet him someday. Today, we brought you a treat."

She pushed her blouse and the cloth aside to pull out a daggart. The child rose immediately and grabbed the offering. She darted off, but another child ran out from between the buildings. He pushed her, knocking her over. Stepping on her wrist, he leaned over and wrenched the prize from her hand. He ran off.

"Oh!" Ellie ran to Soo-tie's side. "Are you all right?" She helped the child sit up and dust off her clothes. Then she handed the girl another daggart.

Bealomondore surveyed the area, looking for more children ready to ambush Soo-tie. He heard a rush of stomping feet behind him, but he only managed a half turn before three sweaty boys barreled into him and knocked him over. The basket of daggarts left his hand and made its way down the street amid hooting and hollering by the successful raiders.

He rolled into a sit and saw Ellie and the small child surrounded by a ring of girls. The barrier did not face inward, threatening the dag-gart carrier, but formed a defensive circle. Boys surrounded them. They stayed out of reach of the girls' clawing hands, but feinted attempts to charge the defensive band of six-year-olds. The girls carried sticks, and the boys hefted rocks.

Bealomondore got to his feet and drew his sword. "See here," he called. "You are going to back off and treat these ladies with respect. Miss Clarenbessipawl has brought you daggarts. You may each have one, but there will be no fighting."

One of the boys turned and hurled the rock directly at Bealomon-dore. He raised the sword and knocked the stone away before it could hit him. He heard Ellie squeal and saw that the girls had converged upon his friend and the smaller child she attempted to protect in her arms. The boys joined the fray, hitting the girls as well as Ellie.

The girls pounded on Ellie and Soo-tie with the sticks. The boys didn't need any weapons other than their fists. Some of the girls turned and attacked those attacking them. Besides poking and hitting with their weapons, the girls pinched and slapped at the boys.

Bealomondore roared and charged. The flat of his sword swatted the backsides of several boys. They hollered, but it took more than one swing to dissuade them from their rough game.

The tumanhofer wielded his sword with precision. It didn't even come close to cutting one of the children. Bealomondore gave thanks for the sword that had taught him how to fight and, in battle, directed his aim. To maneuver among this crowd without really inflicting harm required concentration and precision. But he suspected the edge was as dull as it had been the last time he used his sword to ward off grimy urchins.

One bully reached through the fray and grasped the handle of the basket. He wrenched the prize of daggarts from Ellie and took off. Screeches of protest filled the street, and most of the children raced to catch the successful thief.

"Why are you crying?" asked Soo-tie. She looked at Ellie with concern. "No one is supposed to cry. They're extra mean to you if you cry. You need to stop. They'll come back and pull your hair if you keep crying."

Bealomondore sheathed his sword and came to help Ellie get up.

"Oh, look." She pointed after the gang.

Two children lay in the street. One held his head and moaned. The other wiped a bloody nose on his sleeve. Ellie limped to where the first one was stretched out on his back. Blood dripped from between his fingers where he had them buried in his long, tangled hair.

She knelt beside him while Bealomondore went on to the second child. Soo-tie followed, seemingly more interested in the tumanhofers than in her fallen comrades. Bealomondore helped the boy with the bloody nose get up and come back to Ellie's side.

She pulled out a handkerchief, folded it, and applied it to the first boy's head. The child interfered by trying to get his hands back to the wound.

"Stop it," Ellie fussed. "Your hands are filthy, and the cut will become infected. It's a small wound, but head cuts bleed a lot. Stop it and let me hold this. It'll quit bleeding if you just let me hold the pad there. Am I going to have to sit on your hands? Stop it!"

Soo-tie laughed. "Sit on his hands!"

Bealomondore sat the other boy down, told him to lean his head back and apply pressure under his nose. He found the abandoned cloth from Ellie's basket, wadded it up, and shoved it into the boy's hand. "Use that."

He moved closer to the boy with the head wound. "Let me see, Ellie."

She pulled the cloth pad away for a moment.

Bealomondore inspected the boy's scalp. "It probably could use stitches, but it will have to do without. If we keep it clean, he'll heal up just fine."

Ellie returned the pad. She took a deep breath and sat down next to her patient. Leaning him against her in a more comfortable position, she managed to get a better hold of the wiggling child to keep pressure on his wound. Tears still stained her cheeks, and she hunched first one shoulder and then the other to scrub them away.

She sighed again. Bealomondore couldn't quite determine whether she was weary or disappointed, disgusted or resolved to carry through with her agenda.

"My name is Ellicinderpart Clarenbessipawl. What is yours?"

Bealomondore looked away, grimaced, and turned back. She hadn't given up.

The boy sniffed. "Porky."

"Well, Porky, you and your friends have no manners. But that is going to change." She addressed the bloody-nosed boy. "And what is your name?"

"Cinder."

"Cinder, you are going to learn to enjoy life. You will find it is good instead of bad, fun instead of boring, and safe instead of dangerous."

He lowered his head to look straight at her. The rag muffled his question. "Do you have more of them daggarts?"

"I do."

He put his head back again. "I don't think we want manners. Daggarts are all right. But I don't know about the manners."

"No manners, no daggarts," said Ellie.

Bealomondore shook his head. How did she plan on withholding daggarts until she got the manners she wanted? So far, they'd engaged in two battles with the horde.

And the horde had won both battles.

# 28

# Good? Good!

"The bleeding has slowed." Ellie dabbed at Porky's wound with another clean cloth.

"There's an apothecary a few blocks over." Bealomondore looked up from washing Cinder's face. "We could walk over there and get some sticking plaster."

"Where are the dragons of the watch?" Ellie looked up and down the street as if they would suddenly appear. "It would be handy if they kept tabs on us instead of on all the empty parts of the city."

"Are you proposing to organize the little band?"

"I bet they have followed the same routine for decades."

"You're probably right, but I don't know how easily they can be persuaded to adopt another schedule."

Ellie pushed on the boy leaning against her. "Come on, Porky. We're going to take a walk."

Soo-tie jumped up to go with them. "Does he need stitches? Are there stitches at that place? Are you going to make stitches? What kind of stitches? Like sewing? Eww! Will it hurt?"

Porky scowled at the girl and put up clenched fists. "You think I'm going to cry. I'm not. So you won't have a thing to tell on me."

"Hush, children," said Ellie. She patted Porky's shoulder. She had to look up to see his face, but she determined to treat him just like Gustus. "You chomp down on all those angry words. Think of something nice to say. You too, Soo-tie."

Cinder snickered.

Ellie pointed a finger at the boy tagging along. "You aren't out of it, Cinder. You think of something nice to say to both Porky and Soo-tie."

Cinder made a face like he smelled cooking cabbage. "I don't know anything nice to say." He glowered at Soo-tie. "You go first."

She lifted her chin and let a smug smile set on her lips. "I do know something nice to say. Since you chose me to go first, you know I'm smarter than either of you two. Else you wouldn't have said for me to go first."

"That's squatty poop," yelled Cinder.

"Hold it!" Ellie's voice sounded loud and clear. "No one is to say another word until I give you permission."

The three children clamped their mouths shut.

"Soo-tie, I appreciate your willingness to be first. However, you didn't make it clear that you admire Cinder's choice because *he* is clever enough to recognize that you are gifted in conversation and would be perfect to be the first to try a new way of speaking."

"Huh?" said Cinder and Soo-tie.

Bealomondore winked at Ellie. "She means since Soo-tie talks more than the boys, then she probably could talk the way Miss Clarenbessipawl wants her to."

"How does she want us to talk?" asked Porky.

"She wants you to talk in a way that makes the person talked to feel good."

Puzzled glances passed between all three children.

"Why?" asked Cinder.

"Remember what I told you?" said Ellie. "You are going to learn to enjoy life. You will find it is good instead of bad, fun instead of boring, and safe instead of dangerous."

Porky snorted. "Talking like you want us to is going to do all that?"

The other two snickered.

"Speaking politely will put you on the right road. Instead of being covered with the slime of destruction, you will be lifted above the mire."

The three children turned to Bealomondore.

"She means that every time you speak in the way she doesn't like, it's like you fall in the mud. It gets in your clothes, in your hair, in your mouth. Sometimes it gets in your eyes and makes it hard for you to see. Sometimes it clogs up your ears so you can't hear."

"And if we talk like she wants us?" asked Soo-tie.

"The more you talk her way, the more dirt and grime and muddy slime drop off you."

The children looked at themselves and the grubbiness that clung to each of them.

"This stuff washes off," said Porky. "We don't have to talk different. We just have to jump in the fountain."

Bealomondore smiled. "Ah, but it's not the dirt and mud you can see that is the problem."

Cinder narrowed his eyes and looked suspiciously at the male tumanhofer. "What do you mean?"

"It's invisible," said Ellie.

"Invisible *and*"—Bealomondore let his voice drop to a deep, solemn whisper—"it goes inside you and sticks to your innards. Particularly your heart."

"And in your blood," added Ellie.

"You can't wash it off," said Bealomondore with a sad shake of his head.

"It has to wear off." Ellie nodded with encouragement. "Sometimes it does fall off in chunks, but then you can't see it, so you don't know by what you see whether it's here or there."

Cinder blustered. "If I can't see it, why should it worry me?"

"Because of what it does."

Cinder held out his hands, covered with grime and dried blood from his nose. "It's just dirt. It don't do anything. Just because I can't see it doesn't make it more dangerous than plain dirt. If you're trying to trick me into a bath, it's not going to work."

"A bath?" asked Bealomondore with a more vigorous shake of his head. "Hadn't even crossed my mind."

Porky looked at Ellie. "Are we going to be late for noonmeal?"

"I don't think so."

"We're almost there," said Bealomondore.

Ellie patted Porky's arm. "I'm going to give each of you a sentence to say. We'll practice saying nice things."

"I don't want to," said Porky. "I have a wound."

"The wound isn't in your mouth," said Bealomondore.

"I'm tired and hungry, and I don't feel like talking like she wants me to. Why should I?"

Ellie heaved a giant sigh.

Bealomondore's face became a mask of formidable adult determination. "Miss Clarenbessipawl, give him his sentence."

"All right, Porky. This really won't be hard." She paused. "Your sentence is, 'Thank you for staying to help me, Miss Clarenbessipawl.'"

Porky's face darkened, and he didn't say a word.

Bealomondore stepped in front of him, turned abruptly, and stopped. He spoke between clenched teeth. "Thank you for staying to help me, Miss Clarenbessipawl."

Porky clenched *his* teeth while still glowering at Bealomondore. With his chin still looking like a donkey's jawbone, he growled out, "Thank you for staying to help me, Miss Clarenbessipawl."

Bealomondore's face immediately melted from ice to sunshine. He thudded Porky on the shoulder, announced, "Good job," and turned to Soo-tie.

"What do you have for our brave Soo-tie, Ellie?"

Ellie smiled. "Cinder, I'm sorry you had a nosebleed, and I'm glad it stopped."

Horror washed across Soo-tie's face. "I don't care if he had a nosebleed. That's his goings-on, not mine."

Bealomondore spoke before Ellie could begin the lecture forming in her head.

He put his arm around Soo-tie's shoulders and gave a friendly squeeze. "That is one of the keys to what Miss Clarenbessipawl is talking about."

"What? What is she talking about? She talks a lot."

"This one is, 'You are going to learn to enjoy life. You will find it is good instead of bad, fun instead of boring, and safe instead of dangerous.'"

"Huh?"

"You can't enjoy life unless you can see good, have fun, and be safe. First key! Are you ready for it?"

Soo-tie looked skeptical, but she didn't say anything to stop Bealomondore. Ellie wondered what the key would be.

"You are not alone," he announced. "First key is that you do not live without others. First key is that you are blessed with people around you. First key is that you are not alone."

Soo-tie stopped in the street. Bealomondore stopped as well, and so did the other three.

"Look around you, Soo-tie," Bealomondore instructed her as he slowly turned her in a circle. "Who do you see?"

"You, her, Porky, and Cinder."

"Excellent. Now you must realize that it is good that you are not alone. What would it be like if none of the other children were here?"

Porky wiggled in Ellie's grasp. "She'd get more to eat at noonmeal."

Bealomondore threw a comment over his shoulder. "There probably would not be enough for others if she were the only one."

"Oh," said Porky with a distinct air of disappointment.

Bealomondore turned back to the girl and his point. "What if there were no children here but you, Soo-tie? No one to talk to, no one to run with, no one during the night when it's dark."

He waited. Ellie leaned forward, anticipating the girl's response.

Bealomondore asked, "Would that be good?"

Soo-tie shook her head.

"You are so right, Soo-tie. Having people around is a good thing. Because you are smart, you can see that the other children being here is a good thing."

They started down the street again.

"I can have fun all by myself," she pointed out.

"Yes, but it is the law of the universe, Soo-tie, that some things are more fun when done with others. You can't dispute that. On occasion, the addition of more players multiplies the fun."

She nodded vaguely. Ellie figured she'd have to think that one over for a while. Soo-tie probably couldn't add or subtract, let alone multiply. However, Bealomondore's grand way of explaining ideas made them sound acceptable.

Soo-tie looked with big, wondering eyes at Bealomondore. "The others make me safe?"

Ellie answered. "When all of you learn manners, you will be safe. Because manners are the demonstration of respect for one another. Respect for one another grows courage. Respect sprouts determination to preserve what is good. Respect builds love and compassion."

Three sets of eyes again turned to Bealomondore.

"She's saying that manners help you be good, and when you're good, others tend to be good too, and pretty soon you will all be good to one another except when you make mistakes. Then one of you will choose to be good about the mistake, and that starts everyone being good again."

Porky looked very doubtful. "And all of this good is not boring?"

"Not boring at all," Bealomondore reassured him.

Porky hunched his shoulders and let them drop. "We'll see. I'm not sure manners are going to be fun."

"Me neither," said Cinder.

"I bet we miss noonmeal," said Porky.

Ellie sighed. Bealomondore winked at her.

He pointed. "There's the apothecary."

# 29

# Snips and Snails

Ellie used her fingertips to brush Porky's hair out of his eyes. "Now keep your hands away from the wound. Don't pick. Don't scratch. The sticking plaster will keep the sides of the cut together until Laddin can heal it tomorrow."

Porky reached for the plaster on his head. "Who's Laddin?"

Ellie batted his hand away. "A dragon of the watch."

"A real dragon?" Soo-tie asked.

Bealomondore looked over his shoulder at the three children. His attention had been on the rows and rows of small medicine bottles. "Yes, a real minor dragon, not a bird."

"Fairy tales," said Soo-tie.

Porky squinted a glare at Bealomondore. "We know about fairy tales."

Ellie put a hand under Porky's chin and turned his face back to look at her. "What do you know about fairy tales?"

Cinder balanced on one foot with his arms sticking out. "They aren't true."

Soo-tie plopped down on the floor. "Pepper used to tell fairy tales every night."

Ellie thought Soo-tie sounded sad. "She doesn't anymore?"

"*He* doesn't anymore."

"He's gone," said Porky.

Ellie almost asked where he'd gone and then realized that the child must have died. She busied herself cleaning up the bits and pieces left over from plastering Porky's cut.

"When did he leave?" asked Bealomondore.

Three little bodies gave three shrugs.

"A week ago," said Cinder.

"Nah," said Porky. "Longer. Two weeks ago."

Ellie and Bealomondore looked to Soo-tie for a comment. She shrugged again, perhaps with a little more vigor than the first time.

Ellie knew fairy tales as well. Maybe some of them might be ones these children recognized. "Do you remember any of the names of the fairy tales?"

Soo-tie nodded, and her face lit up. " 'Rando and the Blue Fan.' 'Koomee-Kootah.' 'The Hill on the Mountain.' 'Five Little Brothers.' "

Porky bounced on the stool he sat upon. " 'Seven Tin Cups.' "

" 'Nine Days of Trouble,' " sang Cinder.

"I'm afraid I don't know any of those." Ellie looked at Bealomondore. "Do you?"

He shook his head.

"Can we go now?" asked Porky. "It's awful close to noonmeal."

"Yes," said Ellie, "but meet us here tomorrow."

They charged out the front door, leaving Ellie and Bealomondore to examine the contents of the shelves, taking note of things they might need in the future.

Ellie held up a squat green jar. "Here's some ointment for Old One's sore knees."

"Look at this shelf."

Ellie came to stand beside Bealomondore. "Bug pills?"

Bealomondore grinned and picked up one that read "Powdered

Eggstram Snails." He shook it, held it up to the light, and turned the bottle to see how much it contained.

"What are Eggstram Snails good for?" asked Ellie.

"Temper tantrums in toddlers, anxiety in adults."

"I think I'd throw a temper tantrum if you suggested I consume that powder."

"You put it in a beverage, and you can hardly taste it."

Ellie examined his expression to see if he might be pulling her leg. "*You've* tried it?"

"Yes, for fear of heights."

"You don't seem to be afflicted with any fears. You climbed up to get my blouse this morning. That drainpipe didn't look safe to me, but you didn't seem to have any qualms."

"I'm talking about significantly higher heights."

She arched her eyebrows at him. Surely he was baiting her to have her plead for more complete information. She wouldn't beg.

His manner charmed her, but his words brought her back to old suspicions. "I never got the hang of riding on a dragon. I get airsickness."

Ellie's trust wavered. In spite of the mischievous gleam in his eye, the look on her fellow tumanhofer's face registered as sincere. Either she was the most gullible of country misses, or he told the truth. She decided his telling the truth was more acceptable to her all the way around.

She held up the ointment jar and turned it back and forth. "Let's take the ointment back to Old One and check on making more daggarts."

"More daggarts? Ellie, I hate to tell you this, but I don't think the daggart strategy is working."

"We'll work out a system. We're smarter than the average six-year-old."

"These children have practiced being six for centuries. The only thing I'm sure of is that we run faster." He put the bottle of snail powder in his pocket. "They have more stamina, but we are more strategic in evading them."

"Just listen to you," Ellie scoffed. "You sound like the children are an enemy and you're making plans for battle."

"I have to admit that I do think of them in terms of minimizing losses during an engagement."

He held up a hand to ward off her protests. "The assumption may be the aftereffects of spending a lot of the last two years in the service of our king, defending Chiril."

"Our community wasn't much affected by the war. Some of our neighbors experienced odd shifts in attitude. My brothers became extra feisty, Gramps was morose, my sisters and I lacked the energy to do our chores."

"That strange malady of soul struck all over Chiril. The three statues being out of alignment caused the personality disorders. The invading army took advantage of our weakness, but they didn't trigger the disruptive behavior."

They walked back to the library and joined Tak in the library park. The goat jumped and skittered and playfully head-butted the tumanhofers.

"He sure is glad to see us," said Bealomondore.

"He's definitely a people goat."

"How's that?"

"He prefers to be with people more than with other goats. I hand-fed him as a kid, and I think he assumes he is more tumanhofer than goat."

Bealomondore gave Tak a vigorous back scratch. "He is unquestionably intelligent."

Ellie frowned. "He acted more like a goat at home. He liked to be around people, but he didn't interfere with what I had to do. There have been times since we came into the bottle... He's directed me."

She didn't want Bealomondore to think she was tetched, so she hedged her statement. "Sort of, you know. Not really, but kind of."

Bealomondore laughed out loud. Ellie crossed her arms over her chest and thrust her chin out.

He stifled his laughter. "Since I met Tipper Schope and, through her, Verrin Schope, Lady Peg, Wizard Fenworth, and Librettowit..." He chuckled. "Well, things have not been what they seem, 'sort of, not really, but kind of.' I know exactly how you feel. Any time a wizard is involved, reality slips and slides and has a hard time staying steady."

"And that's the magic at work?"

"No, no, wizards, good wizards, don't delve into magic."

"But—"

"Wizards like Verrin Schope and Fenworth spend years developing an intimate knowledge of how Wulder organizes the universe. Then they facilitate His order without going out of the boundaries of His regulation."

"If that's what good wizards are doing, what are bad wizards doing?"

He pulled her into his arms and swung her around, then kissed her.

She protested halfheartedly. "What was that for?"

"For asking intelligent questions and for believing I have the answers."

"Kissing me is a fine distraction, but I haven't forgotten the question." He stood smiling at her until she felt the urge to prod him back to the conversation. "So what do bad wizards do?"

"First, what they do, they do with dreadful motives. A core of self-ishness colors all their actions. Good wizards desire to serve. Bad wiz-ards desire power to make others subservient to them. Good wizards improve the situations of others. Bad wizards improve their own situ-ations without regard for whom it may hinder or harm."

Old One's roar from the library startled them. They turned as one to learn what caused the commotion. The urohm stood at an open win-dow at the very top of the building, his face red and his white hair streamed around his head as if tousled by a strong wind. The calm air in the garden chilled Ellie.

"Come. I need your help," he called. "Hurry! There's more than ever before!"

Bealomondore, Ellie, and Tak all ran for the gate, then down the short walkway to the back entrance. Tak led the way and clambered up the grating with no help. Ellie followed, with Bealomondore giving her a hand.

Old One's bellows reverberated through the library. By the time Ellie and Bealomondore ran into the rotunda, Tak was bounding up the last few steps of the stairs to the second floor.

He stood at the top, complaining loudly and stamping his feet. His eyes focused on the second staircase. The tumanhofers on the ground floor could not see what he saw. With a final long blast of objection, Tak turned and plunged down the way he had come. The tramping of heavy footsteps announced Old One's rapid descent.

A swarm of fist-sized, black batlike creatures poured from the upper floor and chased the goat.

Bealomondore drew his sword. "Take cover," he ordered Ellie. She ran to the vestibule, snatched an umbrella out of the umbrella stand, and came back to his side.

Tak rushed past them, and they began to swing at the throng of black beasts that followed. Orli appeared among the cloud. He spat at the opponents. Once hit, the animal would squeal and fall to the ground. Ellie quit batting at the air for fear of hitting the white dragon. She backed up a little and surveyed the scene.

Old One collapsed halfway down the last staircase. A cloud of creatures attacked him. He made an effort to bat them away, but put up little fight. She dodged through the melee and scrambled up the oversize steps as quickly as she could. Once beside Old One, she grabbed at the beasts with her bare hands. Their soft, scaly bodies crumpled in her clasp, and she dropped the dead creatures as quickly as she picked them off his body.

Two of the horrid creatures swooped in and grabbed her hair, instantly tangled in her locks. She screamed and struck them with frantic slaps. As soon as one fell away, more swooped in to torment her.

As she struggled, Tak came to her side. He took over butting at the beasts clinging to the old urohm. The round hall quieted, and Bealomondore arrived to help. He dispatched the last live animal stuck in her hair.

He put his arm around her. "It's over. They're dead."

"Old One?"

Bealomondore reached to touch the urohm's neck. "He's alive. Some nasty bites." Examining her arms and legs and face, he asked, "You? Are you hurt?"

She put her hand to her head and grasped a dead creature still tangled in her hair.

"Get it out," she cried. "Oh, Bealomondore, get it out!"

She covered her face as he worked to free not only the one she'd discovered but two more. As he worked at the frustrating task, she sobbed. "Cut it out. Cut my hair."

"Now, Ellie." He sounded more stressed than reassuring. "Ellie, we're all right. This will just take a moment. One left."

When he threw the last one down, she turned into his embrace and allowed him to cradle her as she cried.

"Pull yourself together, love. We have to see to Old One, Tak, and Orli." She lifted her head and made herself look. Old One lay where he had fallen, covered with red wounds no bigger than the end of her thumb. Tak had doubled up his legs, fallen on the step, and lay with his head extended before him, eyes closed. On the floor of the rotunda, still, lifeless black bodies surrounded an unmoving Orli.

Ellie jumped to see to Tak. Bealomondore moved to examine Old One.

"Tak," she whispered.

His eyes slitted open. A weak "maa" answered her. His eyes closed again. She ran a hand over his white coat. Tiny red spots of blood exposed the many bites he'd suffered. She only had a few scratches. She looked at Bealomondore. He had no visible bites. Apparently, the creatures did not like the taste of tumanhofer blood.

# 30

# A Goal, No Two

Bealomondore swept dead bodies into a pile. He had no idea what these black creatures were called or where they came from. Old One was still sprawled on the steps. Bealomondore and Ellie could not move him. They'd cleaned his wounds and applied an ointment they thought would help. Then they had worked on Tak, who had numerous bites but didn't seem to be as afflicted as the urohm.

Now Ellie soothed Orli, his spots less significant than the goat's. Clearly the minor dragon suffered from nerves, so Ellie sat cross-legged on the floor, humming to Orli, with Tak tucked up next to her.

She interrupted her tune. "Bealomondore?"

"Yes?"

"We must figure out a way to signal the watch when we need them immediately."

"If Orli felt brave enough to venture forth, he could locate them quickly."

"Well, he doesn't right now." She drew him closer. "And I don't blame him. That was a nasty attack. And I suppose it was unprovoked. I can't imagine Old One or Orli inciting such furor."

Bealomondore took his broom with him as he struggled up the steps to check on Old One again. He knelt beside his head and felt the pulse in his throat.

"The same." He answered Ellie's question before she asked. "I agree.

I'd be more comfortable if we could summon the watch. Surely there was a system in place years ago."

Ellie picked up his theory and continued. "And everyone's forgotten how to use it or even what it was for." She went on with her own train of thought. "I don't think it's useful for the dragons of the watch to do daily rounds of the city. Obviously nothing is out there to cause harm."

"Perhaps these little black monsters attack the city." Bealomondore sat on the step next to Old One's shoulder. "I'll ask Det and Laddin about the duties they need to perform and what they encounter on these tours."

He eased himself down to the next step and swept away the crumpled creatures. "They're disintegrating."

Ellie tilted her head and furrowed her brow. She looked at his pile. "Oh, I see. Not so much substance anymore. They're more like bits and pieces and dust." She crinkled her nose. "When I picked them off of Old One, they broke in my hand, like a crumbly biscuit."

Bealomondore didn't want her to get suddenly remorseful over slaying an enemy. He knocked the mound of coarse black powder off the step. "It's a good thing their bodies crushed on contact. There were way too many for us to defend ourselves if they'd been sturdier."

He moved down to clean up the next level. "Has Orli calmed down?" At her nod, he went on. "See if you can communicate with our dragon friend and find out what happened. Where did these things come from? Does he know what they're called?"

Bealomondore tidied two more steps before Ellie had the answers.

"Orli says that these are wusstbunters. They are thoughts from the wizard. Bad thoughts. They reflect his frustration."

"They aren't real?"

Ellie lifted one shoulder. "They are, just as the food is real, the real shoes never wear out, and the clothing's real but does not fall apart even as old as it is. Orli says the wizard sustains it all, but sometimes he gets irritated at the urohms, and then these wusstbunters escape."

He'd thought he had it all figured out, but this put a new page in the book of Rumbard City. "So Wulder is not our provider?"

"Indirectly. Wulder put the wizard in charge of the city's maintenance. The wizard was charged with establishing the new generation of urohms as followers of Wulder. The children are to be educated in the Tomes and instilled with a commitment to stand for love, mercy, and honor."

Bealomondore snorted. "Those children are to be like knights? That's what he's saying, you know. That those riotous, willful, unruly, wild, unmanageable horrors are to champion the innocent, protect the weak, right the wrongs inflicted on the lowly, and lift the humble to a better station."

He paused for a moment, unable to imagine the little beggars turning from selfishness to selflessness. He lifted his arms and let them fall again. "No wonder the wizard gets frustrated. The task given to him is impossible."

Ellie cuddled the dragon close to her neck, and he rubbed affectionately along her chin. "Orli says that we can do two things that will change the course of Rumbard City."

"Us? You and me? We're going to be pulled into this mess?"

She gave him a quizzical look. "I think you walked and I *fell* into this mess."

Bealomondore stared at the ugly white dragon enjoying Ellie's attention. He no longer looked quite so frightened and frail. Rather, he looked as if the delivery of this news had taken a lot off his mind. In

234 Donita K. Paul

fact, was he smug? relieved? pleased with himself? Bealomondore narrowed his eyes and studied the dragon. Orli gloated. That was an expression of pure gratification. The dragon had shed the responsibility
of aiding the wizard and dumped his duty on two gullible tumanhofers.

Bealomondore pointed a finger at Orli. "Ellie, mind my words.
This dragon intends for us to bring about this miracle."

"Yes, I know."

"You know? How can you know?"

"He told me."

Bealomondore tried to catch up. Didn't he just recently enlist Airon
to help her learn to mindspeak? Was the bond that sometimes caused
them to finish each other's sentences not constantly in play? How did
Ellie become more informed of the secret workings of Rumbard City
when he'd searched for months for clues? And why hadn't Orli, suddenly a fount of knowledge, come forward to tell him a thing or two
before Ellie fell into the bottle?

It wasn't her fault. He tried not to sound as irritated as he was.
"What did he tell you?"

"Old One was given the task, as the last living adult, to train the
children. But they had been too long on their own. He went out to
speak to them, decided they could not be tamed, came back into the
library, and has shunned them ever since."

"Then his assessment of the situation is very close to mine. The
whole lot of those hooligans is incorrigible. The job of civilizing them
is hopeless."

"Well, it would be, except there is a bottle of memories we can find
and unstop."

Bealomondore unclenched his jaw to speak. "I suppose that is the
first thing we can do to 'change the course of Rumbard City.'"

"Actually, that's the second. First is to gain the trust of the children and guide them toward more acceptable behavior."

Bealomondore stood in a daze, shaking his head. Ellie sounded quite ready to attempt the unattainable.

"It's what we were planning to do anyway, Bealomondore."

She sounded pleasant and determined.

He'd try to be obliging. "Yes, I recall. The amazingly successful Daggart Tactic."

"You're sounding very snide, Bealomondore. That attitude will not get us anywhere."

So much for hiding his mind-set from Miss Ellicinderpart Clarenbessipawl. He jumped off the last step, leaving the mound of disintegrating wusstbunters. He put his hands on his hips and stared at the skylight. What could he possibly do? He had the gnawing suspicion that the key to getting out of the bottle rested with the taming of this crew.

"There's one more thing, Bealomondore."

He closed his eyes. "Go ahead. Tell me."

"When we establish a sense of order among the urohm children and find the bottle of memories and open that bottle, then the bottle around the city will dissolve."

"And we'll be free to go?"

"Yes. We'll be free to go."

# 31

# Realization

After the Battle of the Wusstbunters, Ellie and Bealomondore spent hours cleaning up. The fine dust left from the wizard's uncharitable thoughts drifted with every little puff of air. The dust had a slightly unpleasant smell and caused them to sneeze, which only complicated cleaning up.

Ellie's latest attempt to gather and dispose of the black powder involved getting down on her hands and knees and using a damp cloth. The sooty residue got more and more difficult to scoop up.

She straightened, putting her hands against the small of her aching back, and glared at the smear she had just made. Ellie wanted to leave the smudge, leave the library, and move to another dwelling. Whoever heard of anyone living in a library? She and Bealomondore had seen lots of unoccupied residences in their meanderings through the town.

Of course, living where they were had many advantages. A wealth of information surrounded them. On the other hand, the size of the books meant they were not quite easily accessible. But another plus outweighed that inconvenience. Old One sometimes helped them, and because of the gruff curmudgeon, the children would not sneak in and attack. Perhaps after she and Bealomondore gained the children's trust and developed a friendship, they could move to a real house.

With a gasp, Ellie dropped her cloth on the floor, right in the middle of her latest smurpy gray spot. She stood and looked around the room. Her sudden realization colored everything she saw with a new light.

Old One had yet to move or make a noise, not even a groan or the rattling snore he produced when he fell asleep in his chair. That worried her. They needed Old One, and he needed them.

Tak had made it known he wanted to go outside. He probably felt safer in the fenced library park. With fewer, less severe bites, he had returned to normal quickly. His sores scabbed over almost as soon as she applied the salve.

Orli's numerous wounds required more attention. The beasts had viciously sunk their teeth into both Orli and Old One as if they were the main targets of the attack. Orli lay on the step next to Old One. Ellie could probe his mind enough to determine that the minor dragon suffered from discomfort but not nagging pain. She picked up his concern for the old urohm. It would be good for the watch to come in early tonight. Not only Orli and Old One needed the ministering of the minor dragons. She wanted their comforting presence, and Bealomondore probably felt the same.

She tilted her head and listened. Bealomondore hummed as he worked on the second floor. He was getting more adept at scaling steps, chairs, cabinets, and anything else that got in his way. She didn't recognize the tune, but she took comfort knowing he was close enough to call to if she needed him.

She walked slowly to the children's area, determined to make tea, sit in a comfortable chair, and think. If they lived here for a long time, she wanted to live in a home, not a library. When she envisioned moving into a house, she pictured Bealomondore and herself in one of the smaller residences along one of the quiet streets farther from the center of the city. That was wrong.

Not the house. Not the street. But the two of them setting up house together.

Ellie felt her cheeks burn.

She put water in the kettle from the tap, placed it on the heating circle on the counter. While she waited for the water to boil, she got out the teapot and teacups. Then she sat down and stared out the window at a cloudless sky. At this time of day, she could see a place in the distance where the blue shifted color and marked the boundaries of their habitat. She couldn't actually see the glass, but something different could be detected if she really concentrated.

Her mind drifted to the royal wedding and coronation ball. The excitement of such a grand celebration rippled through her calm pretense. She'd dreamed of her own wedding. In the village, among family and friends, her father would give her to some gentle and loving man. Bealomondore easily fit into the picture.

If they were to decide to marry, how could they do the ceremony part? Who would say the words that were always said? Who would ask the questions about their commitment? Her father would not be there, so who would possess her hand? Then who would take her hand from the entrusted one and place it in Bealomondore's hand? The symbolism made the ceremony special.

She squeezed her eyes shut. What was she thinking? As long as they stayed in Rumbard City, their romance was acceptable. Who would object? The children? Old One? The dragons?

But should they ever escape, she would return to the village, where marriage ceremonies were simple and sweet. He would go to Ragar, where marriage ceremonies required elegance and style.

So…if she really hoped for their eventual escape, then kissing

Bealomondore, holding his hand, leaning against his shoulder had to come to an end. No dreams about happily ever after.

She'd been raised in a no-nonsense household. If things were realistically within reach, then it was all right to try for them. But no daughter of her father would waste time, energy, and plans on something that could not possibly come to pass.

She'd almost forgotten who she was.

She opened her eyes and whispered to the empty room. "Ellicinderpart Clarenbessipawl of Glenbrooken Village—not within the village, mind you, but within walking distance if you've got the day free for such a trip.

"Ellicinderpart Clarenbessipawl, daughter of Naperkowson Clarenbessipawl and Emmademgotton Clarenbessipawl. Oldest sister in a brood of eight, trained in such practical things as cooking and sewing. Knows enough herb lore to cure most common ailments. Has enough experience to tend most needs of the animals on the farm. Shows a green thumb in the garden and a white thumb in the kitchen.

"No one will go hungry, have an illness ignored, nor suffer the discomfort of an unregulated home with Ellicinderpart Clarenbessipawl as woman in charge.

"And that is who I am, and I am content to be that person here in Rumbard City, back home with Da and Ma, or visiting Ragar during festive times." She quoted the stitched sampler on her family's wall, " 'A person who knows who she is, is comfortable being who she is, in any place she is.' "

She slapped her hands against her knees, stood, and strode to the kettle. She'd hidden a few daggarts from Bealomondore and Old One, saving them. Now would be a good time to share the sweets.

Grabbing a potholder, she lifted the partially filled kettle and poured hot water into the teapot. She lowered the tea infuser in and hooked it on the rim, then set the lid on while it steeped.

Retrieving the daggarts required pulling a chair over to a cabinet. She climbed up and opened both doors at once. A cloud of wusstbunters flew in her face. She screamed, lost her balance and fell to the floor. Lying on her back, she covered her face, but the swarm ignored her and flew through the children's area, headed for the rotunda.

Ellie yelled, "Bealomondore!" She scrambled to her feet and ran after the wusstbunters. "Bealomondore! They're coming! More coming!"

She entered the round hall and saw that the beasts had covered Old One and Orli as they lay on the steps. She couldn't see either of them, but their outline showed in the contour of the blanket of biting wusstbunters.

Bealomondore appeared at the top of the staircase, took off his coat, and hurried down, jumping from step to step. He swung his coat as if beating a blazing fire. She grabbed the broom, struggled up the stairs, and began thrashing the nasty creatures. As in the first encounter, each blow dispatched one or more of the wusstbunters. The creatures never turned to defend themselves against Bealomondore and Ellie.

Ellie's arms grew tired, and the broom seemed heavier with each swing, but finally none of the wusstbunters remained alive.

Ellie collapsed next to Old One and brushed the black bodies off. "Oh, Bealomondore, look!" She touched Old One's face in one of the few places not raw from bites. "If Laddin doesn't come soon, I don't think he'll survive."

"I'll go get warm water, clean rags, and the ointment."

She sniffed, trying not to cry. "Can you hear me, Old One? Please, hold on. Laddin and the others should be home soon. The sun is low-ering in the west. Please, please hold on."

Bealomondore returned, and together they bathed Old One's hands and face.

Ellie pointed to his legs. "His trousers are torn. We'd better check for bites under his clothing."

Lifting the ragged, bloodstained shirt, Bealomondore grimaced. "I'm going to cut away his shirt so we can reach more of his wounds. Those monsters ripped his skin to shreds."

Ellie gulped back a sob and could only nod. The urohm had been crotchety from the outset, but she'd grown fond of him. He reminded her of Gramps on the days when his old bones kept telling him he'd passed his prime.

Gramps had a bit more humor in how he faced the trials of a fail-ing body, but Ellie saw the same type of normal concerns in this old man. He just didn't handle it as well. If Gramps could have befriended him, Old One might have had a better attitude.

But what did it matter now? She wanted him to open his eyes, give her a scowl, and gripe about anything and everything.

Bealomondore reached across Old One and patted her arm. "Can you see to Orli?"

She nodded and picked up a fresh rag. She dipped it in the warm water and began bathing Orli's battered body.

A tingle in her ears made her lift her head. "They're coming, Bealomondore."

"I know. I just heard Det and Laddin. I've told them to hurry."

She realized that with Bealomondore close by, she heard the dragon's mindspeaking much clearer. Their odd mixture of words and pictures communicated dismay over the attacks. She soon heard their approach, leathery wings flapping at great speed. She leaned back.

Laddin landed on Old One's chest. The minor dragon turned in a tight circle then moved slowly down the old man's legs and up again. He did another check of the abdomen and chest with that measured circle, then he went to the head and spent a moment studying the extent of damage done there.

He settled across the old man's forehead.

"We can help," said Bealomondore. "Place Orli on Old One's chest. Take my hand as I rest it on Orli, and with your other hand, touch both Laddin and the urohm. The healing energy will multiply as it flows through Laddin, you, me, Orli, and Old One."

Ellie followed his instructions. Bealomondore placed his right hand over Laddin and Old One's temple. His left hand held hers and rested on Orli.

"Relax," said Bealomondore. "You aren't required to know what to do. You only have to allow the energy to pass through. Laddin does the healing. He knows what to concentrate on."

"What will he do?" she whispered.

"Ease Old One's breathing, repair the torn tissue to stop the bleeding, and help any traumatized organs. He'll do the same for Orli."

She shook her head, trying to clear her mind and take in Bealomondore's explanation.

He smiled at her. "You may understand some of what Laddin is doing as you experience it, but our role is to provide support. Laddin will coax Old One's body to return to the functions Wulder has ordained. Take deep, slow breaths. Close your eyes. Allow Laddin to work. Allow Wulder's presence to strengthen Old One while He guides Laddin."

What if she did something wrong and interfered with Laddin's work? But the bond with Bealomondore eased her worries. She found herself relaxing. At first she felt a slight buzz in her hands. Gradually the sensation smoothed out to a soothing hum and extended up her right arm and down her left. She shifted to recline in a more comfortable position.

How long would this take? It didn't feel like work but was tiring nonetheless. Memories of fields of spring wildflowers came to her mind. She heard old man Lemeterndern's mellow fiddle as he played at a gathering in the village. She smelled and tasted her mother's lemon cake. Scenes of peace and contentment drifted through her mind.

She sighed and wondered at the warmth that radiated among those providing the healing circle. Each entity in the ring produced a thread of energy that flowed with the others much like strands in a piece of yarn. They merged to make one stream. She could identify her own and Bealomondore's. Soon she identified the two dragons' energy lines. Old One's thin thread barely pulsed. Once she felt it, she didn't lose it again, even when the stronger, warmer, brighter, unidentified stream entered the flow.

She laid her head on Old One's shoulder. Totally relaxed, she allowed the coursing stream to fill her as it passed through. Joining energy felt natural, and she didn't want the experience to end.

The last thread, the strongest thread—who generated that beautiful peace? The answer came, and she could not tell if Bealomondore had whispered the name in her mind or if the last entity had spoken. Somehow, as soon as she was told, she knew that was what she had expected.

Wulder, Bealomondore's Wulder, had joined them. But not Bealomondore's Wulder. Ellie now knew Wulder in her own way. And she knew she would recognize Him anywhere. He was *her* Wulder. No, still not quite right. *She* was Wulder's.

She had a vision of a strong young man writing her name on a huge banner. He stood back and admired the cloth sign as it hung in the sky on nothing. A breeze fluttered it like a flag. The young man, Wulder, gathered the banner, then wrapped it around His body. The sign bearing her name became one with the robe He wore. She could no longer distinguish it from the material of His clothing. She would never be able to pull the two weavings into what they had been, a robe and a banner. No one else would be able to separate them. She was safe.

Wulder not only accepted her, but chose her and gave her a purpose. She believed He had more to tell her, to show her, and she wanted to learn it all. He turned and faced her. No words came from His mouth, and still she heard His gentle command.

"Rest."

She drifted away from the comforting image and into a pleasant sleep.

# 32

# Morning Revelations

Ellie opened her eyes and realized that someone had put her to bed. She still wore the clothes she'd had on yesterday. Her stomach growled, and she squinted at the window. Morning sun! No wonder she was hungry. She jumped up, pushed her fingers through her unruly hair, and ran to the rotunda. Old One sat in his chair with a tray on his lap.

He frowned at her. "You needn't look so surprised."

"Oh, I'm so glad you're better." She rushed forward and hugged what she could reach, her arms surrounding his leg and her head resting against his knee. Her forehead bumped his breakfast tray.

"Get off! Get off!"

She grinned at his gruff voice and backed away. "You look so much better. I was afraid you were going to die."

"I can't die until it is time to open the bottle."

"Which bottle?"

"The wizard's bottle."

"I think both bottles are of the wizard's making."

Old One's face creased into an even more fearsome scowl. "I don't remember the details of the bottles. One was small and the other surrounds the city."

Ellie sat on a stack of books. "Yes, that's right. One holds the memories of all the people outside the bottle, the ones who came to the city to see what the urohms had built."

"I remember that time. The city was glorious. Bree Dan had the hull of the ship packed with art and instruments and books. He brought an ample supply of material, not only for clothing but also for constructing the fine furniture we'd left at home." His face softened, and he sipped his tea. "Urohms are master carpenters and inventors of all sorts of machines, things that save time and effort and money."

Ellie arched her eyebrows but tried to make her voice soft, not accusing. "Isn't that what got you in trouble with the wizard?"

Old One's teacup clattered against the saucer as he put it down. "Utter nonsense! Wulder was never displeased with our cleverness. He encourages innovation. He takes delight in the work of our hands as we master different aspects of His world. The wizard should know that. After all, the wizards get the power to do incredible feats through knowledge of how Wulder has established the universe. A good wizard only manipulates what Wulder has already given. Their first rule is 'Do Not Destroy.'"

Old One stuck out his lower lip.

"Did you think of something sad?" asked Ellie.

"Disappointing."

"But you remembered something, and that's good."

"It's easier to remember things from long ago. Harder to keep track of yesterday and the day before."

Ellie watched his face and saw confusion as he tried to remember something. The confusion gave way to frustration, and she wondered how to distract him. A question had been on her mind since she first met him. She used her gentlest voice. "Why can't you remember your name?"

"You are a clever one. It's from long ago. You'd think I could remember. It would make more sense if I could." He closed his eyes and tilted his head back. He breathed deeply several times, then let his chin drop and reopened his eyes. "It's no use. I can't grab it from the pesky thoughts that flitter in no pattern around my tired brain. I think the wizard took my name from me."

"I bet Orli knows what it is."

Old One made a growling noise in his throat. "He's not allowed to tell me. If he does, the wizard will take him away, and I'll have no one."

"I think there's a good chance that Bealomondore and I will be around for a while."

"Of course you will. Can't get out, can you?" He chuckled.

She gritted her teeth at his smugness. Did Old One still have enough reasoning to deliberately keep them from discovering the clues that would lead to their escape? She couldn't blame him for wanting company, although he never played the part of gracious host. But she had places to go and a coronation to attend and a wedding to see.

She didn't want to spend the rest of her days bottled up in Rumbard City. If she couldn't marry Bealomondore, she didn't want to be continually tempted by their romantic relationship. The man was the most charming she'd ever met. He made her toes curl when he kissed her.

She wanted out!

Fleeing the emotions that confused her, she sought another subject. "Is Orli better this morning?"

"He went with Bealomondore and several of the other dragons to fetch breakfast."

"Didn't it arrive upstairs for you to bring down?"

Old One glared at her. "I've suffered a trauma to my system. It was all I could do to bring myself down. Bealomondore made tea."

Ellie shivered at the thought of the black beasts. "Have you ever seen those wusstbunter things before?"

"Of course I have. The wizard thinks them."

"He must be a very disagreeable wizard."

"No, he's ordinary."

Ellie felt her eyes widen. "An ordinary wizard? I shouldn't think those two words go together."

"I mean he's like most wizards. Bent on doing what pleases Wulder, but weak enough to fall into doing exactly what doesn't please Wulder."

"But sending those wusstbunters is evil."

"He doesn't send them. Not on purpose anyway."

"I guess you're going to have to give me more information."

Old One's face sagged, and he looked incredibly sad. Again, Ellie came close to hug his leg, carefully avoiding bumping the tray this time.

"You wouldn't believe it now," said Old One, "but I used to be quite a talker. Too many years alone, I guess. Too much confusion in my brain." He sighed. "I'll try."

"I appreciate it."

"Bree Dan crossed the wizard, determined to do things his own way. At the time, I was caught up in the plans and didn't weigh the consequences of our actions. You see, the wizard's plan was actually Wulder's plan. So by tossing aside what the wizard told us to do, we tossed away what Wulder had ordained. That's a pretty serious act of disobedience. But we didn't see it, although all of us knew better. We made plans, and we rushed forward."

"I don't know much about Wulder." Knowing the urohms had a great reverence for Wulder, Ellie watched Old One's face to see if that admission bothered him. He appeared not to be disturbed by her confession, so she continued. "Last night, when we did the healing circle with Laddin, I felt His presence, and I don't ever want to be too far from that feeling. I want to learn more about Him. What I did come to know in that brief encounter is that Wulder is good, not someone to be afraid of."

"He is good. In fact, in the Tomes, it is said that there is no hint of darkness in Him. He casts away evil." Old One nodded his head, seemingly lost in thought.

Ellie was about to suggest that she find Bealomondore when the urohm spoke again.

"Wulder doesn't have a temper so much as a clear-cut sense of right and wrong. When something is wrong, He will do what is necessary to make it right."

"Like what?"

Old One was silent. Ellie waited, wondering if he would continue with his explanation. He picked up his cup.

"My tea is cold."

"Do you want me to get you some more?"

"No. If you go away, I may forget what it is that I have to tell you." He grabbed the tray and twisted to set it down on the table at his elbow. "Come sit on the arm of the chair."

He helped her get situated before continuing.

"Have you ever taken care of a baby?" he asked.

Ellie rolled her eyes. "I am the oldest of eight. I've taken care of lots of babies."

"Suppose you came to the cradle and found a dozen snakes in with the babe. What would you do?"

"I'd scream and pull them out. I'd probably stomp on them or whack them with something."

Old One nodded. "Only the venom would hurt the baby. Why kill the snakes?"

"The snakes carry the poison. The baby could be killed."

He nodded again. "The horror you feel toward the snakes is something like the horror Wulder feels when evil threatens His good creation. Sometimes He acts swiftly, and sometimes He allows time to pass as the situation unfolds. With His great wisdom, He knows which method is best in each circumstance."

"I think I understand what you're telling me, but I am not sure how it relates to the wizard's wusstbunters."

"Is that what we were talking about?"

"Yes."

"I'm afraid I don't remember."

"You said that the wizard is not evil but ordinary and that he doesn't really send the wusstbunters to harm you."

"No, he doesn't."

Ellie fought down her impatience. "Then why do they come?"

Old One looked her in the eye. "Have you ever said something that you wouldn't have said if you'd thought about it before you opened your mouth?"

She nodded. "Oh yes, plenty of times."

"But you're learning to control your tongue?"

"It's hard."

"Yes, I agree. But we can clamp our lips together and forbid the uncharitable words to come forth."

"Some people are better at that than others. Gramps would never say a hurtful thing. Ma rarely does. But Da not only says it, he says it loud and clear." She made a face. "I used to speak way too often when I should have been quiet. I'm learning."

"Consider the callous words you think. For the wizard, it does not matter if he immediately regrets his unsympathetic thoughts. They become the wusstbunters, and they take the first opportunity to attack the subject of the wizard's displeasure."

"Oh my." Ellie took a moment to think of the many times she'd had cruel thoughts about her siblings. "None of my brothers or sisters would be alive today if wusstbunters flew from my mind."

A fluttering noise caught their attention, and they both turned toward the back of the library. The dragons of the watch came into sight first, then Bealomondore and Tak. Orli flew to the armrest and perched next to Ellie.

She placed a hand on Orli's back. "How do you feel?"

The answer came rapidly, and she had to concentrate to catch it all. The minor dragon had physically recovered, but emotionally, he was all atwitter. He told her his spiritual being had been assaulted and only because of his own negligence. He'd allowed Wulder to slip into a corner of his life where He was seldom thought of and seldom consulted.

The minor dragon reasoned that since he'd blocked out Wulder, Wulder wasn't paying attention. With Wulder removed from the picture, then he, a lowly minor dragon, was in charge. The overwhelming weight of such responsibility had disabled him completely, befoozled him. He was paralyzed in a state of constant dither. He'd ignored his duties to the children and Old One. And humiliation had engulfed him, so he'd refused to tell all he knew to the newcomers.

"We're the newcomers?"

With his eyes turned away, his shoulders signaling shame, and his head hanging so low that his chin touched his chest when he nodded, he looked so much like one of the high races, like one of her brothers when he'd been naughty, that she almost laughed.

"So what do you need to tell us?"

A rush of images almost knocked Ellie off her seat on the arm of Old One's chair.

Dark tunnels. A key. Hidden closets. Bottles. A book bound in purple leather. A key. A gate. Dirty children. A sleeping wizard. Glass walls dissolving. A huge city decorated with colorful bunting. A key.

Ellie held her breath, but Bealomondore spoke, "You know the way out."

# 33

# Tuck

Orli's denial came swiftly, too swiftly for Ellie to understand his torrent of explanations. Bealomondore slowed him down with a series of questions.

"The key?"

*"Opens door. Many keys, one door."*

"The tunnels?"

*"Under city. Always been there. Old, very old."*

Bealomondore and Ellie looked at each other and said in unison, "The lost city of Tuck."

"What's this?" asked Old One. "I've never heard of any lost city."

Bealomondore turned his attention away from the frantic minor dragon and addressed the old urohm. "Tuck is a legend, but many believe the legend is based on fact. Tumanhofers lived underground centuries ago. They built entire cities with elaborate tunnels and snug dens carved into the earth. Most were close to the surface and, once abandoned, collapsed, making odd valleys in the landscape. But the lost city of Tuck is said to remain intact. The underground tumanhofer city was not so deep in the earth, so it did not have tons of dirt weighing down on the ceilings. And rock walls supported everything."

Orli forced his mindspeaking into the conversation, interrupting Old One.

*"Yes, yes! Homes, tunnels, lightrocks."* He bounced.

Ellie had never seen the minor dragon so excited. His usual calm made the other minor dragons seem exuberant. Some of them now wore befuddled expressions as they stared at Orli.

"Do we need the keys to get into the tunnels?"

Orli drooped, his previous enthusiasm zapped by the question.

Again, Bealomondore and Ellie responded with the same words. "Don't worry. We'll find it."

Ellie's head hurt. She'd been straining to get as much information as possible out of the dragons of the watch. The glimpses of their thoughts in pictures and the garbled string of words came at a rapid tempo. Bealomondore's talent for mindspeaking shored up hers, but even with that boost, she deciphered little.

The colorful dragons perched in no particular order all around the rotunda—some in trees, some on shelves, one on a cushion on the floor, and the rest on tables. Not only did they all mindspeak at once, but they also battered her from many different directions.

Old One snored softly from his chair, a book open in his lap. Tak, too, ignored the fuss.

Ellie would have liked a nap, a rest, anything to get away from this mental bombardment. She glanced at her tumanhofer friend. Lines marred his forehead, showing concentration. He looked up, and an idea formed between them. They needed a break.

Bealomondore held up a hand and stood. "We need to meet some children who were hurt yesterday."

The clamor in Ellie's mind abruptly ceased. Most of the dragons tilted their heads, waiting for more explanation.

Ellie eagerly reported the progress they'd made. "We were able to talk with three children yesterday. Soo-tie, Cinder, and Porky went with us to the apothecary shop. Laddin, would you go with us to heal their scrapes and bruises? I kept a few daggarts for our tea, but I promised the children I would bring them more. We'll deliver those too."

Bealomondore put a hand on her shoulder.

"Before we go, we should ask some questions of the watch and see if we can figure out a system whereby we can communicate during a crisis."

Ellie beamed at Bealomondore. He'd remembered when she'd forgotten.

She turned a serious face to the gathering of the watch. "Several times we've needed you. Would one of you be able to locate the others in an emergency?" She felt the consensus among the dragons. They were capable of the task but hesitant for some reason. She plowed on. "Could you arrange for at least one of you to be with us at all times?

Silent tension spread across the rotunda. Ellie turned to Bealomondore. *What's wrong?*

"*I'm not sure.*" He studied the eight dragons for a moment. "*I think they're having a conference, deciding what to do.*"

*Do you hear them?*

"*Not really, just a hum.*"

*Can't you ask Det or Laddin what's going on?*

"*They aren't open to my mindspeaking. It would seem that there is some watch protocol that we have abused.*"

Old One snorted, and Ellie jumped. Still sound asleep, he wagged his head back and forth, mumbled, then settled down again.

At that moment the giant of a man reminded her of her somewhat

scrawny Gramps. "I don't like leaving him alone with those wusstbunters showing up."

The minor dragons flew into the air, circled the huge round skylight, then came to rest in a line across one table.

Orli addressed them, and Ellie knew Bealomondore heard the same
words and received the same pictures.

As newly appointed leader, he would negotiate the duties. The others had chosen him because he was the oldest, and if they were to go
somewhere dark, he would already be in the lead since he was the only
one who glowed.

Both Bealomondore and Ellie thought the reasoning behind the
choice amusing, but they refrained from laughing. Ellie refused to look
at her friend lest she giggle.

Orli stated that the number of the patrol watch would be reduced
to four, the chosen minor dragons touring an established part of the
city. They had marked off each territory roughly, according to the points
of the compass.

Laddin would stay with the tumanhofers. Orli would stay with
Old One. The two remaining dragons would pursue information about
Tuck and the keys and any means of escape.

Orli finished his announcement with pictures of gloom. He did
not think the extra activity would yield any results. They would all live
in Rumbard City until the end of their days.

Soosahn hobbled across the table, imitating a very old man walking. He tottered on his rear legs and even held one front leg out as if he
used a cane. His yellow and orange scales flashed in the sun. Laughter
filled Ellie's head.

With her eyes opened wide, she looked at Bealomondore for confirmation. *Am I hearing the minor dragons laugh?*

*"Yes, isn't it a merry sound?"*

She giggled, then laughed out loud.

She heard Orli's admonition not to wake Old One. He needed his naps.

Bealomondore took her arm and guided her out of the rotunda and to the children's area. They packed a few daggarts in a cloth bag and went outside, followed by seven dragons and a goat.

# 34

# Birth Day

Laddin flew ahead of Ellie and Bealomondore as they made their way to the apothecary shop. Tak tagged along, examining flower boxes and piles of debris along the way.

"Someone cleans up," said Bealomondore.

Ellie surveyed the street. "They don't do a very thorough job."

"Consider how long it has been since adults were in charge. The accumulated trash is minimal."

"Maa." Tak had stopped beside a mixed pile of leaves, paper, and cloth. He looked at Ellie, then lowered his head to nose through the mess.

Bealomondore changed directions to investigate. "What did you find, Tak?"

The goat caught hold of something in his mouth and pulled it out of the pile.

Ellie gasped. "Oh! My snood. I've never gotten to wear it. I've never had a snood before. I've never even worn one."

Tak brought her the intricately netted bag that would have adorned her hair on special occasions. She would have worn it with her day dress when she and her aunt did the promenade. Tak carried it in his teeth and gave it up readily when she reached for it.

She turned it over in her hands. "There are only a few little snags. I can mend it."

She remembered sitting in front of Aunt Tiffenbeth's vanity the night before their travels began. Her aunt had gathered up Ellie's long, curly tresses and captured them inside the snood. She'd then secured the elegant bag with many hairpins. The mirror reflected the image of a cultured young lady.

Tears welled up in Ellie's eyes. "Bealomondore, do you think the wedding has already taken place? How many days have I been here?"

"Two weeks tomorrow."

Ellie sat down on the curb and sobbed, burying her face in the crumpled snood.

Bealomondore sat beside her and put a comforting arm around her shoulders. "What is it? What's wrong?"

She stifled her crying and said, "It was only ten days"—she gulped down another sob—"until the wedding and coronation"—she pulled in quick breaths and hiccupped—"when I fell through the glass wall."

He patted her with one hand and dug in his pockets for a handkerchief with the other. She took the offered hanky and blew her nose. Sitting close to Bealomondore lessened the disappointment of missing the only coronation and royal wedding that was likely to happen in her lifetime. But his sympathy reminded her how excruciatingly nice he was and how totally unsuitable she was to be his wife. She cried some more.

"Hey!" A child's voice penetrated her despair. He repeated the trumpeted whisper. "Hey! You gotta get out of the street. Yawn and his gang are looking for you."

Ellie sniffed and wiped her nose on the white handkerchief, then scoured their surroundings. She spotted Porky.

He waved. "Did you bring those daggarts?"

She nodded.

He gestured with his hand impatiently. "Well, come on then. The others are waiting in the apothecary."

Tak butted her from behind, and Bealomondore helped her to her feet. She sniffed one last time and used her sleeve to wipe tears from her cheeks. Porky had already disappeared. Bealomondore offered his arm, which she took in exchange for a quivering smile.

He made a clicking noise with his tongue and winked. "That's my girl."

They entered the apothecary from the back. Cinder and Soo-tie sat on the floor playing a game.

"Where's Porky?" asked Bealomondore.

Soo-tie looked up. "He didn't want to come."

Ellie exchanged a puzzled look with Bealomondore. The bond between them pronounced the oddity of the boy's telling them to hurry and then not being there.

Laddin flew in the open door and landed on Bealomondore's shoulder.

Both children squealed.

"It's one of the ugly birds."

Ellie felt Laddin's immediate indignation and hurried to smooth over the offense.

"Indeed, Laddin would be a very ugly bird, but he is a dragon, a very handsome dragon."

The children stood and slowly came closer. Both looked ready to flee should the dragon attack.

"He's green," said Soo-tie.

Cinder snorted. "Of course he's green. Can't you say something smarter than that?"

Soo-tie didn't respond to the barb. "Do his claws hurt your shoulder?"

Bealomondore moved Laddin down into his arms. "No, he doesn't want to hurt me. He's a healing dragon, very important and very friendly. He's agreed to heal your cuts and bruises from yesterday."

Cinder put his hand over the bandage, now crusted with dirt. "Are you going to take the cover off? Won't the blood run all over again?"

Ellie stepped forward. "Yes, we will take the binding off, but the wound should be scabbed over, so no blood. And when we are finished, I have daggarts to give you."

Cinder's eyes brightened. "Shouldn't we have the daggarts first, in case we get all golly-wobbled and can't eat after?"

Soo-tie nodded. "Sometimes looking at blood and sores and oozy stuff makes my stomach wanna hurl. We should eat the daggarts first so we don't miss out."

"If you have sensitive stomachs," Ellie said as she maneuvered Soo-tie to take a seat on a bench, "then you should definitely not eat the daggarts first."

"Right," said Cinder. " 'Cause then you'd hurl the daggarts. You want me to go first, Miss? I can show Soo-tie how to be brave."

Soo-tie gave Cinder a mulish face. "And then you'd eat the daggarts while it was my turn. I'll go first. I can go first, can't I, Ellicinderpart?"

Soo-tie's pleading face turned to disgust as she looked into Ellie's eyes. She closed her eyes for a brief moment and wagged her head back and forth. When she again looked at Ellie, she displayed a play-acting air of extreme patience.

"You've been crying again," said Soo-tie. "I told you you'd better not cry. Crying gets you in big trouble."

Sitting beside the dirty child, Ellie managed not to wrinkle her nose against the soured smell of her clothes. She hugged the child, bringing her close in a hearty embrace. "Where I come from, children are allowed to cry."

Soo-tie didn't resist the hug but leaned toward Ellie. "But you're a grownup."

"Grownups are allowed to cry as well."

"Do you cry a lot?"

"No, I live a very happy life. There isn't much to cry about."

"Then why are you crying here? Is this an unhappy life?"

"I missed an important celebration."

Soo-tie moved away and looked at Ellie with big eyes. "Birth day?" She said it like it was two words. "Our birth day should come pretty soon." She looked at Cinder for confirmation. "In a week or two. Right, Cinder?"

Cinder rolled his eyes. "We just had the birth day."

He also said it as two words. Ellie raised an eyebrow at Bealomondore. He shrugged. In the time that Ellie and Bealomondore exchanged their bewilderment, the children had come together to better yell in each other's faces.

"We didn't just have a birth day," said Soo-tie. "You don't know nothing."

"I know more than a sissy girl, and you cry at night when no one is listening."

Soo-tie pulled back her arm, made a fist, and hit Cinder in the face. The blow knocked him over backward. "You're dumb," she yelled. "That birth day was months and months and months ago."

"Oh," said Ellie and started forward.

Bealomondore put a hand on her arm. She knew he wanted to watch how the children interacted. He noted their expressions, and she pictured a canvas with the two facing each other and ready to fight. The image formed in her mind. She had to dismiss it to concentrate on the real drama in the apothecary.

Ellie thought Cinder would spring from the floor and tackle Soo-tie. Ellie stepped closer to the angry children and spoke loudly. "How old are you going to be?"

Neither answered. Cinder stood and faced Soo-tie, their noses nearly touching and their faces screwed into fierce expressions.

"I said, 'How old are you going to be?' On your birthday, how old?"

They answered in unison without breaking eye contact. "Six."

Bealomondore rested against a large wooden barrel. "How old were you on your last birthday?"

"Six," growled Cinder.

Bealomondore seemed pleased with the answer. "So that means on this next birthday, you'll be…"

"Six," said Soo-tie.

"Nah!" Cinder challenged. "Can't be."

Soo-tie's face lost some of its ferocity. She relaxed her defensive stance. "That's not right, Cinder," she said. "If we were six on our last birthday…that was a long, long time ago."

"Yeah!" said Cinder, still holding on to his belligerent tone. "So long ago, you don't even remember. That had to be the birth day for being five, 'cause this time we're gonna be six."

Soo-tie walked away from her antagonizer and stared out the huge window at the front of the store. Ellie saw her fingers twitch as if she used them for counting.

The child sighed and turned to face Cinder. "When Ellicinderpart asked me how old I am, I said six. You said six too, Cinder. How can we have the birth day to be six if we are six?"

Cinder's cantankerous attitude melted. He frowned in confusion. Irritation slowly replaced the puzzled look. "What does it matter?" He flapped his arms up and let them slam against his sides. "Nobody asks us. It's not something we have to know for sure like some important things."

Soo-tie nodded toward Ellie and Bealomondore. "They asked."

"Yeah, but they're just dumb grownups."

"What's more important than knowing how old you are? I think that's important."

Their voices were getting louder.

"Lots of stuff," Cinder said.

"What?"

Cinder put his hands in his pockets. "Your name's important, and we know our names. Knowing when there's food at the fountain. That's important. Going to bed before the moon's all the way up. Lots of stuff's important."

Soo-tie returned to Ellie's side. She took Ellie's hand and led her back to the bench. Her shoulders drooped as she sat on the bench and scooted back. "I want Laddin to heal me."

Ellie squeezed the rough and dirty hand of the child. "He'll be glad to help."

"And when he's finished with the bloody stuff, can I ask him to do one more thing?"

Ellie took Soo-tie's grubby arm and started to remove the bandage. "I'm sure if you ask nicely, he'll try."

"I want him to heal all of me so I can be seven and then eight and grow up."

Ellie felt tears pushing behind her eyes. She kept her head down so

Soo-tie wouldn't have to lecture her again about not crying. When she could speak without giving away her emotions, she said, "We will all work to make that happen, Soo-tie. Not just Laddin, but the other dragons, Old One, Bealomondore, and me."

# 35

# Where Is Porky?

Ellie hauled a cushioned chair from the front of the apothecary to the area behind the counter. She curled up to wait, drawing her knees up under her chin and wrapping her arms around her legs. She kept her eyes on the two sleeping children.

After Laddin healed their scrapes and bruises, he informed Ellie and Bealomondore that the children needed milk and sleep. He couldn't do anything about the milk, but he would see to their rest.

He sat first in Soo-tie's lap. The girl had no idea what the green dragon intended. She talked softly to the small creature, gently stroking his wings. She yawned and continued to jabber even more quietly. In the end, she curled up on the floor and fell asleep.

Cinder snorted. "Girls! Soo-tie's all right for a girl, but even she gets squashy."

Ellie whispered her question. "Squashy? What's squashy?"

"You know, soft, sappy, tired." He pointed at the sleeping girl. "Run out of go, way before it's time for bed. We haven't even had noonmeal."

Bealomondore stood and went to Soo-tie. He covered her with a large linen towel that had been hanging next to the sink. Laddin hopped onto his shoulders as he straightened. Tak moseyed over and lay down beside her. He shifted a bit, then closed his eyes.

"Is it my turn to hold the dragon?" asked Cinder.

"I suppose it is," said Bealomondore.

Cinder sat cross-legged on the floor. Bealomondore handed Laddin to the boy and went to sit with Ellie. When he sat close to her side, she resisted the temptation to enjoy his being so near and wiggled away just a bit. Then she immediately started thinking about something else. She didn't want that special bond they had to give away why she was resisting his charms.

Cinder stroked the top of the dragon's head, between his ears. "You're an ugly thing."

"That was rude," said Ellie.

"I tend to believe," Bealomondore said, "that the dragons have every right to believe *we* are ugly."

Cinder's head jerked up. He looked affronted but then broke into a grin. "Maybe you, being a tumanhofer, is ugly. But not me. I'm a fine-lookin' lad."

Bealomondore laughed, but Ellie wondered who had said such a thing to Cinder. Could it be he remembered what a parent or grand-parent said centuries ago? The whole idea saddened her. These children needed adults, needed to be praised for their good deeds and trained not to hit each other and yell.

Soon Cinder had succumbed to Laddin's influence. The boy stretched out on the floor with only his arm for a pillow. Daggart crumbs stuck to the corners of his mouth and his chin. He looked vulnerable.

"And dirty," said Bealomondore.

"You're listening to my thoughts again."

"Not on purpose."

"Well, maybe you should, on purpose, not listen."

Bealomondore put his arm around her and pulled her closer. "Doesn't it happen to you? I relax, and suddenly I'm thinking alongside you, as if we were enjoying a pleasant conversation."

"Yes, it does." Ellie did her best not to think about how comfortable she was with his arm around her. "I'm worried about Porky."

"See? I was just thinking about the boy. And you say, 'I'm worried about Porky.'"

"Well, what do you think happened to him?"

"I don't know, but I've thought about going out to look for him."

"I think you should. It just seems to me that he was eager to have the daggarts. He wouldn't have gone off and missed his chance. Plus he had some injuries from yesterday as well. And he would want to see Laddin up close."

"That's too many reasons for a selfish young urohm to wander off." Bealomondore stood. "I'll go scout around, pick up our noonmeal, and come back after I check the fountain to see if he shows up for his midday sustenance."

Ellie nodded. Bealomondore leaned over and kissed her cheek. "You mustn't worry, Ellie love. You are the perfect tumanhofer lass for me." He turned and walked out the back door.

Bealomondore ducked into the closest alley quickly. He was more concerned about Porky than he wanted to admit to Ellie. He had spent their hours with the injured children trying not to reveal his anxiety. More than one scenario that would explain Porky's absence ran through his thinking. None of them were pleasant.

He went to the fountain first, knowing he would have to return when the sun shone straight above the city. His assumption was correct. Porky did not play among the few children gathered near the fountain.

Bealomondore sought out the places he usually avoided, places he knew often attracted the gangs. In each case, he didn't find Porky. At the third spot commonly used as a playground, he noticed something else besides the absence of the missing child. Fewer hooligans than usual gathered in their rough bands.

In all, he guessed half of the children were missing. He stopped to scrutinize this small collection of the mob. They played, but no one seemed enthusiastic about the games. No fights broke out. Commonly, losers attacked the winners, or winners drove home their victory by bludgeoning the losers.

He shook his head at the memory of one conflict he'd observed. Two children rolled on the ground, each with a death grip on the other. Ellie hadn't witnessed this type of vicious attack and therefore didn't realize the immensity of the task she'd taken on. Since the children had become increasingly uncivilized over a century or more, a few daggarts and some etiquette lessons were not going to change them overnight.

Another thought occurred to him. These children left behind were the more placid of the horde. He wouldn't call them gentle by any means, but they were not the instigators of cruel mischief.

Had someone taken the more unruly six-year-olds?

Had the wizard come out of hiding and snatched them up?

Had he loosed the wusstbunters on them?

More than likely, the wizard had nothing to do with this. After all these years of detachment, why would he return?

Had the worst of the bad children forged an alliance to plan an attack?

What terror could these permanently six-year-old hooligans conceive?

Whatever it was, it would be outrageous, reckless, and bound to cause destruction to property and probably people. Ellie would not like that. She would want him to stop it if at all possible. He sighed.

Now he wanted to find Porky *and* the missing children. On the battlefield he'd learned that a smart soldier knew where the enemies were and what they were up to. He'd had Det to help him, and between them, they'd saved their unit more than once. He couldn't depend on Det at the moment since he was off doing the rounds of the watch. Bealomondore didn't think he had time for the dragon to rejoin him.

He didn't know where the brats were lurking.

He didn't know the extent of the danger Porky had fallen into.

He could use some basic knowledge of the territory he sought to invade.

He could use reinforcements.

He wanted clear direction.

And now, he wanted his sword.

# 36

# Rescuing Porky

A rustle of wings announced a minor dragon's approach. Amee dived from above the empty shops and businesses, coming straight at Bealomondore. Her black and white scales blurred into gray. Whatever her mission, it was urgent.

Bealomondore glanced at the children playing and noted that they seemed unaware of Amee's approach. He ducked into an empty building, out of sight, and waited for the minor dragon to join him.

As soon as she landed, Bealomondore's mind filled with her chatter and flashing pictures. Porky had been caught by the bullies. They wanted to know where Ellie and Bealomondore would meet Porky, Soo-tie, and Cinder. So far, Porky had not told. Amee showed Bealomondore the location of the dismal building Yawn had chosen as a jail.

The temptation to go get his sword wiled its way through Bealomondore's thinking. But Ellie would have a fit, and truthfully, the prospect of inadvertently hurting one of the children turned his stomach.

Once she'd delivered her message, Amee waited patiently for him to decide his course of action. He pondered only a moment more.

"Gather the rest of the watch. I'll go see what I can do immediately about Porky's sticky situation. Bring Laddin, too, when you come. I predict it will be impossible, but try to keep Ellie out of this. She should guard Cinder and Soo-tie."

Amee flew off toward the outer city, and Bealomondore began a stealthy advance on the nasty group of bullies who tortured Porky. The outside of the store they'd chosen as their hideout matched the pristine architecture of Rumbard City grandeur. The furniture emporium fit in well with the other city shops in the area.

When he'd first explored Rumbard City, Bealomondore had peeked inside this establishment. By the signs of rampant destruction, he'd surmised that the horde of children had used the inside for wild games. They'd broken most of the furnishings, pulled cushions off chairs and sofas. Mattresses had been dragged hither and yon and used as walls of fortresses. Sheets, blankets, and anything else they could find draped over banisters and tables. They resembled untidy tents.

Now he entered the premises with caution. The state of the showroom hadn't changed. Crude constructions blocked a straightforward view to the back of the store, where a great commotion was taking place. He used his ears instead of his eyes to locate his target. As he listened to the rowdy boys, he wished again that he had his sword.

Bealomondore edged through the obstacles. A clutch of boys shouted at Porky and at each other. He knew he was close and crept carefully to avoid being detected. Straining to hear Porky's part in the drama, he could not distinguish his childish voice. Then he heard a thud and a grunt and the cruel laughter of a bully. Without thought, he jumped from behind the counter with his hand up in the air.

"Stop!" he commanded.

And he realized that his hand was not empty. His fingers wrapped around the hilt of the Sword of Valor. The brats circling Porky on the floor turned startled faces to the tumanhofer. He grinned and swished the rapier through the air. In the form of a long, slender blade, it made a wicked sound.

Bealomondore glared confidently. He wanted the boys to think he was in control and not in the least bit flummoxed by being outnumbered. The state of his sword bothered him as well. This blade was designed to pierce the chest and stab the heart. He'd rather have the blunt, broad blade suitable for paddling. But Bealomondore advanced, swishing his weapon, which had never appeared out of nowhere before, and grinning like a madman.

The boys backed up a step or two, all but Yawn.

Bealomondore stopped and regarded the six-year-old, whose thrust-out chin displayed his defiant attitude.

Bealomondore sneered. "Do I take you on one at a time or all at once?"

The scalawags who'd stepped back deserted their leader with hoots of fear and scrambling feet. Yawn glanced to both sides and saw that he was alone save the poor beaten boy curled on the floor. He licked his lips, clenched his fists, and tried to stare Bealomondore in the eye.

"You can go," said the tumanhofer. "There's no shame in walking away from a fight that makes no sense."

Yawn puffed out his chest, lifted his chin, and glared at Bealomondore. "This isn't the end of this." He turned and marched out, following the route of his mates.

Bealomondore looked at the hilt of the shining sword. Among the gems along the guard, words etched an axiom: "Show them strength, and you may not need to show them your prowess." He wasn't surprised to find the sword's scabbard attached to his belt. He put the long blade into the leather case and pushed it all the way in. Then he knelt next to Porky. The boy rolled toward him, and he took the shuddering child in his arms.

Porky let out one sob. "I didn't tell them where you were." He had to gasp for breath. "And I didn't cry."

Tears threatened to disgrace Bealomondore. He leaned his cheek against the boy's head and held him closer. "We'll take care of you, Porky. Laddin will be here soon, and he'll make you feel better. Where does it hurt the most?"

"My eye."

Bealomondore looked at the battered flesh on Porky's face. The left eye had swollen shut, and discoloration showed how severe the bruising would be. "It'll be fine. Laddin will fix it."

"My belly hurts too. Yawn kicked me."

Bealomondore bit back the fury that rose like a crashing ocean wave. Fortunate for the bullies that they had already fled. Bealomondore put his hand on the urohm boy's stomach.

"I'm sorry, Porky. I wish I'd gotten here sooner."

"I hurt so bad. Am I gonna die?"

"No, no. Laddin will heal you. After a good night's sleep, you'll be fine. Tomorrow you won't feel any different than you did yesterday."

"Then I'll be scared. 'Cause yesterday I was scared."

"Scared of Yawn and his gang?"

Porky grunted and Bealomondore took it as a yes. He mumbled and Bealomondore leaned closer. "I'm sorry. What did you say?"

"I used to be scared of dying, but now I'm not." Porky moved cautiously, as if to get into a more comfortable position. He groaned and grimaced. "I'm more scared of Yawn than dying."

"We'll take you in at the library. You'll be safe there."

A tear rolled down Porky's cheek. "Great. Old One will kill me instead of Yawn."

"Old One is grouchy, not murderous."

The child shuddered. Two ragged breaths preceded his next question. "Do you have to ask your mother if I can come?"

Bealomondore wished he could see the boy's face. What did he mean? "My mother isn't here."

"Isn't Ellicinderpart your mom?"

"No, she's much too young to be my mother."

"But if you're the father, then she's the mother."

"We're not—"

"Do you have children in the library? Do you have babies? I've never seen a baby."

Bealomondore's thoughts zigzagged among several paths. How could he answer this? Of course he didn't have babies, children! Babies? The sound of the word urged him to stand and back away, but he maintained his position.

He'd seen babies but never held one. What did Porky need out of this conversation? What was the child searching for?

He took a stab at answering the big lump of a miserable child overflowing his lap. "I'm not really familiar with any babies, so I only know general things. Babies are cute when they're not crying. I think they cry a lot. They smell funny. Women seem to like them, and fathers seem to like their own, but…well, men often don't pay attention to babies much."

Porky didn't answer.

"Are you all right?" asked Bealomondore.

He heard a muffled, "Yeah."

Bealomondore chastised himself for the absurd question. Porky was not all right. Now he seemed drowsy, and that was not a good sign.

Bealomondore reached with his mind, trying to make connection with either Ellie or one of the dragons. To his relief, Laddin answered. He was close.

Bealomondore sighed. "It's all right, Porky. Laddin is just a few blocks away."

He hugged the boy a little closer and patted his arm. Porky didn't respond.

"Porky?"

Nothing.

Bealomondore eased the boy out of his arms, allowing his shoulders and head to rest against the floor. Blood trickled out of the urohm's ear. The bruising around the eye looked horrid compared to unnaturally pale skin.

"Porky, can you hear me?"

No answer.

# 37

# Gray Phantom

Laddin swooped in and landed on Porky. Bealomondore recognized the minor dragon's concern as he examined his patient. The scene reminded him of the many times he'd seen Laddin aid soldiers on the battlefield. Bealomondore had witnessed the small dragon work in a frenzy to bring back a young man from the brink of death. Most of the time he succeeded. Most.

The other minor dragons except Orli, who guarded Old One, soon arrived and took up positions around the furniture store. Amee reported her conversation with Ellie. His tumanhofer lass would stay put until the two urohms in her charge woke up. Then she would come to Porky and Bealomondore. Amee had not revealed how badly Yawn and his bullies had hurt Porky. Bealomondore had no doubt that if Ellie knew, she'd have been here even before the dragons of the watch.

Laddin summoned Kriss, Maree, and Amee to help with a healing circle. Bealomondore joined them with a directive to Det and Soosahn to keep a sharp lookout for the ruffians. He entered the circle between Porky and Kriss. The feeble strand that represented Porky in the flow of energy shocked the tumanhofer. A few more minutes and Laddin wouldn't have been able to do anything for the boy.

A hand on his shoulder pulled Bealomondore out of the healing circle. It took him a moment to regain his bearings. Porky breathed easier, some color had returned to his cheeks, and the minor dragons still draped themselves over his body, providing the restorative dose of energy.

Bealomondore leaned back and broke his connection. He looked up to see Ellie's concerned face.

"I think Laddin can return him to health." He looked again at the young urohm. "It may take more than one treatment. I want to try to take him back to the library."

"That's the right thing to do, but Old One and Orli will probably object."

A muffled squeal alerted Bealomondore to Cinder, Soo-tie, and Tak standing near a stack of wooden chairs. The girl had her hand over her mouth. Cinder glared at her. Tak chewed his cud with half-closed eyes.

Bealomondore cocked an eyebrow at them. "Do you want to go with us? I don't like the idea of leaving you out here where Yawn could capture you."

Soo-tie's eyes grew big. "We can't go in the library. Old One'll kill us."

Bealomondore sighed. "As I told Porky earlier, Old One is grouchy, not murderous."

"We still can't go in there." Cinder puckered his lips and squinted his eyes. "If we aren't in our beds by the time the moon comes up, we won't have food."

Ellie put her arm around Cinder's waist. Her cheek rested against his shoulder. "Don't worry, Cinder. We'll feed you."

"Maa!"

Amee sat up on Porky's chest and shook her head as if clearing her ears of water. She bobbed a couple of times, then took off to sit on Tak's head.

"Maa."

Amee's thoughts intertwined with a confusion of input running through Bealomondore's brain. "Ah yes, the wagon. Excellent idea."

Bealomondore turned to his companion. "Ellie—"

"I know. I heard it too. But I think you deciphered all that information faster than I did." She knelt beside the unconscious boy. "We'd never be able to carry him."

Bealomondore nodded. "Are you comfortable with the idea of staying here with Porky and the dragons while Tak and I go get the wagon?"

"Yes, we'll be fine. Better take Det to scout."

He smiled. The thought to take his minor dragon with him had just formed in his mind. He could see a long future where he'd never know which one of them had thought of an idea first. He leaned over and kissed her temple, then moved toward a smashed entryway with Tak following.

He stopped just outside the door and looked back at Soo-tie and Cinder. "You should come with us when we move Porky."

"Yes," Ellie said. "We would be less anxious about your well-being if we had you under our care."

The two children turned puzzled faces to Bealomondore.

"She means we'll be worried sick unless we can see that you're all right. Come with us to the library."

Soo-tie nodded, but Cinder muttered, "Maybe."

"Think about it." Bealomondore followed Tak.

As he took a step into the sunshine, he felt Ellie's reaction as she noticed his sword. Strangely, she didn't object. Apparently seeing Porky, bruised and bloodied by "just children," had altered her belief that the gangs could be reasonable and won over with love and daggarts.

Det flew high, circled, and then returned with a report that a group of ten children had congregated nearby. Bealomondore darted into an alley in an attempt to circumvent the ambushers. Det made another surveillance flight and came back with news of two more clutches of possible assailants.

Bealomondore brought up an image of the streets in his head. The map reflected how Det saw the city from his aerial point of view. Bealomondore couldn't see a route that would avoid all three bands of children. "Do you have any suggestions?"

Det chittered as his opinion flowed into the tumanhofer's head.

"I know they're kids and will lose patience soon." Bealomondore tilted his head while he took in Det's comments. "I suppose we could wait a few minutes."

Following Det's lead, he walked to the closest point of safety. Tak butted the back of his legs, but he refused to go any farther until he got the all clear.

He dodged into the empty building at the corner and climbed the stairs to get a view of the surrounding area. If he could go across the rooftops, he'd be back at the library in a few minutes. But even if he did find a route, Tak wouldn't be able to follow him.

The view from the top floor didn't help. The group of children farthest from the front of the library looked like one of the leaderless bands, playing lethargically at the stone and twig game.

A movement caught his eye, and he focused on an area several blocks away. A flicker of gray appeared between two buildings then, but it passed too quickly across an alleyway for Bealomondore to determine what it was.

By watching the next gaps between buildings, Bealomondore caught glimpses of the shadow as it made its way toward the center of Rumbard. With each sighting, he became more convinced that the being was from one of the high or low races. It advanced with purpose, with a long deliberate stride, giving the impression of a man on a mission.

The agile figure was too quick and too short to be Old One. His build was not thick enough to be one of the urohm children. His wispy form floated, and his robes swayed as he moved forward. At times he seemed to have no substance at all.

"If I believed in ghosts, Tak, I'd say we're looking at one. But I don't believe in ghosts, and I doubt you have formed an opinion."

Whoever he was, he didn't travel alone. Tiny, shimmering birds of many colors swarmed around his head. These creatures drifted apart and re-formed, very much like Verrin Schope did when his three statues were not aligned correctly. The flickering made it hard for Bealomondore to determine which species they were, and it piqued his curiosity.

"I wish I had a spyglass."

The gray figure came into view once more. He drifted toward the fountain, with his hovering assembly swarming close to the peaked hat on his head.

Bealomondore whispered his suspicion. "A wizard's hat." He patted Tak on the back. "Let's go get a better look."

# 38

# Sighting a Wizard

Tak kept up with Bealomondore as he plunged down the stairs. The tumanhofer stopped at the door and listened. He heard nothing that sounded suspiciously like undisciplined ruffians, so he peeked out. Seeing nothing to deter him, he dashed down the alley in the direction of the mysterious visitor.

At each corner, he paused to make sure no gangs of children lurked between him and his goal. Det circled, bringing back information. Sometimes Bealomondore had to make a detour as the young varmints wandered in their play. Tak seemed to have a sixth sense about which direction would be safest. Finally Bealomondore realized that the minor dragon communicated to the goat.

The tumanhofer laughed at himself as he rubbed the fur between Tak's horns. "That explains a lot. I suppose Amee, with her special talent, facilitated your ability to hear the dragons mindspeak. But if you start mindspeaking to me, I won't be responsible for my reactions."

"Maa!"

"Don't do that. It makes it seem like you understand me."

"Maa!"

"Well, I suppose you do to some extent, but I refuse to have conversations with you." He rubbed between Tak's stubby horns. "At least not when someone might hear me."

Det flew back and perched on Tak's back. The goat looked over his shoulder. "Maa!"

Bealomondore objected. "Let's have a conversation I can understand."

Det's description of the elusive figure raised even more questions. The apparition was neither man nor beast. It had no substance. Det could see right through it and through the colorful winged creatures hovering about its pointed head. Det made it clear that they were not birds but were more like the wusstbunters that had attacked Old One and Orli.

"Well," said Bealomondore to his audience of two, "wusstbunters weren't phantoms. They were real enough to leave bites the size of my thumb, and plenty of them."

Whatever they followed managed to keep just beyond a point where Bealomondore could round a corner and get a clear view. The pictures Det projected with his mindspeaking reflected the information he'd conveyed, a hazy shape somewhat the build of an o'rant. And the pointy top could be a wizard's hat.

"I believe he's going to the main fountain." Bealomondore acted on his hunch and took a quick, direct route through a warehouse and a fancy eatery to one of his favorite lookouts.

Det reported that the figure continued on a path that would take him to the circle.

In a moment, the shadow appeared a mere dozen feet from where Bealomondore hid. Still, the precise nature of the being eluded the tumanhofer.

Yes, the thing looked vaguely like an o'rant. But no o'rant Bealomondore had ever encountered could be seen through.

Up close, the objects in flight around the pointed form looked more like tiny bats than birds. Their iridescence indicated their bodies to be translucent, having more form than the thing they hovered over. As an artist, Bealomondore acknowledged the fact that light could not sparkle off a nonsubstance. The mystery figure must be an illusion, whereas the flying creatures were actually there.

The vague shape stood still. At his sides an appendage rose like an arm and swept through the air in a gesture encompassing the scene before Bealomondore.

Baskets and platters of food appeared. The horde's meal had been delivered. As the shape's arm fell to his side, the entire image sharpened for a second before he flickered out.

A wizard. Long white beard and hair. Pointed hat. Robes embroidered with elaborate scenes of mountains.

Bealomondore could not see the wizard's face. But this had to be Wizard Pater on one of his daily rounds, providing sustenance for those in his bottle city.

The tumanhofer watched from less than a dozen feet as the man strolled through the open area surrounding the fountain. He never stopped. Nor did he make another gesture, or even say a command, yet more food appeared in baskets and on platters.

The wizard strolled on in the direction of the butcher shop. The tumanhofer stayed where he was.

Children poured into the fountain circle from all directions. They tore into the food greedily.

Bealomondore remembered the nature of his errand. He and Tak must get the wagon. With the streets empty, they could transport Porky in safety.

Ellie sat in the healing circle. She'd insisted that Soo-tie and Cinder join them as well. The children objected to having to sit still and didn't seem to care much whether Porky lived or died.

"Isn't he your friend?" asked Ellie.

Soo-tie shrugged.

"Sort of," said Cinder.

Ellie feared the children would hear the exasperation in her voice. She took a deep breath before asking, "What do you mean by 'sort of'?"

"I don't know."

Another deep breath. "Is Soo-tie your friend?"

Soo-tie giggled.

A look of horror chased away Cinder's sullen expression. He jerked his head back and forth. "No, double no, and triple no."

"What's wrong with having friends?"

Cinder's shrug could have knocked clinging cats off his shoulders. "Don't know."

Soo-tie squeezed Ellie's hand. "Yawn says no friends."

"Why?"

Soo-tie stared at Porky's pale face for a moment before speaking. "Friends disappear. I cried when Lulu was gone."

"You've had lots of friends disappear?"

Her childish face scrunched with concentration. "Sometimes I think so, but I only remember Lulu."

"There was Tad," said Cinder.

Soo-tie's grip tightened on Ellie's hand. "I don't remember Tad."

A rustle at the door made them all jump.

Soo-tie squeezed hard at the noise then relaxed. "That's Toady and Grim. They're nobody special."

Ellie, who considered each of her bothersome siblings special, examined these two newcomers with a different perspective. Shaggy hair, dirty faces, wary eyes, tight-lipped and anxious, the children looked very needy and special. She smiled and gestured for them to come in.

One spoke. Ellie didn't know it if it was Toady or Grim. "Do you have food?"

"Not here," answered Cinder with a smug grin. "But we're going to go live in the library, and there's lots of food there."

Ellie's eyes widened as she looked at the boy who minutes before had not wanted anything to do with the library and Old One.

The child in the door narrowed his eyes to glare at Cinder. "Nah! That ain't true. You wouldn't go in there."

The other child spoke up. "I would. If'n there's food, I'd go."

Ellie decided from their voices that the first was a boy and the second a girl.

"You're hungry." Ellie reached in her basket and pulled out two daggarts.

The children moved quickly and sat beside her, licking their lips, eyes glued on her hands. She held out the daggarts, and the two children snatched them. Each one crammed the crunchy treat into a mouth drooling with anticipation.

Ellie did her best not to look affronted by such bad manners. "What's your name?" she asked the boy.

"Grim." His answer sprayed her with crumbs. He still chewed. "You got more?"

"More daggarts?"

He nodded vigorously.

Ellie laughed. "Yes, one more for each of you. When Bealomondore gets here, we'll go to the library. We always have full meals there." She frowned. "I thought you were provided with plenty to eat as long as you obey the curfew and go to bed when the sun goes down."

Toady wiped the back of her hand across her mouth. "There is plenty, but sometimes Yawn has a big hunger and takes food from the smaller children." Her face twisted in disgust. "Today he took my food right out of my hand. Two of his boys held Grim, and Grim got one right in the face."

"Got one?"

Grim made a fist and slammed it into the flat of his other hand.

Horrified, Ellie noticed a slight bruise on the boy's cheek. She'd thought it was a smudge of dirt. No words came to her mind. What could she say about such bullying? Worse, what could she do? Nothing. The children needed manners, instruction, and uncompromising adult guidance.

Ellie held out the daggarts. Then she snatched them back as the two ruffians lurched for them.

She would start with the children she had within her reach. "I am going to give you these. There's no reason for you to grab them." She looked the children in the eye. "Reach for them slowly, take them politely, and say thank you before you put them in your mouths."

Grim rolled his eyes, but he took the daggart gently, said thank you, then looked at her with questioning eyes. She nodded. He crammed it in his mouth. Toady giggled.

Cinder let go of Porky, pushed past him, and inserted his own grubby body between Ellie and Grim. "Don't give 'em all to him. He's probably a snitch. Gonna tell Yawn where we are so's Yawn'll leave him alone for a while."

Toady turned big eyes to her companion, then squinted as she looked mean at Cinder. "How's he gonna snitch if he's sitting here?"

"When he leaves."

Around the cake, Grim declared, "I ain't leaving."

Cinder shouldered Grim hard enough to knock him over.

"Enough," said Ellie sternly. "We will all go to the library as soon as Bealomondore and Tak get back with the wagon."

"You've got a wagon?" asked Grim.

"Yes."

"What are we going to use the wagon for?" asked Toady.

Cinder gestured with his thumb, indicating Porky. "Him."

"Ain't he dead yet?" asked Grim.

"Nope." Cinder grinned, enjoying being the one who could tell what happened. "The little dragons saved him, brought him back from the darkworld, healed him almost properly, 'cept he hasn't woke up yet. He could still be addled. Don't know that yet."

Grim sniffed and pointed with his chin to the minor dragons. "Them's ain't stuffed?"

Soosahn hissed from her lookout post on a stack of furniture.

Grim scrunched his head between his shoulders and looked up, spotting the minor dragon for the first time. "They're all over the place." He came out of his defensive posture and put on an arrogant grin. "Just birds."

Toady glowered. "How can you be so dumb? Do you see feathers? You don't see feathers, do you? No feathers, not a bird. I believe Cinder. These are dragons. And they'll eat your innards when you go to sleep if you don't treat 'em right whiles you're awake."

"Hush now," said Ellie. "Someone's coming."

"Tak and the wagon?" asked Soo-tie.

Soosahn made a series of chittering noises.

Ellie motioned for the children to scatter. "Soosahn says hide. You'd better do as she says."

The children dodged behind the boxes and big furniture. Ellie moved to sit beside the one child who could not move. Determined to protect Porky from whoever entered the building, she took a loose chair leg and tucked it under the edge of her skirt.

# 39

# The Gang

Yawn stepped between two towers of chairs. Ellie sighed at the sight of his tough expression. She reminded herself that he was a little boy, just like her brothers. But he was a little boy who had bullied his way to the top of the heap of uncivilized monsters. He needed someone bigger, stronger, kinder, wiser, and more stubborn to guide him out of this trap he'd forged for himself. Surely he wasn't happy being the top dog. His face certainly didn't express any joy.

The daggart ploy was worth a try anyway.

"Did you come for a daggart?" she asked.

He snorted.

She examined his dirty face, hoping to see a glimmer of innocence. The boy looked hard, unforgiving, and unreachable. She wouldn't give up quite yet. "You're alone?"

He sneered. "I've got lookouts scattered about. Your man with the sword won't be coming to rescue you."

"Why would I need rescuing?"

Yawn clenched his fists and took a step forward.

"I could beat you up. I could smear you across this floor. I could—"

Ellie suppressed the fear that shivered her spine and smiled. "But you won't." The words came out sounding more positive than she felt. All the years of bluffing her brothers paid off.

Yawn stopped. His mouth worked as if he thought of several things to say but rejected each utterance. Finally, he held his fists up in front of him. "What makes you think I won't?"

"Well, you do know that hitting a girl is a sissy thing to do, don't you? Everyone knows that. Only stupid boys hit girls. It's a well-known fact. I'm sure you wouldn't actually hit me because you don't want your gang talking about you behind your back."

Pausing, she was gratified to see he puzzled over her statements. "So if you're too dumb to get what you want with words and have to use your fists"—she raised her eyebrows—"that tells everyone you aren't a good leader. And if you pick on girls, that shows you're afraid of a real fight with a real opponent, someone the same size and someone who has as many muscles as you do. And you *know* what they'll be saying about that."

Yawn cast a sweeping glance around the showroom. Ellie did too. All the children had either fled or found a good hiding spot. Yawn must have been satisfied that they were alone.

He growled at Ellie. "What? What will they be saying?"

"The muscle thing," said Ellie. She stroked Porky's brow and was glad that his bruises had faded and he breathed easily. He looked very relaxed. She wished she could relax. She hoped Yawn would relax.

Yawn glared at her and shouted, "What's the muscle thing?"

She was going to make him very angry or very flummoxed. She was hoping for the latter. "Oh, they say how big your muscles are—the ones in your legs, the ones in your arms, and the one in your head. The one in your head leaves no room for the brain, so you become a muscle head, who is, of course, without a brain and therefore stupid."

"I'm not stupid."

"Well, *I* didn't say you were. I said that everyone knows that boys who hit girls aren't brave and aren't smart, and that's why I know you won't hit me. I believe you're brave *and* smart."

His fists clenched and unclenched. He sputtered under his breath, and she suspected his muttered rant was not a nursery rhyme. His eyes darted here and there, looking for something.

Ellie speculated. Witnesses?

The boy spun around and made for the exit. He bumped into Bealomondore as he passed through a narrow opening. The bulk of the urohm child knocked the tumanhofer backward. Ellie rose to her knees with the table leg clutched in her hand. But the bully charged on, and Bealomondore righted himself.

He came into the area where Ellie knelt beside Porky and, with one arm around her, pulled her to her feet. His hand on the make-do club worked to get the weapon away from her. She finally let go, and he dropped the wooden leg to the floor. She ducked her head under his chin, felt the warmth of his protective embrace, and heard his gentle whisper, "It's all right now. I'm here. We have the wagon. We're going back to the library."

She hiccupped as she suppressed a cry. "I was so afraid I'd hit him. I didn't want to hit him."

"Of course not, but it would be nice to have a parent around for these children. Most of them could stand a well-administered spanking." He hugged her tighter and kissed the top of her head.

A chorus of giggles surrounded them.

A chuckle rumbled in Bealomondore's chest. "We have an audience. Say, are there more children here than when I left?"

Ellie nodded. "Yes, two more arrived while you were gone."

"Two?" Bealomondore harrumphed. "I'm going to have to teach you to count."

She lifted her head and gasped. A quick head count revealed that the group had grown to more than a dozen children.

"Are all of you hungry?" she asked.

Without exception, they nodded.

Cinder put a hand on her arm. "Don't listen to them. They're always hungry. Most of them came here from the circle, so they've eaten."

A curly-topped redhead jumped twice to position herself opposite Cinder. "We could eat again." Her hopeful eyes traveled from Ellie's face to Bealomondore's and back again. "We could be your children, and you could fix us supper."

Ellie let go of Bealomondore to put her hand on the child's shoulder, but the little girl grabbed her arm and hugged it. Ellie looked around for Soo-tie, who was always admonishing her not to cry. She wasn't in sight. But still, Ellie sniffed, blinked back the tears, and offered the big angel a reassuring smile. "We'll take care of you."

Out of the corner of her eye, she saw Bealomondore grimace, but he didn't say anything about her offer. Still, his reservations transferred to her awareness through their bond.

He released her and bent over to examine Porky. "Well, he looks better. I think we can safely transport him to the library."

"We're coming too," Red Curls announced. She looked around at the other children, and as if on signal, they all bobbed their heads up and down. She grinned at Bealomondore. "You'll protect us from Yawn."

Another child dared to step forward. "And you'll protect us from Old One."

Bealomondore rolled his eyes. "As I've said before, Old One is—"

"Not murderous," said Cinder.

"Just grouchy," added Soo-tie.

Ellie beamed at Bealomondore. "We've convinced two of them. That's a start."

Bealomondore clapped his hands together and looked over these huge six-year-olds. "I think we have enough muscle power here to do some good." He pointed at some boys. "We need to clear a path wide enough for Tak to bring the wagon in and a large enough space for him to turn around once he's in here. You boys push furniture back on the route to the door." He pointed to more children as he spoke. "You girls clean up this area right around Porky. Boys, dismantle that tower of chairs and get them out of here."

The children obeyed immediately.

"He's the boss," said one boy to another.

"Yeah," the second boy answered. "A real boss, not like Yawn."

Ellie settled beside Porky instead of helping. She felt she needed to protect him from small objects being thrown and toppling furniture. She ducked twice and once caught a fancy carved box before it landed on Porky's head.

The shifting of furniture caused a lot of noise, from the heavy pieces scraping across the wooden floor and from the loud voices of the enthusiastic children. The minor dragons flew about chirping and chittering as if giving orders and offering suggestions. In spite of the urgency of the situation, giggles and laughter accompanied Bealomondore's orders.

Ellie smiled. This is what children should sound like. This was a worthwhile project. And look at how many children had joined them. Perhaps her plans would work in spite of Bealomondore's grim predictions.

Grim! Who would name a child Grim? She shook her head.

This was a most peculiar circumstance she'd found herself in. Parts of it were delightful, and most of the time she forgot she was missing the coronation. And the wedding. She sighed.

"Maa!" Tak greeted her as he pulled the wagon into the widened space.

The furniture still encroached upon the area. Bealomondore walked into the room and shook his head. "We'll have to unhitch Tak, turn the wagon, then hitch him up again."

The children surrounded Tak, pushing and shoving to be the one to unbuckle the harnesses.

Tak stamped his feet. "Maa! Maa! Maa!"

"Here now," Bealomondore's raised voice brought sudden order to the chaos. He pointed to two boys. "You and you take off the harness." He pointed to two girls. "You go to Tak's head and talk soothingly to him. Tell him you're sorry for scaring him and that everything is going to be all right."

The rest of the children pouted.

"Don't worry, you'll all have to help turn the wagon, and there will be more opportunities to help from now on. You're no longer a bunch of scalawags. Miss Ellie has decided you are family. And each member of a family does important jobs."

The about-face of the cart came off without any big problems. Tak was rehitched with the help of two different boys, then many hands made light work of hefting Porky into the bed of the wagon. They trooped to the back door. The children skipped and darted in and out of the stacks of furniture on either side of the path. The dragons flew above them, swooping and doing aerobatics. The children giggled and squealed their appreciation of the show. Ellie walked beside the cart with a hand on Porky.

Bealomondore led the way but made them all wait while he consulted with Det.

"This is going to be a perilous journey," he announced soberly.

The children's eyes grew big.

Ellie knew what he was going to say, and it made her mad enough to spit. Yawn couldn't just leave them alone.

"Yawn has set up ambushes along the way," Bealomondore said in a deep and serious tone. "We can avoid them with Det's help."

"Let's ambush the ambushes," said Cinder, with no fear but a lot of excitement.

A chorus of enthusiastic agreement came from the cluster of children.

Ellie saw and felt Bealomondore's waning patience. His face clouded, and the irritation that passed to her signaled a possible explosion. She decided to intervene.

"We will avoid them as much as possible," said Ellie. "It is not our intention to match their ferocity. We will behave as civilized people. They can be barbarians if they choose."

"What do civilized people do?" asked Cinder.

She could feel Bealomondore's sudden shift in attitude. Her tumanhofer hero fought to keep from laughing. Ellie ignored him.

"Civilized people mind their manners," she answered the boy.

Cinder shook his head in disgust. "I think barbaring would be more fun."

Old One in the library could probably hear Bealomondore's guffaw. Ellie closed her eyes and counted.

# 40

# Run!

Bealomondore stood at the door of the furniture emporium. He could feel the impatience of the children behind him, urging him to move. But the situation outside the old building stirred up caution. Det said the renegade children had collected rocks and left them in strategic places along the route to the library. He contemplated waiting until nightfall, but Ellie's objection registered in his mind.

*"Oh, please, Bealomondore. I want Porky settled. The children are hungry. Isn't there some way we can make it?"*

*Yes, we can make it, but it won't be a straight path. Are you ready?*

*"Yes."*

*One minute, and we'll be out of here.*

He mindspoke to the minor dragons. They flew into the air, and he watched as they bombarded the boys bent on mischief, who were crowding the flat roof of a shoe shop across the street. The dragons dived and grasped the boys' hair, giving a yank before letting go and flying upward. They spat at any child who threw a rock. Their colorful saliva stung, and they rarely missed.

"This way," Bealomondore said as he gestured toward the alley. "Stay together and don't dawdle."

The clatter and bang of the wagon wheels on the rough descent from sidewalk to street alerted the children above. Bealomondore saw them dart away from the edge of the roof.

298 Donita K. Paul

He guided his entourage down the alley. Det returned to report another corner armed with rock-throwing six-year-old thugs. Bealomondore turned away from the library to avoid the attack. Det took off and soon reported that the marauding urohms were perplexed. They had lost the wagon and its escorts when they didn't approach the library along any of the obvious routes.

"Good," said Bealomondore.

"What's good?" asked Cinder.

"Yawn and his gang don't know where we are."

"How do you know what he knows and what he doesn't?"

"Det told me."

"The dragon?" Cinder opened his eyes wide and stared at the dragon now riding on the front rim of the cart. "Tiptop parnot snot! I never knew they could talk." He squinted his eyes and examined Bealomondore's profile.

"Why are you staring at me?" asked the tumanhofer.

"Do you understand that noise they make? Do you speak that twitty kind of talk?"

"They understand each other with the language they use out loud. I understand what they are thinking, words and pictures. It takes some getting used to, but if you have the gift, you can learn to fashion the information together to make sense."

Amee flew around the corner, a black and white blur of scales and wings. She passed overhead without stopping.

"What'd it say?" demanded Cinder. "What'd it say?"

"She said to go through the theater. Yawn has no one guarding that area." Bealomondore approached the street and paused to look over the immediate vicinity. "Det?"

The dragon took off and circled above the intersection. He came back, and Bealomondore signaled for his followers to move forward.

Cinder seemed to be jumping rather than walking. His excitement burst out in small leaps. "He said no one was here, right? He looked and didn't see anyone, so you knew we could move, right?"

"Right, but you'd better be quiet, or Yawn's gang will hear you."

Bealomondore opened one of the front doors of the theater. Cinder held the other while Tak and the children and Ellie entered. They stopped in the lobby and waited until they were all gathered.

Soo-tie squirmed through the knot of people to get to Bealomondore. "I know the way. I play in here a lot. There's a back door behind the stage." She pointed. "On that side."

Bealomondore nodded. He'd explored this building several times during the months before Ellie came. He went to Tak's head and led the goat and cart through the doors into the theater proper. The rest of the crowd followed.

He saw Ellie start at the sight of the cavernous room. The rows and rows of huge seats looked like markings on a scalloped seashell. Large glass windows allowed light to come in through the slanted roof above. He knew that a catwalk led to the windows, and these could be covered during a performance.

In this light, enough of the great hall could be seen to admire its glamour, but the shadows along the edges caused a trickle of wariness. The children hushed and tiptoed down the slanted, carpeted aisle. They probably imagined spooky creatures, more ominous than their rough playmates.

He looked ahead and grimaced. He'd forgotten that the only way to the back was to either climb the steps on either side of the orchestra pit or to enter narrow doors at each side and climb even more constrictive stairways.

He halted his companions as the floor leveled off at the front row of seats. "I need a couple of boys to come with me to carry wide boards."

Three jumped to be his helpers.

He nodded at Ellie. "We'll be right back. There are boards backstage we can use for a ramp."

She acknowledged his plan with a dip of her head and climbed into a huge theater seat. The other children followed suit. Even before Bealomondore and his three volunteers left, the children had discovered that jumping back and forth between the rows was much more entertaining than sitting.

Bealomondore felt Ellie's indecision about whether to make them sit quietly or let them play. She relaxed when he mindspoke to her that the children probably could not be heard from outside.

He and the boys found several sturdy boards long enough to make the ramp. Ellie led the nervous goat, speaking softly. Bealomondore pushed from behind, steadying the cart and keeping the wheels from coming between the boards and pushing them apart. He gave a number of boys the job of keeping the boards from shifting, and he had to remind them often to keep their fingers from getting smashed. The other children laughed as Tak clambered up the wooden incline, and they danced up the boards once he was onstage.

Bealomondore and the boys brought the boards with them to get down the steps from the rear entrance to the theater. Maree swooped into the alley and landed on Tak's back. His bright blue scales caught the beam of light slanting into the broad passageway from above. Tak's fur glistened. When a beautiful sight caught his eye, Bealomondore's artist instincts always surfaced. He sighed. He would never again be that fop that barged into Byrdschopen, looking for the great Verrin Schope to be his mentor.

For now, he enjoyed the contrast of the clean colors against the drab background of old bricks while he listened to Maree's report. The male dragon had been closely observing Yawn's allies until they began to disappear.

Maree's last statement made Bealomondore frown. "What do you mean by disappear?"

"What did he say?" asked Cinder.

"That the children go into buildings and don't come out. Our friends fly into the buildings and can't find them."

Cinder shrugged. "They're using the subter."

"What's a subter?"

Cinder rolled his eyes. "It has a longer name, but I don't know it. Something like 'subter-ran-he-in.' We don't usually go down there because it's scary."

Several of the children nodded their heads in agreement.

"More scary than the theater," said Red Curls. "More dark places. More spooky noises."

Grim pushed to the front. "And sometimes when you're down there, you can't find any doors unlocked so you can get out." His eyes expressed remembered panic. "That's the scariest thing of all. That never happens in the theater."

Confusion pushed Bealomondore's ordered thoughts aside. For a moment the sensation baffled him. He smiled after a moment of shock. The confusion was not his, but Ellie's. This was something he'd have to get used to as they went on in life together. The intrusion of disorder had been disconcerting.

He turned to face his followers. "While Yawn's forces are down in the subter, we shall make progress to the library. Come now. Be brave and quick."

He headed toward the inner city, taking the shortest route to their safe haven. After several blocks of no interference, the children relaxed and added skips to their hurried pace. They turned the last corner and saw the library at the end of a long stretch of avenue. The large, white, columned building sat at the end of the street they were on, where it teed at a cross street. Everyone quickened their strides.

Bealomondore studied the windows of the stores they passed. Surely there would be one more attempt to stop them. He caught sight of movement out of the corner of his eye, but when he turned his head, he saw nothing suspicious.

With his mind, he called to the dragons of the watch to close in on this area. Almost immediately, Kriss reported children on the only flat roof available to the ambushers. Airon reported evidence of a trap a block away.

"Hurry!" Bealomondore commanded.

He and his troops trotted.

Det sounded an alarm from above.

Bealomondore shouted, "Run!"

A barrage of rocks showered them from the flat roof. A swarm of children poured out from the alleys. Yawn's thugs had wooden shipping crates over their heads. The wide slats in the sides allowed them to see.

The flying dragons could no longer pull hair nor spit in the faces of the army of six-year-olds. He hated to admit it, but the leader of the horde was quite clever.

Bealomondore separated himself from his band, his sword already in his hand. "Run!" he called again.

Bealomondore stayed behind, swinging his weapon with the determination to protect Ellie, her goat, and her children.

# 41

# Sanctuary

Ellie's head whipped back and forth as she tried to keep an eye on what was happening to Bealomondore behind her and the children in front of her. Whimpering, the children dashed for the safety of the library. Some cried out as they were hit by the stones hurled from above.

Ellie held tight to the side of the cart. One rough spot in the pavement and the wagon would tilt. Too much of an upset would send it over. She knew she couldn't hold it up, of course, but she'd try. As soon as she had the children, Tak, and the cart carrying Porky hidden at the back of the library, she'd return to Bealomondore and try to help.

A rock caught Tak on the hindquarters. He jerked and sprang forward. Ellie saw the cart tip away from her. The wheels on her side left the pavement. She lunged to hang her body on the edge and grabbed hold of Porky as he rolled toward the lower side. Her weight pulled the wagon back and the wooden rim jarred against her stomach as two wheels bounced on the street.

Ellie jumped, landing on her feet. She ran beside the cart with her hand on the rough side, aware that any minute the wagon could tip again and Porky might topple out.

Glancing over her shoulder, she saw Bealomondore surrounded by the gang of boys. The minor dragons flying above looked totally helpless to deter Yawn's forces. She stumbled and used the cart to keep from falling.

The pitch of child-shrill hysteria rose. The children racing in front of her now screamed and howled as they ran. Their outcry changed to even higher shrieks. Ellie focused on the library ahead and saw red-faced and snarly Old One standing at the top of the deep steps between two tall white columns.

"Oh," was all she managed to get out before he came charging down the steps, a huge unfurled umbrella in his hands.

The fleeing children screeched, and their swarm split in the middle, some veering off to the left and the others zooming to the right.

"Go to the back of the library!" she yelled. The rescue plan was turning topsy-turvy. The scattering children escaped in two directions, getting away from her. Would she be able to herd them back together? Gasping for breath, Ellie charged on.

Old One hurtled down the library steps, coming directly at her with his umbrella raised. Tak bleated a complaint, the attacking children behind her whooped and hollered like wild heathens, the children fleeing in front of her yowled like injured pups, and the dragons made noises she couldn't identify. Were those shrill wails a war cry?

As Old One approached, she heard his deep, ominous growl. She flinched and desperately looked around for a way to retreat. Ignoring her, he passed on the opposite side of the cart.

Ellie let go of Porky's wagon and slowed enough to be able to safely look back. Old One charged into the melee that centered on Bealomondore. With his umbrella closed now, he bopped the children around their middles, hitting sides, stomachs, rumps, and arms. When close enough, he yanked the wooden helmets off their heads. He threw the boxes away.

Most of these young warriors froze when exposed. Old One took advantage of their fright, leaned over, and growled in their faces.

Ellie smiled, glad that ferocious Old One had no more intention of hurting these wayward children with his umbrella than Bealomondore did with the flat of his sword. She let a giggle escape as she watched two terrorized hoodlums take off for the alleys. Amee and Maree chased them for good measure, then returned to find another victim whose armor had been jerked off by Old One.

Confident that Bealomondore was no longer in danger, Ellie followed the trail Tak had taken to the back of the library. She found her rescued children gathered around the wagon. Porky sat, staring at his surroundings.

"He woke up," Soo-tie announced.

Cinder snorted. "She can see that."

Soo-tie delivered a slug to his arm. Cinder raised a fist.

Ellie pushed through the pack of overexcited youngsters, trying to reach the combatants before a free-for-all broke out. "Stop that!"

The children stared at her. Exasperation welled up in her chest. Didn't these monsters have any idea of civility?

She leaned into the wagon and put her arms around Porky. "You're going to be all right. We're safe here."

Eying the mob around her, she took a calming breath, but still her tone sounded harsh in her ears. "You're not supposed to fight all the time."

"What are we supposed to do?" asked Soo-tie.

"Speak kindly, encourage each other with words, help one another, and do things that make your life better, not worse." She sighed, remembering all the times she'd heard Gramps utter similar words. She pulled out of her memory the edict most often quoted. "Construct, do not destruct."

"I'm hungry," whined one of the children.

A murmur of similar complaints rose from the gang surrounding her. Obviously her lecture had not registered.

"Help me get Tak into the park and Porky into the library. Then I'll see what I can find for a snack." She released Porky from her hug, giving him a kiss on the cheek as she did so.

A scuffle erupted over unhitching the goat.

"Stop!" Ellie shouted.

Their movement ceased abruptly, but Ellie sensed the squabble would explode again if she didn't think of some incentive to thwart them.

"There will be no food for anyone who hits, pinches, or pushes." She looked at their confused faces. "Or anything else mean and hateful."

They waited. What did she expect them to do? She'd have to teach them how to cooperate. Otherwise, they'd stand there and glare at her until sundown.

"Cinder and Grim, unstrap Tak. Toady, open the gate and let him in, then close the gate behind him. Soo-tie, you and some of the girls help Porky walk to that opening over there. That's where we'll go into the library."

She placed a hand on Porky's shoulder. "Do you think you can walk with their help?"

His eyes were big in his pale face. "Into the library? We're going into the library?" His lower lip trembled, matching the quiver in his voice.

"It's all right. Old One is a friend of mine. He likes Bealomondore and me." Ellie thought that might be a bit of a stretch, but Old One had shown up to help battle against the militant troops under Yawn's control. "We'll be safe inside the library. Yawn and his gang won't come in."

Det, Airon, and Maree swooped out of the sky and landed on the cart. The children emitted squeals of pleasure. One lurched to grab Airon. She hissed and flew up, avoiding capture.

"Don't touch the dragons," Ellie ordered.

She heard running feet, and Bealomondore appeared from around the corner of the stately white building. The rest of the dragons arrived and took perches in the trees.

Bealomondore panted. "Well, that's taken care of." He leaned over, his hands on his knees. "We made it, thanks to the unexpected help from Old One." He stood and grinned at the crowd around him. "The old man swings a wicked umbrella."

Reminded of their nemesis, the pack of nervous children seemed to shrink as they scooted into a closer knot. Bealomondore ignored their apprehension and moved to help the girls maneuver Porky out of the back of the wagon.

Ellie made sure Tak entered the park, looking him over for injuries from the hurled rocks. She checked to see that he had water before following Bealomondore and the young refugees through the vent opening.

The children remained subdued as they entered the library. She even saw several holding hands, which both surprised and pleased her. They weren't as callous toward each other as they would have her think.

Ellie clambered in after the last child, Red Curls. She had to shove a bit to get in. They had all stopped just inside the opening.

"Excuse me. Move a little, please. Excuse me."

She got her feet under her and stood. "What's going on?"

Red Curls leaned close and whispered in her ear. "I gotta go."

That didn't explain why the group had stalled just inside the library.

She took Red Curls's hand and plowed through the bodies wedged in the small space in front of her.

"Coming through. Excuse me. Move aside. Excuse me."

She dragged Red Curls to the front and looked around in amazement. "There's nothing here. Why are you standing around in this back room instead of moving into the children's area?"

Bealomondore's expression showed that he was as perplexed as she was. Through their bond, she felt his irritation rising. Her annoyance fed on his. Her eyes widened as their gaze met.

*We'll have to be careful,* she mindspoke. *I feel like I could wring their necks without an ounce of remorse.*

Bealomondore's brow furrowed, then cleared. *"Yes, I felt my anger surging in a manner that is totally out of proportion to the situation."*

*Doubled!* Ellie smiled her understanding.

*"And then doubled again."*

She nodded. *Twice the emotion for half the cause.*

Cinder cleared his throat. "Are you two just going to stare at each other? You look silly."

Ellie broke out of her private communication with Bealomondore and surveyed the frightened children.

Toady's anxious voice barely reached her. "He's in there."

For a moment, the identity of "he" eluded her.

"Oh, you mean Old One."

Red Curls jerked on Ellie's arm. "I gotta go."

"Right," said Ellie. "We'll go to the children's area. I've never seen Old One there. After we get settled in, I'll introduce you to him. He might even read to you. He is a librarian, not a grawlig, you know."

Bealomondore's thought interrupted her. *"I believe he said he was a guardian."*

A communal gasp turned Ellie's attention from Bealomondore to the place where they focused all eyes. Old One stood in the doorway to the main library area.

"You will obey all the rules," he bellowed, and the children cowered.

"You will not shout, yell, or scream. You will maintain a quiet attitude. You will not run, skip, or dance. You will move sedately through the book stacks. You will treat the books with respect. No chewing, throwing, or stepping on. You will sit in chairs and on the floor. No climbing is allowed in the library. No running."

Cinder spoke up. "You said that one already."

The glare Old One pinned on the unfortunate boy scared even Ellie.

"No running," Old One repeated.

# 42

# Fairy Tale

Tense faces stared at Old One as he sat beside the desk in the children's area. He scowled at one in particular, and that child shrunk and wiggled to the back of the group. Bealomondore thought Old One was doing an admirable job of keeping order.

Ellie didn't. "He's scaring them. There's no need to scare them."

"Then you should explain to the children that they're not allowed to scare me. Being attacked by that mob in the street took ten years off my life."

"These are the peaceful children, not the hooligans."

"I recognize some of these innocent-looking cherubs as wranglers in a few scuffles I've seen," he said.

Ellie looked at Bealomondore. "What are we going to do? We can't let the children and Old One stare darts at each other."

Bealomondore thought better of the sarcastic remark that sprang to his mind. The sad thing was that before he could shut it off, Ellie heard it.

"Humph!" She squinted at him sternly.

He thought she looked adorable, and she heard that too. She blushed. He laughed.

"The first order of the first day in your new abode," said Bealomondore, "is to have noonmeal."

Ellie turned her hands up and shrugged. "Where do you suppose the food is?"

Bealomondore didn't sound worried. "The wizard that provides our sustenance seems to know what we're doing and when. He always puts the correct amount of food where we can find it."

At the mention of food, the children's attention had shifted from the grouchy librarian to the tumanhofer. Some of them nodded to his statement, some stood with their mouths hanging open, and some wagged their heads, indicating they didn't have a clue what he was talking about.

Bealomondore debated revealing his sighting of the wizard at work. The children evidently were unaware that a wizard watched over them. Then he'd need to explain the history of the city. How much could this young audience absorb in one sitting? He decided against getting into anything too complicated.

He took a deep breath and let it out. "So"—he examined the grimy faces suddenly attentive to his every word—"I suggest we have a scavenger hunt. Holler loud if you're the first one to find the stash of food, and we'll all come to help cart it back to the children's area."

He lifted his hand to count on his fingers the rules he wanted them to follow, but the children dispersed with wild whoops and cheers before he said another word. The dragons of the watch took off from their various perches and joined in the riotous hunt. They flew above the children's heads, chirring lively tunes and doing aerial acrobatics as if caught up in the children's exuberance.

Ellie grinned, but Old One growled, muttering under his breath. "No loud voices. No running. No rough-and-tumble play allowed within the library walls." His eyes widened, and he turned his head abruptly in the direction most of the children had taken. He bellowed,

"You aren't allowed to go up the steps. Never go up the steps. Off-limits to the likes of you."

A squeal resounded through the hallowed halls of Old One's literary institute. "I found it! I found it! Come see. There's buckets of food here. Buckets!"

Wizard Pater had provided plenty of food. Enough for the children to have seconds. Usually he avoided giving them desserts, but a beautiful cake, iced and decorated with pictures of the minor dragons, sat on a shelf directly behind the buckets of food in the broom closet.

"And where's my broom?" Old One groused.

Ellie pointed to the wall behind the big door. "Right here."

He growled and stomped back to his rotunda.

After noonmeal, Ellie had her new family sit in the children's area and pulled out the many pillows hidden in a cupboard.

"These are for you to keep," she said. "Find a place and that will be your place to sleep."

"Nah!" objected Cinder. "We don't sleep during the day. That's for babies."

"I didn't say we were going to have a nap. I'm going to read to you, and I want you to be comfortable. We'll sleep tonight, but you can claim your space now."

The children accepted the brightly colored cushions and scrambled to get the best spots.

Bealomondore watched with amazement. He couldn't decide what attracted the children to a particular location as superior to another. The disputes became violent, and he had to step in and negotiate peace several times as the young tyrants zeroed in on one site and then another. Ellie scooted up close to Bealomondore and whispered in his ear. "Sit on this side of the room, and I'll sit on the other while I read."

"Why?"

"Your presence will keep them under control."

"What if they squirm and wiggle?"

"Just touch them."

He couldn't resist teasing her. "With the point of my sword?"

Her exasperated look pleased him. She had more appeal than any society damsel he'd ever met.

She patted his arm. "Your hand will be sufficient. Just lightly touch them."

Ellie crossed the room, crawled into a huge rocker, and opened the book she had left there. Bealomondore noticed that Old One had parked his huge frame in a chair near the entrance of the children's area.

"Quiet now, so you can hear." She opened the book, and from the first sentence, her voice captured the room.

Bealomondore found the story she'd chosen to be enchanting. The tale was not a legend he was familiar with. The urohm characters fought an evil monster to free their children from its cave.

He never had to settle any of the children. Her audience listened without stirring. After the heroes brought home the rescued children, Ellie read from a children's poetry book. One by one, the listening children fell asleep.

When she looked up and saw the quiet room, she closed the book, slid off the chair, and with a signal to Bealomondore, tiptoed into the main library. Old One stood and followed her. Even he seemed to understand the need for quiet.

The old librarian settled in his favorite chair. Orli flew in and settled on the back of his chair, close enough to wrap his tail over Old One's shoulder.

"You two had better be careful," said Old One.

Bealomondore scrunched his forehead as he turned his attention to the librarian. "In what way?"

"You're getting too close to that wizard. He's treacherous, not to be trusted."

Bealomondore didn't understand Old One's suspicion. "He's provided food for the citizens of the city all these years."

"Because he had to, not because he wants to."

Ellie sat on a stack of books she had cushioned with a blanket. She folded her hands in her lap and gave her full attention to Old One. "Why is that? Surely if he arranged the situation of Rumbard City being isolated in a bottle, he could free us. Why shouldn't we get close to him in hopes of persuading him to break the bottle?"

"He's trapped as well." Old One shifted uncomfortably, as if the conversation bothered him. "He has to keep us alive. We are his only hope of being free himself."

Bealomondore sat beside Ellie and put an arm around her shoulders. "Do you mean *we* as in Ellie and me, or *we* referring to you and the children?"

Old One pinched the bridge of his nose, eyes squinted shut. "Anyone alive in this city. That's probably why he trapped you. So you would help him escape. He knew I wasn't going to do it. I don't care if he's trapped for eternity. Ha! Serves him right for acting like he's Wulder Himself. Setting a punishment on us as if he's not just as prideful as the ones he punished." He nodded. "But Wulder sees right to the heart of each man, woman, and child. Wizard Pater is confined just as we are."

"Where?" asked Bealomondore.

Old One shook himself. "What'd you ask?"

"Where is Wizard Pater trapped?"

The librarian waved his hand in front of him, dismissing the question. "That was years ago. Why do you want to dredge up the past?"

Bealomondore stood. "We want to get out of here."

"This isn't such a bad place. A bit livelier than I like now that you're here." He nodded toward the children's section. "You'll soon turn those out. They cause trouble."

Ellie peeked around Bealomondore. "We will not be throwing the children out."

Old One scowled at them. "What are you going on about? I'm tired, and you two are nattering. Leave me alone."

Bealomondore sat down again. They watched the librarian settle in his chair, preparing for an afternoon nap.

Bealomondore placed his arm around Ellie's waist and leaned closer. "I think that's all he'll tell us today. But if we could get him to talk, to remember things, he could help us get out."

She whispered back. "I wonder what triggered this memory. I'd be willing to testify that he didn't 'remember' the bit about Wizard Pater being trapped yesterday or this morning."

"I doubt he remembers what we were talking about two minutes ago." He rested one hand on his knee. "I know some people who own an insect emporium. They probably have some mixture that would stimulate his memory."

"And I know a woman in the village who mixes up dried herbs. She probably has something for memory."

Bealomondore sighed. "And neither source is available to us."

"We could look for a book on herb lore. I know a little bit but not enough for something like this."

"After we found a book, then we'd have to find the herbs. We might be old and gray by then."

Ellie shuddered. "I don't want to live here for always, Bealomondore."

"Neither do I."

"Let's talk about something else." She looked at Orli, who watched them, not at all relaxed like his urohm. Then her eyes went back to the children's area. "The dragons stayed with the children," she said.

Bealomondore hugged her closer. "Now they finally have something to watch."

Old One sat up suddenly, startling them both. He prefaced his statement with his usual growl. "Why did you choose that story? Why not educate them with the history of Amara? There are two excellent volumes detailing the journey to Chiril."

"I picked a legend, a fairy tale, for a specific purpose. And I picked 'The Monster Held the Children' because I wanted to educate them."

"Bah, it's nonsense. Monsters and caves and cunning trickery. No substance."

Bealomondore felt the tension bubbling in Ellie. He rubbed his hand up and down her arm.

She took a deep breath to calm herself. It was one of the many habits he'd grown to recognize. Through their bond, he sensed her ordering her thoughts.

"My gramps attended Dorminhale University. He calls himself a wood and prairie scholar. That means he's wise in practical and not-so-practical things. He taught me to read in defiance of my father, who is a field, farm, and natural scholar."

"So?" Old One's glare sharpened, as did the challenge in his voice.

Ellie chafed. The tumanhofer's condescension irritated her. She wouldn't be rude, because rudeness proved ignorance. She'd politely mention her upbringing.

"So," she said with a smile, "Gramps taught me material from many of the courses he attended at Dorminhale. He especially liked literature. He said that fairy tales are found in every culture. Each group of people uses story to define their world. The story we just read tells the children that families are natural. How would these children know about families if we didn't read books where families are normal?" With a direct look at Bealomondore, then at Old One, she challenged them to dispute the fact. "The story also establishes that parents love their children and will risk all to protect them. These children have not seen that."

Bealomondore had to strain to hear Old One's response. "They once had families. A mother and father who cared. Homes to live in. Older brothers and sisters. Babies born and needing tending. But Wulder took that away."

"Do you know why?" asked Bealomondore.

"Because we had it all and didn't cherish it."

Bealomondore frowned. That didn't fit into the picture he had of Wulder from reading the Tomes and talking with those who came from Amara. "Really? That's the reason?"

Old One stirred himself enough to glare at Bealomondore. "Part of it, boy. Part of it."

Ellie stepped in to prevent an argument. "The fairy tale also establishes the culture's sense of nobility. It declares right and wrong, differentiates between kindness and cruelty, and points out the futility of selfishness and the blessings of selfless behavior."

"Now that's where the urohms outdid themselves." Old One grinned. "Right from the moment we began building Rumbard City, our sole intent was to give the benefit of our society to the backward people of Chiril."

Bealomondore was amused as he and Ellie both took umbrage at

Old One's arrogance. They looked at each other, and he felt an understanding pass between them. They wouldn't verbally attack the ancient urohm's belief. It would do no good. Sometimes he remembered more clearly how they had disappointed the wizard. The wizard had banished them to the bottle.

"And," said Ellie, turning her attention back to Old One, "the stories propose that to pursue moral ethics, to stand for the weak against tyranny, is praiseworthy."

"Succinctly put," answered Old One. "Through a good tale, you can convince these heathens of what is good and create in them a desire to be better than what they are right now."

Bealomondore raised his eyebrows.

"You two needn't look so surprised. Of course I know the purpose of the different types of literature. I am a librarian after all."

He struggled to his feet. "I know these books better than you. Since they are mostly from my culture, you'd have to dig and dig to find the right urohm texts. I know which stories will suit your purpose." He stopped and stared at them. "Well, are you going to just sit there? I'm offering to guide you to the right shelves."

Bealomondore and Ellie hopped to their feet. He whispered in her ear as they followed Old One. "Spoken like a true librarian."

# 43

# The Clan

Bealomondore hid his thoughts. He didn't want his girl to know how much he enjoyed dunking these filthy boys. The more they hollered, the more he enjoyed himself. During the two months before Ellie came, the street gangs had made his life miserable. He'd been forced by children to skulk through the alleys of Rumbard City like some cowardly criminal. The maintenance room of the library provided the "tub," a huge, deep sink screened in by Ellie's ingenuity with some curtains she'd found on one of their foraging expeditions. While Bealomondore scrubbed, Ellie held Porky in the tub of water. His shrieks could probably be heard outside the library. Bealomondore noted that the minor dragons had made themselves scarce during the hullabaloo.

"Be quiet," Bealomondore ordered. "You'll have Yawn and his gang thinking we're torturing you."

"You are!" Porky screamed. "All this soap ain't good for me. Water's just fine, all by itself." He squirmed harder. "Don't touch my head. Not my hair."

"Oh, quit acting like a baby." Ellie lost her grip on his arm, and he splashed and twisted, trying to get out.

Bealomondore solved the problem by pushing the wet child clear under, then letting him up. "Are you going to quit struggling?"

Porky howled and thrashed. Bealomondore pushed him back

under. He only held him beneath the water for a moment, but he could feel Ellie taking exception to his methods. This time he used *his* strategy. Daggarts and fairy tales would not make a dent in these kids' determination to remain squalor-crusted.

He let Porky up and asked the same question with an explanation of what he expected. "Are you going to quit struggling? Start behaving, boy, because I'm going to keep dunking you until you stop this nonsense."

Bealomondore won the battle of the wills. Porky settled down. The performance was repeated with Cinder, Grim, Ostes, Barm, Laska, and Jep. Some struggled more than others. Some gave up sooner. They all protested.

Ellie sensed that Bealomondore had lost most of his patience, so after supper she tackled the girls' baths alone. She instructed Bealomondore to keep the boys busy and out of her hair and sighed with relief at his demeanor with the shiny-clean boys.

He introduced them to a game of cards called Climbing Mountains. She'd learned the same game as a child. Perhaps their backgrounds were not so different. Most Chiril children played this game. Bealomondore used the numbered deck to teach the illiterate crew how to add quickly. Like the baths, some took to addition easier than others.

Ellie waved sweet-smelling powder under each girl's nose and used it to bribe them into the tub. She'd found the floral-scented talc while exploring one of the closer abandoned homes. She'd gone scavenging with Bealomondore many times. Even this was a part of the routine they'd fallen into. Their outings were precious moments alone, without the cumbersome burden of young children. Still, she thought Bealomondore would soon explode with frustration. Finding the way out of the glass bottle occupied most of his thoughts.

Soo-tie volunteered to go first into the sudsy water, and with her good example, the others tried to be calm. They squealed some, but did not physically fight like the boys had in a water war against her and Bealomondore. The colorful dragons hung around to sing and chitter while the gals soaped up and rinsed off.

Red Curls's name was Carrie. She wanted her hair clean and shiny like Miss Ellie's. Aval, Fister, Lisby, Fronna, and Disnat got in and out as quick as Ellie would let them. And the last child, Toady, wouldn't get out of the tub, she liked it so much.

After a few days, baths became part of their routine, even if overall hygiene remained an ongoing battle. But a child who made the effort to be clean received special treats. Ellie spent a lot of time in Old One's kitchen.

"I'm glad you've come to help," she told the librarian one day.

"My library is overrun by hooligans," he complained. "I come up here to escape the chaos. It's not by choice I come to be a kitchenmaid."

"No one's forcing you to help me make daggarts." She grinned at him, recognizing that he enjoyed being with her and actually doing something rather than sitting and reading all day.

"Daggarts?" He pronounced the word with a growl. "It's not just daggarts but boiled tarts, finger pies, and anything else you come up with."

She went over to him and hugged his upper calf, which is where her arms reached when he stood.

"I like having you here. And you're changing. You are less grouchy, more agile, and"—she leaned back to look all the way up to the grouchy face staring down at her—"you aren't as forgetful as you were when we first came."

"Self-preservation. I've got to keep sharp, or you'll bring in the rest of those ruffians."

"We do get one or two more members to our clan as each week goes by."

"I know it," he snapped. "I'm not blind."

A month passed, and Bealomondore tried not to act out his frustration. He endured the routine established by the inmates of the library, but just barely. He preferred digging through the books and exploring the subter.

Every morning, he and Ellie fed the children in the children's area. Old One refused to take part in their meals, but he always sat within hearing distance. After breakfast, the girls tidied up and had baths. The boys had cleanup duty after supper and got plunged into soapy hot water just before bed.

Ellie taught the children how to play with the few toys in the children's area. She also taught them to write numbers and letters. Airon helped teach songs they found in the children's books. After noonmeal, Ellie read to them. And after they woke from a nap, Bealomondore took them outside to play games he'd played as a child.

But Bealomondore chafed at the time taken in the care of the little clan. His determination to get out of Rumbard City grew with each exasperating day of child-sitting.

He pored over the journals of Old One and of some of the deceased citizens of Rumbard City.

"What are you reading now?" asked Ellie during one of the afternoon rest times.

He held up the book in his hand. "Somas."

"The architect." She sat on a footstool opposite him.

Bealomondore looked at her dimples and smiled, welcoming her company. Her hands went to her cheeks, resting on the little dents beside her mouth. She blushed.

As much as he liked to famfoozle her, he didn't like to keep her in a state of embarrassment. He continued on the subject at hand.

"Right." He paused. Where to go from here? How much did she want to escape their confinement and the onerous job of running an orphanage for huge six-year-olds? "Ellie, I keep finding references to an underground city. It has to be real. Old One doesn't remember, but Airon knows tumanhofer songs she said she learned in the 'old' library. I can only believe the 'old' library is beneath us."

"Why would finding the old tumanhofer city be helpful to us?"

"Because the city would have more than one way to the surface. A dozen exits or more." He leaned forward. "I've been through miles of the subter."

He felt her frisson of fear as she frowned.

"I worry about you when you go exploring."

"No need. Det is always with me, whether we are on the streets of Rumbard City or in the tunnels below. He always knows right where we are and the fastest way back to the library."

"He's a remarkable dragon."

Bealomondore slumped against the cushions of his chair. "We haven't come across one door that sounds like the one described."

"What about the key? Who had it last? Where was it kept?"

"Mysteries." Bealomondore puzzled a moment over their predicament. "But finding the key without locating the door would do us no good."

She finished his thought. "Finding the door without the key would not be much better."

Bealomondore tapped the closed book in his lap. "Somas gives the best clues yet. He talks about an underground cool-water stream. If we follow the stream, we come to the door."

Ellie laughed. "Now we have to find a key, a door, and a stream. This doesn't seem to me to be an improvement."

"I'll ask Old One again. Sometimes he remembers things."

"And most of the time he doesn't."

"You're being a pessimist, Ellie. That's not like you."

She looked down at her hands, shoulders drooping. "I hate to admit it, but I think I'm tired of caring for these enormous, demanding children."

He refrained from commenting on what he considered to be the futility of their efforts. Ellie leaned forward. "Did you notice we have two new members in the clan again today? I'm quite positive we have more children in the library than Yawn commands outside our little sanctuary."

He nodded. "I always smell them before I see them."

She giggled. "Soo-tie and Toady have already told them they are going to have baths after story time."

He grinned. "How'd they take the news?"

"Quite well. It seems Yawn is being particularly nasty and they'd rather be with us."

"Understandable." He hopped out of the chair and came to sit with his girl. "Ellie, Yawn is dangerous. If he ever gets hold of one of these children who has defected to the library, he'll pound him or her."

"I know." She shuddered. He saw the image she dwelled on, the injured Porky when they first rescued him. She clutched Bealomondore's hand. "They don't venture out farther than the fenced park. But I think they are getting dangerously restless. Mischief erupts out of boredom."

He hugged her and kissed her forehead. "So wise for one so young."

She laughed.

He gave her a quick peck on the lips, a move that always produced a sweet silence and glowing eyes. Her beauty radiated around them in a way that demanded to be painted. But they had work to do before he could jump full-time into his art. "I have an idea."

"And you're keeping it from me. I can't hear your thoughts."

He nodded. He'd kept the notion to himself until he'd planned out the details. Now was a good time to share, and if he waited much longer to be freed from Rumbard City, he might become loopy like Old One. "Let's set up a hunt. The children are to find any and all keys and bring them to us."

She raised her eyebrows.

"When the search goes outside the library, we will accompany them."

"Where will they look?"

"Here first, then the homes of the prominent citizens of Rumbard City."

She nodded, thinking of the possibilities of his suggestion. She hadn't guarded her thoughts. Bealomondore followed them with little effort. She came to what he had thought would be their next step after a successful key hunt.

"And when we find the key," she said, "then we turn to the exploration of the subter. Together we'll find the stream and the door." She grinned and clapped her hands together. "Oh, they're going to like this, Bealomondore."

# 44

# Keys, Keys, Keys

Ellie's head swiveled as she tried to keep an eye out for any of Yawn's gang. At least she had four dragons with her, circling and scouting the roofs and alleys. Half of their forty children scampered around her, glad to be out of the confines of the library. Ellie had hoped to find the key inside their sanctuary and not have to venture into the streets. It was through no lack of trying that they had to extend the search. The children found dozens of keys but not the one Orli could identify as the right key.

Bealomondore had gone one direction with twenty urohm children and Det, and she'd gone the opposite with minor dragons, children, and Tak. They planned to seek out the more affluent neighborhoods where the city founders who'd held important posts had dwelled. Old One had actually been helpful, locating a directory from the town council.

They turned down a side street where mansions loomed under stunted trees. Outside the bottle, these morgym trees would be twice as tall. The delicate leaves shadowed the street with shifting dapples. Ellie took a big breath, savoring the rich, spicy smell of the morgyms. In the spring, the sap would rise. She could see signs on the tree trunks of having been tapped in the distant past.

"Let's check the first house on the right," she called to her charges.

Carrie stopped. "What right?"

Ellie didn't scold the children for not knowing right from left. She mentally added it to the things she would teach them. "The yellow house."

The children ran up the broad steps to the front porch and attacked the door.

Several called out. "It's locked."

Then, as if driven by a wild shepherd, they dashed down the steps and loped around the side of the house.

Ellie followed. "Wait for me! Remember Bealomondore wanted me to show you how to search."

She hurried around the corner and almost cheered when she saw the children lined up before an open door. When she came to the steps, she saw Kriss, Maree, and Amee blocking the entrance. The children had not exhibited a rare display of self-control. She shrugged. She'd take what she could get. A month ago they would have plowed over the small dragons in their way.

She entered the kitchen and turned to make sure the children gathered in such a way as to be able to see her demonstration. When they were settled, she pulled open a drawer.

"Never dump the contents of what you are looking through. We'd just have to pick it up off the floor, and that would slow us down."

She lifted a stack of tea towels carefully. "See. I pick up the towels, look underneath, then carefully replace them." She picked up hot pads next. "I can go through the whole drawer without making a mess." She raised the next stack of cloths.

"Why do we have to be so neat?" asked Jep. "Who cares?"

"It's a matter of respect. These items belonged to someone at one time. Out of respect for their feelings, we take care of their belongings."

"But they're long gone," said Lisby. "They don't know."

"The simple answer is that Wulder would know. Bealomondore

says Wulder sees everything we do. Wulder favors order and disdains destruction."

Lisby scratched her scalp under the tidy ponytail Ellie had gathered on top of her head. "What does that mean?"

Carrie elbowed her. "It means He likes neat and doesn't like mess."

Ellie looked Lisby over, trying to find something that the girl counted as valuable. Untied shoes, scruffy leggings, a faded dress, and a wisp of a yellow scarf were the girl's only possessions. Ellie pinched the edge of the scarf and pulled it gently from Lisby's shoulders.

"Let's say that it is three hundred years from now. I don't know you, and you aren't here, but I find your scarf." She held it up for all to see.

Alarm opened Lisby's eyes wider. Her eyebrows arched into her bangs.

"Now," said Ellie, looking around the kitchen but not at the children, "I don't see anyone here. Obviously, this yellow scarf belonged to somebody, but that was so long ago. I have mud on my shoes. Maybe I'll use this rag to wipe the dirt off."

Lisby grabbed for the scarf. Ellie deftly pulled it out of her reach.

"Or," Ellie said, "I might cut it into squares and make handkerchiefs to blow my nose."

Lisby made another desperate attempt to recapture her scarf. Again, Ellie eluded her.

"Or I might play tug of war with the scarf. Tak loves to play tug of war."

"No, no!" cried Lisby.

Laska grabbed Ellie's arm. "Don't do it! She loves that yellow thing."

Ellie patted his hand on her elbow. "You don't have to worry." She handed the scarf back to Lisby. "I wouldn't damage the scarf, or throw it on the floor, or burn it in the stove. It is something that belongs to Lisby. And I don't have the right to destroy it."

"But you take stuff from the houses all the time. So does Bealomondore."

Ellie nodded. "I do." She looked around and picked up a bar of soap from the sink rim. "This soap belonged to the people who owned the house. I want to take it and use it. I don't think they would object to my taking it since I really need it. I'm not going to destroy it. I'm going to use it."

Laska wrinkled his nose. "So that's different? Just because you're going to scrub us with it? You can take it?" He shook his head. "Nah, Miss Ellie, it's the same. You ought to respect that soap and leave it here."

Ellie fought the giggle that rose to her throat. He'd turned her argument against her. "No, Laska, I respect the people, not the soap. And in respecting the people, I recognize that most people are generous enough to share a bar of soap. I'd give you a place to sleep if you needed it. I would give you my coat if you were cold." She let a grin spread across her face. "And I would give you a bath if you were dirty."

Laska put his hands up in front of him and backed away. "No, Miss Ellie, I'm fresh scrubbed."

The other children laughed, and Ellie joined them.

She hugged the two closest to her, then released them. "All right. Let's search this house. And remember to leave everything the way you found it."

"Except the keys!" shouted one of the girls.

"That's right," Ellie said. "Collect the keys for Orli to examine."

They worked their way down the street and had crossed to come back on the other side when Det flew over, circled, and landed on Ellie's shoulder.

Her mindspeaking abilities had sharpened over the weeks, and she understood him easily.

"They think they've found the right key. We're to meet the other half of the clan at the library."

Their dash back to the center of Rumbard City included laughter and happy squeals. Ellie tried to calm them as they approached the area where Yawn and his few remaining thugs hung out, but she couldn't contain the children's excitement.

Ellie panicked. What would she do if those ruffians jumped out at her and tackled the children who had deserted Yawn and come to the library? She didn't want a fight. She didn't want anyone to get hurt.

"Shh! Be quiet!"

The children heeded for almost a full minute before they broke into noisy games of chase and tag as they walked through the wider, empty streets of abandoned shops.

Ellie remembered Bealomondore's calm voice as he spoke to Wulder. He put a lot of trust in Wulder being real and interested in what Bealomondore said. Often her tumanhofer friend would list the things he liked, thanking Wulder for His provision. And he would list his concerns.

Sometimes he sounded like he was thinking things over aloud, but most of the time it sounded as if he was actually talking to someone. And he often sat, with his eyes closed, a small smile on his lips. Ellie would notice through their bond that a peace flowed through him, a peace she had never felt on her own.

In imitation of what seemed to work for Bealomondore, Ellie began to pray. "Wulder, please keep us safe. Keep Yawn occupied somewhere else. Allow more of the children trapped in Yawn's hold to escape and come to us."

For a moment she stopped praying. Did she really want more children to care for? No, if she was honest, she didn't. Where did those words come from? She decided to try again and to keep control of what her mouth said.

"Wulder, please keep us safe. Keep Yawn away. Help us get to the library quickly and without any trouble. If any of Yawn's brutes have decided to leave him…"

There it was again. She didn't want to pray this way.

"Wulder, please let the key we need be among the keys we found. Help Orli identify the right key, and help us find the door to the underground city. Help us to decide what to do with all the children." She stopped before she could add "even those from Yawn's group." What was the matter with her?

"Please help us to get the children safely out of the city. If we have to find the wizard first, please lead us to him. And there's a bottle of memories we should find as well as the key. I guess we need help in a lot of things."

She stopped speaking again. Her heartbeat no longer raced. She scurried behind the small band of children and Tak with an air of excitement instead of fear. Det said the key looked like the one Orli had shown them in mental images. They might soon be out of the bottle and back with friends and family.

Who would take care of the children they rescued? There were very few urohms in Chiril. She and Bealomondore had decided that a few urohms must've been away from the city when the wizard set up his punishment. Urohms were living in Chiril, but in very limited numbers. Surely they would adopt these children. But who would take care of the children still caught in Yawn's snare? How could they possibly leave without them? And Yawn, such an unhappy child, filled with anger and pride.

"Wulder, please rescue *all* the children."

She hesitated once more, the library steps visible at the end of the street.

"Yes, Wulder. All the children. And Old One. And the minor dragons."

"Maa!"

"And Tak."

# 45

# Doors, Doors, Doors

Out in the streets of Rumbard City, Ellie had felt exposed. She'd expected Yawn and his gang to pounce. The sun had shone brightly, the birds sang, the dragons chittered, the air smelled fresh, the flowers bobbed their heads in the gentle breeze. And still she had expected disaster. Now that she was in the underbelly known as the subter, she *knew* this was where Yawn would attack. The setting held dark corners, unidentifiable noises, and the chill in the air brought goose bumps on her arms.

Each of the children had a lightrock. Bealomondore carried a lantern. Orli's body glowed as he flew above them. Still there was not enough light to suit Ellie. The plastered walls were dank and mildewed, with long brown stains flowing from top to bottom. Pipes and girders crisscrossed the low ceiling. How would a grown urohm stand up straight in these tunnels?

Bealomondore squeezed her hand. "This is man-made. When we get to the tumanhofer city, you'll see something more along the lines of caves and caverns. Of course, the tumanhofers widened tunnels and flattened floors and enlarged caves to accommodate the citizenry. Have you ever seen drawings of Tuck?"

"Yes. Gramps has a *Torrabendarah's History of Tumanhofers*."

A clunking noise like metal against metal echoed through the dark tunnel. She jumped, and the children froze.

"What was that?" a voice whispered out of the group of boys and girls.

Bealomondore stretched a bit to look over the crowd around them. "Probably nothing."

"It sounded more like something than nothing."

Ellie recognized the child's voice. "Let's just keep going, Toady. The quicker we find the door, the quicker we can get out of here."

Det flew back from scouting a passage ahead of them.

Bealomondore passed the map dragon's instructions on to the clan. "We're going to turn right at the next intersection of tunnels."

"What right?" came back in a variety of forms. Ellie still had not taught them left and right successfully.

"When you get to the crossing, stop," she told them. "We'll tell you which way is right."

Bealomondore spoke quietly to Ellie. "Det says he can hear running water. Perhaps he's found the cool-water stream."

"You've never been down this way in your explorations?"

"Never this far. I always had in mind that I must get back to help you with the children. I didn't want to leave you at their mercy for too long."

Soo-tie giggled. "Mr. Bealomondore, you shouldn't be so worried. We aren't murderous."

Several voices joined hers, finishing the phrase in unison. "Just grouchy."

Ellie patted Soo-tie's shoulder. "Most of the time you aren't even grouchy. Everyone has been trying to get along. I appreciate that."

Soo-tie laughed louder, and those around giggled as well. "We know how to get treats from you, Miss Ellie. That's why we're good."

"I don't care why you behave, just so long as you're practicing your manners and they're becoming a habit. A good habit."

"We found the crossing," said Grim from the front of their pack. "Which way do we go?"

Bealomondore let go of Ellie's hand. "I'm coming to the front. I'll lead from this point on. Let me through, please."

"Where do you think we are?" asked Porky.

"Det says we are east of the library by about three miles."

"Three miles?" One of the boys wagged his head back and forth in disbelief. "We walked three miles already?"

"That's right."

"Right? Where?" Cinder screwed up his face in disgust. "And we haven't even tried one door yet."

"The doors we've passed so far are doors made by urohms. We're looking for a door made by tumanhofers."

"What's it gonna look like?" asked Tolly, the newest child to join the clan.

Bealomondore looked at the girl as he answered. "We don't know what it will look like exactly, but we do know that it won't look like all the doors we've seen in Rumbard City."

"It'll be shorter," said Laska. " 'Cause tumanhofers are shorter even when they're grown up."

"Good observation, Laska." Bealomondore gestured for the children to follow. "Let's find that door."

They'd walked quite a ways when Bealomondore held up his hand for them to stop. "Be very quiet and listen."

All the children stood still. Ellie heard water running, much like the brook near her home.

"We're close," she said.

Det returned and landed on Bealomondore's shoulder.

"Did he find the stream?" asked Soo-tie.

Bealomondore grinned. "Yes. Only a few more yards and a turn to the left."

The children cheered.

He and Ellie exchanged an amused look as the inevitable voice asked, "What left?"

Bealomondore shrugged. "I'll tell you when we get there."

The need did not arise. As soon as they came to the crossing of two tunnels, the din of rushing water called to the children. They turned the corner to the left and took off running.

"Don't fall in," Ellie called.

Bealomondore waited for her and Tak. He took her hand and followed the excited clan. The mass of six-year-old bodies churned with the thrill of running water.

"Why is it," asked Ellie, "that a stream, a river, even a little brook causes such fascination?"

"Water is very hard to paint, but I confess I am drawn to moving water. Waves on an ocean are the same."

"I've never seen the ocean."

"Not even in pictures?"

"Well, yes."

"Pictures can't do justice to the majesty of the sea. I shall take you to the seashore."

"When we leave Rumbard City, I'll go back to my parents' farm and herd sheep."

"Never. Ellicinderpart Clarenbessipawl, I want you to be my wife."

She had expected this, but not in a dark and gloomy man-made tunnel with exuberant giant children just a few yards away. She'd already decided what she'd say. She had to turn down his offer to marry her because her reputation was now tarnished by their stay in Rumbard

City without a proper chaperone. But she had hoped the proposal would be a little more romantic. It was probably the only one she would ever receive. She steeled herself to do what she must.

"No, Bealomondore. I won't marry a man who *has* to ask me to marry him."

He stopped, and though she resisted, he turned her to face him and lifted her chin so she had to meet his eyes.

"Ellie, I am going to drop all my defenses so that you can experience exactly what I'm feeling. I will not hide any of my thoughts. Are you ready?"

For a moment, she didn't think her heart would allow her the experience. Looking into his eyes melted her resolve not to let him be a martyr and marry the country lass he'd been stuck with. The love she saw in his expression filled her with a surge of like emotion. There was more?

She nodded.

The full volume of Bealomondore's emotions struck her.

She gasped.

Oh yes, there was more.

She felt as if she were drawn into his soul. In an instant, her being melded with his. Her tentative belief in Wulder burst like fireworks into full-blown awe. The sparkling background became a jumble of giddy feelings, elation, and jubilation.

As this myriad of emotions danced in ecstasy, a solid base formed beneath them. She felt like she could skip on the edge of a precipice with no fear because Graddapotmorphit Bealomondore loved her. He *loved* her.

She willingly went into his arms. He kissed her, and a kaleidoscope of bliss swirled through her. Because of their special bond, she felt her own pleasure and his. Happiness doubled and twined a ribbon of color between them, through them, and all around.

"Hey!" Cinder hollered at their shoulders. "What are you doing? We found the door."

Reluctantly, she and Bealomondore pulled apart.

"Well?" said Cinder. "Are you coming?"

# 46

# The Bottle Wizard's Bottles

Bealomondore pulled the keys out of one of his deep pockets. Orli had sorted the dozens of keys brought in by the children. The minor dragon eliminated those that were too small, too plain, or too shiny according to his memory. Bealomondore banked on the fact that dragons have long and accurate memories. Seven old, cumbersome keys remained. Each looked like the others with only slight variances in the etched design along the shank.

The light dragon now sat on Bealomondore's shoulder, as eager as any of them to see the door open. Only Tak seemed disinterested. He sat off to the side, refusing to be a part of the press of onlookers gathered deep in the subter. Ellie stood at Bealomondore's side, and the crowd of witnesses pushed forward, each trying to see as he placed one key in, gave it a twist, and tried the door. He handed the used keys, one by one, to Carrie.

He came to the seventh key, and the group as a whole held their breath. This would be the final attempt. The door would finally yield to the hand unlocking the plain mechanism.

When the knob did not budge for the last key, a disappointed sigh escaped from them all.

Bealomondore shrugged. "I guess tomorrow we'll search for more keys."

"Couldn't we kick it in?" asked Grim, bouncing his foot against the stubborn door.

The tumanhofer laid his hand on the solid wood. "Son, a tumanhofer craftsman fashioned this door. Not only does the lock work, but there's probably a simple device that also prohibits entry."

Carrie stooped, examining the design across the bottom of the door. "Hey! These look like keys."

She took one key and placed it in the first indentation. It fit. The children who could see cheered.

Porky jumped, trying to see from his position at the back. "What happened?"

Ellie glanced over her shoulder, then balanced on her toes to look above the children. "Carrie found a place to put the keys." A murmur of excitement buzzed through the gathering.

Carrie stood and held up a key. "I've got one left over."

Bealomondore held out his hand, and she placed it in his palm.

He lifted his eyebrows and grinned at Ellie. With no more ado, he inserted the key and turned it. Even the burble of rushing water didn't drown out the click of the mechanism. Bealomondore twisted the doorknob, gave a push, and the door swung open.

With shrieks of excitement, the children stampeded past Ellie and Bealomondore. She lost her balance, and he grabbed her around the waist, pulling her close to avoid being trampled.

After the charge passed, a commanding voice rose above the din. "Be still."

Silence. Absolute silence. Except for the stream behind them.

Bealomondore looked at Ellie's startled face and answered her unspoken question.

"We'd better find out."

They darted through the door and stopped.

Lightrocks studded the walls, making the great hall bright. The children stood in various poses, seemingly trapped by the authoritative words. Frozen in flight, the minor dragons hung like suspended hot air balloons above their heads.

On the opposite side of the large cavern sat an old man on a throne. If Bealomondore had any doubts as to who the gentleman might be, the pointed hat and elaborate robes pronounced a wizard.

Bealomondore bowed. Ellie, taking her cue from him, gave a small curtsy.

"Come, come." The wizard gestured for them to cross the expanse between them.

As they passed under Det and Airon, Ellie looked up in amazement and mindspoke, *"How'd he do that?"*

*We could ask him to explain, but if he's like Fenworth, the explanation will be indecipherable.*

"Wizard Pater?" Bealomondore asked as he guided Ellie through the field of statuelike children.

The wizard nodded.

Walking beside Bealomondore, Ellie's expression reflected horror as she studied the frozen faces of the children. At the foot of the wizard's dais, she rounded on the old man with an outraged tone. "What have you done?"

He laughed, a pleasant sound in the eerie stillness. "Do not worry, Miss Clarenbessipawl. It is not permanent. The cease-action command will last no more than five minutes. So we have less than five minutes to have our adult conversation uninterrupted."

She lowered her accusing finger. "All right."

He smiled, and Bealomondore felt Ellie's acceptance, and perhaps even approval, of Wizard Pater.

Bealomondore stepped up on the small platform and extended his hand. The wizard took it to shake with a firm but gentle grip.

"Wizard Pater," said Bealomondore, "we would like to leave Rumbard City. And according to Old One, you too would like to be free."

"Old One? His name is Humbaken Florn. Yes, you have freed me from the city of Tuck, and I am grateful. But without the bottle of memories, none of us can slip through the glass walls of the city."

Ellie frowned. "Don't you know where you put it?"

"I do," said the wizard, "and I don't."

Neither Bealomondore nor his bride-to-be spoke.

"Yes," said Wizard Pater. "I put the bottle on a shelf in what I have taken as my storeroom."

Bealomondore realized that their silence would prod the old man to explain more than a stream of questions they might ask. Of course, Ellie joined him without verbal prompting.

"And…many years have passed." He looked at the children. "And I have placed other bottles on the same shelf."

The wizard sighed with a huge gust of air. The emotion on his face piqued Bealomondore's artistic interest. If he could capture that expression of regret, the portrait would resonate with every person who had ever done a foolhardy deed.

The wizard continued, "I arranged for the isolation of the urohm population without consulting Wulder. I was rather peeved at their lack of obedience. Therefore, being an o'rant and given to pride just as completely as were the urohms, I sought to teach them a lesson. In other words, I committed my own act of arrogance by judging and sentencing and carrying out the punishment in my own self-righteousness."

He paused to rub his hands together, as if warming them. He then rested one on each knee. "Wulder was not pleased." His hands rubbed forward and back several times before he uttered another word. "And Wulder, in His infinite wisdom, gave me the task of maintaining the city until only those children who were under six at the time remained. It would seem Wulder agreed that the urohms required discipline, as I had determined, but discipline given by the master, not the servant. Over the years, the people grew old and died off, quite naturally. You mustn't think they chafed terribly under my reprimand. They seemed very content."

He grimaced. "I must confess, that irked me even more. I'd devised retribution for their folly, and I seemed to be the one chastised most heavily."

He smiled again at his audience. "The children are beginning to stir. I must be succinct."

Bealomondore and Ellie surveyed the still unmoving crew. An eye twitched on a girl, and a lip curved a little on another. None of the children stirred significantly.

"Where was I?" asked the wizard. "Oh yes. The adult population dwindled until only the librarian walked the streets. At that time, Humbaken Florn was charged with seeing to the children in the city. I continued my service by providing sustenance and such that is needed, still trapped under the city. Humbaken's response to the call was to barricade himself in the library. He seemed to suffer most. And you would think that finally I would get some satisfaction as he endured penance."

Wizard Pater shook his head sadly and rubbed one hand across his face and down his beard, giving the chin hair a firm jerk. "No, I felt sorry for him. So I bottled his memories as well."

A giggle behind them brought Bealomondore and Ellie around to face the children.

Another giggle answered the first, then snickering bounced from one child to the next.

Through his laughter, Cinder remarked as if he had a mouthful of food, "I can hardly move my lips to talk."

"Me too."

"Me too."

"Me too."

That set off another round of snickering.

"I got my toe to move," one child reported with glee.

Now claims of movement of different body parts were conveyed with more titters and giggles and chuckling.

Ellie smiled at the wizard. "They don't seem to have been harmed by your cease-action command."

Wizard Pater's eyes twinkled. "They never are. Of course, I haven't used the command for eons. I used to teach at The Hall in Amara."

"A university?" asked Bealomondore. "I think Fenworth mentioned The Hall."

The old man's eyebrows lifted. "Fenworth? Fenworth is here?"

"Yes, along with his librarian, Librettowit. Although by this time they may have returned to Amara."

"Oh, I hope not. Fenworth can help us dissolve the bottle around the city. He is quite a master of our trade. Not the Master, of course, but very knowledgeable in Wulder's ways."

Two of the children managed a step forward with one leg. Cheers broke out among the others.

The wizard stood. "All right, children. Listen to your wizard, and all will be well." He pointed down a hallway on the side of the room.

"I'm going to take the grownups down that hall and serve tea. As soon as you are able, follow along, and I'll have cakes and daggarts and candied fruit for you."

"And punch?" asked Porky.

"Definitely punch," answered the wizard. "Now come along as soon as you've worked out your kinks, and don't go into any of the rooms along the way. Come straight to the kitchen. You can't miss it. It smells dandy, like roast and gravy, rolls and butter, cinnamon, licorice, and vanilla."

As he mentioned the spices, the scents floated through the room. Several of the children expressed their appreciation with a word: "Yum."

"Follow me," said Wizard Pater.

Bealomondore glanced into the rooms as they passed, seeing spaces that looked like the entryways to homes. Typical tumanhofer furniture declared the residents' race.

He stopped at the opening of a smaller door and pulled Ellie back to peer inside. Shelves lined a long, narrow storage room. Bottles of every size, shape, and color crowded every inch of the space. Some had twist tops. Others had corks. Some had rags stuffed in the opening. On the floor, dust covered bottles large enough to stuff a baby pig inside.

Wizard Pater called from ahead, "I did say I have a few bottles, didn't I? There really isn't much to do as a hobby here in Tuck. Of course, maintaining Rumbard City is an onerous task, but I did have a spare moment here and there where I tried my hand at something different."

Ellie raised her voice to question him. "What do you have in all these bottles?"

"Elixirs, music, scenery, letters, books, atmospheres from different worlds, flowers, mountains, bits and pieces of time. And one bottle of memories."

# 47

# A Wizard's Way

The wizard served their tea in a large dining room. Ellie thought the children behaved rather well considering how excited they were.

Toady was fascinated by the old man and followed him everywhere, helping some and getting in the way more often.

"How did you know what we were doing? How did you know if we were in bed on time? How did you know to feed Mr. Bealomondore and Miss Ellie when they first came? Did you know about Tak, the goat?"

He showed them a flat bowl on a pedestal. "Come, Ellie and Bealomondore. This will interest you. Through this device, I can see the inhabitants of the aboveground city reflected in still water. This is how I've kept track of my charges. I can't go myself, of course. But I send the essence of me to deliver supplies."

Ellie doubted they would see anything.

Bealomondore scolded. *"Don't be such a naysayer. These men of Wulder can do amazing things by understanding the great mysteries of our Creator's handiwork."*

"Gather 'round," called the wizard to the children. "Watch. It's time for me to take the evening meal."

The wizard stood beside the large basin with his eyes closed and his hands held over the bowl, palms down. The scene within the water changed.

"There's the fountain," said Cinder. "We're seeing it just like we're walking into the center of town."

"No one's there yet," said Laska. "But look! There's our baskets and platters. They just appeared."

"The wizard did it," said Toady, and she gave the old man a look of admiration. He didn't notice, so she shrugged and went back to gazing at the changing scenery in the water.

Porky leaned way over the rim of the bowl to see better. "Not as much food as there once was."

Laska had an answer. "There's not as many children as there once was."

Toady tugged on the wizard's sleeve. "Are you going to feed Old One?"

The wizard did not answer. His pleasant expression remained unchanged. The children fell into silence as the reflection jumped from first one child, then to another. They also saw Yawn and two toughs walking with him and, lastly, several children playing in an alley.

According to the basin, the wizard checked in at the library. For a moment they saw the back door. An instant later they saw Old One's kitchen, where a basket of food appeared on the table.

"Well, then," said the wizard, breaking the silence in a loud voice.

Ellie jumped in response to the sudden noise. The picture in the basin had been mesmerizing. How could Wizard Pater stand here and see up there? How could she and the others see it as well? The experience amazed her but also made her a little nervous.

Bealomondore's arm tightened around her. *"Don't be afraid, Ellie. This wizard, like Fenworth, leans on Wulder's understanding, not his own."*

*I'm not really afraid. Well, maybe a little. But he could decide to do bad things with this trickery, couldn't he?*

*"Yes, and I've met wizards who have turned their gift of knowledge to their own selfish pursuits. Fortunately, there are not many wizards, and fewer wizards who choose evil."*

The children had surrounded Wizard Pater and were pelting him with too many questions for him to hear and answer.

He held up his hands and commanded. "Silence."

The children's mouths still moved, but not a peep could they utter.

"Very good," said the wizard, smiling. "We shall have a question and answer period before bed. Then Miss Ellie will read one of my interesting books. After a good night's rest, we'll hunt for the bottle of memories." He put his hands on his hips and with good humor continued, "It would seem I may have accidentally included a bit of my memory in the bottle because I have no clear idea of where I put it."

He led them to his throne room, and the children sat on the floor. He pointed to Toady first and released her voice. She asked her question, got an answer, and the wizard moved on to another child.

Ellie thought about how good his method would be for handling children in a classroom or even her own large family around the dinner table. The thought instantly made her think of her little brothers and sisters. Her heart ached to hear their voices. Hopefully she and Bealomondore would leave Rumbard City and the lost city of Tuck soon.

Bealomondore woke to the smell of baking bread and frying bacon. He looked around the room where he'd slept with several other boys. The tumanhofer beds were the right size for him, and a comfortable fit for six-year-old-sized urohms. Several were still asleep, but three had deserted the bedroom.

Bealomondore got up and checked the closet, hoping to find fresh clothing. The cupboards were bare. But thankfully, from the sounds and smells coming from the kitchen, the pantry was well stocked.

A few minutes later, he entered the kitchen through the dining room. He greeted Ellie and Wizard Pater and the two girls who helped with the cooking, then voiced his concern.

"I thought there would be more children at the tables."

Wizard Pater brandished the fork he used for turning sausages. "Some have finished eating and already embarked on the quest for the bottle."

Lisby looked up from buttering biscuits. "The bottle has a stick figure man on it with his head in a cloud. That is the symbol for memories."

Bealomondore nodded. He could see how that would represent someone with a cloudy memory.

"Of course," explained the wizard, "not all the memories are gone, just those pertaining to urohms and Rumbard City."

Ellie's smile was extra bright this morning. "When we open the bottle, people in the neighboring villages and countryside will remember long ago, when the urohms first came and the time they spent building."

The wizard winked at her. "And the glass bottle around the city will dissolve."

Bealomondore took the warm biscuit Lisby offered him. "Thank you, pretty girl." She giggled and he turned to Wizard Pater. "Is there any trick or ceremony that needs to be done?"

"No, just take out the cork, and let the liquid evaporate into the air. It's gradual, but that's better for the populace who are doing all the remembering. Don't want to rush something like that."

"Of course not."

Bealomondore settled at the kitchen table to have breakfast. He asked about clothing and learned that the wizard had no stores of that type. Tuck was deserted when he found himself the sole inhabitant.

The morning passed comfortably. He and Ellie strolled through the well-lit tunnels of the unique city. They admired the architecture and visited home after home with an eye out for a bottle marked with a man whose head hid in a cloud.

The children searched as well but soon lost interest and occupied their time with a few toys left by tumanhofer children. Most of these were broken, and the wizard stopped his inventory of the bottle closet to patiently mend them.

Bealomondore sent Orli and Det back to inform Old One about finding the underground city. Some of the minor dragons returned to Rumbard City to perform the duties of the watch.

After hours of roaming from one house to another, visiting closed stores, and locating the public records building, Bealomondore and Ellie returned for noonmeal.

Wizard Pater had not bothered to prepare their food in the kitchen, even though he said cooking breakfast had been a pleasant experience. He didn't relish assembling meals three times a day, every day, by that method. Instead, he handed them meals in baskets and on platters just as he had always delivered while they were aboveground.

As they ate, Bealomondore became quiet.

"What's wrong?" Ellie asked. "You're shielding your thoughts. That makes me nervous."

"I don't want you listening to me worry. I had expected Wizard Pater to reach in a hollow of his robes and pull out the bottle. It never occurred to me that he would have misplaced it."

"Tuck is a not as big a city as Rumbard. And I don't mean in size. It never housed as many citizens as the city above."

"It is still a sizable amount of territory to search. Once we've been through it in this perfunctory manner, we will have to do a second, more meticulous search."

"Or…we could possibly find it on the first round."

"Oh, it's good to hear you being optimistic. I believe I've accused you of pessimism. I apologize. Today I'm the naysayer."

Wizard Pater returned from his distribution to Old One and Yawn's gang. Although he'd only been in the next room, he appeared tired.

"I shall take a nap. The mental exercise of my duties tires me."

Ellie stood and hugged the old man. "We'll try to keep the children quiet so they won't disturb you."

"No need for that, dear girl. If they suddenly go quiet, you'll know I took the matter in hand."

He waved as he wandered out of the dining room.

Ellie said, "I like him."

"He's very different from Wizard Fenworth."

"How?"

"Fenworth is much older."

Ellie's eyes widened, and Bealomondore laughed.

"I know it is hard to fathom, but I think Fenworth might have been around when Wulder created our world."

"Really?" Her voice squeaked.

"No, not really. He is just terribly, tremendously old."

Hours later, after more unrewarded searching, Bealomondore and Ellie sat in a small room off the dining room and discussed whether or not some of them should go check on Old One.

Bealomondore didn't want the group split up. "He's managed without us for centuries."

Wizard Pater came out of his rooms. "I had the most pleasant dream."

They turned their attention to him.

"Don't we have a child named Cinder?"

"Yes," said Ellie.

"In the dream, Cinder found the bottle."

A scuffle interrupted the wizard. The noise came from the hall. A moment later, Yawn appeared in the doorway, his arm wrapped around Cinder's throat. "Well, he didn't."

"Let go of that boy," commanded the wizard.

Yawn complied, looking surprised, as if his arm had loosened its grip of its own accord.

Cinder stumbled over to Ellie.

"I found it, Miss Ellie, but he has it now."

"And I'm going to keep it. You were going to leave me and my gang in the city. Alone! Well, now we'll leave you to rot down here. I'm gathering up my people and walking out of here. I'm going to shut and lock the door when I do."

"How long have you been down here?" asked Bealomondore.

"Just this afternoon." He made a face at them all. "We've been spying, and we're good spies. Nobody caught us. We could have kept on spying forever, and you stupid people never would have known."

"Do you want to go with us?" Ellie asked. "You could come live here. We have good beds, and you could help us search for the bottle."

"I told you I have the bottle. Don't you listen?"

"You said you have the bottle, but I haven't seen it. And I don't see a place where you could have put it away. You don't have pockets, do you?"

"Of course I've got pockets." He lifted up his shirt and dug in a side pocket to his pants. He pulled out the bottle and held it up. "See?"

The wizard took a step forward and spoke quietly. "Be still."

Yawn froze, triumphant grin on his face, bottle held aloft.

Cinder charged forward and tackled Yawn's arm, trying to pry the bottle from his clenched fingers.

"No need for that," said the wizard.

"I can get it," answered Cinder. "He's letting loose."

"I doubt that he could let loose in that short of time. It takes five minutes to even begin to move."

"I—," Cinder grunted.

The force of his struggle caused the stiff Yawn to wobble.

"I almost"—Cinder grunted again—"got it."

His breath came out in a *whoosh* as he slipped the bottle out of Yawn's fist.

Just as he turned to show his prize, Yawn fell forward. He toppled like a statue, falling against Cinder, knocking the boy forward and sliding down to hit the ground. The bottle flew up in the air, sailed halfway across the room, and landed at the feet of Bealomondore and Ellie.

The sound of shattering glass told the rest of the story.

# 48

# Journey to the Other Side

Ellie jumped to her feet and ran to Yawn, then knelt beside him to see if he'd been hurt.

Wizard Pater passed her on the way to the broken bottle. "We must hurry. No time to lose."

"He's not bleeding," Ellie announced, then realized that only Bealomondore seemed interested. He called for Laddin.

Stooping beside the leader of the gang, Bealomondore felt the boy's head for a bump. "Yawn couldn't put out a hand to break his fall. Our bodies' instinctive reactions save us more than we realize."

Ellie heard Bealomondore call Laddin again and realized that both this time and the first time he'd been mindspeaking. Perhaps when the message was loud, it should be called mindshouting.

Bealomondore must have heard her frivolous thought. He winked at her.

Aloud, he said, "Laddin'll be here very quickly, and though he can't reverse the wizard's still command, he can check for injuries and keep bruises from forming."

Wizard Pater came to them with the shattered bottle in a cloth he'd also used to wipe up the liquid. "We must get to the surface and to the bottle before this dries, or all is lost."

"We can't leave Yawn!" Ellie clasped the stiff hand of the young gang leader.

"We will, indeed, leave the rapscallion," said Wizard Pater. "The dragons of the watch will take good care of him until I return."

"When do you plan to come back?" asked Ellie as Bealomondore lifted her to her feet.

"Only you and Bealomondore will go through the wall at this time. With the bottle broken and the liquid rapidly evaporating, we can only send two safely through the glass." He started for the door that led to the great hall and the entry to the subter. "Listen carefully as we walk. I have instructions for you, and it is imperative that you remember."

Ellie and Bealomondore kept pace with the wizard's long legs. The children ran in order not to be left behind.

"Some of the contents of the bottle fell on your shoes and lower garments. Do not wash them. Put them away someplace safe until you have contacted Wizard Fenworth. He may be able to reconstitute the substance and engineer our escape. The residue on your apparel will also help you move through the glass."

"Why were we able to come into the bottle without any special liquid?" asked Bealomondore.

"Ah! Don't you know that it is always easier to get into a predicament than to get out of one?"

They passed into the tunnel through which the stream flowed. The wizard turned away from the route they'd taken to get to Tuck.

Ellie pointed over her shoulder. "Shouldn't we be going that way?"

The wizard answered without pausing. "We'd be walking back to the center of the city, and then we'd have to walk out of it again. This way is shorter. We'll climb the steps to the surface a few yards from the glass wall."

They had neglected to grab the lightrocks. Without them, they had only the glow given off by embedded globes along the walls and down the center of the tunnel ceiling. Ellie could see the others vaguely. Tak's white coat gleamed blue as he passed under each lit orb.

Ellie worried about the children. "Be careful of the stream." That only covered one of her concerns. "You're to stay with Wizard Pater after we leave, and we'll be back for you as soon as we can. Be good for him. Use your manners. And never come down to this part of the subter without an adult. You could drown in that river."

"Miss Ellie," Cinder complained, "that's not a river. It's just a trickle of water."

"You can drown in two inches of water, young man. Don't argue with me."

They reached stone steps, obviously built by tumanhofers. Ellie and Bealomondore climbed to the rough door easily.

Cinder rushed to help lift the wooden planks upward. It swung open like the cellar door on Ellie's family farm. Slanted golden rays of sun greeted them from the west. Their shadows stretched out across the grassy plain.

The children romped like springtime rabbits in the meadow. Tak settled in to trim down the abundant growth.

"They've never been in the country," Ellie said. "Look how excited they are."

"Come, hurry," called Wizard Pater. He charged toward the glass wall.

"I can see it," said Ellie, huffing a bit as she kept up. "When I first passed through, I turned around and couldn't see the glass."

"Neither could I," said Bealomondore.

"Angle of the sun," Wizard Pater yelled. "No time to talk about diffusion, reflection, and refraction. Fascinating, but I judge we only have three minutes to get you through to the other side. This rag is all but dry."

He stopped by the wall. Ellie and Bealomondore caught up. The wizard showed no signs of strain. The tumanhofers panted. Ellie's knees buckled, and she sat in the grass.

"Get up, girl," demanded the wizard. "You can collapse on the other side."

She struggled to her feet with Bealomondore's help.

The wizard unwrapped the glass shards. "Aaah! Just enough moisture within the cloth to get you through. Ready?"

Ellie turned to the frolicking children. "I need to say good-bye."

"No time," the wizard said.

"Tak! I have to get Tak."

The goat still foraged near the open door to the subter.

"Too far, no time." Wizard Pater gave the bottle fragments and cloth to Bealomondore. "Now hold Ellie's hand and just walk through. No problem."

Bealomondore started to speak, "Thank you—"

"No time. Walk!"

They stepped toward the barrier, Ellie looking over her shoulder. "You will watch the children? They've made such good progress. And take care of Yawn and his little toughs. They really are just children."

"Yes. Yes. Go, girl, or you'll be left behind."

Ellie felt Bealomondore tugging at her hand. She turned to find herself pressed against the glass. Part of Bealomondore had already penetrated the barrier.

Both hands were empty. Bealomondore spun around, but there was no sign of Ellie. Instead, he could see two wagons, his and another traveling cart that reminded him of caravan wagons the wanderers lived in, a tiny house on wheels.

He looked down at his clothes. His sword was at his side, even though he had not been wearing it in Tuck. He had on the same ragged shirt, coat, and pants that had been his uniform while away.

But his wagon and the old slow horse were right where he'd left them in the shade. The sun hadn't even moved enough to change the direction of the shadow.

A marione came out of the back end of the large cart. He waved. "There you are!" He beckoned him closer. "Come. Have some refreshments."

The voice sounded familiar. The man looked familiar. Bealomondore squinted to read the lettering on the wooden side of the wagon. "Rowser and Piefer Insect Emporium. The finest supplies in medicinal bugs."

"Rowser?" Bealomondore dashed across the field. "How did you get here? What are you doing here?"

"Vacation." He smiled and held out his arm, gesturing to the lovely countryside around them.

"*He's* on vacation," fussed another voice Bealomondore remembered. "He sits and reads."

Rowser held up a finger. "And records."

"While I run around with a butterfly net, catching specimens for our shop."

Bealomondore came to a halt beside Rowser. "Piefer, where are you?"

He heard a scraping noise from under the wagon. Soon Piefer's head popped out. The bug man was on his back, and he grinned up at the tumanhofer. "I was just checking on the night beetles. We have to keep them cool and alive."

Bealomondore made a disgusted face. "Surely you don't feed them to your patients alive."

Rowser looked up from the book he'd opened. "Alive? The patient or the bug?"

Bealomondore looked over his shoulder again. Where was Ellie? To Rowser, he answered, "I assume the patient is alive. A corpse would be uncooperative when asked to swallow your brew of medicine."

The emerlindian Piefer climbed out from under the wagon and slapped the loose dirt from his pants. "I look like I've been working in the field. But then, I have been working in the field. Why do you look like you've been wallowing in nature?"

"I—" Bealomondore stopped. He'd been in Rumbard City, trapped in a bottle. How was he to tell these men he'd met several years ago about his latest adventure?

He searched the horizon, the edge of a small wood, and the distant meadow.

"What are you looking for?" asked Rowser.

"Tell me"—Bealomondore would wait for an appropriate time to go into his lengthy tale—"have Paladin and Queen Tipper married yet?"

"She's still Princess Tipper until the coronation, and that's still months away."

Rowser tapped his finger on the open book. "Just barely seven weeks."

Piefer took exception to the correction. "Seven weeks is almost two months. Thus the plural is necessary. Singular would mislead

Bealomondore. They will not be married in a month. She will be crowned, and they will be married in almost two months. Plural."

Bealomondore scratched his head as he once again scanned the fields. "I came out on the same day I left. She either did the same, or she wasn't able to get through."

"What's that, Bealomondore?"

"I've lost a friend, and I'm not sure if she has vanished to a different time or a different place or didn't make the journey at all."

"Ah, I see," said Rowser.

Piefer nodded his head in agreement. "He's been gadding about with wizards again."

Rowser's eyebrows arched. "Only explanation. Did you want tea or something stronger?"

"I'll stick with tea. Your something stronger might still have bits of legs and antennas in it."

# 49

# Rendezvous

Ellie stumbled over a runt bush and landed hard on the palms of her hands. They stung. She quickly turned over and sat up. The rock ridge she'd thought looked like a stone dragon rose out of the ground right in front of her. Her feet touched the part that looked like the tip of the tail.

She recognized this spot.

She could see quite well across the valley. No misty cloud hung over the land now. But water soaked the ground, and she stood up to avoid getting any wetter.

No sign of Bealomondore. No sign of the bottle. Over to the south she could see smoke curling out of the Hopperbattyholds' cabin. To the west, she caught a glimpse of the road to Pence. Her aunt and uncle would have long ago passed that crossroads village.

She searched the terrain once more, looking for Bealomondore. Should she turn back to walk home or go on to the road? Stopping in the village seemed the best thing to do. She could ask what day it was, if the royal wedding had been magnificent, and if anyone had been looking for her.

As she trudged over the rough moor, she wondered if she should go looking for Bealomondore or go home to see if he came looking for her.

"He will," she said aloud, then felt foolish. Tak wasn't with her, so she couldn't pretend she was talking to him and he understood. "What are people going to say?" She raised her arms a bit and let them fall back to her sides. "What am *I* going to say?"

She thought perhaps she should go to Ragar and find Wizard Fenworth. She had a message to deliver from Wizard Pater. But so did Bealomondore. A clump of coarse wire grass slashed her ankle as she walked by. Tiny cuts above her sock bled a little, not enough even to wipe away. She returned to mulling over her immediate future and stumbled over a tangle of bracken.

With her eyes on the ground, paying better attention to where she put her feet, Ellie reached the road and turned toward Pence. Perhaps she could get a ride back to Glenbrooken Village and walk home from there.

She moved to the side of the road when she heard a carriage approaching from behind. She didn't bother to look as the coach rumbled past. It splashed mud on her clothing, and she jumped farther out onto the sloped grass beside the road. With her head down, examining the new stains on her tattered skirt, she heard the order to stop.

A screeching rendition of her name caught her attention. "Ellicinderpart!"

*Aunt Tiffenbeth?*

The carriage looked very familiar. She trotted over to stand next to the coach and look up at the people inside. Her aunt and uncle stared at her in disbelief. Aunt Tiffenbeth's face had turned a horrid shade of reddish purple. Her eyes were wide and slightly unfocused. Uncle Stemikenjon looked perplexed.

"It is indeed your niece." He patted his wife's hand, which clutched the open window's edge.

She jerked her hand away and used both to cover her face. She moaned.

Uncle Stemikenjon merely raised his eyebrows and addressed Ellie. "How did you reach this point before us? And what happened to your clothes and your carpetbag?"

"Have her get in," Aunt Tiffenbeth ordered from behind her hands. "Before someone sees her."

"Oh, right," said her uncle. He opened the door, descended, and gave his arm to support Ellie as she stepped on the small runner beneath the door. "I apologize for being tardy in bringing you in. I'm a bit baffled by your appearance. Not just your physical appearance, your clothes, your missing carpetbag, but also that you managed to come all this way in the inclement weather and get here first. An appearance out of nowhere, so to speak."

"Where is the goat?" asked Aunt Tiffenbeth, her words still muffled behind her hands. "She doesn't still have the goat, does she?"

Uncle Stemikenjon gave a quick glance around in all directions. "Apparently not."

Ellie settled on the upholstered bench beside her aunt. "Tak is…is being taken care of."

The coach swayed as her uncle climbed in and took his seat opposite the ladies. He shut the door, leaned out the window, and ordered, "Drive on."

The carriage jerked into motion.

Aunt Tiffenbeth took her hands from her face, shuddered when she once again saw Ellie, and turned her eyes to the scenery passing.

She whispered in a dramatic undertone, "Tell me what happened, Ellicinderpart."

Ellie couldn't think of a good place to begin. Fortunately her aunt prodded. "What happened to your carpetbag?"

"A gang of wild children stole it."

Her aunt nodded as if she heard of such things every day. "And your attire?"

"I'd gotten muddy, so I stopped in a cave to change." She paused. "And to get out of the rain for a while."

Aunt Tiffenbeth's eyes drifted back to survey her niece, then darted back to the more pleasant view of grass and trees and cottages. They approached the crossroads village.

"And why did you choose that particular combination of clothing?"

Ellie looked down at her mismatched outfit. What she was wearing hadn't concerned her for the months she'd been in Rumbard City.

"The children pulled my clothes out of the bag and threw them all over the place. They carried off most of my belongings. This is what I could find to wear."

"Stemikenjon, you shall inform the magistrate of this area about this barbaric crime."

"Of course." He nodded his head, and Ellie realized he'd picked up his book and was reading again. Perhaps he and Old One, or Humbaken Florn, could discuss books. Master Florn could use a friend with similar interests. Maybe she could arrange for Gramps and Humbaken Florn to meet. Once she found Bealomondore and Wizard Fenworth and they broke the bottle around the city.

Aunt Tiffenbeth's expressions reflected the different emotions she sorted through before she could handle the situation in her usual sensible, ordered manner. The family often counted on her to rise to any challenge that faced them. "The clothes in the trunk on the roof are too fancy to wear on the journey. We shall have to stop at a dress shop in one of the villages."

Ellie's former appreciation for her aunt crept back. She'd resented being dumped beside the road to take care of a wayward goat, but her aunt would come through for her. The shock was wearing off, and the practical details became the focus of attention.

Her aunt went on to describe how they would manage to buy clothing and get Ellie changed without causing a stir. Aunt Tiffenbeth would purchase the needed garments, then Ellie would change inside the coach with the windows in place and the curtains drawn.

Ellie gasped at a sudden revelation. She'd come out of the bottle at the same place she'd fallen in. And she'd also come out on the same day. She blurted a question out without thinking. "Are we still going to the coronation, to the wedding?"

Aunt Tiffenbeth frowned at her. "Of course. You aren't to be punished for this little mishap. Obviously you ran into circumstances beyond your control. It is fortunate that you are not hurt. Clothes can be replaced."

Ellie started to throw her arms around her aunt but stopped. Her aunt wasn't quite ready to accept an embrace from a dirty ragamuffin niece.

Ellie settled for words. "Thank you, Aunt." She smiled at the top of her uncle's head as he bent over his book. "Thank you, Uncle."

He grunted.

"Aunt Tiffenbeth, do you know of a society artist named Graddapotmorphit Bealomondore?"

"Oh, my girl, you are unsophisticated. Everyone knows of Bealomondore. He's famous for various escapades. He was important in the war and helped save the country. He's been on quests with Paladin. Perhaps that's where you've heard his name. He's a good friend to the princess and is mentored by Verrin Schope himself."

"Do you think we can meet him in Ragar?"

"Oh, dear girl, no. Your uncle and I don't belong to that circle of society. They are rather above us. Not that I would want to be caught up in that level of our culture. So much is done merely to impress. An inordinate amount of expense is involved in dressing and providing hospitality and traveling to galas. I'd rather your Uncle Stemikenjon spend his money on our own little comforts that please us and make us comfortable. The alternative is to spend it to garner the favor of people you hardly know and to accrue praise of little worth."

Ellie pondered her aunt's words. Perhaps she was right after all. Perhaps she and Bealomondore had been parted as the gentlest way to end their relationship. The chances of meeting Bealomondore in the crowded city, among all the high society people, were slim. Nonexistent.

Then she remembered Bealomondore's proposal in the subter. And his kiss. The tingle in her toes at the memory determined her course. She was going to look for him and hope he was looking for her.

# 50

# The Ball

Ellie stood with her aunt and uncle on a balcony overlooking Palace Fairway, the street that led directly to the Amber Palace. Thousands of people lined the streets below. The coronation parade proceeded slowly along the plotted route. Aunt Tiffenbeth's friend pointed out the personalities in each open carriage as they passed in front of the hotel.

"This carriage has the councilors and their wives. I'd name them all, but I only want to name a few of those participating in the parade. You'd be overwhelmed by a hundred or so names you'll never need to know."

Aunt Tiffenbeth smiled and nodded. "I do want you to point out Sir Beccaroon."

"All grand parrots look alike, but I will try. Dikendraval has a program."

She leaned forward a bit to look down the line of people watching the parade to where her daughter stood with Ellie. "Dikendraval, let us know when the carriage with Sir Beccaroon comes by."

"Yes, Mother."

Ellie bounced on her toes. "There!" She pointed to a carriage way down the street that had just turned the corner to make the approach to the palace. "That's him. That's Bealomondore!"

Aunt Tiffenbeth arched an eyebrow at her. Ellie saw the look and interpreted what her aunt wanted. Ellie refrained from bouncing like a country bumpkin and folded her hands demurely in front of her waist. Aunt Tiffenbeth nodded her approval.

Ellie closed her eyes and tried to reach Bealomondore by mind-speaking. When she listened with her mind, she heard thoughts from all the people around. The sudden uproar shocked her, and her hands came up to cover her ears. That didn't help at all, so she closed her mind against the cacophony.

She turned to her new friend, Dikendraval. "I've got to go down there. I must speak to him."

Dikendraval's eyes grew big, and she clamped both hands on Ellie's arm. "You can't. It's not safe for you to be down there in the crowd. You could get knocked over. And there are thieves who would steal your reticule. And"—Dikendraval stretched out her last objection with a dramatic flair—"you could ruin your reputation."

"I don't have a reputation, Dikendraval. I'm nobody."

The city tumanhofer schooled her face into an expression of haughty sophistication. She leaned forward and whispered, "My mother would tell. I love my mother, but she is a gossip, and the juicier the tidbit, the more she will chew on it." Dikendraval let her staged face slip. "We'll have to attract his attention from up here."

"How?"

Dikendraval leaned forward to look at her parents. Her mother cast her a severe look, and she straightened up. "It's hopeless, Ellicinderpart. My mother would catch us for sure. I never get away with anything."

Ellie's eyes had been on the progression of the parade. She turned back to look straight at Dikendraval. "I'm going down there."

"No!" Dikendraval's grip on her arm tightened. "I have a better idea. We'll go be servants at the Muskagillians' Ball."

"Servants? Your mother won't let me go down to the street, but she'd let us masquerade as servants?"

"Everyone does it. Well, all the young women. You get a chance to see all the fabulous ball gowns, hear the music, and all you do is carry trays into the public rooms and offer refreshments to the guests. It's the only way you or I will ever get to see such grandeur. My mother and probably your aunt did the same thing when they were young."

Ellie looked at Aunt Tiffenbeth's flushed face. Her aunt admired the people parading past. Her own heart had been set on seeing this pageantry, but after months in a bottle city with Bealomondore, all she wanted was to see him.

She heard Dikendraval's mother say, "The people in the next carriage are friends of Princess Tipper. The skinny old man is Wizard Fenworth. The tumanhofer beside him is a librarian and works for the wizard. His name is Librettowit. I thought Sir Beccaroon would be in this coach, but he may be in the parent carriage later on. The tumanhofer in the red coat is Graddapotmorphit Bealomondore, a very talented man who has a varied career from warrior to society darling. Five years ago, everyone who was anyone wanted a Bealomondore portrait hanging in their homes. Now he is more of a statesman than a pet of the upper classes."

The carriage passed directly under their balcony. Ellie and Dikendraval jumped up and down, waving their arms in the air, and calling out to Bealomondore.

"Girls!" Aunt Tiffenbeth and her friend shoved past their spouses to bring the two young women in line.

Dikendraval's mother went so far as to wrap her arms around her daughter and hold her still. "You must be an example to our country guest. She doesn't necessarily know how to behave, but you do."

Ellicinderpart and Dikendraval had listened to a three-hour-long lecture about correct behavior in polite society. The aunt and mother even pulled out a book on etiquette and read chapters from between the covers. Ellie agonized over whether or not they'd be allowed to serve at the Muskagillians' Ball. In the end, Dikendraval's father and her uncle took pity on the poor young ladies, cut short the scolding, and sent them off to get dressed.

The uniforms for service were a deep purple with a white apron, white collar, and white band around the hem. They looked better than the few dresses Ellie had owned before joining her aunt and uncle. Her aunt had wrangled her curly hair into a snood to keep it back from her face as she served.

Now she entered the back door of the Muskagillians' mansion and could hardly contain her anticipation. Surely Bealomondore would be here. Dikendraval said *everyone* would be here.

The house chef explained their duties. Each of the volunteer servants had a silver tray. They arranged the appetizers on the tray themselves from a huge table laden with mouth-watering morsels of food. They would tour the public rooms of the mansion until their trays were half empty. The young ladies would then return to replenish the appetizers. The cycle would be repeated until the guests sat down for a late supper. A few of the experienced servants would wait on the tables. The other girls were encouraged to gather in the kitchen and sample the leftovers.

On her first foray into the public rooms, Ellie spotted Wizard Fenworth's pointed hat. She meandered in that direction, hoping to deliver the message given to her by Wizard Pater. She also hoped to find out if Bealomondore had spoken to him about the bottle city and where her tumanhofer friend might be.

Guests wanting a sample from her tray delayed her progress. She became impatient and had to laugh at herself. After all, the only reason she could mingle with this crowd was because of her duty to hand out the fancy slivers of food. She had to go replenish her refreshments twice before she finally found herself next to Wizard Fenworth, Lady Peg, and Librettowit.

"I know you," said Lady Peg. "I'm Lady Peg, but perhaps I don't need to say that if I know you. And I do know you. I'm Princess Tipper's mother. Do you know me?"

"I know who you are, Lady Peg, but I don't think we've ever met."

Tipper's mother turned to Wizard Fenworth. "Do you know this young lady, Fenworth?"

The wizard looked at Ellie with squinted eyes. He patted his robes, dislodging a lizard that crawled back into the folds of the elegant material. The wizard located the pocket he wanted and pulled out a pair of glasses. He perched them on his nose and studied Ellie.

He nodded. "I know her."

"Who is she?" asked Lady Peg.

"Perhaps we should ask her."

"But if we know her, we shouldn't have to, should we?"

"Definitely not." The wizard took off his glasses, a bug sitting on one lens, and addressed his librarian. "Librettowit, what is the etiquette in this society when you meet someone you know at a formal gala event but the person in question comes to you without a proper name?"

Librettowit shook his head. "We do know her name."

Fenworth turned to Lady Peg. "Not to worry, dear lady. We do know her name."

"We do?"

"Librettowit says we do."

Ellie felt like she was the birdie in a game of birdnet. The conversation bounced around among the three friends and left her standing there, holding the appetizers. Would jumping into this conversation between royalty and distinguished guests from another country be rude?

"Well," said Lady Peg, "I'm certain I know her face. I don't know this dress except that it is being worn by all these lovely, helpful young women. But the face was on another dress. I'm certain of it. Not actually on the dress but above it. Not exactly above the dress as in floating. That would be unsettling. But attached to a body that was in the dress."

Ellie started to giggle. Bealomondore had tried to explain Lady Peg's penchant for wandering thoughts. Now Ellie understood.

Her laughter caught their interest, and the three focused on her.

She smiled at them all. "I have a message from Wizard Pater for Wizard Fenworth."

Wizard Fenworth clapped his hands together. Butterflies escaped from his wide sleeves. "Bealomondore's mysterious lady in the portrait. Ellicinderpart Clarenbessipawl. His bride-to-be!"

Lady Peg's face glowed at the announcement. "You're right, Fenworth. But Bealomondore gave you the message, did he not?"

She stepped forward, and Ellie just managed to keep from spilling her tray as she was embraced by the royal mother of Princess Tipper.

"Ellie!" The voice behind her sent shivers up her arms and through her heart. Lady Peg released her and turned her around.

Bealomondore grabbed the tray and thrust it into Lady Peg's hands. He gathered Ellie into his arms and kissed her. Her first thought was relief and pleasure. He still loved her. Her second thought was that she was a serving girl being embraced by one of the elite. This should be done in private or perhaps, some would say, not at all. Her third thought was she didn't care.

He released her enough to look into her eyes. "I've been here for two months. Two long months, waiting for you. Fenworth explained that you came out of the bottle at your own time. We couldn't go back to dissolve the bottle because we needed your soaked clothing as well to have enough of the memories." He pulled her close again, her head on his shoulder. "Oh, it feels good to hold you."

Ellie heard Lady Peg behind her. "Yes, isn't this sweet? Long-lost love. Not years, of course, but months. Still, that's hard for young lovers. Would you like an appetizer? These little lemon cakes are especially tasty, but I haven't tried those brown crinkly ones because they look like bugs, and I always associate bugs with headaches or upset stomachs. Would you like to try one of these brown things, Fenworth? Librettowit?"

Her voice faded, and Ellie peeked. The princess's mother had taken over her job, circulating among the guests, offering refreshment.

Bealomondore gave her a last squeeze and let her go, with only his arm still around her waist. "My parents are here." He stretched his neck and looked around. "I want you to meet them, and then we can dance and feast and dance some more. I'll introduce you to many of my friends."

"I can't meet them now. I'm supposed to be serving."

"You can't. Lady Peg went off with your tray."

She felt the bond sizzle between them as if reconnecting. He studied her face, then nodded.

"This is my cousin's house. I'll find her, and she'll take you upstairs to her room where she has dozens of ball gowns. Then when you're comfortably attired, our evening can begin."

Bealomondore sat in the foyer at the base of the grand staircase and lit-erally twiddled his thumbs. When he became aware of what he was doing, he stopped. Then his knee jiggled. He kept trying to reach Ellie through mindspeaking, just to tell her to hurry up. There were too many people in the house, and she was too far away and probably busy. His cousin had hugged Ellie and dragged her off with the enthusiasm of a young hostess with a special guest.

He thought they might never come down. Surely they weren't doing the hair and nails and all the other falderal women normally did before a ball. If they were, he'd get to dance only the last dance with his fiancée.

He felt her coming. Her spirit felt like a spring bubbling out of a forest glade, fresh snowmelt providing crystal-clear water. He stood and waited at the bottom of the steps until she came into view.

She looked stunning, a portrait of grace and innocence. How could he have found someone so perfect? He thought about the chances of them both falling into a bottle city and smiled. This was not by chance. This meeting was orchestrated by Wulder.

Floating in the wide skirt of golds and browns, with a snug bodice of pale gold satin, she looked like a doll his sisters had played with, a beautiful porcelain doll with perfect form and dark coloring. He'd have to start another portrait of Ellicinderpart tomorrow. The first did not do her justice.

He took her hand at the bottom of the stairs and nodded to his cousin, who had accompanied Ellie. He led her into the ballroom and swirled her onto the dance floor the minute they stepped through the doors.

Her words breathless with excitement, she protested. "I don't know how to dance like this."

"But you're dancing."

"I think it's the bond we have between us. I think your mind is telling my body what to do. Bealomondore, we are even breathing in rhythm."

He pulled her closer for a tight turn. "I think our hearts are beating as one as well."

"Bealomondore, I love you."

"And I love you, Ellicinderpart."

They maneuvered through three steps that parted them and brought them back together. Words passed between their minds and hearts, unspoken but truly committed.

*"May it ever be so."*

# In and Out of the Bottle

"I'll just do this little thing I call a swirl." Fenworth lifted his arms while Ellie and Bealomondore watched.

"Wait!" Ellie reached for the wizard's arm. "I've been told about the swirling. Where are we going?"

Wizard Fenworth shook his head as if clearing it. "To rescue the inhabitants of Rumbard City. Isn't that what we're supposed to be doing? I had it clearly marked on my calendar. Today the urohms of Chiril who wish to participate in assimilating the orphans into society will gather at Bellsawyer. That's their part of this endeavor. Am I not right?"

"Yes sir," Ellie said. "But are we going to swirl into the bottle, or next to it on the outside?"

Fenworth looked at her for a long moment. "Inside. I've tried to understand your reasoning, but you are thinking like a tumanhofer. When Librettowit pulls that trick, it always bamboggles me."

He rubbed his hand down his beard. Ellie watched to see what would crawl out and was disappointed when a reptile head poked through the shanks of hair and then pulled back.

"Quite possibly you should ask your questions of him, not me. Where is he? Shouldn't he be here? I seem to remember him going on about studying Tuck."

"Yes," said Ellie, "that's another reason we need to wait."

"I'm here! I'm here!" Librettowit rounded the corner, carrying a portfolio of papers. "Let's go."

Bealomondore squeezed with the arm he had around Ellie. She squeezed back. The tales she'd heard about swirling were disconcerting. She closed her eyes as the room seemed to whirl around her. Random sounds punctuated the roar of wind: cattle mooing, a crack of thunder, a child crying, and someone singing, not very well.

The odd sensations ceased, and she opened her eyes. Children sat at the long dining hall tables. Wizard Pater read as he ate, his face buried in the pages, unaware of their arrival. The minor dragons flew from their perches and did circles above their heads, chittering a happy melody. Tak bleated and ran to greet Ellie. She let go of Bealomondore and wrapped her arms around the goat's neck.

She looked over his body at the children. They smiled and waved in between scooping spoonfuls of soup into their mouths. She wondered what this spell was called.

Librettowit was already making notes, examining the architecture and sketching things of interest.

"Pater," said Wizard Fenworth. "It's been centuries since I've seen you."

The trapped wizard lifted his head from the reading and slowly took in his visitors. He smiled, closed the book, and got up. "Do you require sustenance? We have a fine pot of green stew."

"No, no," said Fenworth. "We've come to dissolve the bottle. I will need a few things from you, but I think we can manage it. My librarian brought along some notes on bottle cities and the dissolution of such."

Ellie looked up at Bealomondore and whispered, "He *thinks* they can manage it? Bealomondore, are we stuck in the bottle again?"

Bealomondore shook his head. "They'll take care of it."

As the children finished eating, they got up, took their dishes to the kitchen, then walked quietly to the door leading to the big hall. Once beyond that door, they shook off the spell.

Toady gave a leap, twisted in midair, and came barreling back into the room. She threw her arms around Ellie. "Don't go away again. He makes us behave!"

"We're all going to get out of here, and there are urohm parents waiting to take you to a new home."

"Really?" She jumped up and down, then tore out of the room to inform the others. "We're going to have parents!"

The last boy at the table finally emptied his bowl. He got up and moved to the kitchen as if he were being led to his own execution. Ellie wondered if he had to do the dishes. But he deposited his bowl in the sink. He made his trip to the door of escape with his shoulders slumped and his chin on his chest.

"Yawn?" Ellie said as he passed.

He didn't respond, but she thought it was because of whatever spell Wizard Pater had used to influence his behavior.

When he crossed the threshold to the other room, he turned and looked at Ellie, Tak, and Bealomondore. Ellie smiled at him, and he slunk back into the room to stand before them.

"Do you know who Wulder is?" he asked in a gravelly voice.

Ellie and Bealomondore answered in unison, "Yes."

"Wizard Pater told me lots about Him." He paused and shuffled his feet. "Do you think there's going to be parents who will take me?"

Ellie's heart hurt. She put an arm around the tough leader of the gang. "Yes, I think so."

Yawn didn't look at her. He studied Tak. "Do you think we could find parents who can forgive like this Wulder does? I think I'm going to need parents who know how to forgive. At least for a little while."

Ellie nodded. "That's what we'll look for."

"Wizard Pater says I have bad habits but that they're just habits, they aren't really me. And you can get rid of habits." Yawn put his hand on Tak's head and rubbed between the horns. "I'm doing better. Wizard Pater says so."

"I'm sure," Ellie said, praying that it was true, "that you will do better and better now that you don't have to be with only children all the time. And your parents will teach you things. That will be interesting. It's harder to be good when you're bored. You'll get older. It's easier to decide to do right things."

"It's the practice," said Bealomondore. "The more you practice doing good, the easier it is to make the right choices."

Yawn nodded. "Yeah, Wizard Pater says something like that."

A low rumble vibrated the floor. The dragons jumped and chittered.

Ellie looked at Bealomondore.

"Let's go check it out," he said and started toward the door.

Ellie took Yawn's hand and pulled him along with them. Tak dogged her steps as if to say she couldn't leave him behind again. The minor dragons made a ruckus as they flew over their heads and sped to the source of the noise.

The air became thick.

Dust poured in through the door to the subter. The children coughed.

"Put cloth over your noses," Bealomondore ordered. He put his own nose in the crook of his elbow and rushed to the open door to close it. "Let's move away from this room."

"Tut, tut, no need," said Fenworth from the hallway. "It will clear away in no time. I've summoned a stiff breeze from the ocean. I think it was the ocean. Not being on the surface obstructed my accuracy."

The wizard went to the door and opened it. After sticking his head out and looking in both directions in the tunnel, he motioned them forward. Everyone followed him as they made their way out of Tuck and into Rumbard City. When they stepped on the surface, Old One and Orli were there to meet them.

"The city's gone," exclaimed Cinder, the first of the children to see outside.

Old One looked around and nodded in agreement. "It never should have been here in the first place."

Wizard Fenworth put his hands on his hips. "I wasn't expecting this. How about you, Pater?"

The wizard nodded. "I thought Wulder would take our spell one step further. I've been asking Him for years to wipe away our mistakes and give us a new chance."

Yawn approached Wizard Pater and looked up into his face. As an o'rant, he was taller than the young lad. "Does everybody get a new chance, sir?"

"Yes, everyone."

"Me?"

"Yes, you."

"Everyone?" The boy persisted.

"Everyone who wants it."

"I want it."

"So do I!" said the adults in unison.

"Is that group mindspeaking?" Librettowit asked. "I've heard of it but never seen it played out."

Bealomondore's arm went around Ellie's waist. "I've seen a lot of things in the last four years. I think I'm just getting used to the idea that Wulder works wonders. And I'm expecting more surprises down the road."

"Wise thinking," said Fenworth as he clapped the tumanhofer on the back. He turned to Pater. "Should we try a double swirl, Pater? Do you think we can move all of these people to Bellsawyer between the two of us?"

Pater nodded.

Librettowit secured his portfolio under his arm. "Wizards! Why can't they stick with the things they *know* they can do? Why do they have to experiment? Why do I always have to be along when they do?"

The wind picked up, and the swirl began.

# Appendix

## ❧ People ❧

**Airon**
Purple minor dragon, has a talent for music.

**Amee**
Black and white minor dragon, communicates with animals.

**Aval**
Urohm girl.

**Barm**
Urohm boy.

**Graddapotmorphit Bealomondore**
Tumanhofer artist, warrior, diplomat, and part owner of the family mining business.

**Sir Beccaroon**
Grand parrot, magistrate over his district, former guardian to Princess Tipper.

**Stemikenjon Blamenyellomont**
Ellie's uncle, husband of Tiffenbeth.

**Tiffenbeth Blamenyellomont**
Ellie's aunt, wife of Stemikenjon.

**Carrie**
Urohm girl.

**Cinder**
Urohm boy.

**Ellicinderpart Clarenbessipawl**
Tumanhofer country girl who uses the name Ellie.

**Gustustharinback Clarenbessipawl**
Ellie's younger brother.

**Letterimdebomm Clarenbessipawl**
Ellie's younger sister, next in line after her oldest brother.

**Nabordontippen Clarenbessipawl**
Ellie's ornery oldest brother.

**Da**
Ellie's father. His full name is Naperkowson Clarenbessipawl.

**Dabryhinck family**
Neighbors to the Hopperbattyhold family.

**Det**
Blue minor dragon, good with geography.

**Dikendraval**
Ellie's friend. Her mother is friends with Aunt Tiffenbeth.

**Disnat**
Urohm girl.

**Wizard Fenworth**
Ancient o'rant wizard from Amara.

**Fister**
Urohm girl.

**Fronna**
Urohm girl.

**Gardie**
Urohm girl.

**Tilly Genejolly**
Urohm girl who sailed from Amara to Chiril. She kept a diary of her journey.

**Gramps**
Ellie's grandfather, taught Ellie to read.

**Grim**
Urohm boy.

**Hopperbattyhold family**
Ellie's neighbors. They live in a cabin in the country.

**Prince Jayrus, Paladin**
Dragonkeeper and prince of Mercigon Mountain Range, Princess Tipper's fiancé.

**Jep**
Urohm boy.

**Kriss**
Light green minor dragon, chef, and food scavenger.

**Laddin**
Green minor healing dragon.

**Laska**
Urohm boy.

**Lemeterndern**
Plays the fiddle in Ellie's village.

**Librettowit**
Tumanhofer librarian and friend to Wizard Fenworth. He is from Amara.

**Lisby**
Urohm girl.

**Lulu**
Urohm child who died.

**Ma**
Ellie's mother. Her full name is Emmademgotton Clarenbessipawl.

**Maree**
Blue minor dragon, predicts the weather.

**Porta Mellow**
Urohm girl who sailed to Chiril from Amara.

**Muskagillian family**
Bealomondore's cousins. They host Princess Tipper's coronation ball.

**Old One**
Ancient urohm librarian.

**Orli**
Old One's gray and white minor dragon, shines in the dark.

**Ostes**
Urohm boy.

**Wizard Pater**
Guided the Amaran urohms to Chiril.

**Pepper**
Urohm boy who died. He told fairy tales to the other children.

**Phee**
Urohm child.

**Piefer**
Emerlindian man, co-owns the Insect Emporium.

**Porky**
Urohm boy.

**Rowser**
Marione man, co-owns the Insect Emporium.

**Gordman Rumbard**
Leader of the urohm expedition from Amara.

**Salm**
Wizard Pater's major dragon. Flew him from Amara to Chiril.

**Lady Peg Schope**
Mother of Tipper, wife of Verrin Schope, daughter of King Yellat and Queen Venmarie.

**Princess Tipper Schope**
Young emerlindian woman, princess, daughter of Verrin and Lady Peg Schope, Prince Jayrus's fiancée.

**Verrin Schope**
Artist, sculptor, scientist, explorer, wizard, father of Tipper.

**Somas**
Urohm architect, kept a journal.

**Soosahn**
Yellow and orange minor dragon, has a talent for humor.

**Soo-tie**
Urohm girl.

**Tad**
Urohm child who died.

**Tak**
Ellie's goat.

**Toady**
Urohm girl.

**Tolly**
Urohm girl.

**Queen Venmarie**
Mother of Lady Peg, wife of King Yellat.

**Winkel**
Kimen who gave Bealomondore a moonbeam cape.

**Wulder**
Supreme Being, Creator, God.

**Yawn**
Urohm boy, a bully.

**King Yellat**
Ruler of Chiril, Lady Peg's father, deceased.

## ⌒ Glossary ⌒

**Amara**
Country surrounded by ocean on three sides. Located in the northern and eastern hemisphere.

**amaloot**
A warm, soothing beverage.

**bundle-up bug**
An insect similar to a doodlebug.

**button grain**
A type of grain commonly fed to livestock.

**daggart**
A baked treat in the form of a small crunchy cake, often served with tea.

**Eggstram Snails**
Used for medicinal purposes. It cures temper, reduces anxiety, and prevents tantrums.

**emerlindians**
One of the seven high races, emerlindians are born pale with white hair and pale gray eyes. As they age, they darken. One group of emerlindians is slight in stature, the tallest being five feet. Another distinct group is between six and six and a half feet tall.

**hollow**
A nondimensional space used like a pocket for storage.

**kimens**
The smallest of the seven high races. Kimens are elusive, tiny, and fast. Under two feet tall.

**lightrock**
Crystals that produce light, most common color is blue.

**mariones**
One of the seven high races. Mariones are excellent farmers and warriors. They are short and broad, usually muscle-bound rather than corpulent.

**moonbeam cape**
Cape woven from moonbeam plant fibers. It can be used for camouflage if it remains still.

**morgym tree**
A tall, leafy tree.

**nightflyer**
A bird similar to an owl.

**o'rants**
One of the high races. Five to six feet tall. They are most likely to become

wizards because they hold Wulder in esteem.

**parnot**
Green fruit like a pear.

**quaken tree**
A tree very similar to an aspen.

**razterberry**
A fruit that can be eaten fresh, baked into pies, or made into jam.

**tumanhofers**
One of the seven high races. Short, squat, powerful fighters, though for the most part, they prefer to use their great intellect.

**urohms**
One of the seven high races, gentle giants up to fourteen feet tall. They are well proportioned, and very intelligent.

**watch of dragons**
A unit of dragons (like a gaggle of geese).

**wusstbunters**
Batlike creatures. They are fragile and disintegrate when touched.

# More of the Chiril Chronicles Series

**Book One:** *Dragons of Chiril**

Before the DragonKeeper Chronicles, a young emerlindian's mistake may spell the end of the world unless she and her ragtag band of adventurers can find three lost sculptures.

*previously titled
*The Vanishing Sculptor*

**Book Two:** *Dragons of the Valley*

In this spine-tingling adventure, Tipper and Bealomondore are faced with a new threat to Chiril—one that is tearing their land apart.

### Read the book that started it all!

*DragonSpell*
Book One of the epic
DragonKeeper Chronicles